THE HEALING PLACE

THE HEALING PLACE

SHARON DOWNING JARVIS

Deseret Book Company
Salt Lake City, Utah

For all those who need,
at one time or another,
a "healing place" in their lives

Special thanks to
Linda Nimori, Sheri Dew, Richard Peterson,
and all those who work so skillfully
to bring my stories to publication

"In the Hollow of Thy Hand"
© 1977 Janice Kapp Perry and Monita Turley Robison
Permission granted for use of lyrics on page 79.

Library of Congress Cataloging-in-Publication Data

Jarvis, Sharon Downing, 1940–
    The healing place / Sharon Downing Jarvis
      p. cm.
    ISBN 0-87579-817-9
    1. Community life—United States—Fiction. 2. Women—United States—Fiction. 3. Neighborhood—Fiction. 4. Mormons—Fiction.
    I. Title.
    PS3560.A64H43   1993
    813'.54—dc20   93-40089
                                              CIP

Printed in the United States of America

10 9 8 7 6 5 4 3 2

1

Anger tightened her lips as Liz Ewell watched for a break in the traffic and eased her compact car back onto the Nevada highway.

"Rotten little man," she muttered, still smarting from her encounter with the owner of the gas station (in no way had it been a *service* station) who had watched her pump the gas and then demanded cash.

"No credit cards, lady," he'd said, pointing to a tiny sign high on the rusty canopy above the pumps.

"Oh," Liz said, fishing in her shoulder bag. "Well, I have traveler's checks."

"Nope, don't take them neither. Might be stolen."

"They're certainly not stolen, and I have two forms of picture ID."

The man shrugged and spat a stream of tobacco juice. "Might be forged. Cold cash is all I can trust."

Liz flipped open her wallet and handed him her last ten.

"Are you sure you couldn't cash just one traveler's check? I hate to be totally without cash when I travel, and this is the last of it."

"That's your lookout, lady. You'll make Wendover pretty

soon, or maybe them Mormons over in Utah'll trust you. Me, it's cash or nothin'."

An angry lump rose in her throat. "Keep the change," she told him, not wanting to wait for the sixteen cents she had coming. Then she paused, one hand on the door handle of her car, curiosity momentarily surpassing anger. "What would you have done if I hadn't had any cash?"

The man let his rheumy brown eyes linger on the slim figure in jeans, turtleneck, and jacket. "Oh, I've got me a siphon over there," he smirked. " 'Course, maybe you'da had some other idea as to how you could make it right with me."

"Sorry I asked," Liz said bitterly and got into her car, locking the door as she started the engine. A swift glance in the rearview mirror showed the man heading back into his dingy office, shoulders shaking with laughter.

"All right, Elizabeth," she chided herself, disgusted with the tears that kept filling her eyes. "This is the bad old world, and you're a big girl now. You can't let every petty little creep you come across get to you. You'll never see this one again, and he's not worth a second thought. Besides, you knew what a woman on her own could expect to encounter. Marla told you. Sue told you. Plus, you've read all those magazine articles. You knew, and you chose to be divorced. So hang tough, lady."

The trouble was, she wasn't tough, and she knew it. She felt fragile, vulnerable, and brand-new, faced with decisions and problems she wasn't ready to handle. "I need a warm, dark cave to crawl into," she muttered. "But if I found one, there'd probably be a bear already in residence."

She tried to concentrate on the landscape, which was drab and stark at the moment—brown, bald hills with occasional patches of tired snow, and the eastern horizon shrouded in threatening February clouds. By the time she crossed the state line into Utah, she was heartily sick of all the billboards warning her that she was about to pass up her last chance to gamble at a real Nevada casino.

"Bet *they'd* be willing to cash a traveler's check," she said, hunching over the steering wheel in an effort to ease the burning tiredness between her shoulder blades. "And gambling? I'm probably taking the biggest gamble of my life right now."

The hills receded into the distance, and she saw, on either side of the road, flat white stretches that looked like snow or ice. When she spotted the sign for Bonneville Speedway, she realized the white stretches were salt. If she had been traveling with Brock, she reflected, they would have stopped for the casinos *and* the speedway. But she had little interest in either. She merely wanted to get to Salt Lake City before it began to snow or rain.

She almost made it. The gray clouds made good their threat and rolled across the valley floor, producing a steady shower that turned the city lights of early evening into a colorful, runny blur on her windshield. The left wiper needed replacing. She tried to peer above and below it, and finally rolled down her window and poked her head out, searching for the motel that held her reservation. By the time she spotted it, her hair and face were cold and wet, and she pulled under the canopy with a sense of relief and accomplishment.

It seemed strange to be registering alone at a motel; it wasn't something she had often done. Even when she'd finally left Brock, she had stayed with friends and then her cousin in San Francisco until the divorce became final. She hadn't meant to stay so long at her cousin's, but Marla had insisted, and Liz had been too tired to resist.

In her room, she flopped on the queen-size, extra-firm bed and closed her eyes against the familiar motel decor—the long dresser, the wall-mounted television, the round table under the window.

"So what did you expect?" she asked herself. "A roaring fire and a shelf of good books?" She laughed a little at the notion and stretched luxuriously. "Throw in a chintz-covered chair and needlepoint footstool—maybe a tray of French pastries. How about a tall man in a tweed suit with one arm resting casually on the mantel? No—scratch the man. He's bound to be a cad."

Liz rolled over and stood up, kicking off her shoes. "Settle for a good hot shower and a sandwich," she counseled herself.

The shower did wonders for her comfort and well-being. Toweling her short blonde hair dry, she put on a forest green sweater and matching pants. Her gold chain and matching loops in her ears made her look a little braver than she felt, but she went easy on the eye shadow. Her greenish eyes seemed enormous and shadowed enough, and the new hollows under her cheekbones accorded with the present gaunt fashion. The finished product looked reasonably presentable, she decided. Ironic that Brock, who had always been after her to lose ten pounds, shouldn't be here to witness the result. Would he be pleased? Likely not. Little she had done had ever really pleased him. Oh, well, that was all over—if an eleven-year investment of a person's time, energy, and emotions could ever truly be over and done with.

"Okay, Liz—you're thirty years old and divorced. Time to grow up, right? So take a deep breath and go to dinner."

Obediently she shouldered her bag and remembered her room key just in time. In the restaurant she debated with herself. She was hungry after driving all day, but surely, a woman dining alone should content herself with a quick sandwich or salad and be done with it, shouldn't she? After all, one's first dinner alone (not counting the one on the plane) was hardly an event to be celebrated—or was it? With an air of defiance, she ordered a veal cutlet, potatoes, and salad, and then settled back to observe the people around her. She always speculated about the origins and lives of people she encountered when traveling, a habit that Brock had ridiculed. Eventually, she learned to keep her imaginings to herself, but the habit had survived.

A young family with three red-haired children worked their way through hamburgers and spaghetti, keeping her amused through her own dinner. All was well until the youngest grew sleepy, rubbed her eyes with spaghetti-stained fists, and began to scream. The young mother quickly dipped her napkin into her water glass and wiped the child's eyes. As the baby's cries subsided into hiccuping sobs, the mother gave her husband a meaningful look: "About these family vacations . . ."

Liz smiled to herself. *How would I cope?* she wondered. *Oh, well—idle speculation. I'll never have the chance to find out.*

She paid for her dinner and walked out to the car to retrieve a forgotten paperback. The rain had stopped, and the misty air was cool against her face. She hesitated, suddenly unwilling just yet to return to her carbon-copy room. On an impulse, she slipped into her car to take a short tour of downtown Salt Lake City. The wide, surprisingly clean streets were shared by the usual motor traffic and a few elegant horse-drawn carriages. The shops and restaurants seemed similar to those in any American city, and she noted a couple of theaters advertising interesting-looking stage productions. At one point she passed under a bronze archway topped by an imposing eagle and, glancing straight up the hill, saw what she assumed must be the domed state capitol building. She turned left at the next signal, drove past a high-rise office building, and stopped for the red traffic light. She caught sight of a building with lighted turrets rising from behind a wall, a golden statue topping the highest turret, or spire. Liz was entranced, but a horn sounding behind her alerted her to the green light, and she moved her car forward with a slight jerk. Following the wall, she noticed other buildings within its enclosure, and people, many obviously tourists, passed in and out of the iron gates that stood open.

Wanting a closer look at that spired church, or whatever it was, she circled the block, and pulled into a parking spot just as someone vacated it. It seemed to strike a chord in her memory, but she couldn't quite get the association to jell.

A metal plaque beside the nearest gate proclaimed that this was Temple Square, The Church of Jesus Christ of Latter-day Saints, and that visitors were welcome. Liz hugged her short jacket closer to her and walked in. She stood for several minutes looking at the delicate strength and beauty of that magnificent building—*cathedral, more likely*, she corrected herself—with its golden guardian lifting his slender trumpet to the heavens. Liz was intrigued and inexplicably moved. She had been awed by the grandeur and workmanship of several great European cathedrals she had visited with Brock, but somehow this structure spoke to her on a deeper level. Possibly, she told herself wryly, it had something to do with Brock's not being there to tell her to stop daydreaming and hurry up and snap a picture if she liked it that much. Or maybe it was because she had come upon it so unexpectedly, and it was in such contrast to the rest of her day.

She walked around to view it from another angle, and then turned to an elderly couple who stood arm in arm nearby, also admiring the scene.

"Excuse me," she said. "Do you happen to know what hours that building is open to the public? I'd love to see inside."

"The temple?" asked the man, in some surprise. "Oh, it's not open to the public. It's in use seventeen or eighteen hours a day, five days a week, for special ordinance work for Latter-day Saints." He smiled and patted his wife's hand. "The wife and I were married in that temple nearly forty-three years ago."

"Congratulations. Forty-three years is a long time," Liz said, dredging up a tight little smile.

"Oh, well—we expect our marriage to last for eternity, so forty-three years is just the short haul, you might say." He smiled genially.

"Eternity!" she repeated. *And you couldn't take it for more than eleven years*, something inside her mocked.

The woman leaned forward to touch Liz's arm. "My dear, it is lovely inside. I hope one day you'll be able to see it for yourself, but meanwhile, there are slides and photographs you can see in the Visitors Center, and someone to explain what takes place. Have you been there yet?"

"Um, no—I just barely walked in, because I wanted a closer look at the—temple. Who is the statue on top?"

"The angel Moroni," explained the man. "He's proclaiming the everlasting gospel of Christ to the world."

"That's a new one for me," Liz commented. "I've heard of Michael and Gabriel, but I don't know any other angels. He isn't wearing his wings," she added whimsically, "or I might at least have classified him."

The man chuckled. "We don't believe angels have wings, you know," he confided. "They apparently travel on beams of brilliant light. When the Prophet . . ."

"Edgar," his wife admonished. "Milk before meat, dear."

"You're right, of course," he agreed. "Would you like us to show you around the Visitors Center, young lady? Be our pleasure."

"Oh—no, I couldn't. That is, I don't have much time right now. But it's very kind of you."

"Good night, then," they called as she smiled and moved away.

Eternity! she thought, and shook her head. She surprised herself by vaguely recognizing an oval-shaped building with a rounded top as the home of the Mormon Tabernacle Choir and organ. It, too, stood closed and silent, but northward a well-lit building, obviously the Visitors Center, beckoned her in spite of the excuse she had made. Time, indeed. Time was what she had the most of! Besides, where else was there to go? She hated going to movies alone, and it seemed too early to sleep, even though she was tired. The February chill was seeping into her bones, and she decided to go in just to warm up for a few minutes.

People moved around inside singly or in groups or families.

"Hello," said a personable young woman as Liz approached a desk to one side. "Welcome to Temple Square. Have you been here before?"

"No—may I just look around?"

"Oh, you bet. There are guides to answer questions and direct you to various exhibits, and tour groups form right over there every little while if you're interested. Have a pleasant time."

Liz nodded, accepting a brochure the young woman handed her, and followed a small group of foreign tourists around a curved gallery, viewing a display of religious paintings. She thought they were remarkably well-done and life-like—the faces could be those on the street outside—although she didn't recognize all of the scenes represented. Curiously she followed another group and their guide up a curving, carpeted ramp, the walls of which gradually became a star- and planet-studded mural. Under the domed ceiling stood a magnificent white statue of Christ, arms outstretched in loving welcome, expression intent and gentle, the prints of nails visible in the feet and open hands.

Liz almost expected to see people kneeling, but no one

was. People stood about in silence or subdued conversation, and she stood beside a long window to contemplate the statue.

What a serene place, she thought, *and how appropriate that we should have to climb to get here. Leave the world behind and make a little effort, and then suddenly there he is, reaching out . . .* Quick tears stung her eyes and she blinked them away, lest anyone should notice, but no one was paying her any attention. *Is it really that simple, that easy, to find the real Christ?* It had been so long since she'd tried, made any effort at all in that direction, though she had always believed.

Dear Lord, she prayed silently, *forgive me if I've done wrong.* Then, remembering a childhood teaching that everyone had sinned and done wrong, she amended her prayer. *Forgive me for all the wrong I've done, and help me to move ahead in my life and to find peace. Amen.*

"Folks," urged the quiet voice of an older gentleman nearby, "if you'd like to step this way, we'll be just in time to catch the last showing for tonight of a very special film—a thirteen-minute feature that has long been a favorite among visitors to Temple Square."

Liz rose and followed the group to a well-appointed little theater on a lower level. The film simply and movingly portrayed a man and his close and loving family enjoying life together and experiencing the death of a beloved grandfather. When the spirit of the grandfather moved into heavenly realms and was joyously welcomed by waiting relatives, Liz felt that the lump in her throat was going to burst into audible sobs. Discreet sniffs throughout the audience told her she wasn't alone in her reaction.

Sentimentalist! she scolded herself, swallowing back tears. *What a place for you to be—what a film to be seeing now, of all times! It's incredibly idealistic. Nobody's really like that family.*

She hardly heard the words of the guide as he bade the

group good night, but he was at the door by the time her row filed out, and disconcertingly, he smiled directly at her. He was a middle-aged man, plump and serene with twinkling blue eyes above a gray business suit.

"What did you think of the film, young lady?" he asked.

Liz paused. "Do you really want to know?" she asked, with an apologetic smile.

"Yes, I do. I'm very interested," he replied, taking her elbow to steer her to one side, out of the way of the crowd.

"It was beautifully done," Liz said slowly, "and very touching. But I didn't find it very believable."

"Oh? How so?"

"I don't believe there are families anywhere that close and that loving. Maybe in years past, but not now. Not in these times."

The twinkle came back to the man's eyes. "I assure you, my dear, there are such families. I know several, and I happen to be blessed to have one myself."

"How very lucky you are, then."

"I can tell you're not quite convinced. These are difficult times for families, it's true, and many are struggling. In fact, I'm sure every family has its problems and challenges, but most difficulties can usually be worked out with patience and diligence and the help of the Lord. The result is a family like the one portrayed in our little story, experiencing peace in this life and eternal life together with loved ones in the hereafter."

"It's a beautiful concept," Liz admitted. "But so far, it hasn't been a part of my experience."

The man reached out to shake her hand and pat her arm in a fatherly gesture. "Then I hope you have that yet to look forward to. Come see us again, won't you?"

"Thank you," Liz said and made her way through the crowd and out into the evening. The drizzling rain had returned, and she caught the collar of her jacket close against her throat, sparing only a glance up at the spires of the temple as she passed through the open gate. She had forgotten, she realized, to look for the temple display inside the Visitors Center. *I will come again*, she promised herself. *Sometime. When I'm ready.*

2

Liz slept well that night and woke feeling kindlier toward her rented room. She had, after all, been exhausted after her long drive of the day before and prone to overreact to practically everything. After a quick breakfast, she cashed several more of her traveler's checks before striking out on a day's exploration.

"Warm for February," commented the man who sold her a map of Utah.

"Is it? I feel quite chilly—but then I've spent the last few years in Florida and Hawaii."

"How would it be?" the man wondered, but his contented smile belied his envious words. "Never been to either one myself."

"Mild and moist and flowery," she told him. "But also busy and touristy and much the same all year round."

"Nice places to visit, but it seems natural to me to watch the seasons change. Believe I'd miss that."

Liz nodded. "That's one reason I'm here. In fact, I hoped to catch a taste of winter."

"Oh, I expect you're in time for that. Planning to do a little skiing? It's still real good."

"I've never skied, but maybe I'll try one day. Right now I'm just looking for a place to settle where life isn't too hectic. I need a change of pace."

"Salt Lake's hectic enough—more of a big city all the time. We've even got a few gangs, and smog, and commuter traffic jams."

Liz smiled. "All the comforts of home," she said, tucking the map in her purse.

"It's still a great place. But you might want to look at some of the smaller towns either north or south of here. Logan's pretty, but the winters up there are a bit longer and colder than here and points south."

"I'm heading for Provo today," Liz said. "I have a friend from there."

"Provo-Orem area's nice. Growing fast, too, though."

An hour later, Liz agreed with him, as she drove off the freeway into a busy but not frantic main street and stopped beside a park where the winter-weary grass was greening under the influence of melting snow and relatively mild air.

"So, Dorrie Stanford, this is your town," she said softly, getting out of the car to look around. Massive trees proclaimed the age of the park; it was no new project introduced by a socially conscious city council. A bandstand with peeling paint had obviously been the setting for many summer concerts, and children had swung in those sturdy swings for years. Provo was, she knew, a university town, with attendant advantages and disadvantages. It was like Dorrie, Liz reflected, as she drove up and down the streets—warm and busy and neat, unpretentious and friendly.

"Just a bit big for my taste," she decided aloud. "Though I think I'll want to be close by."

She stopped at a supermarket and bought a packaged sandwich and a couple of apples. The sense of adventure with which she had begun her journey, and which had been so

easily dampened, was now returning. It was really a heady feeling—all this freedom to be able to travel where she pleased, to
pick and choose her own times, places, and people. She
planned to be especially careful about the people. She needed
to be alone for a while—maybe a long while—to *feel* alone, to
be at peace, to live quietly and simply. Probably she could have
done that anywhere, she admitted to herself, but she had kept
thinking of Dorrie's tales of growing up in Utah. In Hawaii,
where soft breezes and tropical fragrances were intertwined
with the bitterness of Brock's poisonous influence and the misery that had led to her divorce, Utah's crisp winters and dry
sweet air had sounded refreshing. Liz craved Utah; she had developed a need for Utah, born of Dorrie's uncomplicated
warmth and acceptance.

Dorrie had reared her four healthy children with love,
laughter, and good sense and had made a pleasant home for
her husband, Jack, whom she teased and cajoled out of taking
himself or others too seriously. She had little interest in the social functions that seemed to occupy the time of so many Navy
wives—the teas, luncheons, and cocktail parties. She laughed
when they tried to get her to play bridge, and said she wasn't
bright enough, but Liz suspected she coveted her spare time
and needed it for her own projects. Dorrie read widely, gave
hours of volunteer service at hospitals, and when the Officers'
Wives had a Christmas project of dressing dolls for needy children, she found time to do eighteen or twenty. Her house was
always abloom with numerous houseplants and atumble with
puppies or kittens, and her kitchen exuded wonderful aromas.
Liz had spent many afternoons—and a few mornings, too—in
that kitchen, watching Dorrie make cinnamon rolls or homemade noodles or a gourmet tropical salad and listening to her
stories of a girlhood spent skiing and tobogganing and camp-

ing in the canyons and of going each spring to her grandfather's farm to see the crop of new lambs.

Liz felt guilty, on occasion, that she had taken so much
from Dorrie and given so little in return, but Dorrie had
seemed to sense her need and had welcomed her whenever she
came, unquestioning, simply "rattling on," as she put it, allowing Liz just to sit and absorb. She never pried into Liz's problems with Brock, and Jack was transferred before the final
break came. Liz rarely heard from Dorrie, but Dorrie's influence
was still strong—strong enough, Liz reflected, that she found
herself driving down a Utah highway at the earliest opportunity! Maybe it was silly, she thought, but there had been no
other place she particularly wanted to go, and Utah seemed a
good enough spot to begin trying to get herself together.

She left the freeway at an exit announcing the route to
Price and Manti and drove east for a while. The afternoon sun
warmed her car, and soon she put her window down, in spite
of the frozen blue-gray marsh ponds on either side of the road
and the patches of snow still lingering in the shade of cedars
and rock overhangs. In one spot, a miniature waterfall had
frozen in midcascade just beside the road, and scattered boul-
ders gave credence to the Falling Rocks sign she had seen.
When she sighted a herd of deer grazing on a sloping hillside,
she pulled to a stop to watch them. Two or three raised their
heads to gaze at her for a moment and then returned to their
nibbling.

"No more afraid than cows," she marveled and dared to
ease quietly out of her car. She had caught the attention of a
magnificent stag, however, who gave whatever signal the does
understood. In seconds they were gone, springing and bound-
ing like ballet dancers in a carefully choreographed exit.

Liz stood for a few minutes breathing the sweet air and
then climbed a short distance to a patch of snow that she

examined with the toe of her shoe. It was crusty on top but soft and thawing underneath. She picked some up and sniffed it and then made a loose, wet handful to throw against a fence post. It had been years since she had seen snow, and she had never seen much of it, having grown up in southern Alabama where snowfalls were rare and light. Brock's tours of duty with the Navy had been mostly in California, Florida, Puerto Rico, and Hawaii, which had suited him fine because he hated cold weather, but Liz had begun to yearn for it. That was Dorrie's doing! Liz smiled to herself as she rubbed her reddened palms together and climbed back down to her car. It surprised her how breathless she felt.

"It's the altitude," she comforted herself as she leaned against the door. "I'm not *that* out of shape."

A cloud covered the sun, and the breeze went suddenly chill. She got back into the car and studied her map. She was straying a bit too far from the towns she knew she would want to visit from time to time—and besides, this canyon didn't look very promising for house-hunting. She chose a town at random because she liked the name—Mapleton—and after one wrong turn and the help of a man fixing a flat on his truck, she found it. It was a charming community with a number of older homes and many gracious new ones. There were a few stores, a community center, and several churches. She asked around for a house to rent, but the only place anyone seemed to know about was an elegant family home with seven bed-rooms, and a three-year lease available while the owners served a mission for the Mormon Church in Argentina. There were five acres, horses, a swimming pool, and a huge trampo-line.

"Not my place, I guess," Liz decided, leaving Mapleton regretfully and driving randomly down country road after coun-try road, envying the people who lived in the neat, peaceful-looking houses surrounded by space and fresh air. She checked out another town with a definitely New England-type name—Salem—and laughed when she saw that the town had been built around a pond. "At least they don't dunk witches in this one, I trust," she murmured, biting into her last apple. Salem didn't seem to have much more to offer in rental properties at the moment than Mapleton, however, and she turned her car in what she hoped was the direction of Provo, thinking to secure a motel for the night. Then she saw the sign. It was a small, fluorescent red on black, House for Rent sign tacked lopsidedly on a corner fence post beside yet another lane that curved away up a hill. Liz braked and pulled to the side of the road, her tires kicking up gravel and mud. At first she was disappointed, because the sign seemed to refer to a sprawling and dilapidated old farmhouse that nested among huge, bare-branched trees, but then she noticed a hand-drawn arrow on the sign, pointing up the lane. She glanced in that direction, but little was visible beyond a mature-looking orchard that followed the gentle curve of the hill. She backed her car and turned up the lane, noting on her right a modern, well-kept church building.

Beyond the orchard, set well back from the pavement behind several tall evergreens and a brown lawn, stood a bungalow built of yellowish brick. A generous front window displayed the red and black twin of the sign on the fence post. Liz parked in the driveway—more damp dirt and a sprinkle of gravel—and got out, slinging her bag over her shoulder and staring at the house.

It certainly wasn't very modern—and with its dry lawn and empty, gaping windows, it wasn't especially inviting, either—but there was something about it that appealed to her. *Maybe it's the ivy that's grown over the east wall and the stones of the chimney,* she thought, *or the fair-sized front porch, its base built of* the same stones. Probably a local rock, she decided, wondering how old the house was. Even the windows, baleful and empty-eyed though they appeared at the moment, would give plenty of cheerful sunlight to the rooms inside. She tried to get a toehold on a stone of the chimney base to boost herself up to peer into a side window, but her foot slipped, and she twisted her ankle slightly as she came down.

She limped around to the small back porch where she could get a partial view of the kitchen through a window in the door. The other side, toward the orchard, displayed windows that she assumed would belong to two bedrooms and a bath.

"Private enough, really," she told herself, looking around. When the orchard was in leaf, the house would be totally hidden from the farmhouse down the hill—not that it looked as if anyone lived there, anyway—and except for one newer home across the lane, there were no other houses closer than a distance of about a block. "Which is exactly how I like it," she affirmed and returned to the front porch to copy the phone number from the For Rent sign.

"Hello," called a cheery voice, and she turned to see a stocky man in denim work clothes walking up the drive. Her first impression was that he had the cleanest, pinkest skin and the whitest teeth she had ever seen. His smile was infectious, and he held out a calloused hand to shake hers heartily.

"Looking for a house?" he asked, nodding toward the bungalow.

"I am," Liz responded. "Do you own this one?"

"That I do. Or at least, my wife does. Used to belong to her uncle. I'm LeGarn Tucker. That's my place across the road."

He gestured toward the white brick rambler set among rich-looking farmland, backed by yet another planting of meticulously symmetrical rows of fruit trees.

18

"My name's Elizabeth Ewell," Liz said, deciding that she might as well lay her cards on the table. "I'm recently divorced and I have no children. I live very quietly and privately, and I'm looking for a place where I can do just that—preferably a place like this, where there's room to breathe. I grew up in a rural neighborhood, and I never learned to enjoy city living. I detest apartments and condos. I don't care to know my neighbors' business nor to have them know mine."

LeGarn Tucker's smile had faded, but his expression was still pleasant, and the crinkly lines around his blue eyes were still there. His eyes, intent and farseeing, never wavered from hers as he listened.

"B'lieve you might enjoy it here, then," he said. "Real nice folks in this little neighborhood—nobody to bother you, I'd judge—and we're kind of out of the way, so it's plenty quiet. Too quiet for some," he added with a chuckle and glanced around. "Day like today it looks kind of drab and ugly, but along about May when them orchards bust into bloom, it's a sight to see. Want to look inside? Got the key right here. Saw you pull up and thought you might want a look."

"Thank you," Liz said, following him as he unlocked the front door and stepped inside. The house smelled musty, and dust motes swirled with their entry, but it was not unpleasant. The living room had three painted walls and one of knotty pine, and as she had surmised, it was light and roomy. The fireplace was faced with brick that someone had painted white and was topped by a wooden mantel. The floor was hardwood, painted dark brown. A small dining room came next, with double windows across from an arch that led into the bed and bath area. The bathroom fixtures were old and plain but seemed to function properly, and the bedrooms were livable. The kitchen, located behind the dining room, was rather old-fashioned, but it had been scrubbed spotless. A small pantry contained a furnace, water heater, and shelves to the ceiling.

"There's no basement, but there is a fair amount of storage space," Mr. Tucker said, looking around critically. He ran one finger across a countertop and examined it for dust. "Me and Lolly, we give it a good cleaning when Uncle Ned went into the rest home, but a place standing empty collects dust. Blows in off the fields in dry, windy weather and just seeps right in. Basically, though, this is a sound little house. We had the wiring checked, and the roof's fairly new. Plumbing works good, furnace is adequate, and the fireplace draws."

"How much?" Liz asked.

"We're asking four hundred, plus gas and power. We pay water."

"Four hundred—so around sixteen a month," Liz mused, half to herself. "That's a little higher than I hoped, but for a private house . . ."

"Land, no, young lady—it rents by the month! Four hundred a month, plus gas and power."

Liz blushed at her error. "Sorry, I guess I'm too used to rents in California and Hawaii. That must have sounded stupid. And for that price, I am definitely interested! What will you want for a deposit? I'll need to cash some traveler's checks."

"First and last months' rent will do, and no need to sign a lease unless you want to. I've got a simple rental agreement written up, over to the house. Why don't you just plan to stop by when you're ready, and we'll make it official. You plan to move in right away?"

"As soon as I can pick up some basic furniture to get started with. What may I do in the way of decorating—painting, papering, and so forth?"

"Well, Lolly and me, we hadn't figured on doin' any painting, but if you want to do some on your own, why, we don't mind—anything short of pounding a lot of nails in the walls or tearin' up the floorboards, you go ahead and please yourself. I know Lolly never gets through fixin' up our place."

His grin told her he was proud of Lolly and her "fixin' up."

"Thank you," Liz said, a rising enthusiasm bubbling inside her.

The February afternoon was moving toward an early evening. She glanced at her watch. "Will tomorrow morning be all right? By the time I find a bank today, it will probably be too late."

"Tomorrow's fine. You'll want to see the power and gas companies, too." He pulled a scrap of paper from his pocket and wrote on it. "Here's the address of this place, and here's the utilities you'll need to see. I'll get the water turned on for you. And it's a good ward we have here, too, if I do say so."

"A good . . ." Liz echoed, confused. Had he said "good water," or . . .

"Good ward. I'm the bishop. Oh—but maybe you're not a member."

"A member? Oh—a Mormon, you mean? No, I'm not. Did you say you were—a bishop?" LeGarn Tucker, with his denims, crinkly smile, and homely speech patterns, didn't fit any image of the word *bishop* that had ever existed in Liz's mind. She had vague notions of priestly vestments and headdress.

"A Mormon bishop is the leader of the congregation," he was explaining. "We call each neighborhood congregation a ward, and the bishop is the appointed leader for a few years." He chuckled. "Keeps me busy enough to stay out of trouble, but at least I don't have to preach every Sunday like a paid minister would."

"Oh—who does that?" Liz asked curiously.

"Ever'body takes turns. We usually have a couple of youth speakers, and two or three adults each Sunday. Just short talks,

21

generally, on whatever gospel topic they choose. Gives us all a chance to grow and take part, and nobody gets bored listenin' to the same voice each week. Works out real well."

Liz stared at him in amazement. "You mean, if I were a member of your church, I'd have to stand up and talk—give a sermon—in front of the whole congregation?"

"Oh, sure, your turn would crop up sooner or later," he said cheerfully. "And I bet you'd do fine. Somehow, with the Lord's help, we rise to the occasion."

Liz shook her head. "I could never, ever, be a Mormon," she declared. "I'd be petrified. I barely made it through my high school speech class."

He laughed, and she liked the unself-conscious way he threw back his head in enjoyment. "Actually, we don't force folks who are really reluctant to get up and talk. But why don't you stop in sometime and listen to a few of those talks? Just to see what it's like. Eleven o'clock Sunday mornings, just down the hill here. Visitors are always welcome."

"Well, thank you. I don't know—maybe I will, one day. I appreciate the invitation. Now, I wonder—may I stay here for just a few minutes longer to look around and try to decide what I need to buy?"

"Take your time, but it'll be dark soon. Door locks when you pull it to. Our place is across the way, like I said, and whenever you get here tomorrow will be fine. Let us know any way we can help you get settled."

"Thank you very much, Mr. Tucker."

He scratched his head and then smoothed his thinning grayish blond hair. "You know, I answer to Mr. Tucker, Brother Tucker, Bishop Tucker, and LeGarn," he said. "But mostly I'm just called Tuck. We're Tuck and Lolly to our neighbors and friends—be pleased if you'd call us that."

He held out his hand and shook hers firmly again.

"Then you and—and Lolly must call me Liz," she responded, trying to sound friendly in spite of her reluctance.

"Happy to. Hope you'll enjoy the place, now—and we'll see you tomorrow."

Liz hugged her arms against the cold and watched Tuck cross the road to his and Lolly's neat brick rambler. Was it really good, she wondered, to be on a first-name—nay, even a nickname—basis with one's landlord so soon? Maybe this was how things were done in Utah. Dorrie had a friendly, casual way of greeting new people, too, exemplifying the motto she had worked in counted cross-stitch and hung in her home: "A stranger is just a friend we haven't met." There was another way in which Tuck reminded her of Dorrie, too. She thought it was the intense but understated personal interest she felt from both of them, as if they cared deeply about her and wanted to know her well but respected her privacy too much to pry. But perhaps it was too soon to be sure of that with Tuck.

Oh, well, she thought, turning to survey what was about to become her new home. *I'll have to keep all the Tucks and Dorries at bay. The last thing I want right now is to form any close attachments. I need time and peace and freedom to learn to be me.*

The next half hour was spent in jotting down notes and approximate measurements, but finally the chill of the unheated house drove her away. She left reluctantly—happier, she realized, than she'd felt for eons.

A wry smile twisted her lips as she thought of Brock and imagined what his reaction to her unpretentious little house would be if he were to see it. Actually, it didn't matter anymore what Brock might say—or at least it shouldn't. But Liz knew one thing: this little house would contain no chrome and glass coffee tables covered with cubist sculptures and empty cocktail glasses. There would be no canvas director's chairs and no huge expanses of vivid primary colors hanging on the walls. She hadn't realized for years how much she disliked Brock's taste in contemporary decorating, how it had grated on her nerves like a spoon across the bottom of a pot, and how little she had ever felt at home in any of the houses they had lived in. He had insisted on glaring, stark white kitchens for her with perhaps a splash of yellow, and naked windows to catch all possible light. Perhaps it was natural for a flier to crave all that light and space in his home, but it had made her feel inadequate and exposed. She liked sunlight, too, but she preferred it somewhat filtered and controlled inside a house. *One more thing*, she promised herself, *if I put up a clock in my house, it will have numbers on its face!*

3

The next morning, with rent money and a brand-new checkbook tucked safely in her purse, Liz almost got lost retracing the way back to her new neighborhood. She finally spotted the turn, noting with some satisfaction that the red and black For Rent signs were missing from the fence post and the front window of "her" house. The sky seemed to be clearing, and only the last wisps of clouds clung to the mountaintops. She stepped out of her car and stood transfixed. Clouds had obscured her view of the mountains since her arrival in Utah, and now as the rugged slopes and snowy upper reaches stood unveiled, she marveled. They were far grander and more imposing than she had imagined, and incredibly more beautiful, with shades of white and lavender-gray against the pale blue sky and delicate black etching here and there to indicate stands of evergreens and outcroppings of jagged rock.

"Looks like a clear day," announced Tuck as he came around the corner of his garage, peeling off lined work gloves to shake her hand.

"The mountains are *incredible!* I had no idea they were so close and so huge," Liz told him.

He chuckled. "We're a ways from 'em here, actually. I've always liked to watch 'em. They change, you know, with the

25

weather and the seasons and the time of day—different colors and contours. Funny thing is, some folks who come here can't seem to get used to 'em. Feel intimidated, I guess, like the mountains are going to fall on 'em. Me, I've always felt like they were a kind of protection, though to tell the truth, that doesn't make a lot more sense than the other, I guess." He had been shepherding Liz toward his front door during this comment, and now he opened it and called, "Lolly! Our new neighbor is here."

The small foyer and living room were exceedingly tidy and furnished with careful good taste. A ceramic figurine of Christ graced a gleaming cherrywood piano. Liz recognized it as a copy of the impressive figure she had seen in the Visitors Center on Temple Square.

Lolly appeared from the kitchen, wiping her hands on a towel. She was a small, rounded woman with apple-red cheeks and dark hair going to gray—a perfect partner, Liz thought, for the cheerful Tuck.

"This's Liz Ewell, Lolly. Liz, my wife, Lolly Tucker. Real name's Laura, but she's been Lolly ever since her baby brother started to talk."

Liz was a little surprised when Lolly put out her hand for a handshake almost as firm as Tuck's.

"Liz, I'm just so glad to have someone nice move into Uncle's place. It's seemed lonely to have it empty since he left. Come on back to the kitchen where we can talk."

Liz followed her and looked around in delight. There was indeed a kitchen with shining appliances and beautifully crafted oak cabinets. It opened onto a family dining area with red-cushioned rocking chairs on either side of a black wood-burning stove on a flagstone hearth. A canary trilled from a bamboo cage by a sunny bow window.

"What a wonderful room," Liz said.

"Oh, we enjoy this part of the house, all right. In fact, we practically live in here in the winter," Tuck responded. "Sit here at the table, Liz, and I'll get the papers. You certain, now, that four hundred a month's all right for you? We could prob'ly adjust it a little, if need be."

Was he worried that as a woman alone, she couldn't meet the rent?

"Thank you, but four hundred seems fine to me. I—um, I received a pretty generous settlement on my divorce, and the Navy sees to it that my alimony check arrives on time—so there shouldn't be any problem."

When her money had been exchanged for a receipt and one of the two signed rental agreements, Liz started to rise, but Tuck waved her back into her chair.

"Believe Mother's got a little something she'd like to serve us," he said with a twinkle. "Don't want to deprive her of that chance, now do we?"

"Don't want to deprive yourself, is more like it," Lolly said, smiling as she set a tray on the table.

"Oh, my," Liz said as she was given a mug of hot spiced apple juice and a plate of warm bran muffins. "Who could refuse? Thank you."

"Seems like a warm bite goes good about this time of the morning," said Lolly, joining them. "Tuck, he's been up since five, and it's still a while till lunch. You have any children, Liz?"

Liz stiffened. "No," she said simply.

"We had four," Lolly continued. "Eighteen grandchildren now—can you believe it?" She indicated a grouping of photographs on the wall opposite, above a small table and chairs and toy box tole-painted with elves and flowers. "It's a three-ring circus when they all get here, but that doesn't happen very often. Only one lives close—our daughter Susan, in

Orem. Boys are in Connecticut, Seattle, and Arizona, but they come when they can. Now, Liz, what can we do to help you get settled? Tuck, he called the water company already, so that should be on soon. I know I can't do a thing in a house without running water. Tuck, hand her the keys before we forget. The one with the string is to the back door, Liz, and we've got duplicates if you need one anytime. We'd better have Tuck go over and show you how to work the furnace—or maybe it'd be better if the gas man does that when he comes. Here, have some more butter with your muffin. How about some apricot jam?"

"No, thanks—these are wonderful just plain." Liz let herself relax. Lolly was busy but not a busybody. She finished her muffin and took the keys Tuck handed her.

"There you are, Sister Ewell," he said and then caught himself. "Whoops, pardon me. We call everybody brother and sister in our church, and it comes so natural to me it just slips out sometimes. But we *are* all brothers and sisters anyway, aren't we?"

"That's—fine," Liz said faintly. She paused to look at the pictures of the Tucker grandchildren on her way out. Small, happy faces of blondes, brunettes, and one redhead smiled from the variety of frames. Liz wondered how it would really feel to be able to lay claim to such treasure.

Tuck and Lolly both walked her to her car, where Tuck opened her door for her with unaffected courtesy. "Let us know if you need anything at all," he told her.

"Thanks. I think I'll be just fine," she told him.

"Sure will be good to have you there," Lolly repeated.

"I'm afraid I'm not a very good neighbor," Liz warned, smiling to soften her message. "I'm terrible about visiting. I stick pretty close to home."

"That's all right, dear, you suit yourself. It'll just be a comfort to know you're there. There's nobody, you know, in the big old Parrish place down the hill—hasn't been for years. Up here, there's just us and the Ashcrafts, and across the field, there, is Woodbines', and Mr. Earl Christensen above them. The newer house down across the highway is the Johansen boy's place. He built on the lot his dad left him. Just a young family. We're not isolated here, but we're more country than town. I could live right in town, I think, but Tuck, he's sure he'd get claustrophobia."

Tuck shrugged. "Old country boy, that's me. Live close to the land, you live close to the Lord."

"That's as may be," Lolly retorted, cuffing his arm lightly. "But sometimes you get so close to the land it's hard to scrub it off!"

Liz's smile broadened as she waved and got into her car. She turned into her "own" driveway and walked through the house again. Already it seemed warmer and cheerier with the February sunlight streaming through the south and east windows. She jotted down a few notes of more things to buy and then locked up and hurried away to complete her errands. With the utilities arranged for, she turned her attention to some serious shopping in Provo. One of the most immediate necessities, she decided, was a bed, and she chose a comfortable single one with an intricately scrolled white wicker headboard. Brock would have hated it. She bought a white chest, bedside table, and cushioned wicker chair, and on impulse, a wicker fern stand and a fluffy, pale green area rug. To celebrate her new home, she treated herself to a grilled steak dinner, with a paperback mystery for company.

"Only one more night in a motel," she promised herself. The bed would be delivered the next day, and the electric and fuel company representatives had agreed to come then, too.

Early the next morning she picked up a few groceries and

cleaning supplies, mailed a request to the transfer and storage company in Hawaii that was holding the few belongings she had chosen to keep from her life with Brock, and drove, with certainty this time, back to her house to await the arrival of the furniture and utility trucks. She wiped down the cabinets and stored the few cans of food on the shelves. It was cold enough outside that the perishable items would keep in her car until her refrigerator could be turned on. She dusted and swept, but it was difficult to do any serious cleaning without hot water, so she went out to wander around her yard, utterly charmed to discover the first green shoots of unknown spring bulbs pushing their way up into the air. She would have flowers, she decided. Not the rank growth and wild abandon of the tropics, but gentle, controlled, civilized flowers—daisies, roses, pansies, marigolds. Maybe she could even get some blue asters.

On the north side of the house, a rectangular patch of ground showed evidence of having been a vegetable garden.

Shall I? she asked herself. *Do I dare? I know next to nothing about gardening. But I could learn, couldn't I? There are books, and I can ask nursery people, and use what common sense I may still possess. I will! I'll do it. I wonder when you can begin here . . .*

Her thoughts were interrupted by the arrival of her furniture, followed not long after by someone from the gas company. With the eventual advent of hot water, she set about scrubbing the bathroom, which didn't really need it, but the activity made her feel more confident and in charge of her home.

Later, stretched out on her new bed in a wonderfully warm and well-lit house, she laughed at herself. She had bought a bed but not a pillow. She had a cozy rug for her feet but no sheets or blankets to cover her, so here she was, curled up on a bare mattress with a couple of sweaters for a pillow and her bathrobe and longest coat for blankets. Well, that would be remedied first thing tomorrow, as would the matter of bath soap, towels, and toilet paper.

She wondered how long it would take for her things to arrive from storage. There wasn't a lot, so they would have to travel with someone else's load. She had taken only the items that were truly hers—her grandmother's little rolltop desk and needlepoint footstool and several items she had kept from her girlhood. She would need new cookware, dishes, linens, and such—it would be fun choosing, she thought. Like a bride, except there was no groom. *And that's just as well, too,* she told herself sternly as she drifted off to sleep.

The next day, Saturday, she toasted a slice of bread under her broiler, drank a glass of juice, and rushed off to resume her shopping. By evening she was exhausted but returned with a car full of packages and sacks. She spent the evening making her bed with real sheets and blankets and set white ginger jar lamps on her chest of drawers and bedside table. She had chosen paper for one of her bedroom walls—pale green with a white bamboo pattern—and a tall ceramic jar with yellow and white silk daisies to stand in an empty corner. The bedspread and curtains would have to wait, but at least there were old-fashioned pull shades at the windows—not, she reflected, that there was much need to worry about privacy on this side of the house. The only place visible at all from her bedroom windows was the empty house down the hill, and the orchard of bare-limbed trees separated her from that.

Liz unpacked boxes of cookware, stoneware, and flatware. A peach rug and fluffy floral towels made the bathroom more welcoming, and a couple of braided rugs softened the austerity of the kitchen. She had chosen nothing as yet for her living or dining rooms, but at least the back part of the house didn't echo quite so hollowly at her footsteps.

Her last stop had been at a bookstore, where she had

bought several books on gardening, and, on impulse, a small framed photograph of the statue of Christ that had so moved her on her visit to Temple Square. It would go in the hallway, she decided, where it would be visible from her dining room.

It was sheer pleasure to snuggle between new percale sheets—though she would have preferred to wash them first and let them air-dry on the clothesline in the backyard. Her house didn't have plumbing for a washing machine, however, so she would have to locate a laundromat on her next outing.

A fitful little wind had kicked up outside, but her new lamp cast a cozy glow over her bedroom, and she huddled deeper into her goose-down pillows and read of peas and lettuce and eggplant and onions and ways of controlling earwigs and squash bugs. It was informative and useful material but not highly stimulating, and it wasn't long before she slipped into the contented slumber that follows a busy and satisfying day.

Sunday morning she washed her hair and then stood at the window watching people stream into the church down the hill as she deftly used her blow-dryer and a round brush to shape her short hairstyle. It was surprising how many people went to church, she thought. Somehow she had pictured a very small congregation. One family walked by from the house farther up her own road, the parents tall and slender, holding hands, followed by a blond boy and girl. The boy was as tall as his father but not so filled out, and the girl, a preadolescent, had shoulder-length shining straight hair and long legs that gave her an awkward grace. What was the name Lolly had told her? Yes, Ashcraft. That must be who they were. *That'll be easy to remember,* Liz thought with a small smile. *I'll just think of them as the "Ashblond" family.*

Presently Lolly herself drove by, at the wheel of a late-model Buick. Liz assumed that Tuck, as bishop, must already be at the church, doing whatever bishops did. After a while, all looked quiet at the church, and Liz grew restless. She dressed and went out for a long, exploratory drive, promising herself dinner later at the Chinese restaurant she had spotted the day before in Provo.

The day was sunny but chill and breezy, and Liz was glad of her short, fake-fur jacket when she parked her car in a visitors' area on the Brigham Young University campus. She got out to stretch her legs and look around. She had expected to find the buildings deserted but was surprised to see groups of students in Sunday dress going to and from what must have been church meetings in various classroom buildings. Several nodded and spoke pleasantly to her. There was a feeling of peace on the campus that relaxed her immeasurably, and she sat on a bench in a sunny, sheltered spot, listening to a medley of hymns being played from a tower of carillon bells. Recognizing one tune from childhood, she closed her eyes and tried to recapture the words to "What a Friend We Have in Jesus," but most of them were lost in time. All she could come up with were the words, "Oh, what needless pain we bear" and "what a privilege to carry everything to God in prayer."

There she was, she thought, being reminded again to pray. Well, why not? It was Sunday, after all, and heaven knew—and so did she—that she had prayed seldom enough in the last few years. She had practically forgotten how, if she'd ever truly known.

Dear God, she began silently, *Thank you for this peaceful time—for my new house, for my health, for the chance to rest and learn who I am. How can I say thanks for my divorce? I think you probably don't approve of divorce. But surely you didn't approve of my marriage, either. Please—please help me in all I do. Amen.*

It was a feeble attempt, she acknowledged to herself, but somehow she felt better for having made it. She went to find her Chinese dinner and enjoyed it immensely, knowing that she had a cozy home of her own to return to.

She found a slip of white paper tucked into her front screened door when she got home. "Come for Sunday dinner at three if you have no special plans," the note read. "Love to have you." It was signed "Laura Tucker." It was already past four, Liz noted with relief, though it was kind of Lolly to invite her. She must remember to thank her. Tuck and Lolly, she had already decided, were the sort of people known as the salt of the earth.

I will have to see about a phone, Liz told herself. I hate to, in a way; I'd love to be perfectly private here, but I suppose I must, for emergencies and for situations like this. I could call Lolly and explain easily, but if I walk over to speak to her, she'll persuade me to stay, and I don't want to. Oh, I hope people will leave me alone here! That's really all I ask of them.

4

Liz spent the evening studying her garden books with an
eagerness that amazed her. She made notes and charts of
what to plant and when for the Utah climate and how to prepare the soil. Her parents had always had a garden when she
was growing up, but it had been her father's project, and she
had never taken much interest in it. During her married life,
her gardening had been limited to a few temporary houseplants that she gave away to neighbors when Brock's transfers
came. But this would be her own garden, her own project, and
she couldn't wait to begin. It would be an interest, a hobby—
and a practical one, giving her fresh food for her table and
fresh air and exercise for her body.

Monday, still mild, found her buying hoes, rakes, seeds, and
fertilizer, as well as jeans, long-sleeved shirts, and warm sweat-
shirts. She also found time to visit an antique shop, where she
paid more than she suspected she should have for a sturdy, used
(but by no means antique) drop-leaf dining table and four
matching chairs, which she was confident she could strip to
the original wood and stain to suit her taste.

By two-thirty, she was home, clad in her new work clothes
and taking advantage of the afternoon sun to begin preparing
her garden soil. It wasn't long before she realized that she had

forgotten to buy one necessary item—gardening gloves—and blisters rose in several places on her palms by the time her back also told her it was time to quit. But the ground had been workable enough after the recent rain, and she was pleased with the results of her labor: a portion of the plot spaded and hoed and raked, fertilizer mixed in according to directions, and three neat rows of peas planted.

Liz yearned for a good hot soak in her tub, but before she could get it ready, a knock sounded at her front door. A young woman stood there, strands of brown hair escaping her scarf to whip across her face, and two small children tugging at her coat.

"Hello," Liz said uncertainly.

"Hi," the young woman replied, a friendly smile replacing the rather hassled expression she had worn. "I'm Marilyn Woodbine. I live across the field, in that big old house to the north, there—had you noticed it? We just walked across to say 'hi' and welcome to the neighborhood."

She offered a loaf of bread, still warm to the touch.

"Oh—well, thank you so much. Um—will you come in? The wind's really kicking up, isn't it?"

"It is," Marilyn agreed, ushering her children across the threshold before her. "We'll only stay a minute. I wanted to get the bread to you while it was still warm. I think it's best then, don't you? And what's your name? Lolly mentioned it, but . . ."

"I'm sorry—Liz Ewell. And you actually baked this bread? From scratch? I've never dared try—that's really a special treat. It smells heavenly."

Marilyn laughed. "Not so special at our house—we do it three times a week. When you have ten kids, it pays to be able to produce your own basics. Not so much running to the store."

"Ten?" Liz repeated, stunned. "Ten kids?"

"Yep. These are my two youngest, Kenny and Kimberly. My eldest is seventeen."

"You don't look old enough to have a seventeen-year-old," Liz said. "But if they're all as cute as these two, you must have a beautiful family." She winked at the little boy peeking around his mother's legs. He grinned and hid his eyes.

Marilyn smiled again. "You have my undying friendship for saying so," she said. "We have been blessed. They're good kids. Do you have children?"

"No, I never had any, and I'm recently divorced. I'm sorry I can't ask you to sit down," she added, by way of changing the subject. "I'm just beginning to collect a few pieces of furniture, and I haven't even started on the living room yet."

"It takes a while. Where did you move from?"

"Hawaii, most recently, with a stop in San Francisco to visit a cousin for a while. But tell me about your bread—is it hard to learn to make?"

"Not really. I do all our bread and rolls, different varieties. This is part whole wheat, part unbleached white flour. I have my own grinder and bread mixer, so it's not like kneading by hand. It doesn't really take long. Saves money, plus we like it better, and there are no preservatives and junk."

Liz looked at her with respect. "I think that's remarkable. But did you say you have a grinder? Do you mean you grind your own flour?"

"Sure. We have about three tons of wheat stored in our basement, so we can grind just the amount we need, fresh, every time we bake."

"Forgive me—I'm probably sounding stupid—but were you anywhere near serious when you said three *tons* of wheat in your basement?"

Marilyn laughed again. "Absolutely. Blows your mind, doesn't it? Did mine, when I first learned about doing it. Part of it's our year's supply, of course, but we rotate it to keep it fresh. You'd be surprised how fast it goes. Listen—why don't you run over sometime, on a baking day—that's Monday, Wednesday and Friday—and I'll show you the whole process. I usually start about nine in the morning. It'd be fun to show you."

"Thanks, I'd like that," Liz said, surprised to find she meant it. She liked Marilyn Woodbine, with her open, frank face, freckled nose, and ten children. She was not quite like anyone Liz had ever met.

"I need to run. I've left soup on the stove, and Tom will be home soon. He teaches at BYU. But really, why don't you plan to come over anytime you can, and we'll get better acquainted."

"I'm a terrible neighbor," Liz warned her, as she had Lolly. "I hardly ever get around to doing much visiting. It's not that I don't like people. I just . . ."

Marilyn reached over to pat her arm. "Oh, listen—no pressure, okay? Just if you feel like it and want some company, or to see how we do bread—please know you're welcome. I'm not a very social, outgoing sort myself, so I know exactly what you're saying. But I just had to run this over and say hi, before the storm broke."

"I'm very glad you did. It's nice to meet you, and I'll enjoy some of this with my supper. Is the weather supposed to get interesting? I haven't heard a forecast lately."

"There's a storm front moving in, but they're not sure how much punch it has. We've had a pretty mild winter so far—but then, any winter is a lot of winter when you've been used to Hawaii and California!"

"True," Liz agreed, watching as Marilyn scooped up her youngest under one arm, took the hand of the other, and jogged across the empty field that separated their yards. The wind had a new bite to it, and gray clouds moved once again to obscure the mountain peaks.

Liz had her bath, changed into soft pajamas and robe, and began to prepare a salad to go with the chicken breast she was broiling. Another knock at the door startled her, and she peered out her front window into the breezy blue dusk to see who was calling now. It was a young girl carrying a plate. One of Marilyn's children?

"Hi," the girl said shyly, as Liz opened the door. She had cornflower blue eyes and long, straight blonde hair. Liz realized who she was before she spoke again. "I'm Missy Ashcraft. I just brought you some cookies to say hi."

A Utah custom, apparently, Liz thought. Or maybe a good old custom, in any state. Country hospitality. Or was it country curiosity? "Come in, Missy," she invited, accepting the plate.

Missy stepped inside. "Oh-h," she said softly, looking around the bare room. "It looks so—sad! I mean, I haven't been here since Uncle Ned left, and he had this room full of such fun stuff. He had Japanese dolls and ivory elephants— little tiny ones, with their tails and trunks hooked together, you know? In a line? And over there, he had the neatest old organ with carved wooden flowers and red velvet behind them. He used to let me pump the pedals while he played, 'cause his knees were too bad."

"You must miss him," Liz said sympathetically.

"Yeah, he was nice. I was real sorry when he had to go away, and then he died. He always said when he had to leave his home, it'd be time for him to leave this world. And he did."

"I—see. Well, thank you for the cookies. Did you make them?"

"Yep. I cook a lot. I made spaghetti today, but Dave said I shouldn't have put chili powder in the sauce because that's

39

Mexican and spaghetti's Italian. Do you put chili powder in the sauce?"

"Usually I season it with oregano and sweet basil," Liz said, suppressing a smile.

"Would you write that down? Then I can get some at the store next time. I mean, Dave ate a whole lot of it, anyway, but maybe next time I'll try it your way. I like to experiment around with food."

"I imagine your mother appreciates your help in the kitchen."

"Yeah, I guess. Dad says she used to like to cook, too. She doesn't anymore, because she doesn't feel too well. But it's okay, 'cause I like to, and Dave's pretty good about helping wash up."

"Dave's your brother?"

"Yep. Do you have any kids my age? I'm eleven."

"No, I'm afraid I don't. There's just me."

"Oh, baloney. I mean, it's nice *you're* here, but I was hoping there'd be somebody to play with."

"What about the ten Woodbine children? I met their mom today."

Missy wrinkled her nose. "The ones near my age are all boys," she said scornfully. "And they're a pain. The closest girl to my age is Suzanne. She's fourteen and thinks she's all grown up. I mean, she has a crush on *Dave,* and he's way too old for her. He's almost nineteen and ready to leave on his mission. Even when he gets back, she'll only be about sixteen. You know? So I was hoping for a girl."

"Right. Um—I need to check on my dinner. Would you like to come back to the kitchen with me?"

"Sure." Missy tossed her shiny hair and followed Liz to hover at her shoulder while she basted her browning piece of chicken.

"It's almost ready," Liz remarked.

"What're you putting on it?"

"A little melted butter, lemon juice, and pepper."

"Is it good? It smells yummy."

"I like it."

"Maybe I'll do that the next time I fix chicken. Which bedroom did you pick? Oh—wow!" She answered her own question by peeking in each room. "How gorgeous!"

"Well, thanks," said Liz, half pleased and half annoyed. Without being sure why, she picked up a roll of her bamboo wallpaper and spread it out for Missy to see. "I thought I'd put this on one wall and paint the others pale green, with white woodwork. I'll probably have white eyelet curtains and spread."

"It's just like you'd see in a magazine. It looks real different already. Uncle Ned, he had a lot of big, dark furniture and piles of clothes and stuff in the corners. His wife—her name was Ethelyn—had been dead a long time, you see," she said earnestly. "But he really loved her, and he couldn't stand to give away all her things. I mean, he kept an old box of her face powder on the dresser and a little bottle of cologne that had gone all strong and smelly, you know how it does, but he kept it anyway. It was awful sad but kind of sweet, too. He was a nice man."

"Really," said Liz, who would much rather not have known quite so much about the history of her fresh new bedroom. She rolled the wallpaper back up and placed it in the corner. "Well, Missy, thanks again for the cookies. And I expect my dinner is ready now," she added pointedly.

"Yeah, it smells done," Missy agreed. "Don't you even have a husband?"

Liz swallowed. *Get used to it*, she told herself. *Children only voice what adults don't dare.*

"I'm divorced," she said evenly. "Just recently."

"Oh-h," Missy said. She cocked her head to one side, pursed her lips, and regarded Liz with a critical eye. "Well," she said, "I expect it was his fault. Anyway, you're pretty enough that you won't be single long. I mean, probably you'll meet somebody nice and get married again real soon."

"Oh—no, I don't think so."

"Really? Do you still love him? Were you married in the temple?"

"In the—oh, no, I'm not a Mormon. Neither is he."

"But do you love him?"

"Missy, I don't think—well, no, I don't, not really. But I don't think I'll be able to love anyone else, either. So I'll probably just stay single. Anyway, I enjoy being by myself."

Missy didn't take the hint. "It's fun, sometimes," she agreed. "Because you can do whatever you want. But after a while it gets awful lonesome. My dad got real lonesome when Mama was away. He still does, but it's not so bad because at least he can talk to her and see her and all, and sometimes things are almost like they used to be."

My girl, Liz thought, *if you can be nosy, so can I.*

"Missy," she said, "what's wrong with your mother? Didn't I see her walking to church with you, yesterday?"

"Oh, she's not sick. She's fine. It's just that she has—problems, you know? So she isn't quite herself these days."

It sounded rehearsed—a canned speech.

"Is she mentally ill?" Liz asked quietly.

"Well, kind of like that," Missy said, stubbing her shoe against the bottom of the cupboard. "I mean, she isn't wild or anything. She's really sweet. She just sort of isn't—quite with us. She kind of lives in a dream world, my dad says."

"That must be hard for all of you."

"Not so bad," Missy said, looking away toward the corner

of the kitchen. "Not for me, because I can't really remember how she used to be. But Dave can, and it upsets him sometimes."

"I would think so," Liz said, subdued. She set out her dinner on the countertop. Missy watched her in silence.

"Guess I better go," she said finally.

"Um—wait a second, Missy." Liz rummaged in her bag for a scrap of paper and hastily wrote from memory her favorite spaghetti sauce recipe. "Here you go—try this on Dave sometime."

"All right! I will. Thanks, you're really nice. It'll be almost as nice having you here as Uncle Ned. Tell you what—I'll stop by when I can and keep you company."

"Oh, no, that's not necessary, Missy. I don't want . . ."

"You don't want me to come?"

Liz looked at the cornflower blue eyes and rounded cheeks. Missy was a pretty child who wouldn't be a child much longer, and she was apparently growing up without a mother's guidance. Inwardly, Liz cursed the compunctions that made her reach out to squeeze the girl's hand.

"I *meant*," she said, "that I don't want you to feel obligated to come over too often. You must have a lot of responsibilities at home. But stop by for a few minutes when you can and want to."

Missy's face cleared. "Oh," she said. "Sure. You know, you'd better eat your chicken before it gets cold. 'Bye!"

"Aren't you afraid to be out in the dark?" Liz called after her retreating form.

"Not here!" Missy shouted back over her shoulder.

Liz ate her supper in a thoughtful mood, washed her few dishes, and then retired to her room to plan her next section of garden. After the second time she nodded off over her books and charts, she turned out her lamp and snuggled luxuriously

43

under her blankets, realizing that she was more tired than she had thought. Certain back and shoulder muscles told her in no uncertain terms that the physical side of having a garden was much harder work than the mental preparation and planning for one.

She awoke once during the night, startled by a ghostly "woo-oo" sound—almost two threads of sound in eerie harmony, weaving through the darkness somewhere behind her. For a few moments her heart beat frantically, and she lay perfectly still, trying to will her sleep-laden mind to identify the sound and to stop creating images of the erstwhile Mrs. Uncle Ned Whoever's powder boxes and perfume bottles. Gradually her pulse slowed; it was, of course, the wind prowling about the corners of the house, prying and crying at her window and sending little eddies of icy air through any available crevices to mock her comfort. One of her pillows was warm against her back, and she thought of how comforting it had once been during the many tropical thunderstorms they had weathered to sense Brock's solid presence in the bed beside her—even if all she had really gained from it had been the nearness of a fellow human being.

You're on your own, she reminded herself for perhaps the hundredth time and applied herself to sleep—practical, necessary, blessedly forgetful sleep.

5

A s she awoke the next morning, Liz became conscious of
two more unfamiliar sounds. Something was hitting the
window with a faint "zing," and somebody was doing something on her back porch: scrape, crunch, crunch, *thunk*. She
stepped out of bed, grateful for her soft rug, although even that
felt cold to her bare feet, and shrugged into her robe, wincing
at the now thoroughly stiff gardening muscles of the previous
day. Holding aside her window shade, she found her visibility
was almost zero on account of water trickling down the glass
and tiny bits of ice (could it be sleet?) being flung and clinging until they, too, melted and ran. The world looked white.

"Snow!" she cried softly and hurried to the back door to
check on the other noise. Tuck was carrying small armloads of
neat logs and stacking them under the shelter of her porch.
His pickup was backed close to the house. She ran a hand
quickly through her tousled hair and over her face and then
opened the door to admit a whirl of icy air.

"Hello! What's this?" she called, half-closing the door
again to ward off the wind.

"Mornin'!" replied Tuck, his cheerful face red under his
hunting cap. " 'Pears like we're in for a day of this—maybe
two—and it occurred to Lolly and me that you didn't have

anything to burn in your fireplace and you might just want a fire, day like today. Use the small sticks for kindling, and twisted-up newspaper does pretty good, too, and that ought to catch the bigger logs all right. Oh, and Lolly sent you over these, too. She likes a good mystery on a stormy day—thought you might enjoy them." He handed her three paperbacks, one an Agatha Christie, together with a small box of matches, and left with a wave before Liz could do more than gasp a surprised "Thank you!"

She put water to heat and hurried into jeans, a sweater, thick socks, and soft slippers. The cold made her hungry, and she prepared oatmeal, toast, and juice, and then finished off with one of Missy's cookies and coffee. Finally she sat back, re-plete, and listened to the soft ping of the snow as it was flung against the windows. She eyed the three paperbacks in a mo-ment of temptation and then set them aside and stood up. "Later for you," she told them. "First I'd better earn my leisure. Today for wallpapering."

She felt relatively confident in her papering skills, having once helped Dorrie paper several rooms, and she had acquired the needed equipment the day before. By noon, she had a bamboo grove flourishing on the east wall of her bedroom. Feeling pleased with herself, she decided to get acquainted with the snow. The wind had died down, and the snow was now falling in large, lazy flakes, floating like feathers to cushion the earth. Having no boots, Liz put on a pair of thick-soled walking shoes, fastened her jacket high under her chin, and, as an afterthought, stuck an apple in her pocket.

The first thing that struck her was the sweet smell of the snow; the second was the utter quiet and peace of the world. She stood absolutely still and listened. The only discernible sounds were the occasional soft plops of dollops of snow drop-ping from overladen twigs and branches. There was, she judged, at least three inches, and it was still falling steadily. She looked upward, trying to determine how far she could see into the swirling onslaught.

White on white, she thought, watching flakes appear as if by magic just at the limit of her vision.

The evergreen trees were Christmas cards come to life, the fragrance of their needles clean and exhilarating. By her front steps, Liz brushed the snow from a little purple flower, tightly closed and nestled cautiously among its spiky green shoots of leaves. "Brave little thing," Liz told it. "Blooming all by yourself in this climate. Or maybe you're just foolhardy, like me."

She followed the road to the top of the hill, the snow squeaking under her soles. She passed Tuck and Lolly's home, the smoke rising from the chimney of its cozy kitchen, and finally came abreast of the Ashcraft house—a simple ranch-style with gray siding and peeling white paint on the trim. A few bare-limbed fruit trees stood to one side, and a middle-aged blue pickup before the closed garage collected a mantle of snow. No smoke rose from the chimney here, and no lamplight gleamed from the windows. Liz wondered about the woman within. What did she do all day? How ill was she? Did she know she was not well? Did she have any measure of happiness?

Liz shivered inside her jacket. The road ran past the Ashcrafts' house for perhaps another two hundred yards or so—it was hard to judge in the snow—and ended at a gate in a barbed-wire fence that enclosed more farmlands. *Tuck's?* she wondered. She turned and tramped back down the hill, stopping to watch as the joyous barking of a dog at Woodbines' alerted her to action there. Three brightly clad little bodies tumbled out the door with glad cries, falling and rolling in the snow as the dog plowed through it with his nose, running circles around them. There was smoke rising from that chimney, right enough, and the air began to take on a tang that reminded Liz of roasted hot dogs and crusty brown marsh-mallows. She pulled her apple from her pocket and bit into it with a satisfying crunch.

By the time she had walked back down the hill, circled around the church grounds and back up to her house, her cheeks were warm and glowing, but her feet were soaked.

"Why shouldn't I have a fire, too?" she asked herself aloud. "I'd be ungrateful not to, after Tuck brought me all that wood." She pulled open the firescreen and examined the black grate. It had been brushed clean, so she laid the best fire she knew how, with logs and dry twigs and some wads of paper for kin-dling. She would drag the wicker rocker from her bedroom, she decided, and have an afternoon of fireside mysteries.

The fire caught well enough, but it soon became apparent that the chief mystery of her day was why the grayish smoke insisted on pouring into the room instead of rising up the chimney as it should. Alarmed, she yanked open the front door and then ran to the kitchen for a pan of water to douse the flames.

"It's not drawing!" she exclaimed, staring in dismay at the ruins of her lovely fire. "I'll have to tell Tuck—he thought the fireplace was in good order."

Wrinkling her nose at the acrid odor of wet ashes, she closed her front door and repaired to her room with the three mysteries to read behind a closed door. Throughout the after-noon and evening she blessed Lolly for sending the books and promised herself that she would lay in a supply of reading ma-terials at the next opportunity.

For supper she sliced a thick piece of Marilyn Woodbine's excellent bread and melted cheese on it to have with a bowl of tomato soup. It seemed good to enjoy such simple, homely fare after the restaurant meals and quick snacks of recent days.

Two days later, the snow was all but gone, dripping from

the eaves in constant splashes that gave Liz the sense of having left water running somewhere. Fitful rounds of sunshine showed patches of grass that were, if anything, greener than before, and the little purple flower opened its yellow heart to the warmth. Close by, a similar patch of orange-throated white buds also began to open. Liz wondered what they were called and decided to consult her gardening library.

Armed with accurate room measurements and a few general ideas, she set out to select a few things for her living room. By the end of the day she was tired but satisfied with her efforts. She chose a large Oriental-style rug and two smaller ones to adorn the dark brown floor. A delicate rose-striped paper would cover all walls except the panelled one, and when her little rolltop desk arrived, it would fit perfectly between the windows. Comfortable chairs and long Priscilla curtains could be complemented by a few cozy lamps and plants. Among her things were a couple of counted cross-stitch pictures she had made under Dorrie's tutelage but had never hung because they didn't fit with Brock's decor. They would fit with this room, and she had even ambitiously selected wools and a book of afghan patterns to crochet. *Cozy,* she decided. *Cozy and mine. A reflection of my personality, for a change. A haven of peace and silence and solitude.* She hugged herself, looking around the bare living room and imagining how it would look with everything in place. She wanted to wrap the little house around her like a comforter and hide in it.

By Saturday morning, the living room was papered and ready to receive its furnishings. When the furniture van pulled away, Liz discovered that the room exceeded her expectations. She loved it. It was warm and friendly and, at the same time, delicate and feminine. *Hers.* Even Uncle Ned, she suspected, would have approved.

She had made a creditable start toward the dining room

49

project, as well, choosing colors to complement her new dishes and the warm wood tones of her newly stained table. By the windows she would have more plants—ferns and African violets, tuberous begonias and trailing ivies. She had seen them in her gardening books and wanted several varieties. The brave little flowers by the front steps, she had discovered, were called crocus.

When she could bring herself to leave, she put on her jacket and walked across to the Tuckers' house, Lolly's mysteries tucked under one arm. The sun, red in the west, gave a pink glow to the snow-covered mountains across the valley. The air was still and cool, and the moment seemed fragile and precious. Liz stood still and let the beauty of it wash over her and leave her refreshed. Then as the sun slowly disappeared, she turned up the Tuckers' drive.

Lolly answered the door, flushed and warm from kitchen work, and led her back to that large and cheerful room. The round table was set for two, and Tuck rose from his place to shake her hand heartily and reach for a third plate.

"Haven't had your supper yet, have you?" he asked.

Liz smiled. "Haven't even thought about it," she confessed. "I've been too busy today. But you folks go right ahead. I just dropped by to return the books, which I loved, and to say thank you for the firewood. I . . ."

"Sit down right here," Lolly insisted. "Been meaning to have you over for a meal ever since last Sunday. Sorry we missed you then. We're eating early tonight because Tuck's got a stake meeting, and we've got plenty—it's just sloppy joe hamburgers. Kids always wanted that for Saturday supper, and we kinda got into the habit. Still in the habit of making a lot, too, so don't think there isn't plenty. I'll tell you, it's hard to gear back down to just cooking for two—guess that's part of the empty-nest syndrome you keep hearing about. Will you take milk or fruit punch?"

"Punch is fine," Liz said, allowing herself to be drawn in against her best intentions. It had been years since she'd tasted a sloppy joe. "That was a great choice of books, Lolly," she said, seating herself at the place provided. "I didn't have much reading material on hand."

"Thought you might not," Lolly agreed, looking expectantly at her husband, who bowed his head and gave thanks for their food and their company.

"Amen," Lolly echoed. "Have some potato salad, Liz, and some carrot sticks, while I dish up the burgers."

"Um—Tuck, I tried to make a fire the other day, but something went wrong. I don't know if I didn't do it right, or if the chimney has a problem, but smoke poured out into the room."

"Was the damper open?" asked Tuck, helping himself to potato salad.

Liz grinned. "Probably not, since I don't know what a damper is, or how to open one. I've never had a fireplace."

Tuck laughed and told her about the little door inside the chimney and where to find the handle that controlled it. "It opens in and closes out, just like the door to the house," he explained. "Sorry I didn't think to tell you about that."

"No harm done."

"Saw a furniture truck over there today," Lolly said. "Are you finding everything you need?"

"Yes, I'm delighted with how it's all shaping up. I'd like you both to come and see what I've done."

"We'd like that. Met any of the neighbors yet?" Tuck inquired.

"I had a lovely loaf of bread from Marilyn Woodbine and a plate of cookies from Missy Ashcraft, both last Monday."

Tuck and Lolly exchanged twinkling glances.

"Figured Missy'd be Johnny-on-the-spot," Tuck said. "Missy gets lonesome—pops in and out here and at Woodbines' and just about everywhere. Hope she won't be a nuisance to you."

"No—I don't think she will. She hasn't been back yet, at any rate. I understand her mother isn't well. Is she too ill to communicate much with Missy?"

Tuck sighed. "Sister Ashcraft's a real sweet lady," he said slowly. "Just as pleasant as she can be. She simply lives in a different world than the rest of us. She nods and smiles and answers your question. Trouble is, her answer usually has no relation to what you asked. Or she begins talking about one thing, and by the time she gets to the end of her sentence, she's talking about something else. Makes you feel like you missed something along the way. So you can imagine there's not much real communication going on, and Missy feels the loss."

"What does Mr. Ashcraft do?"

"Used to be in real estate, but he took a night job at the post office up to Provo so he could be home days while the kids are in school. They don't like to leave Helen alone for too long—not because she's ever been dangerous but just for their own peace of mind. She spent three years at the state hospital, and they seemed real tickled to finally bring her home. Nice little family, in spite of everything."

"Missy seems sweet," Liz said, awed at the overwhelming problem faced by the little girl and her family.

"They'll sure miss David when he goes on his mission," Lolly remarked.

Liz was vaguely aware of the custom of sending young Mormon men out for missionary service. "How long will he be gone?" she asked.

"Two years," replied Tuck. "Would seem like he's needed at home, more, but he really wants to serve, and Wynn's always encouraged him to plan on it. Doesn't want Helen's condition to keep the kids from having a normal life any more than necessary. Dave's been called to Austria," he added.

"Does the church pay the missionaries a stipend or anything?" Liz asked.

"Oh, no," Tuck and Lolly said together. "They and their families pay," Lolly added. "The church helps families who can't meet the whole amount, but it's an unpaid volunteer service. We sent all three of our boys—one to Japan, one to Tennessee, and one to Canada."

"That's amazing," Liz said, impressed.

"Well, it's a great maturing experience for the boys, spiritually and socially," Tuck explained. "Not to mention the great good they can do for others in the process."

"Two years in Austria sounds like a marvelous education," Liz said thoughtfully.

"They do soak up a good bit of culture along the way," Tuck agreed. "And they have a little free time to see the sights. Of course, they get a head start on the language at the MTC up to Provo—that's the Missionary Training Center—and knowing a second language is valuable for anybody these days. But what's even more important, they learn to love the people they work with because they serve them. Learn to love the Lord, too, because of course when you're serving God's children, you're serving him. Take some more of this potato salad, now, Liz—you only had a dab!"

"Maybe another dab, then—it's delicious. I enjoyed meeting Marilyn Woodbine, too."

"Marilyn's a lovely girl," Lolly agreed. "Got her hands full with that big family, but she does real well. One of the finest Relief Society teachers we've ever had."

"Tom's a good man, too," Tuck added. "Bit intellectual for some folks around here, but he never puts on airs or lets it go to his head. Real dependable sort—does whatever you ask him. Good dad to his kids, too, even when he might rather be holed up somewhere studying or working on his book."

"He's writing a book?" Liz asked.

"He's into Japanese history. Served his mission there a few years before our boy did and got interested in the country then. Tom's quite the scholar, and Marilyn's not too far behind him. To tell the truth, though, she's just as down-to-earth as you'd want."

"She told me about all the bread she makes."

"Land, yes, those kids go through food like a tent full of lumberjacks! And I thought it took a lot to raise four." Lolly laughed comfortably.

Liz thanked the Tuckers for the supper and hurried back to her welcoming little house. It wasn't complete, of course, but it was coming along nicely. She supposed that eventually she would buy a television and a stereo system, but for now it was still restful to listen to silence and think her own thoughts. She had her car radio, which she listened to while driving, and she had bought a few papers and magazines, so she wasn't entirely out of touch with the world. Just almost, she reflected with a wry smile. With Brock, she had awakened early every morning to a fast-paced cacophony of world news that she wasn't ready to face yet. Half the time, she would remember something later in the day and wonder whether she'd really heard it or made it up from her subconscious. Of course, that had been before she'd begun sleeping in the guest room and not getting up in the mornings until after Brock had gone.

She wandered into her bedroom and stretched luxuriously. It was beginning to feel marvelous to be her own woman, "beholden to no one," as her grandfather would have said.

6

When her peas broke ground, Liz rejoiced, and she ran out to look at them at odd moments throughout the day. Encouraged, she prepared ground and planted lettuce, radishes, and Swiss chard. In one corner of the garden, some volunteer onions had appeared. Nights were still cold, and the wind keened at the corner of her room, but more and more frequently the afternoons warmed up to mere "sweater weather," and then she took long, rambling walks. Daffodils were in evidence everywhere, and the grass was greening up with enthusiasm. There were still patches of snow on the north sides of buildings, and one day more snow fell, but it clung only to those existing patches, otherwise melting into the already soggy ground. Fat robins and a horde of migrating blackbirds investigated the garden and teetered wildly, clinging to utility lines in the March gusts.

Missy Ashcraft had become a regular visitor, popping in for brief chats two or three times a week. Sometimes, with a small twinge of guilt, Liz managed not to hear her knock, and finally Missy commented on it.

"You should get a doorbell," she announced with no preamble. "I was here yesterday, and I knocked really loud. I thought sure you'd hear me, 'cause you don't have a TV or anything, and I know you were home, 'cause I heard the toilet flush when I came along the yard. But maybe you were getting in your bath."

Liz decided to try to level with her. "Missy, um—sometimes I don't feel like visiting with anyone, so I just don't answer the door."

"Have you been sick?"

"No. I just like—well, I told you before. I enjoy being alone."

Missy considered this and nodded wisely. "I get it. You must feel kind of sad, sometimes, and think about your husband a lot."

"No, really, it's not that. I'm very happy, actually. I'm just a private sort of person, that's all. Some people are. I just like to think my own thoughts and choose when I want company and when I don't."

"Well, I think you must be shy. If you knew us all better, prob'ly you'd want to visit more."

Liz gave up. "You may be right. I do like everyone I've met, though."

"Even me?"

"Of course, you! Why do you ask?"

"Well, I mean—not everyone does. Maybe I am weird."

"Oh, I don't think so. Not at all. I think you're rather special."

"Really? That sounds nicer than weird. But I don't know if I want to be special, either. I think I'd kind of like to be just like everyone else."

"Well, we're not really all alike, are we? Everyone's a unique individual. That's what makes people interesting."

"I guess." She paused, sucking on her lower lip. Then, "What was his name?"

"Who?"

56

"Your husband."

"His name is Brock."

"Mm. There's a Brock in my grade at school, and he's a brat."

"Well," said Liz with a wry smile, "maybe it goes with the name. Brock the brat."

Missy giggled and then narrowed her eyes. "Was he cruel to you?"

"In—in a way. But not—he didn't hit me, or anything. We're just very, very different."

"Mental cruelty, then. Was that the grounds?"

"Missy, where do you learn such things at your age?"

"On TV," Missy said simply. "I'll bet he didn't want to let you be a private person, did he?"

Liz sighed. "I'm not sure he even knew I *was* a particular kind of person. Maybe that was my fault, for not being stronger. But that's all in the past, Missy. It's receding farther and farther back into the past every day. I'm working on forgetting all about that part of my life."

"That's good. I like the kind of person you are, you know, even if I'm not that kind, myself. Dave's more like that than I am, and so is Dad. Oh, that reminds me! That's what I really came to ask you about. You know how Dave's going on a mission to Austria? I told you about that, didn't I?"

"Yes."

"Yeah. Well, he's taking this missionary preparation class, okay? And he's supposed to practice giving the discussions to somebody. So he's been giving them to me and sometimes to Dad, when he has time to listen. It's kind of fun, you know? Except I know most of the answers already, because of Primary. And Dad knows all of them, but sometimes he tries to trip Dave up, or act like he doesn't believe it, just for practice, okay? But I thought . . ." She took a deep breath. "I thought, wouldn't it be neat if he could practice giving the discussions to you! Because you really aren't a member, even if you're nice enough to be one, and you'd know the kind of questions to ask him, and all." She rested her case, blue eyes expectantly wide.

Liz swallowed. "Missy, I—no, I don't think I can do that. I'm sorry. I'm sure it would be interesting, but I'm just not ready for that much—I don't know how to explain," she ended lamely, feeling wretched at the disappointment on Missy's face.

"It's okay," Missy said with a sigh. "Dave said I shouldn't ask you."

"Oh? Why?"

"He said it was too—um—obvious, and not fair to you. And another word. Too—presumptish, or something, I don't remember exactly what. But you will come to his farewell, won't you?"

"To—what? You're giving him a farewell party?"

"Oh, no—well, I mean, we *are*, of course, but the farewell is the sacrament meeting at church where the missionary gives a talk before he goes in the MTC. It's going to be April nineteenth, at eleven o'clock. Will you come? You could walk down with us or ride with Sister Tucker."

Liz didn't know why she agreed. Probably, she decided, it was because she hated to give two no's in a row to a little girl who was so obviously excited and proud of her big brother.

"But I'll just walk down by myself," she told her. "April nineteenth at eleven o'clock in the morning? See, I'll put it on my calendar right now."

Hands on hips, Missy regarded her, blonde hair swinging to one side as she tilted her head. "You are the by-yourselfest person I ever met!"

Liz laughed. "I guess I probably am," she admitted. "But you have to understand, Missy—that's one reason I moved

58

here instead of to a place with more people. I came here to be quiet and alone and think things over in peace."

Missy looked chagrined. "I know. And I really shouldn't bother you so much. I'll try not to."

"I'm usually glad to see you, Missy—as long as you understand when sometimes I don't answer the door."

"Tell you what: just holler 'Not today, Missy,' and I'll go away. And thanks for saying you'll come."

"Thanks for inviting me."

"Yeah." She sighed, glancing around the living room. "I love your house. It's so pretty and soft and clean. Well, 'bye for now." Characteristically, she left as abruptly as she had come, running up the road, vaulting over puddles and sliding precariously in the mud. Her cotton dress was short, and Liz wondered about the warmth of the thin sweater pulled around her shoulders.

A day dawned early in April that was a precursor of the summer to come. The sun rose smiling on the bright tulips and hyacinths and the still-bare limbs of the trees. Liz packed herself a lunch and decided to go exploring somewhere new. Having learned a bit about the unpredictability of Utah's spring weather, she took along a jacket and a sweater.

It was a little early for exploring the canyons, but she found a deserted picnic spot at the base of one with a trail that seemed relatively dry. No one else was about, and the clean, sweet smell of last year's leaves and this winter's melting snow was as refreshing as a drink of cold water. She swung her arms, she sang, and she talked to the brown and white chipmunks that appeared from time to time ahead of her on the trail. An excitement mounted in her; she couldn't justify it and didn't try. It was enough that she was alive and healthy and in Utah and it was almost spring.

"Zip-a-dee-doo-dah," she sang, laughing at herself, half-expecting a blue Disney butterfly to come and flutter around her head, but the only thing that flew around her head was a pesky early bee that kept buzzing her hair.

She ducked. "Get away—I'm no flower. It's just my shampoo you like."

She ate her lunch on a large flat rock in the sun, crumbling part of her sandwich on the grass for foraging birds and chipmunks and then lying back on the rock, her rolled-up sweater cushioning her head, for a few minutes' relaxation. She thought about nothing and anything, screening out any images and memories that didn't suit the day. She actually dozed for a bit, but the fickle April warmth fled before an afternoon breeze that soughed through the tops of the trees and brought some high white clouds to cover the sun.

"Nice while it lasted," she said, stretching, amused to discover how much of her little feast of bread crumbs had vanished while she napped. She sauntered back down the trail, slipping here and there on loose pebbles, feeling her hair gently lifted by the cool fingers of the breeze.

Her car was still the only one in the small parking area, and there had been no sign of any other person within sight or hearing, but there beside her car lay a dog. Her first thought was *Who can it belong to?* followed closely by *That is by far the ugliest mutt I have ever seen.*

It was not really a large dog—perhaps eighteen or twenty pounds—and its breed an unfortunate cross of some sort of hound and some other sort of terrier. The hound ancestry was evident in the shape of the body and the short, darkish coat, but the terrier cropped out in a few straggly chin whiskers, a sort of grizzled salt-and-pepper chest and forepaws, and a set of absurd bushy eyebrows that gave the face a look of perpetual astonishment.

"Good grief," said Liz. "Where did you spring from?"

The dog stood up and looked at her anxiously, its longish tail beating against the air.

"Where are your people?" she asked, gazing around. "Must be here somewhere."

She opened her car door and tossed her jacket and empty thermos into the back seat. They landed a split-second before the dog, who sat up and looked at Liz expectantly.

"Oh no you don't," she said firmly, shoving the driver's seat forward and snapping her fingers in a command no dog could mistake. The dog lay down on the seat, whiskered chin between grizzled paws, upraised eyes searching her face.

"I *mean* it," she insisted. "You're not my dog!"

She straightened and looked around in all directions. "Hello!" she called. "Hello! Anyone looking for a dog?"

It was hard to tell how far her voice carried. The wind was coming now in long gusts, sweeping down from the mountain pass to set the treetops rattling and swaying. "Hello!" she called again and again, between gusts, but the only answer was a faint echo. Suddenly Liz felt very much alone and anxious to start her car and get going.

"Come on, doggie," she said coaxingly. "Nice doggie." She reached in to grasp the dog by the scruff of its neck and remove it bodily from the car. There was no growl, no show of teeth, but the dog resisted with every muscle it possessed.

"Passive resistance, huh? What are you demonstrating against? Well, I'm the riot police, so heave-ho!" With considerable effort, she dragged the dog from the car and kept it out with one foot while she maneuvered herself behind the wheel and managed to shut the door. She started the motor and revved it, but the dog sat where it was and looked up at her, a ridiculously worried expression on its face.

"Whoever said animals don't have facial expressions has *not* met this one," Liz muttered, and rolled down her window a few inches. "Listen, pup," she said. "I'm sorry to be mean, but I can't take you with me. I don't want a dog. In fact, that's the last thing I want. And besides, your owners will be looking for you. Okay? Now, *stay!*"

The dog's tail thumped twice. Carefully, Liz backed her car and turned out onto the paved road with a small screech of tires. It was a narrow, winding road with blind curves, and though there was very little traffic, she didn't dare drive fast. She had traveled just over a mile when she caught a glimpse of something in her rearview mirror that gave her a distinct shock. Rounding the last curve and running for all it was worth was the dog. Her first impulse was to speed up and lose the creature by sheer power, but after a brief burst of speed she was annoyed to find herself herself slowing down and pulling into a roadside turnaround. She got out of the car, half hoping the dog would hurtle right past her and continue running toward its home somewhere close by. What a fool she would feel, then!

It didn't pass her. When it saw she had stopped, it stopped too, panting heavily, and limped the rest of the way to lie down at her feet, its sides heaving with the effort it had made.

"Oh, doggie—why me?" Liz asked, reaching down to fondle the silly ears. They were silky soft but matted and burr-ridden. She ran her hand over the body, feeling the prominent ridges of the rib cage, rising with each gasp for air.

"Okay, okay—I'll take you home and feed you, and I'll check the papers and the animal shelter to see if anyone's looking for you, but that's all, okay? If no one's claiming you, into the nearest shelter you go. Is that clear? All right, come on."

The dog climbed into the back seat with much less energy than it had exhibited in its first attempt. As Liz drove, she glanced back occasionally at her passenger. Slowly the panting eased, and the dog slept, stretched full-length on the seat.

"What in the world," she mused aloud, "made that animal attach itself to me? Lying there by my car, just as if it had been waiting for me."

I don't want a dog! she insisted silently. *I just can't love another dog, especially not this one, not after Fleece.*

Brock had sneered when she'd brought Fleece home from the pet shop—a white fluff ball of a poodle with merry black eyes.

"If you want a dog, get a dog," he'd said, eyeing Fleece derisively. "Get a Dane or a Dobie. That thing's no dog—it's a windup toy!"

She had named the puppy Fleece because of her soft woolly coat that needed trimming every so often, and also because, as she confided to Dorrie, it sounded like Felice, which meant "happy." And Fleece had given Liz the happiest moments she had known for a long time. Brock, of course, had insisted on calling her Fleas.

Liz had had Fleece for more than two years, and the warmth and joyousness of her doggy spirit had helped to ease the pain Liz experienced as her marriage went through its final stages of disintegration. Fleece had had her faults, of course. One was that she loved to tip over trash cans and strew the contents far and wide. The other, her fatal flaw, was a common one. She seemed to feel a single-minded compulsion to chase away from the premises anything on wheels, be it paperboy's bicycle or moving van. One early morning when Brock was leaving to go to the base, Liz had heard the soft thump on her floor and then Brock's muttered curse as Fleece slipped past him and out the carport door. A heavy truck was approaching. Liz heard a few frenzied barks and then a sharp yelp. Wide awake, heart pounding, she arrived at the front door in time to see Brock turn the little body over with the tip of his shoe and then pick it up gingerly by the scruff of the neck and fling it into a nearby trash can. The truck hadn't stopped. Brock didn't even glance toward the house. He examined his uniform quickly for bloodstains, found none, and got into his car and drove away. Liz shrank back from the door, shaking in rhythmic shudders that finally drove her to the bathroom in nausea. She didn't cry. She forced herself to dress and go outside to be sure Fleece was really dead. There was no doubt. Liz wrapped her gently in a pillowcase and buried her in a corner of the backyard.

That afternoon had been one that she spent rocking in Dorrie's kitchen, letting the ebb and flow of normal family life soothe and cleanse her spirit. She didn't mention the incident to Brock, waiting to see if he would bring it up, offer any sympathy at all. He never said a word on the subject, and she was determined never to let him know of her grief. He despised displays of any emotions other than anger or amusement, and he prided himself on being totally unsentimental.

That was the day that Liz pinpointed in her memory as the last straw. Brock had his preferences, his lifestyle, his philosophy, and his house, but she no longer felt obligated to share any of them. Looking back, she was amazed at her own—what? Patience, tenacity, perhaps fear? Whatever it was that had kept her hanging on, trying, for so long. Why had she bothered?

7

Impatiently, Liz swabbed at her wet eyes with a tissue and concentrated on her driving. The dog slept on until the car bumped to a stop close to the back door. Then it raised its head, slowly and painfully, and looked up at Liz with dull, pleading eyes.

"That run really wore you out, poor thing, didn't it?" Liz said kindly, and the dog thrust its nose into her hand. "Come on, let's feed you and see if you perk up."

She hadn't really intended to allow the dog into the house, but it followed her closely, slipping by her legs to sit sedately beside the refrigerator.

"You really are something, do you know that?" Liz said, pulling the meat from some chicken bones as she spoke. The dog began to drool, licking its chops convulsively, but sat still until the dish was placed on the floor. It devoured the food in great shuddering gulps and then drank a bowlful of water without stopping before looking hopefully from Liz to the refrigerator and back again, wagging its tail.

"No more now," she told it. "Maybe later. Let's go back outside." She opened the door, and the dog trotted toward the orchard, where it relieved itself, and then proceeded to examine the yard and garden. It was still limping, and Liz sat down on the back steps, calling it to her. It came and sat, trustfully leaning against her leg.

"Let's see that sore paw," she said, reaching for the favored foot, and the dog obligingly rolled over onto its back.

"Oh, my—you're a girl, aren't you? I hadn't thought to check. Now what's the trouble here?"

The pads were rough, and sticky, dark blood had oozed between them. Liz tried to separate them to look for glass or a burr, but the dog whined and jerked her paw away. Then the animal quietly fell asleep where it lay, ribs heaving with deeply drawn breaths. Liz went into the house and located the phone number of a veterinarian in a nearby town, who agreed to check the dog that day.

"You've been to a vet before, haven't you, girl?" Liz murmured as the dog in her arms shrank from the smells and sounds of the small office. A shrill yapping in the distance sounded disturbingly like Fleece, and closer by, the contralto yowls of a cat proclaimed its Siamese ancestry.

"Come on, kiddo, this is for your own good, and all that," Liz said, steadying the trembling body against her. "We'll get that paw attended to and then see what we can do about finding you a home."

The doctor was a short man with a beaky nose, bright blue eyes, and a trace of an eastern European accent.

"So here ve are, den," he said, hoisting the dog onto a stainless steel examination table while Liz explained the situation.

"Ah, hah, I see. So, little girl, you are a wagabond, eh? A gypsy but looking for a home. Steady now, girl, let's irrigate that paw and see vat ve haf, all right?"

Liz stroked and held the furry head while the doctor cleansed and probed carefully.

"Ah, yes, ve haf it." He held up a sharp and bloodied fragment of brown glass. "Beer bottle, I suppose, from somevun who cares little for anyvun's tires or bare feet. Good girl, now steady—some medicine against the infection, and ve vill check over the rest of you."

Liz watched, impressed with his gentle touch as he tended the wound and deftly examined the rest of the animal, whose trembling had subsided.

"So," he said at last, giving a friendly rub to the ears he had just examined. "She is wery tired and a bit malnourished and dehydrated just now, but her temp iss normal, and she seems othervise sound. She should haf her shots, of course, and most probably ve should vorm her just to be sure."

"But what should I *do* with her?" Liz worried aloud. "I looked through several papers from the last week, and there was no ad for a dog of her description."

The doctor riffled through a set of file cards, shook his head, and then made a couple of quick phone calls. He came back shaking his head. "No vun hass called for her at the local shelters," he said. "Most likely she vass abandoned. It happens too much."

"Perhaps I could leave her at a shelter for someone to adopt," Liz said.

The doctor cupped the dog's fuzzy chin in one hand. "She vould not last long, there. She iss not beautiful, nor iss she a puppy—although she iss not old either. She hass good white teeth. But the shelters, you see, are so crowded and so under-staffed. She vould most likely be euthanized soon."

"You mean—put to sleep? Killed?"

"It iss a matter of money, you understand, not cruelty. But better I should do it here, if that iss vat you vish. Easier for her."

"Oh, no, I—don't want that. But—don't you think someone would like her? She's really a dear, even if she is funny-looking."

"You like dogs, I think. Can you not gif her a home?"

"Well, I—had a dog, you see, that I was very much attached to, and she was killed. It was really hard for me, and I haven't wanted another . . ."

He nodded deeply. "Ven ve love, ve open ourselfes to hurt, it iss true," he agreed. "But most folks decide it iss vorth it, after all. As long as it lives, the pet gifs us much love and pleasure, and hopefully, receives the same from us. Ven it dies or iss lost, there iss pain, you see, but also much more remembered happiness—and vun day ve see a nice pup or kitten and begin again. But it iss a matter of time. I do not advise folks to rush out and replace a pet right avay. Ve need a space to grieve—and only you know ven the space hass been enough."

"Mm-m," Liz said noncommittally.

"But in the matter of this doggy, it iss for you to decide. Even if she vere not pregnant, she vill not get a home, I think, so . . ."

"She's *pregnant?*" Liz demanded.

"Oh, yes, did I not say? Not quite halfvay along, I think, and several pups, though after vat she hass been through, they may not all survive, you see. I vould suggest to spay her and destroy the pups, but that vould be hard on her ven she iss already so exhausted."

Liz took a deep breath. She felt as if she had been backed to the edge of a cliff and couldn't turn her head to see whether she'd be landing on jagged rocks or a haystack if she took the plunge.

"So you're going to be a mother?" she said, and the dog's tail thumped against the table as she realized Liz was talking to her. "Is that why you latched onto me—for your babies' sake?"

"It iss part of vhy, I think," said the doctor. "But also she seems to trust you. Iss only today ven she has found you?"

"Yes, only today."

"It iss truly a vonderful thing, this instinct a dog has, how to judge people. She does not treat you like a stranger. She thinks you are her person."

"Oh, well, probably anyone who came along just then . . ."

The doctor shrugged again, and folded his arms. "Perhaps. So—vat shall it be? Shall ve give her the shots to keep her well or de stuff to send her off into eternity?"

We? Liz thought frantically. *What have I got myself into?*

"Vat shall it be?" the doctor asked again, affably, as if he were offering a choice of chocolate or vanilla ice cream.

"Well—maybe I could keep her until her pups are big enough to give away and then advertise for homes for all of them at the same time . . ."

"Oh, good idea! Wery sensible. You see? She vas right to pick you."

Quickly the doctor prepared injections and administered them—before she could change her mind, Liz suspected—and she and the dog left the office with packets of worm medicine, vitamin and calcium supplements, and each other. Once outside, the dog's joy was evident, as she ran in happy circles around Liz and led her unerringly to the car, jumping readily into the back seat. Liz climbed in more slowly and sat for a while with her arms around the steering wheel, her forehead resting on her wrists.

"I'm not sure," she said slowly, "but I have the distinct feeling that I've been snookered." She turned to look at her companion. "You're a lucky dog, you know. Somebody in there likes you." The afternoon sun had reemerged and warmed the closed car, and the dog began to pant gently. Her face took on an astonished, merry expression, the bushy eyebrows above and the silly terrier's goatee beneath the doggy smile.

Some small cold place inside Liz melted just a little. "You are kind of cute," she admitted. "It'll be interesting to see what kind of pups you produce. What am I saying? Let's go home."

There were dozens of times in the next few days that she wished she had never seen Gypsy, as she had spontaneously called her when the vet required a name for his records. It seemed that Gypsy expected to accompany Liz on all excursions by foot or by car. Liz finally resorted to locking her in the house when she couldn't have her along, and that produced its own problems—not because Gypsy had unmannerly habits but because Liz would go and come to the accompaniment of an unearthly keening, a soft soprano howl that spoke volumes of fear of abandonment and loss. Liz could only wonder what miseries the little dog had endured in her short life—and could only be glad that some distance separated her house from others. There had been nothing in the rental agreement to prohibit pets, but Liz, not planning to acquire one, hadn't specifically asked. Now she hesitated, uncertain what she could do if Tuck and Lolly forbade a dog. In the meantime, she was greeted with expressions of ecstatic relief when she returned from even a short walk.

There were also quite a number of times that Liz regretted ever having told Missy that she would attend her brother's mission farewell. She hadn't met Dave; he still was just a tall young man with blond hair, lately worn very short, who roared down the road in an old Mustang of composite colors or who walked quietly to and from church with his family. Nor had she met the Ashcraft parents.

On the first Sunday in April, Liz noted that all was quiet at the church down the hill—no cars, no people came. Had the world ended overnight, she wondered, or did the Mormons take a spring vacation? The next Sunday all was back to normal, however, and the nineteenth approached with what felt like breakneck speed. Liz dreaded the meeting. She dreaded being singled out as a stranger or mistaken for a member. What did the Mormons do in their meetings? Was their worship formal, stylized, emotional, spontaneous? A childhood memory surfaced of once venturing into a tent revival meeting set up in her neighborhood by some unknown denomination and witnessing the whole congregation clapping and swaying while Mrs. Aitken, the mother of a classmate and an ordinarily prim lady who worked at a local dry cleaners, writhed and wriggled her way up the sawdust aisle on her knees, ruining her dress and—the young Liz had been sure—her reputation forever. Liz had backed out of the tent in fear and disgust and had never been able to look at Katie Aitken again without thinking of her mother's torturous progress up that aisle, arms raised and face contorted with some unidentifiable emotion. An older Liz had realized that her fear had probably been generated by the apparent transformation of a known to an unknown—the safe, solid, staid Mrs. Aitken to the totally uninhibited creature toiling toward the preacher in the tent. If it could happen to her, it might happen to anybody—even Liz—and the idea was unthinkable. Besides, how well could you really know a person when people could be that unpredictable? The young Liz liked people to be what they seemed. The adult Liz hadn't changed that much. These people, her neighbors—Tuck and Lolly, Missy, the Woodbines—all seemed so real and uncomplicated and good-hearted. Did they, too, change in some unaccountable way within the walls of a church? She wasn't at all sure she wanted to find out.

The nineteenth came on apace, and she woke that morning with a heavy sense of dread, casting about in her being for any hopeful sign of illness to keep her home. Wasn't her throat a tiny bit sore? Didn't she feel rather queasy—or was that just nerves?

She drank a cup of tea in her kitchen, watching the April sun warm the landscape into the delicate yellows and greens of spring. "Do you know," she said to Gypsy, who was drowsing in a patch of sunlight on the faded linoleum, "that it's been at least eleven or twelve years since I last went to church?"

Gypsy's tail thumped, but there was nothing in Liz's voice to prompt further response. The dog had grown accustomed to being talked to, quietly, off and on, and she had learned to recognize every tone and inflection and quite a few actual words in her new mistress's vocabulary.

"No help from you, I see. You could at least have planned to begin giving birth this morning." Liz put down her cup and went to dress, choosing a lightweight navy suit and silky blouse.

Taking several deep breaths, she closed her front door against Gypsy's mournful protests and walked down the hill. The day was glorious, filled with sunshine and birdsong. Liz would have loved to keep walking past the church and down the highway, but her feet, neatly shod and more obedient than her heart, turned onto the sidewalk leading to the double glass doors of the building.

"If I must," she whispered. "This is for you, Missy."

8

The carpeted foyer seemed dim after the brilliant sunlight. Open doors to her right, attended by a cheerful man offering folded programs, indicated the way to the chapel.

"Good morning," he said, shaking her hand. "Relative of the missionary?"

"Um—no, a friend of his sister," Liz replied. "Does it matter where I sit? Are there reserved pews?"

"What? Oh, no, not at all, except the front two on the left for the deacons."

Liz was a little early, as she had planned to be, and only a few people were scattered around the simple sanctuary that was comfortably decorated in wood and rust-colored carpet and upholstery. The pulpit was situated off-center to the left, and a matching piano and organ stood nose-to-nose on the right. At the organ a woman with dark hair sifted through her music, selecting and setting her choices in order before her. There were no flowers, no candles, and the only stained-glass window was a slender panel of orange, blue, and amber sections to one side of the choir seats.

Liz selected a pew toward the back and slid over against the wall, hoping there to see and not be seen. She opened the program and read the announcements. There was to be a roller-skating party for the YW and YM, whoever they were, and four sisters and two brethren were needed for a cannery assignment on the twenty-second. *Cannery?* Tuesday was to be the stake temple day, and all recommend holders were urged to attend.

The facing side of the program detailed the meeting about to begin. Liz read through it quickly—hymns, prayers, speakers. Missy was to talk—she knew that already—then her father, Wynn Ashcraft. Next was listed a special musical number, "In the Hollow of Thy Hand," sung by Max and Louise Fenton. "Oh, good," whispered Liz. Missy had told her that Dave wanted Uncle Max and Aunt Lou to sing, but it all depended on whether they could get down from Boise. The missionary, Elder David Ashcraft, would speak next, and he would be followed by the bishop, who would offer a few remarks. The closing hymn and benediction completed the program.

Liz began to relax. There didn't seem to be anything too threatening in the planned service. The only real unknown was "administration of the sacrament," but Liz decided she would simply watch what others did. She took a green hymnal from the rack on the back of the pew before her and glanced through it. The only hymns she recognized were "How Great Thou Art" and "Sweet Hour of Prayer."

The organist began a soft prelude, and worshippers filtered in, mostly in family groups—some reverent and others rather noisy, Liz thought, surprised. People greeted each other with smiles and the inevitable handshake, and there was a whispered buzz of friendly conversation. The organ's volume increased fractionally.

If Liz had hoped to remain anonymous, her hopes were short-lived. Missy spotted her right away and bounded into the pew in front of her, waving her family to join her.

"You really came! I knew you would, though, 'cause you *said*."

"How pretty you look," Liz whispered, leaning forward. It was true. Missy's dress was a flowered print with a lace collar, and a matching ribbon tied back her hair, which had been curled for the occasion.

"Do you like my dress? Sister Tucker made it, special for today. Daddy, c'mere. This is Liz Ewell—I told you she'd be here!"

Wynn Ashcraft stepped into the pew and reached to shake her hand. He was thin to the point of gauntness, with a hollow-cheeked face that bespoke years of strain, but his eyes were calm and his smile cordial. "Missy's spoken often of you, Mrs. Ewell, and it's good to meet you. Thanks for coming—and for being so kind to Missy. I hope she doesn't intrude too often."

Liz smiled. "Not at all. We have an understanding."

"Good. My wife, Helen, and our son, Dave, soon to be a missionary."

Helen Ashcraft had lovely features and might have been termed elegant except for a certain expression in her eyes. Liz couldn't have said precisely what it was, but she could tell that all was not well. Helen's smile was sweet as she clung to Wynn's arm and looked at Liz.

"I think the red petunias will do well," she said softly. "But when the mountains fall, I'm afraid we . . ." Her voice trailed off into silence.

Missy's brother leaned across and thrust out his hand, saving Liz the trouble of trying to reply. "Dave Ashcraft," he said with a nod. "Sure appreciate you coming today. Be sure to stop in up to the house later for cookies and punch—around four to six."

"Thank you—and good luck to you," Liz responded.

Dave had a charming grin and the same fair, straight hair

as Missy and their mother. Helen's was just a shade darker and worn pulled back into a large clip at the nape of her neck. Who did her hair, Liz wondered. Who chose her clothing? To what extent did she care for herself? How did they cope?

Wynn led Helen to a pew close to the front, where she was welcomed by two couples, probably relatives, and made comfortable, while he and Dave and Missy retired to seats behind the pulpit.

Liz watched with interest as Marilyn Woodbine shepherded her considerable family into one long pew in the middle section. The children, all with varying shades of thick, shiny brown hair, seemed relatively well-behaved and well-groomed—no small achievement, Liz suspected. And the slender, balding man with glasses who brought up the rear of the procession fit the scholarly description Tuck had given of Tom Woodbine. He discreetly but firmly separated a pair of what looked like twin boys and sat between them, taking a small girl on his lap. Marilyn leaned over to smile down the row at him, and nodded when he apparently said something to her.

Do stop staring! Liz admonished herself. *You're getting to be a regular old Nosey Parker, examining your neighbors like this.*

With the chapel nearly filled, the organ music ceased, and Tuck went to the podium. He took a moment to survey the congregation, catching Liz's eye and giving her a brief twinkling nod. She had the feeling he didn't miss much—that he knew precisely who was there and who was not—and probably why.

"Good morning, brothers and sisters," he greeted. "We welcome you to sacrament meeting this beautiful Sabbath day, and we extend a special greeting to all those who are visiting with us today to worship the Lord and to honor this fine young missionary, Elder David Ashcraft, as he prepares to go forth and serve his Father in Heaven and his fellowman."

Liz's attention wandered as he went on with announcements, but she followed along as the congregation sang, "I'll Go Where You Want Me to Go." Appropriate enough, she agreed. She had never felt such commitment or humility herself, but she acknowledged that there were people who could feel such things, and she suspected she was in the presence of some of them. The sacrament song touched her, too, with its reverent poetry about the sacrifice of Jesus for the sins of the world. She watched carefully as a row of young boys of varying heights stood before a table covered with white damask and received trays of torn pieces of bread. A beautiful blessing had been pronounced upon this offering by a somewhat older boy who had thick brown hair. *Must be a Woodbine,* she decided.

Realizing that the tray would be passed to her, Liz whispered to the woman sitting next to her, "Is it open or closed communion?"

"Beg pardon?"

"Is the communion just for members of your church?"

"Oh—yes, it is." The woman offered an apologetic little smile, and Liz nodded. She sat back, grateful that the woman didn't pass the tray to her but handed it back along the row. A similar procedure was followed with trays containing small paper cups of water, and then the boys sat down, having taken the offering themselves. Liz's neighbor handed her a program on the back of which she had written, "Our sacrament is partly in remembrance of the covenants we made when we were baptized into the church—that's why it's only for members. Nice to have you with us!"

"Thank you," Liz whispered with a smile. She looked up to see Missy at the podium, smoothing a piece of notebook paper as if it were very important to have every wrinkle out before she began to speak.

"Okay, my talk is on service," she began. "Jesus said when

we do something for even the least of his brethren, it's like we do it for him. One way we can serve people is to take care of them when they're sick. Or maybe we can help them with their work. Sometimes we can just talk to them and be their friend. Friends are real important to me, and I'm thankful for all of mine. They help me out a lot. I'm thankful for Sister Tucker who made me this dress, and for Marsha Olsen—she's my friend at school—and for the Woodbines and for Sister German, my Primary teacher, 'cause I know I ask an awful lot of dumb questions and she's real patient with me, and I'm 'specially thankful for my newest friend, Liz Ewell, who lives up the road in Uncle Ned's old house. She's real nice to talk to me even though she's a real private kind of person and all, and I'm glad she's here today."

A strange mix of emotions warred in Liz's heart. Her lips wanted to smile, her cheeks were hot, and there was a definite lump in her throat. She felt, rather than saw, several heads turn in her direction, and she knew she had been identified. So much for blissful anonymity!

"Another way of serving is by going on a mission," Missy was saying. " 'Cause that way you can serve the people you go to teach and help out the Lord at the same time. I'm real glad my brother Dave has chosen to serve a mission. I know he'll be a real good missionary, but we'll miss him a lot at home. I love all my family, but I 'specially love Dave, even though I yell at him a lot and sometimes he yells back, but he still helps me with my homework and the dishes and all . . ." Her voice wavered and broke, and she paused. Then she took a deep breath and plunged on. "But I'm real proud of him for going, and I know the Church is true, in the name of Jesus Christ, amen."

Liz's eyes were moist, and she searched her purse for a tissue. *Oh, I can't—I don't want to get involved with these people!*

she thought rebelliously. Nevertheless, it was true that Missy Ashcraft did something to her on a feeling level, something that she couldn't deny. The child was so vulnerable and yet so optimistic and determined in spite of her problems.

Musing, Liz missed the first few phrases of Wynn Ashcraft's talk and then willed herself to listen. He spoke of sacrifice as necessary to spiritual progress, as a blessing in disguise that opens the floodgates of heaven and allows God to bless us beyond our wildest imaginings. His delivery was quiet and thoughtful, and Liz didn't question his sincerity, but she wondered what in his experience had caused him to believe that concept. Hadn't he sacrificed a great deal to keep his family together, and wasn't he sacrificing further, now, to send his only son far away on this mission? But what great and unimaginable blessings had he received—he, whose children were bereft of their mother even in her presence, whose finances were drained and career interrupted, whose wife was a lovely, pleasant nonperson—how could he stand and boldly declare that sacrifice calls forth the blessings of heaven? Was this what they called blind faith?

Controlling his feelings with some effort, Wynn spoke of his gratitude for such a son as Dave. Dave, sitting behind him, ducked his head and closely examined his loosely clasped hands.

The lump returned to Liz's throat during Uncle Max and Aunt Lou's duet. The words of the song were a parent's prayer for the well-being and growth of a missionary son, poignant and pleading: "In the hollow of thy hand as he grows from boy to man, let him know the special blessing of thy peace."

Handkerchiefs and discreet sniffs were evident throughout the congregation as the song ended, and the missionary himself stuffed a damp tissue into his pocket as he rose to speak.

He, too, expressed thanks to friends and family members who had made an extra effort to share this day with him.

"You all know, I guess, that this hasn't been an easy decision for me," he continued. "Even though I always planned on a mission when I was growing up, when the time got closer I kind of got cold feet. I didn't want to drop out of college, and I had a job I liked, and I kinda figured I was needed at home, too. You probably all know that our situation is sort of unique. But in spite of it all, I had this feeling that maybe I should turn in my papers anyway and just see what came of it. I was really mixed up, and I couldn't figure out what I wanted to do.

"Well, you all know what the scripture says: 'If any of you lack wisdom, let him ask of God; that giveth to all men liberally, and upbraideth not; and it shall be given him' (James 1:5). Sounds familiar, doesn't it? I figured if it worked for Joseph Smith, maybe it'd work for me, too. So I started fasting and praying."

Liz blinked in wonder. This lanky, personable young college freshman who gunned his old Mustang down the road with wild abandon, sometimes several times a day, had been serious enough about a problem to *fast*? She had never known anyone who fasted except a few Catholic friends who had given up something for Lent. What had Dave given up, and for how long? She tuned back in.

"Have to admit I've never been too good at fasting," he said. "I always kinda dreaded fast Sunday and hardly ever made the whole twenty-four hours without food or water, so after my first attempt, I guess it shouldn't have surprised me when I didn't get any answer that I could recognize. About a week later, I tried again. I thought surely then that the Lord would just have to answer me. But I didn't get a thing. All I felt was a greater desire to get an answer. And, I guess, maybe that was my answer at that point, because it made me keep trying. It took seven times, brothers and sisters, seven separate times of fasting and praying, to get my answer. But you know, that seventh time was different. It was special. I felt so humble that I was willing to do *anything* to find out what the Lord's will was for my life. I went up in the canyon to a real neat place I remembered going once with the Scouts, and I just poured out everything to my Heavenly Father. I didn't just say, like I'd done before, 'Please help me to know if I should go on a mission.' I told him *all* the things that worried and concerned me, all my hopes and fears and weaknesses, and I told him how badly I needed to know what to do. And it was different this time. I knew Heavenly Father was listening—I could feel him there. And it wasn't scary at all. In fact, I began to relax and feel pretty wonderful, like—it's hard to describe, but like there was this sort of cloud of love all around me, just pure love, warm and friendly like you might feel from your family or your best friend, only more so—really *great*. I had stopped praying and was just soaking it all in like sunshine, and it was then I heard this voice—in my mind, you know? Not out loud, but speaking to my mind, only very clear and definite, not at all like something I'd just think of, and it said, 'Fear not to go forth and serve me, and all shall be well with thee and thine.'

"Now, you know me, brothers and sisters. I don't talk in words like that or even think in them unless I'm praying. I *knew* when that answer came, and it thrilled my whole soul. It was worth fasting and praying and struggling for—many more times than seven, if necessary. To think that the God of all creation knows and loves *me* and answered my prayer! Of course, we've always been taught that he does, and I guess I've believed it, or I wouldn't have been trying so hard, but now I *know* it.

"Well, after I got through thanking him, I didn't even go

home. I went straight to Bishop Tucker where he was out in his apple orchard and told him I was ready."

Tuck smiled and nodded.

"So I'm excited now to get to Austria and see if I can find somebody there who's ready to learn about the restored gospel of Jesus Christ. I know it won't be easy. The language won't be easy, and I know there'll be adjustments, and it's not a real easy mission anyway, from what I hear—but I'm more excited than scared now—and with that kind of love and backing from the Lord and my family and you good folks, I'm ready to take him at his word and go forth to serve him. In the name of Jesus Christ, amen."

Liz sat through Bishop Tucker's closing remarks and another hymn and prayer in a state of mixed emotions. In fact, as she politely brushed past those persons sitting on her bench and hurried out of the meeting before anyone could speak to her, she decided she hadn't felt so churned up emotionally since she'd left Hawaii. Peculiar new feelings kept rising within her, trying to surface, but something akin to fear kept thrusting them down again. She was sure of only one thing—uncomfortably sure—that the Ashcraft family would never again be to her the one-dimensional paper doll "Ashblonds" that she had tried to keep them in spite of Missy's efforts. Now they were all as real and human as Missy herself.

Oh, please, she prayed fervently as she climbed the hill in the fragile April warmth, *please don't let me get emotionally involved in these people's lives. I just can't. I don't have anything to give them. I'm empty.*

She wasn't at all sure that her prayer was heard—or ought to be.

9

Shortly before five o'clock that afternoon, Liz found herself climbing the rest of the hill to the Ashcraft home. She carried a plate of freshly baked cookies—a favorite recipe full of rich butter and ground pecans that she would never dare make just for herself. As Liz had hoped, Missy opened the door to her knock.

"Here you go, Missy—a little contribution for the party. Please tell your brother I thought he did a wonderful job with his talk—you all did—okay?"

"No, you've got to come in! You've *got* to. You've never been here before—and then you can tell him yourself."

"No, Missy, I . . ." But Liz allowed herself to be drawn into the small living room, which was already crowded with chatting people, several of whom looked up brightly to greet her.

"I'll take the cookies. Mmm, they look yummy. Thanks!" Missy bore the plate away toward the small dining area where a table was laden with goodies. Liz was discomfited to see Helen Ashcraft coming toward her.

"How kind of you," Helen said graciously. "Everyone is so kind at Christmas. I'm afraid the calendar is too full of days, though. How can it hold them all?"

Liz swallowed. "Sometimes it seems that way," she murmured.

"Come and sit down. Here's a spot," invited a woman whom Liz recognized as "Aunt Lou" of the duet. Helen drifted off to another room, and Liz gratefully took the place offered on the sofa.

"Don't mind Helen," Lou was saying. "She's a dear, but her thinking is very confused."

Liz nodded. "Missy explained that her mother isn't well," she said. "Do they know what caused it?"

"Well, she suffered from depression for a long time after Missy was born, and they weren't able to control it. It would come and go, and it got to where some days she'd be fine and able to cope, and others she'd just sort of sit, letting life go on around her but taking no part. She would sit and rock or lie on her bed. It got so that Wynn could tell in the morning what kind of day Helen would have, and he'd call me to come help out if it looked like a bad one. He's my brother, you know. Bless his heart, he spent a fortune trying to get help for her, but nothing seemed to work for long. Then, on one of her better days, they went on a picnic and took a hike up a little path through some bushes. She stumbled into a hive of bees and was stung forty-two times. It put her right into a coma for two weeks, and when she woke up, she was like she is now—just sort of out of touch with reality. They put her in the state mental hospital, but Wynn brought her home when it went on and on without much progress. It's sure been hard on Wynn and the kids. Little Missy's never really known her mother."

Liz sat perfectly still, stunned by the matter-of-fact recital. Such sadness, such frustration and grief, and yet the family seemed cheerful and accepting.

"How—how do they manage?"

"Oh, Helen's not hard to care for. Wynn's devoted to her,

and he helps her bathe and dress. She helps herself, too, at times. She'll eat whatever they put on her plate and take care of herself if they take her to the bathroom. Otherwise she just wanders around the house, but never—you know—initiates anything or does anything. She'll stand looking out the window for a long time or watch television, but nobody knows how much she really notices. Once in a while she'll dance a little, if some music appeals to her. She likes Wynn to dance with her, and she likes to go for rides. She seems happy, in a way, in her own little world, but it's been a great tragedy, of course—for all of us."

"Yes. I meant, I guess, how do they manage to deal with it emotionally? I'm afraid I'd be devastated."

Lou smiled sadly. "Well, life goes on, you know, minute by minute and day by day. Wynn has told me that's how he gets through—just taking one moment, one day, at a time, doing what needs to be done right then, and trying not to think too far down the immediate road ahead. Then, too, he makes the leap beyond and thinks of eternity, when her health will be restored and she'll be herself, and his sweetheart, again. They were married in the temple, you know."

"Meaning," Liz said, "that their marriage is not just for this life? I'm not Mormon, but I've heard a little about that."

"Right. Wynn clings to that and to his memory of what she was like before she got sick. I think he's pretty remarkable that way. Not all men could stick it out, you know? I'm kind of proud of my little brother."

"Yes. Oh, yes—you should be," Liz agreed, thinking of Brock, who almost never got sick and who had managed to make her feel weak and foolish if she so much as caught a cold.

"It helps, too, that they live here among such good, understanding people. I worried when they first came. They had a really nice home up to Pleasant Grove, but they had to give it up, of course, what with the medical bills and all. About the same time, my husband was transferred up to Boise, so I wasn't around to help like I had been."

"I imagine they missed you."

She nodded. "And I missed them. We offered to take Missy to live with us, but Wynn wanted more than anything to keep his family together. Said he couldn't bear to lose his daughter, too. So we just take her for a couple of weeks in the summer. I don't know how that'll work out this summer, though, with Davey gone. She'll be needed at home more than ever."

"Oh, I hope she can go," Liz said. "I think she probably needs the change and looks forward to it."

"Yes, she does, and we love to spoil her a bit. Will you excuse me for a moment? I see my husband trying to get my attention."

"Of course—and by the way, your song was lovely."

"Why, thank you, dear. That's nice of you."

Liz sat back and sipped at a cup of punch that someone handed around on a tray and nibbled a small sandwich, listening to the cheerful bits of conversation that ebbed and flowed around her—laughter and teasing from some of Dave's school friends, shared recipes from a group of women on her right. Tuck and Lolly moved from group to group, greeting and shaking hands, pausing beside Dave to unobtrusively drop a folded white envelope in the pocket of his new dark missionary suit and pat him on the shoulder.

"Hello, Liz, what a pleasure to see you here today," Tuck said, giving her hand a hearty squeeze as he shook it, and Lolly beamed at her.

"Stop over and see my new quilt I've got on," she invited. "I've just finished a couple of new suspense novels, too, if you're up for a good scare." She laughed her jolly, comfortable laugh. "I just love to be scared when I'm safe and secure in my soft old easy chair. Makes me appreciate what I've got. Tuck, he says he doesn't need fiction—he gets scared enough comparing newspaper headlines with scriptural prophecies about the latter days."

Tuck smiled tolerantly at his wife and winked at Liz as he reached to draw forward a tall, striking young woman with short, upswept red hair. "Francie, have you met Liz Ewell? Liz, this here is Francie Johansen, who lives in that nice new bi-level down across the highway. Liz is living in Uncle Ned's old house, Francie, and you ought to drop in and see how she's fixed it up."

He and Lolly moved away, and Francie Johansen folded herself to sit on a vinyl hassock close by, locking her hands around shapely silken knees and smiling to show perfect small white teeth. "I'll just bet you're a career girl, aren't you?" she queried in a low, chatty voice. "I'll bet you're—let's see—you look cool and efficient enough to be an executive secretary. But no—I think you might be a home economics teacher, or—I have it! I'll bet you're a travel agent!"

Liz laughed lightly. "I've never been any of those things. But thanks for the compliment."

"Well, you must have some kind of career to make all us dowdy little housewives feel jealous and unfulfilled. *I* know—you're a writer!"

"Hardly. And dowdy certainly isn't a word I'd use to describe you, housewife or whatever."

Francie shrugged attractively. "That's all I am," she confessed. "Diapers and dishes are not my thing, you understand, but you know how it is. You do what's expected of you—or at least you try to. Men are so hopeless, don't you think? Eric expects me to get everything done and yet look as though I hadn't done anything but my hair and nails. Now I ask you!

Naturally, I can't achieve that, but I try to keep up appearances."

Liz looked at the upswept red hair and wondered how Francie managed to keep it in that position yet still looking soft and shiny. As for her nails, they appeared perfect, burnished with a coppery peach polish. Had she grown them or had them "sculpted"?

"Actually," Liz said, "if we're going to play 'What's My Line?' I'd peg you as a model."

"Oh, you doll!" Francie squealed. "You've absolutely made my day! You see, that was my dream when I was younger. But Eric came along and finished all that for me."

Liz wasn't about to comment on that remark. Instead, she asked, "How many children do you have?"

"Two boys—a three-year-old and one fifteen months." She rolled her long-lashed eyes expressively. "One in diapers and the other in everything else. How about yourself?"

Liz shook her head. "No children. And I'm divorced."

"Never had any?"

"No."

Francie's eyes narrowed, and she leaned forward confidingly. "Might've saved your marriage, if you had," she whispered. "Some men are like that—just won't put up with a woman who won't give them kids. Pride and all, you know. Bad as the Shah of Iran."

"My husband wasn't that sort. He was the one who didn't want children."

"Well, lucky for you, then—you're not stuck with any now. I think it would be really hard to meet men and date and all if you had kids to worry about. Most guys don't want to take on a ready-made family, you know? Support and raise another man's kids. It'd be a handicap."

"M-mm."

"Oh, here's Eric." Francie stood up in one fluid motion and took the arm of a tall, blond man who shouldered his way through the crowd to her side. "Eric, this is our new neighbor just down the road. Liz—what was it—Ewell? Isn't she a sweet little thing? Just a doll."

Liz, who hadn't heard herself described as either a "doll" or a "sweet little thing" since possibly fourth grade, managed a somewhat embarrassed "How are you?" and the obligatory handshake.

"Well, I'll say," boomed Eric Johansen, who was, Liz decided, definitely what her cousin Marla would have termed "a hunk." For her own taste, there was something a bit too smooth about his blond handsomeness, but he looked well matched with Francie.

"It's great to have you in the neighborhood, Mrs. Ewell. Is your hubby here? Like to meet him, too."

"She's currently alone," Francie whispered, snuggling against his shoulder. "Don't we know some neat guys to have her meet?"

"Oh—no, thank you," Liz said hurriedly. "I'm really not interested right now in—in meeting anyone. In fact, I moved here to have some time to myself and do some thinking. To sort of reevaluate my life—you understand?" Liz felt she was babbling in her haste to protect herself from the Johansens' matchmaking, and she wasn't at all sure that they understood.

"Much too good-looking a gal to spend a lot of time alone," Eric was saying, and Francie echoed him: "Can't just let you wither on the vine, Liz. Time's a-wastin', as they say. Speaking of time, honey, we'd better hustle back to the boys. I'm not sure their sitter can handle them for very long. She's only ten."

"It's been nice to meet you," Liz offered, allowing them room to depart and wishing they'd be quick about it.

"Oh, it has," Francie agreed. "How long did you say you'd been here?"

"About two months."

"And we hadn't even noticed! What a shame—we'll have to make it up to you."

Privately, Liz thought it no shame at all and hoped the Johansens would promptly forget about her. Actually, she rather doubted that her arrival had totally escaped Francie Johansen's sharp green eyes.

" 'Bye, now—we'll be in touch."

"See you soon," Eric added, lifting blond eyebrows at her.

They stopped to say good-bye to Dave, whose ears turned red as Francie gave him a quick hug and a kiss on the cheek, leaving a shiny smear of lip gloss.

"Isn't he darling?" she demanded of all within hearing, while his friends wore embarrassed grins. "The girls in Austria won't have a chance. They'll join the Church in droves."

"Yeah, sure," Dave mumbled, rolling away from the friendly punch Eric aimed at his arm.

Liz felt she shared Dave's sense of relief as the couple finally exited, and she planned to do the same thing as soon as they were safely ahead of her. She shook the missionary's hand and wished him well, and then she waved good-bye to Missy, who was adding punch to the bowl on the dinette table. Helen was nowhere to be seen, and Liz assumed she was with Lou Fenton, who had likewise vanished. Wynn Ashcraft seemed engrossed in conversation with two men by the front door, and Liz tried to slip out unnoticed, but he broke away long enough to grip her hand and thank her for coming.

"It meant a lot to all of us that you would come," he told her. "Especially Missy. Thanks again for your kindness to her."

Liz smiled. "Missy's a dear," she told him. "And I was very impressed by the meeting today. I'm glad she invited me."

90

"Good. Come again," he invited cordially and turned back to his friends.

Liz escaped, followed closely by Tuck and Lolly, who walked down the road with her.

"See Francie bent your ear for a while there, Liz. Hope you realize there's no real harm in Francie—you just have to take her with a grain of salt," Tuck said.

Lolly leaned close to Liz. "Sometimes," she confided, "it takes more than a grain. Gets up to a whole spoonful, every now and then."

Liz laughed, grateful to feel understood. "She's very attractive, but she struck a note of fear in my heart when she threatened to bring on all sorts of 'neat guys' for me to meet. I tried to tell her I don't want that—that I need time alone to get my head together—but I'm not sure she listened."

"Listening's not Francie's strong point," Tuck said. "But you just firmly say *no* to anything and anybody you don't feel good about inside. I don't know a whole lot about your situation, of course, but I can tell you're a nice, sensible young woman. So don't let anyone push you into anything."

"Thanks—I won't."

"You know," Lolly said, as they paused in front of Liz's driveway, "it just makes some women plain uncomfortable to have an attractive single woman anywhere nearby. I figure they feel compelled to find her a husband as quick as possible for fear she might look at theirs."

"You mean Francie would be jealous of *me?*"

Tuck smiled genially at her. "Maybe not consciously, unless Eric began to notice you in particular—and I don't really think he's that type. Known him all his life, and he's a pretty good boy. But young Francie's always depended on her looks to make her feel okay about herself, you know? Seems like she needs to feel on top all the time—better looking, fancier, maybe, than those around her."

"Mirror, mirror on the wall," Lolly quoted softly. "A girl like Francie—it's going to go hard with her as she grows older if she doesn't develop some inner resources and spiritual beauty. Her kind of prettiness doesn't last forever, though I'm sure she'll always do her best to stay attractive, and that's fine."

"Well, we mustn't be unkind," Tuck said. "Francie's young—she's not finished, yet. We have to keep that in mind—people change. They can, and they do. In fact, there wouldn't be much point to the gospel if people couldn't change, would there?"

"You're right," Lolly agreed. "But don't let her get to you, Liz. Keep your salt shaker handy!"

"I will," Liz said, smiling as she watched them turn toward their house, holding hands as they stopped to admire a bed of red tulips.

What interesting people, she thought. *They must have been dying to know what I thought of their church service, but not a word was mentioned. They're so patient and sincere. They're dear, really. They're a little like Dorrie.*

10

As Liz walked up her driveway, a familiar sound assailed her ears—Gypsy's mournful howl. It seemed, however, to have a new sense of urgency to it, and she quickened her step. Gypsy greeted her at the door as usual with joyful yips but then ran to her box in the kitchen and wagged her tail frantically. There on the wet and stained papers lay a tiny dark puppy, perfectly still.

"Oh, Gypsy—you had a baby!" Liz cried, kneeling beside the box. "But I'm afraid . . ."

Gypsy nudged the puppy with her nose and whimpered, looking to Liz for help. Liz touched the wet little body gingerly and then lifted it and felt for a heartbeat, but there was none. The rounded head lolled limply back in her fingers.

"I'm so sorry, Gypsy," she whispered. "It's a beautiful puppy, but it's not breathing." She felt Gypsy's distended belly.

"There are more coming, girl, and I think they're alive. I felt them move. I'll just take this one away."

She took the puppy into the extra bedroom, where she found an empty shoe box for its casket. Then she went into her own room to change into comfortable jeans preparatory to digging a small grave. She was tying the laces on her sneakers when she looked up to see Gypsy trail past her door to the kitchen, the dead puppy in her mouth. Liz watched her carefully place the puppy back in the box and jump in beside it, licking it devotedly.

"Just willing it to live," Liz whispered. "All right, Gypsy—I'll leave it until another one's born."

She settled herself beside the box and stroked Gypsy's warm head with its funny beetling brows. Gypsy panted for a minute, braced her hind feet against the side of the box, and pushed.

"Another one coming, old girl. Better luck this time."

It took several hard contractions before a tiny paw appeared and finally one enormous push that wrung a yelp of pain from Gypsy before the puppy was expelled. She immediately began assiduously cleaning the pup and stimulating its breathing, but it gave one little shiver and then lay as still as its littermate.

"Oh, no, Gypsy." Liz began to massage and pat the still-warm body herself. She wiped inside the small pink mouth with one finger in case mucus obstructed the breathing, but to no avail. Recalling the time-honored method of encouraging newborn human babies to breathe, she dangled the puppy by its hind legs and gave it a smart tap on the back. It didn't respond. She tried again and then laid it gently back beside its anxious mother.

"I'm afraid the vet was right—your pups are having trouble. And I'm not much of a midwife. Wonder if he's available . . ."

She went to the phone to leave a message on the doctor's answering machine, and Gypsy promptly left her box to stand beside her, panting heavily. For Gypsy's sake, Liz dragged the rocking chair from the living room into the kitchen, placing it beside the birthing box.

"I won't leave you, Gypsy. We'll see this through together," she promised. Gradually she relaxed, stretching out in her chair as the clean April breeze brought messages of growth and beginnings through the open door. She put her head back and let her hands dangle limply by the armrests, allowing herself to doze sporadically. Between her naps and Gypsy's occasional need for comfort, bits and pieces of her day began to replay themselves in her mind—the conflicting emotions aroused by the church meeting, her closer acquaintance with the Ashcrafts, and the half-amused, half-angry reactions brought about by Francie Johansen's flat assumptions that she wanted a new husband as soon as possible, that she was lucky to have no children, that it had been her decision not to have any, and that she must have a flourishing career.

No, no, no! she cried silently. *No to all of those!* Impatiently she rolled her head from side to side against the chair back as tears squeezed out of the corners of her eyes and wet her face. So Francie was envious, was she? Francie with her handsome husband, comfortable home, and two small boys.

"I could tell her about envy," Liz muttered bitterly. "I could tell her all about envy and wishing and longing and dreaming."

An image came unbidden into her mind. She hadn't thought of it for years, but there it was, still charged with the power to cause her pain. It had been a simple, innocent thing—merely a photograph of a child on the front of a women's magazine at the supermarket. It was the December issue, and it pictured a little girl of four or five, clad in a lace-trimmed red flannel nightgown, her hair a dark tumble of curls down her back. She stood on a ladder, her face a study in concentration as she reached to place a silver star atop a popcorn-garlanded evergreen. A contrived picture, no doubt, Liz had told herself. The little girl was probably a paid child model, and the tree must have stood in the middle of a photographer's studio instead of in a warm and genuine home, but she bought the magazine anyway. She had fallen in love with the little girl and had given in at last to her yearnings for a child, allowing herself to hope that the changes she had noticed recently in her body might mean that, in spite of all the careful precautions Brock had insisted upon, she had conceived a child.

When she could bear the suspense no longer, she purchased a home testing kit. The results were positive. She threw away the kit, concealing the evidence carefully in a bag of trash and hiding her precious knowledge just as carefully inside her heart.

She waited to tell Brock until one evening when the two of them were lying relaxed on the beach after a picnic supper. He appeared to be in a good mood; it seemed safe enough to let him know of his incipient fatherhood.

"I have a surprise for you," she said lightly.

"Yeah? What's that?"

"I think I'm pregnant."

Brock had been lying on his back. He rolled slowly onto his stomach and leaned on his elbows, staring at her.

"You *think?*"

"I—well, I'm pretty sure. I took a test."

His eyes narrowed. "You had better not be," he said quietly and then with growing anger, "Did you forget your pill? Or did you trick me?"

"No! No, I didn't! You know sometimes these things fail— even the pill."

"Why? Why would it fail? Never has before! No, you slipped up, that's what *you* did."

"I did not! I keep track. Besides, is it so awful? I mean, I know it'll be an adjustment, but . . ."

"Liz, you *know* I don't want a kid! You know how I feel about fliers having families—it's way too risky. I mean, it's one thing if *you* were dumb enough to marry a pilot. Maybe you've got a yen to be a merry widow, huh? But I don't believe in creating orphans."

"Brock, that's a cop-out and you know it. What about all that business about being safer in your plane than you are driving to the grocery store? Most of the guys have families. What about Kent? His wife's about to have her fourth, and they're not worrying. And Glen and Chrissie—they've got twins."

Brock's voice was sarcastic. "Oh, yes, and what about Brad and Joan? They're so happy with their two, aren't they?"

Liz swallowed. Brad's plane had gone down into the sea on a training mission, and Joan had been devastated.

"Not fair!" she insisted, her anger flaring again. "Sure, anybody can be killed, whatever their job is. But that's not really your problem, is it? Your problem is, you don't want your comfortable lifestyle to be interrupted by a child. You might even have to miss a party, or an hour's sleep when he cries at night."

"You better believe I like my lifestyle—our lifestyle, I would have thought! And I like you just the way you've always been, nice and flat and firm, with no stretch marks or flab to mess up a good body." He sat quietly for a minute, gazing out over the water. "Listen, Liz, honey—I hate to say this, but I think if you've got a bun in the oven, you'd better plan on removing it—as soon as possible."

"Removing—you mean . . ."

"Just what I said. Do it now, before things get complicated and dangerous."

"You want me to have an abortion—to kill our child."

"Aw, there's no child, Liz! It's a little-bitty mass of tissue, like a—a wart or a tumor. It's not a person, so don't get all sentimental over nothing—that's incredibly stupid. Be a big girl. Grow up and go to the doctor and have the problem taken care of. No big deal."

"No big deal?"

"Of course not. Probably no worse than a trip to the dentist."

"I wouldn't grieve over a pulled tooth."

"Right. It's just one of those things you have to take care of, and the sooner the better. Call tomorrow, okay?"

Liz sat up on her towel and rested her head on her knees. When she looked up again, her eyes were streaming tears. "I'm sorry to disappoint you, but aborting this baby is something I will never, ever do. How can you even think of it—your own child?"

"*I* don't have a child. I don't want a child. And I don't want you to have a child. Do I make myself clear?"

Liz's anger squeaked past her sobs. "I thought all men with an ego as big as yours were eager to perpetuate themselves as soon and often as possible," she flung at him. "Or maybe you already fulfilled that urge, years ago!"

"I don't know about that—and frankly, I don't care. I *don't want* kids, Liz. I thought that was understood."

"I didn't know it when I married you."

"Or you wouldn't have? Baloney. You weren't any more interested in a pack of brats than I was. You never mentioned kids at all when we talked about marriage."

"I just assumed that—that later on, after a while, we'd both want a family—that it would work out."

"No way. Not then, not now. So make your plans, babe. If you can't find a doctor you like on base, I'll ask around."

"No!" She had stared at him, numb with pain and anger. "Not that! I've gone along with you on most things, Brock, but I won't do this. I want this baby—and even if I didn't want it, I wouldn't kill it for my convenience!"

He raised his hand, then, and she thought he was going to hit her. His eyes blazed with fury, but she forced herself to stare him down without flinching. Finally he swept his arm down and sent the remains of their picnic scattering over the sand.

"You want this baby, huh? Then the two of you can go to blazes together, all pink and blue and cuddly! I'm out of here."

He slammed onto his motorcycle and spun off, sending a stinging spray of sand over Liz and her shattered hopes.

She had sat on the beach alone until her body stopped trembling, and then she had sat some more, watching the sun descend into the sea as she planned a life for herself and her baby. At last she had shaken the sand from towels and picnic cloth, gathered up the paper plates, and walked the three miles back to Brock's house—suddenly it was his house, not theirs— ignoring the whistles and rude invitations that her bare legs elicited along the way.

She hadn't even tried to go inside the house, not really wanting to know whether Brock had locked her out. Instead, she had wrapped the picnic cloth around her like a blanket and fallen into exhausted sleep on a patio lounge. Early the next morning, after Brock had left, she crept inside, took a shower, and slept away most of the day. She roused herself to prepare a simple dinner, but Brock didn't come home until after she had gone to bed in the guest room. They didn't speak.

During that night, she woke with a dull ache in her lower back which soon melded into severe cramps that left her ice-cold and shaking uncontrollably. Toward morning, she passed some bloody tissue, and the next day her doctor confirmed that she had, indeed, suffered a miscarriage and prescribed rest and vitamins.

Liz didn't tell Brock. In silence, she mourned the loss of her baby. Hers. It had nothing to do with her husband; he had disclaimed it, wished its death. After a week or so, when they had begun stilted conversations over mundane things, he casually asked if she had found a doctor yet. She replied that it wouldn't be necessary, that there was no baby after all.

"Hey!" he had cried, his eyes lighting in relief. "Good news, eh? Just a false alarm—no problem, after all."

"No problem," she had echoed, but her face felt set in stone.

Later that day, cleaning, she had come across the magazine with the little girl in the red nightgown. She tore the picture to shreds, destroying it as her baby had been destroyed, torn from her through pain and anguish. And, resolutely, she tore from her heart the hope of motherhood. She concentrated on trying to be a wife to Brock, to please him, but her heart just wasn't in it. The fragile thread that had bound her to him had been severed. She had no energy, no sympathy, no desire. A month or so later, she bought Fleece.

A tentative knock sounded at the back door, startling her into an upright position. It was Missy.

"Liz? I brought back your plate—most everybody's gone. What's wrong? Oh!" She plopped down beside the box and peered at the dead puppies. Gypsy, who early on had accepted Missy as a friend, licked her hand even as a new contraction seized her. "They're dead," Missy whispered. "Oh, poor puppies—poor Gypsy. No wonder you're crying," she added, looking up at Liz.

Liz roused herself to blow her nose. "The vet said she might have trouble. I called him, but all I could get was his answering machine."

"Is she going to have more, do you think?"

"I think so, but I don't know how many. Missy, I don't know if you should be here. Have you ever seen anything born?"

"Sure. When Bishop Tucker's cow had her calf I was over there, and he let me watch. It came out all slippery, like it was in plastic wrap, or something. Then while it was still wet, it spraddled its legs and stood right up and looked around! It was so cute—it had the sweetest little white face." She reached a hand to touch Gypsy's straining side. "I guess you've prayed for them already."

"Well, no, I didn't think of that. Do you think it's proper to pray for a dog?"

" 'Course I do! Tuck—I mean, Bishop Tucker—he prayed for his cow and calf."

"He did?"

"Sure. He said it says to, in the scriptures. He says the Lord's always waiting to bless us, but we need to ask him."

"Oh. Well—you go ahead, Missy, if you'd like to. I don't know much about praying myself."

"It's easy. I'll show you."

Missy folded her arms and bowed her head, her shining hair falling forward to shield her face. "Dear Heavenly Father, we thank thee for this beautiful day and all the good things that've happened. But Heavenly Father, we've got a special problem here today. Gypsy's having her puppies, but they're not living. And you know—I mean, thou knowest that Gypsy wants her babies, and she'd be a good mother to them. And we want them, too, so we ask thee to help the rest of them to please live. Please bless Liz—um, Sister Ewell, here, for being so kind and good. We thank thee, Heavenly Father, for help- ing. In the name of Jesus Christ, amen."

She looked up brightly. "See? It's not hard. You just thank him for everything and then explain what you need."

Liz swallowed and cleared her throat. "I'm sure that will help, Missy, if anything can. But you have to realize that some- thing may still be wrong with the pups . . ."

"Oh—and one other thing. You have to have faith, too."

"Oh. Right."

Silently, Liz formed a prayer of her own that Missy's faith would be rewarded.

They didn't have long to wait. Gypsy gave a mighty push and a sleek brown puppy was born. This one was moving as soon as Gypsy cleaned it up, bobbing its silky head in a blind search for nourishment. Panting, Gypsy lay back and bared her considerable milk supply.

"Oh, Gypsy, you did it!" Liz breathed, watching the puppy nuzzle hungrily.

Missy was enchanted. "He's so *cute*," she said over and over, her eyes glowing. "Look at his tiny little tail—it's pointed. And his little toenails. And his soft little ears."

They marveled over the puppy until the next one was born, also living. As Gypsy performed her cleanup ritual, the newborn emerged as a curly-coated black and white terrier type. It was obvious from the first that it would inherit Gypsy's eyebrows and goatee, and Liz felt a small rush of gladness.

"So, you see why I believe in prayers?" Missy asked, beaming. "You do too, don't you?"

"I certainly believe in your prayers," Liz told her gently. "Thank you for today, Missy. And I think you did just wonderfully with your talk."

"I don't know." Missy wrinkled her nose. "I meant to say a lot more about David, but I kinda got a frog in my throat, so I thought I'd better stop."

"I think it was perfect."

"Thanks. Golly, it's getting late! I'd better go help Aunt Lou. She's making us some dinner. Do you think there'll be any more puppies?"

"I don't know. Stop by after school tomorrow and check."

"Okay. 'Bye!"

One more puppy arrived, but it was undergrown and lived only a few minutes. Gypsy was so absorbed in her living offspring that she allowed Liz to remove the three small bodies to the shoe box and carry them outside for burial. By the time that sad task was completed, the sunlight had deepened to a rosy gold and the fresh spring air had cooled considerably. Liz took only a quick glance at her thriving peas and bright green lettuces before locking herself into her house for the night.

Well, Dorrie, she thought, *you'd never believe it, but here I am in Utah, with puppies in my kitchen. I just wish you were here—there's so much I'd love to ask you. But I guess letters will have to suffice.*

11

The days warmed as they passed with occasional lapses into coolness brought by billowing gray rain clouds. In the orchards, swelling buds gave promise to the bees that in the meantime kept themselves occupied with daffodils and hyacinths. The puppies thrived, and so did their mother. Missy visited at least once a day to see if their eyes were open yet, and Liz knew that this was a welcome and healthy diversion for the girl during those first lonely days after her brother entered the Missionary Training Center in Provo.

As soon as the pups began to see, they began to play—clumsy efforts at boxing and biting even before their wobbly legs could bear their weight. Tiny growls interspersed with whines brought anxious looks from Gypsy, whose pleasure it was to keep them well-fed and well-groomed. Tuck and Lolly, who hadn't objected when Liz asked them about keeping a dog, were amused at Gypsy's attentive mothering.

"Now, that's rejoicing in your posterity if ever I saw it," Tuck remarked with a chuckle.

Marilyn Woodbine brought her youngest to see the pups, having been advised to do so by Missy, who had a justifiable proprietary interest.

"They're sweet," Marilyn said. "They must be a lot of company for you."

"They do their best to keep me entertained," Liz agreed. "They're actually a lot more fun than I had anticipated."

"That's kind of how I feel about these two pups," said Marilyn, reaching out to ruffle the hair of Kenny and Kimberly. "Say—have you gathered any asparagus yet? It's on now."

"Asparagus—where?"

"In the old orchard below you, here. It comes up every spring, tons of it, between the trees. It's good stock, too, but we're about the only ones who harvest much. Tuckers have their own, and Ashcrafts don't care for it. Come on, I'll show you. Bring a sharp knife and something to put the spears in."

Gypsy, busy with her pups, was too preoccupied to howl when Liz followed Marilyn outside. Liz was surprised at the wealth of tall, purply green stalks abounding in the orchard. Marilyn showed her how to cut them cleanly at ground level.

"Who planted it?" Liz wondered.

Marilyn straightened up and flicked her long ponytail over her shoulder. "I've no idea. The orchard goes with that house down the hill, but nobody's lived there since before we came, and that was seven years ago."

"Really? I wonder how long asparagus keeps growing."

"Forever, I think, if it's nourished at all. I heard of a bed of it in England that was still producing after hundreds of years. I guess the rotting leaves and fruit provide plenty of compost for this one."

"What kind of trees are these?" Liz asked, touching a swollen dark red bud.

"Sweet cherries, through this section. That's something else we gather freely. Bishop Tucker sprays these trees when he does his own—doesn't want a plague of worms or disease to get started here, I suppose. We bottled two hundred quarts last

July, and dried a lot, too. They're lovely—like big raisins. My kids think they're great."

"Two hundred quarts!" Liz shook her head. "You talk in quantities I can't even imagine. Did you always want a large family, Marilyn?"

"Me? Gracious, no." Marilyn laughed. "I was all set to conquer the world's problems through social work. I got my master's degree in that field and had an undergraduate double major in psychology and English lit. Great preparation for my present job, don't you think? I can analyze my kids' social tendencies and quote Shakespeare to lull them to sleep."

Liz laughed with her. She liked Marilyn's sense of humor, her thin, freckled face, and straight white teeth.

"Then," Marilyn continued, "Tom came to do graduate work in history, and my dad was his advisor. Dad invited Tom to dinner one night to talk over his program, because he'd had to keep breaking appointments with him during the day. That's how we met. Talk about impact! In a puff, I was all changed, it seemed. My views on love, marriage, family, my religion, my future—all whammied."

"Really? You weren't always a Mormon, then?"

"Oh, no."

"Have you ever—regretted any of it? I'm sorry, that's none of my business. I shouldn't ask."

"I never have. Well, almost never," she amended, bending to rescue her knife from the busy hands of her small son. "There are times when things can get pretty discouraging—but no, never any real regret. I feel certain I'm where I'm supposed to be and that Tom's the person I should have married. Just knowing that can be really comforting when things get rough."

"It must be," Liz said wistfully. "Your kids are beautiful—the oldest girl, especially. I noticed them at church."

"Oh, yes, that's our Suzanne, who's fourteen going on twenty-one—she thinks."

"And I've met Kenny and Kimberly, here. That leaves seven more. Who are they?"

"Rod's our eldest—he's seventeen next month. Then Suzanne, and Jess is twelve. The twins, Nathan and Jonathan, are ten; Tommy is seven—almost eight; Martha is six; and Becky just turned five. There—I think I got them all right! So hard to keep ages straight. They keep changing all the time."

Liz smiled. "I'd be the last to know if you missed one. How do you manage to—well, even to relate to all ten on a personal basis?"

"Well . . ." Marilyn stared dreamily across the field at her tall old house. "I could give you a flip answer, I guess, but the truth is, I just keep trying, every day—and I try to let my love for each of them be the determining force behind our relationship. Then too, I try to keep in mind that they're not really mine, in the spiritual sense. You know? They were Heavenly Father's children before he gave them to me, and he knows and loves them better than I ever could. I look at Suzanne, for instance, and I think, 'She's my sister as well as my daughter,' and that helps me to respect her as an individual, even when she's being obnoxious. She isn't just part of me, or a duplicate copy—she's herself, an eternal spirit, just as I am—and she and I may even have made a covenant before we came to earth that I would go before and play the role of mother to guide her through mortality. I think about that a lot, and it helps to keep things in perspective for me."

Liz laid down her knife and sat back on her heels. "Do you really believe that we lived and knew one another before this life? Isn't that a sort of reincarnation theory?"

"Not at all—it's very different from that." Marilyn wrapped her arms around her knees and kept a watchful eye on her two young ones as she spoke. "Reincarnation, you see, implies taking upon us a series of different physical bodies and having several earth lives. But the principle of premortal life is simply that we were all spirit children of a loving Heavenly Father. He had this wonderful planet prepared for us to come to and have experiences that would help us grow and learn to make choices between good and evil. Then, if we choose to, and are willing to follow his counsel, we can prepare ourselves to go back into his presence and eventually become like him."

"Become like—God?"

Marilyn nodded. "When Tom was first teaching me the gospel, these were the things that were most thrilling to me. I know, of course, that some people think it's blasphemous even to think of such a thing. But look at it this way: don't all offspring have the capacity within themselves to grow to be like their parents? I mean, tadpoles become frogs, little boys grow to be men, and the children of God surely have the capacity to become like their Father."

"I've never thought of it so literally," Liz said slowly. "Of course I've always heard the term 'Father in Heaven,' but I thought of us as God's creatures, rather than his actual children—you know, like saying 'Hippocrates, the father of modern medicine.' "

"That's what I used to think too, until Tom expanded my view of things."

Liz thought for a minute. "Doesn't it say in the Bible—and I shouldn't dare to quote the Bible, because the truth is, it's been a long time since I read from it—but doesn't it say that Jesus was God's only son?"

"Yes—his only begotten son in the flesh. But we all are begotten of him in the spirit. We believe that Jesus was the firstborn of God's spirit children, and the rest of us followed. Remember when Jesus said, 'I go to my Father and your

Father—and to my God and your God'? Because of this belief, many church members speak of Jesus as our 'Elder
Brother.' But . . ." Marilyn's eyes grew misty, and her voice
dropped, became almost shy. "Jesus Christ is so much more to
us than that. He's truly our Savior and our Advocate. His love
for us . . ." She stopped, tears tracing patterns down her
cheeks. "To me, he's everything. He makes possible all good
things in this life and the next. Sorry, Liz," she added, reaching
out to squeeze Liz's hand where it rested motionless on her
knife handle. "I'm probably embarrassing you. I embarrass my
kids regularly when I try to talk about these things. It's just
that this knowledge is so precious to me, and so exciting! I can
never get enough of studying and thinking about it. But you
didn't bargain for a sermon, did you?"

"It's fascinating," Liz said slowly. "It'll give me a lot to
think about in my spare moments. And I have quite a few of
those these days."

Marilyn resumed cutting asparagus. "Much as I adore my
family," she admitted, "I could envy you a few of those spare
moments."

Liz smiled wryly. "And as much as I enjoy my spare moments, I could envy you a few of those children."

Marilyn looked up and straightened her glasses. "Come
and see us—please do," she said. "Who knows—you may come
away forever grateful for your childless state!"

Liz shook her head. "I don't really think so," she said. "I always wanted a family. Maybe not ten, but—well, that's neither
here nor there. Anyway, I will come, one day. I'd love to meet
each of your kids. Look, I've got plenty of asparagus for myself,
now. Let me help cut some for you."

She busied herself, working quickly, keeping her back to
Marilyn until she was able to blink away the unexpected rush
of tears and tune out the happy squeals of Kenny and Kimberly

playing a game of chase among the trees. What foolishness was this, she wondered—this yearning for children again when she had thought herself well and truly past that—now that she was divorced and on her own? Was it Missy's unsettling influence or the puppies with their silly baby ways? Probably she had come to the worst possible place, this family-centered state where children abounded like dandelions! She should have chosen New York or Los Angeles—or maybe even Rio de Janeiro. She had liked Rio, when she and Brock had vacationed there once. No, not Rio, she amended, remembering the dark-eyed street children who had caught at her heart there. *Anywhere but here*, she told herself.

But the truth was, she had grown fond of this place. Already it felt like home, more than any other place in years, she realized with surprise. She enjoyed her cozy little old house. It was hers, as none of the houses she had shared with Brock had ever been. She loved the changing faces of the mountains and the sky and the abundance of life that sang and buzzed all around her. Knowing that Tuck and Lolly were across the way gave her a sense of security, almost of family, that had long been missing in her life. And Missy—yes, even disturbing, exasperating Missy—added to her days. She had begun to look forward to the girl's whirlwind visits, though there were still times when she would call out, "Not today, Missy," according to their agreement.

"That's great, thank you," Marilyn said as Liz added another couple of pounds of asparagus to an already overflowing dishpan. "Come out and check every couple of days for more. It shoots up almost overnight, especially if there's rain."

"Thanks for showing me. And—why don't you bring your other kids over to visit the pups, if they'd like?" She regretted this impulsive invitation even as it fell from her lips, but it was out.

"Oh, they'd like. They'll be enchanted. Well—have a good day, Liz. It's been fun to visit. Come on, gang!"

Liz took her asparagus into her kitchen, which seemed small and dim, though safe, after the sunshiny joy of the orchard.

Two weeks later that same orchard burst into bloom. The trees ranged down the hill like so many brides in white lace, nodding and whispering with the breeze. Liz didn't dare go into the orchard on a sunny day, so numerous were the bees at their ordained task. But after quitting time, when the air was still perfumed with the delicate fragrance distilled by the day's sunlight, she loved to wander among the trees and look up at the white or pink blossoms against the deepening blue of the evening sky.

On one such evening she pulled on her sneakers and a light sweater and slipped away from Gypsy and crew, intending only to get a breath of air and a little exercise before settling down with one of Lolly's mysteries. But the night, as it descended, had its own allure, and she found herself walking farther than she had intended. She passed the Woodbines', where lights shone from nearly every window, and three sounds emerged: television, children's high-pitched voices, and the strains of a symphony that Liz could almost identify, but the name eluded her. She smiled as a young male voice rose above the others—"Hey, you guys, cut the racket! I've got exams tomorrow."

An almost-full moon rose over a jagged ridge of mountain like an oversized streetlamp, bright enough to cast shadows and to give a pearly glow to the snow still clinging to the higher elevations. Liz, who had thought herself jaded by the splendor of tropical moons and lush vegetation, caught her breath at the glory of it. This was a beauty that didn't sate one's senses but teased them. It had an elegant restraint that made one want to pursue and capture it.

Liz hugged her elbows and gazed at the night sky. The stars were sharp and brilliant and seemed larger than she had ever noticed before. It was easier to believe that they were suns and planets—worlds in the making, perhaps—than it had been when she had viewed them through the soft humidity of a tropical night. She walked on, following a little lane that she had discovered one afternoon with Gypsy. It was as clearly marked in the moonlight as it had been by day, and she swung along, enjoying the exhilaration that nearly always came when she was out-of-doors alone and free to go where she chose. But the exhilaration had brought a companion feeling this night, and Liz was at a loss to identify it or its cause. It was a vaguely familiar sensation, a nebulous longing, a tender yearning for something wonderful but undefined, coupled with a sense of anticipation that had no basis in fact. It was almost—but not quite—the feeling she had experienced as a young child in the days just before Christmas. It was closer to—but not quite—the happy-sad emotional mix she recalled from budding adolescence.

Mulling over the bittersweet feeling occupied Liz for the remainder of her stroll. She passed Mr. Earl Christensen's mobile home and wondered about him. He was the only neighbor she hadn't met. She walked by Woodbines' again—it was quieter now—and looped around the old farmhouse at the bottom of the hill. Impulsively, too full of the night and her own responses to it to go inside just yet, she left the road and plunged into the fragrant orchard. The beauty was too much—it almost hurt to be surrounded by it. She cupped a handful of white and held it to her face. Then she turned to catch a view of the rising moon through a frame of blossoms but saw instead the plaid flannel shirtfront of a tall man at very close range.

"Oh!" she cried out, startled beyond thought as he caught her arms just above the elbows, steadied her, immediately released her, and stepped back. "Who are you—what are you doing here?" she demanded, searching his face in the moonlight. He was not anyone she recognized—not Tom Woodbine or Wynn Ashcraft as she had momentarily thought he might be, and surely not Earl Christensen, whom she understood to be in his seventies. This man was much younger. He had a longish face with high cheekbones and deep-set eyes. A few strands of dark hair fell across his forehead, and lines on each side of the generous mouth gave it a stern expression.

"I might ask the same of you, what *you're* doing here," he said. "Except that you seem to be simply enjoying the blossoms, as I was. As for my right to be here—this is my property. I have every right."

"Your—but I thought nobody—that is, of course *somebody* had to own it—or did you recently buy it? I'm sorry I barged in, but I didn't think anybody ever . . ." Liz knew she was babbling, but the sudden confrontation had shocked her. She was shaking somewhere deep inside. "Excuse me, I'll just go . . ."

She wanted to escape the stern gaze of this Lincoln of a man who had spoiled her perfect evening. She feared he might even have spoiled her perfect little neighborhood. Had he bought the house, too? Surely he didn't intend to live there! She wanted to know but didn't dare ask. She turned to go, but the brief touch of his hand on her arm again detained her.

"I'm sorry," he said. "I think I've frightened you and gotten off on the wrong foot, which is a talent I seem to have. My name's Will Parrish, and I've just flown out here from Virginia to have a look at this property. It used to belong to my grandfather and then to my aunt—and now it's passed to me, and I wondered what shape it was in and so forth. I hadn't been here since I was a kid."

Liz nodded and let out a long breath that she hadn't realized she'd been holding. "I see. Well, I'm sorry to have trespassed. It's just so pretty here that I got carried away. Good night."

"But wait—you weren't really trespassing. You're welcome to enjoy the orchard whenever you want. You—you wouldn't be Mrs. Tucker, by any chance, would you?"

"No. That'd be Lolly Tucker, across the road up there, in the white brick house. The Tuckers are my landlords. I rent the house just up the hill."

"Then we're neighbors. I understand Mr. Tucker's been looking after this property while it's been vacant. I'll need to speak to him. And your name is . . . ?"

"Elizabeth Ewell. The Tuckers are nice people—you'll enjoy meeting them. Now, if you'll excuse me, I'd better go in."

"If you'll accept my apology for my rude reaction to finding you here. I thought—well, you startled me."

I startled you! Liz thought. "It's quite all right," she said coolly. "Good night."

She brushed past some soft fronds of asparagus fern that had grown from immature, uncut stalks, ducked a low branch, and made her way quickly to the road. She barely heard Will Parrish's belated "Good night!" in her haste to get home.

She sat for a long time in her velvet chair by the fireplace, staring at a pot of daffodils on the hearth, seeing instead the stern set of a mouth that hadn't smiled. Occasionally she shivered.

"I must be coming down with something," she finally murmured, and made herself a cup of herbal tea to sip in bed. As she turned off her bedroom light, she looked out her window to the west, toward the house at the bottom of the hill, beyond the orchard. Barely visible above the trees, the flickering beam

114

of a flashlight appeared first in one upstairs window and then in another, and she imagined Will Parrish going through that ramshackle old house, room by empty room, alone at night. It was more than she would have cared to do.

She got into bed and lay for a long time willing sleep to come. Just before it did, she identified the two things that kept haunting her about the face that had so startled her in the orchard. One was the uncanny feeling that she had seen it somewhere before, though that surely was impossible. The other was the sense of ineffable sadness that seemed to emanate from those deep-set eyes.

12

Some time during the night, a freshening breeze swept in, waking Liz and bringing the cool-scented promise of rain. She closed her window and snuggled deeper in her pillows, sparing a sleepy thought to wonder where Will Parrish had slept. Not, surely, in that empty old house. And why hadn't he waited until morning to look over the place? He had said he'd flown in—perhaps he had an early flight back to—where was it? Virginia. Liz slept again.

In the morning, a tall figure, hunched to keep the cold spring rain from streaming down the back of his neck, appeared on Liz's front porch and knocked lightly on her door. Gypsy ran barking to announce his presence, and from their box the puppies yipped, too, and scrambled to peer over the edge.

"Good morning," Will Parrish said sheepishly as she opened the door. His dark hair was plastered to his head and dripped rainwater down his face, which was clean-shaven in spite of a haggard look that bespoke a night of little sleep.

"Good morning," Liz replied reservedly. "Do you want to come in?" *What is he doing here?*

"Um—well . . ." He slipped off his jacket and left it to drip on the porch, running one flannel shirtsleeve quickly over his face as he stepped just inside the door. "I wondered—I need a little information," he said, gazing intently at Liz, who was suddenly glad she had dressed and combed her hair. "I went over to Tuckers', as you directed, but no one answered, and as I was coming away, I met a little girl on the road, apparently heading for school, and she said, 'They're not home—today's their temple day.' " He shrugged, looking perplexed. "Do you have any idea what that means or when they might be back?"

Liz smiled. "The little girl would be Missy Ashcraft," she told him. "She knows everything about everybody, but I'm afraid I don't. I do know the Tuckers perform some kind of service once a week in the Mormon temple at Provo, but I have no idea how long they'll be away. Not too long, I imagine, because Tuck has his animals to look after. Gypsy, get *down*."

Gypsy was, for some reason unknown to Liz, making an absolute fool of herself, jumping on Will Parrish's long, jeans-clad legs and wagging her tail as if greeting an old friend.

"Hello, girl," he said, extending the back of his hand for Gypsy to sniff and lick. "Does she have pups?"

"Two," Liz replied, trying not to give in to the same unreasoning internal shaking that had seized her the previous night. That, she reminded herself, had been the result of an unexpected encounter in a moonlit orchard. This was the cold, wet light of morning. Still, she gripped her elbows hard against her middle and wished him gone at the same time that some perverse corner of her mind wanted him to sit down and keep talking.

He noticed her protective gesture and was instantly contrite. "Here, I'm sorry—you're freezing, and I'm keeping you from your breakfast." He pushed her front door closed behind him. The unmistakable aromas of coffee and bacon emanated from the kitchen. "Just one more question, speaking of breakfast. Is there a cafe close around where I could get a bite? Within reasonable walking distance, I mean?"

Liz shook her head. "I'm afraid not. We're pretty much between towns, here—just farms and homes in all directions for several miles. Don't you have a car?"

"Not on this expedition. Somehow I pictured the bus running right by the house, on the highway. I almost thought I could remember it that way, from the couple of trips I made here as a kid. But it doesn't. I was able to ride the bus from Salt Lake to Provo with no problem, but then I hiked most of the way down here until a trucker gave me a lift the last few miles."

"So, where did you sleep last night?"

A ghost of a smile crossed his features. "Oh, down at the house. I came prepared, like a good Scout, with a backpack that included a sleeping bag, flashlight, map, and a change of clothes. Somehow it didn't occur to me that procuring food might be a problem! Isn't there even a little gas station that sells bread and milk?"

"Not within walking distance, in this downpour. Listen, why don't you join me? I have plenty of bacon and eggs—it's such a chilly morning that I wanted a hearty breakfast."

"That sounds wonderful," he admitted, the slight smile appearing again. "My head says, 'No, you're imposing,' but my stomach says, 'Eat, numbskull—who knows when you'll get the next chance?' "

"Listen to your stomach," Liz advised. "Come and sit down. It'll only be a minute."

He followed her into the dining room, ducking under the arched entrance. The room and its furnishings seemed to shrink suddenly, wonderland-like. *At least six-three or four*, Liz estimated, as she quickly set a place opposite her own at her windowside table, unaccountably pleased that he should be the first guest to eat there. He looked around appreciatively.

"This is nice," he told her. "Cheerful but calm."

"Thanks. I enjoy it."

He stood in the kitchen doorway, arms folded, watching as she beat eggs in a bowl. His face relaxed into lines of weariness, almost bordering on sorrow, Liz thought. She wanted to see his smile again.

"I think Gypsy wants you to notice her pups," she suggested, indicating the box in the corner where the mother dog stood wagging her tail, watching the new person on her premises.

"Oh, hey," he said softly, going down on one knee beside the box. Liz watched covertly as he fondled Gypsy's ears first and then played gently with each puppy. "Do I ever know a couple of kids who'd be tickled with you guys! At least, I *think* they still would be."

Liz buttered two extra slices of toast. "I think we're ready," she said, and he rose from the floor in one easy motion.

"Coffee?" she asked.

"Please."

Liz poured coffee and grapefruit juice and set out a dish of strawberry jam. Will ate quickly and neatly while outside the rain intensified into a steady stream. It wasn't until he sat back and lifted his coffee mug with both hands that Liz noticed the missing fingers. Part of his left thumb and the tip of the index finger were gone, and the third and fourth fingers of his right hand were without the first joints.

He intercepted her gaze and grinned wryly. "Ever known a shop teacher with all his fingers?"

"Is that what you are?"

"I teach metals and woodworking at a middle school near Richmond."

119

"Sounds interesting, but it must be a rather dangerous profession."

"It can be, in both cases," he agreed evenly. "I'm on spring break right now—that's why the hasty trip out here to check out Granddad's house. I have to teach again on Monday."

"Are you thinking of selling the house, then? You don't plan to move here, I assume . . ."

He gave her a quizzical look and carefully set down the mug. "It depends. I need to go over the house carefully and come up with an estimate of what it would take to make it livable. There's a little money with the estate, but I'm sure it wouldn't cover everything. I'd do most of the work myself, of course—and I'd need to see if I could find a teaching position here. How are the schools? Do you have children?"

"I don't. You should talk to Marilyn Woodbine, in that big house across the field. She has ten."

"*Ten?* As in one, two, three, four, five . . ."

"Six, seven, eight, nine, ten. No kidding. Ages two to seventeen. She can probably tell you a lot about the local school system. And she's very nice, very intelligent."

"Ten," he repeated, still looking stunned. "That's more than three times the size of my family."

Liz swallowed. Of course he had a family. What had ever given her the notion he might not—the fact that he was alone on this trip? *Stupid, really, Liz.* And wouldn't it be nice to have a family living down the hill, instead of that empty old house?

"You have what, then—three?"

He nodded, gazing morosely at the gray rain beating against the window. Reluctantly, it seemed, he brought himself back to the present. "My daughter Megan's nearly twelve, Tim's almost ten, and Nicky is—let's see—sixteen months."

"Oh, Missy'd be so pleased! She's about eleven, and she

longs for a girl her age to play with. And I'm sure Woodbines have boys the right age to play with yours."

"Is it a friendly neighborhood? Not clannish? We're not Mormons. Do you think a tribe of Danish Scotch-Irish English easterners with a touch of Cherokee to boot could be accepted here?"

Liz laughed. It was easier now, knowing he was a husband and father, to relax around him. Now she could stifle the tender new shoots of attraction that she had to admit this man awakened in her. What was the matter with her, anyhow? Were these marriage-minded Mormons getting to her, after all?

"Well," she told him, "I'm not LDS, either, as the Mormons call themselves, and I'm divorced and childless and a terrible neighbor, and they've been wonderful to me. So I'd say you folks have a chance."

He wiped his mouth carefully with a napkin. "After this breakfast, you'll never convince me you're such a terrible neighbor. It was great, and I really appreciate it."

"You're quite welcome. I'm only doing what Lolly Tucker would have done if she'd been home."

"Then I'll have to thank Lolly Tucker as well as you," he said and gave her a smile that warmed his face. It was like turning on a lamp behind his deep-set hazel eyes. She had been wishing for such a smile; now she almost wished it hadn't come. She didn't want to feel envious of this man's wife, her possible neighbor-to-be whose name she didn't even know yet.

He stood up and stretched his shoulders as though they were stiff. "Have to admit, that wasn't the best night's sleep I've ever had. The floor may be ready to crumble in places, but it felt plenty hard under my sleeping bag. Then too, I got the impression I wasn't quite alone."

"Oh? What . . ."

"Just the patter of lots of tiny feet, and a few squeaks."

"Mice."

"Mice," he agreed. "I don't know what they find to eat—maybe the house itself. Excuse me," he added, stifling a yawn. "I suspect I'll have my work cut out for me, if I decide to take it on. Now, how can I compensate you for that wonderful meal? I wash a mean dish, or would you accept a couple of dollars?"

"Neither," Liz told him firmly. "I enjoyed the company."

"Well, I'll find some way to get even." He moved toward the door, stood in thought for a moment with one hand on the knob, then turned to look at her. "About last night," he said quietly. "I really am sorry I was so abrupt. It must have been quite a shock for you to come up against a guy like me all of a sudden. But it was—um—something of a surprise for me, too."

"Please don't give it another thought. I'm afraid we've all grown accustomed to wandering through there, looking at the trees and cutting asparagus. Did you know you have loads of asparagus growing out there?"

"I didn't. Maybe my kids will learn to like it—if we come, that is. In the meantime, please use all you can. Fruit, too, when it's ready."

"Well, then—you see? You've already paid in advance for your breakfast, because I've had several good servings of your asparagus."

He nodded. "That's good. Help yourself."

Stepping out onto the porch, he shook his jacket and put it on. The rain still blew in great gusting sheets.

"Does it do this often here?" he asked.

"I don't think so, but I've only been here since February, so I'm not the one to ask. Would you—would you like to wait until it lets up?"

"I'd very much like to, and I thank you, but no—there's so much planning and figuring to do, and so little time. I'd better get on with it."

"Then here, please—use my umbrella. I'm not going any-where today, and if your jacket gets soaked through, you'll be really cold in that unheated house. You can drop it off when-ever you're through with it."

He struck a movie-cowboy pose and dropped his voice an octave. "Ma'am, ah'm no stranger to wind and rain, but I'll tote your parasol if it'll ease your mind."

Liz laughed, admitting to herself that her blue umbrella looked far too fragile as protection against the storm and far too dainty to shield a man of his size. Nevertheless, he opened it awkwardly and held it close over his head and shoulders as he plunged into the downpour.

"Thanks again!" he called, his clean, limber stride carrying him quickly out of sight.

Liz turned back into the cozy warmth of her home that seemed, for the first time, strangely empty. After she washed the dishes and watered her plants, she cleaned the bathroom with a vengeance and then sat down by her front window to plan her summer vegetables. Gradually the rain abated to an intermittent drizzle as the purple clouds retreated eastward to shroud the mountains.

It was nearly eleven o'clock when Tuckers' car turned into their driveway, and less than an hour later, Liz saw Will Parrish sauntering up the road, skirting puddles, and being received into their home.

She was in her backyard, examining her peas for storm damage, when he and Tuck emerged and headed back down the hill, deep in conversation. She heard Tuck's laugh ring out and wondered idly what Will's laugh would sound like and what would bring it forth.

You see? she chided herself. *You're no better than Francie Johansen thought you were! Don't you remember how it was with Brock? Aren't you enjoying your freedom and independence? Are you so eager to give all that up, just because you met an attractive man? A married man, Elizabeth? You're not going to be that kind of divorcee, are you? Heaven forbid!*

Disgusted with herself, Liz went against the advice of her gardening books and picked a large sack full of plump, wet pods to take to Marilyn Woodbine. She changed into dry shoes and socks and took the long way around by the road to avoid the muddy field. She allowed herself only one casual glance at the sprawling, ramshackle old house as she passed by. There was no sign of the two men.

As she swung along the roadside, breathing in the sweet, rain-washed air, Liz felt a growing confidence that she could successfully stifle her initial attraction to Will Parrish. But she couldn't help wondering how different her life might have been if she had met someone like Will before Brock Ewell had come along.

13

A fitful sun was doing its best to relieve the chill of the day as she knocked at Woodbines' door.

"Liz, come *in!* I've been meaning to call you all day." Marilyn accepted the sack of peas and sniffed them eagerly. "Mmm, they smell so fresh and green. Thank you—ours aren't on yet, and I'll make creamed peas and potatoes with our meat loaf tonight. Tom loves that. I'll just shell them now, while we visit. Do you mind?"

"Let me help. I have to admit, I'm kind of proud of these. They're the first vegetables I've ever grown. I know you're not supposed to pick them wet, but I couldn't resist."

"I don't think they'll suffer—they look healthy. Do you mind sitting in the kitchen? Take my rocker. I'll sit on the end of the bench."

Liz seated herself in Marilyn's chair, which was cushioned in a red checkered fabric to match the cloth on the lengthy picnic-style table and the cafe curtains at the window.

"This is a warm, inviting room," she commented.

Marilyn smiled. "We're going through our Italian restaurant period, I guess. We do serve a good bit of pizza and spaghetti."

"What were you meaning to call me about?"

125

"Well, there's probably nothing to it," Marilyn said, handing Liz a bowl to shell peas into and placing a paper sack on the floor between them for the pods. "It's just that my twins got up this morning full of tales about that old house down the hill being haunted. Seems they saw a light flickering on and off in the windows last night. I thought it might be a transient who'd broken in looking for shelter, or maybe some kids up to no good or exploring on a dare. Tom said he'd tell Bishop Tucker this afternoon, and they can check it out, but I thought you should know there might be some mischief afoot. We hardly ever have any problems around here, but crazy things can happen."

"I know who it was," Liz said quietly, smiling at Marilyn's surprise. "It was the man who owns the place."

"The owner—at that hour? Who, and why?"

Liz fought to conceal the trembling that began again inside her as she told the story of Will Parrish inheriting the property. Marilyn Woodbine was too quick—too perceptive—and Liz didn't want her to know of this absurd weakness in her character.

"He's from Virginia, you say? How interesting—all that way. Older man, or young? Is he bringing a family along?"

"Mid-thirties, I'd judge, and married with three children. He seems nice enough. He said he's a shop teacher—woodworking and so forth. I think he has a daughter about Missy's age and a younger boy and a baby."

"Sounds as if you got well acquainted already."

"Well, we sort of ran into each other last night, and I saw him again this morning. He and Tuck are down at the house now, looking it over with an eye to possible repairs."

Marilyn popped several peas into her mouth. "Yum, these are good. I always eat most of my share before they ever make it to the stove. You know, it really would be nice to see something done to that place before it falls down—and it would be fun to have a family living there, too. I've never thought the place was really spooky, just lonesome. Speaking of houses, would you like to see what we're trying to do with this one? Come on, I'll give you the grand tour while the little ones are asleep. We can finish shelling these after."

Liz followed her into a large space that, Marilyn explained, had originally been three rooms.

"There was a stuffy old square dining room here, an even stuffier parlor, and a tiny bedroom behind that. We knocked down the walls and lowered the ceilings and created this—our living room—and you may take that in the literal sense. It's where we do our living. There isn't room or funds right now to add on a separate family room, so this is it—the 'everything room.' "

It was large and L-shaped, decorated in a functional and comfortable mixture of traditional and early American. A spinning wheel stood in one corner, and a battered baby-grand piano dominated the other end, highlighted by sunlight from three long windows. Scattered sheet music and a flute lay on top of the piano.

"Who plays?" Liz asked.

"Suzanne, mostly. She's really quite something on the piano. I play a little, and I teach all the kids as far as I can take them, but Suzy takes from an excellent teacher at BYU—she's way beyond my level. I love to play the flute when I can, and Suzy and I enjoy duets. Rod and Jess are both pretty good guitarists, and we all enjoy singing, though so far I see no exceptional voices arising!" She laughed. "Of course, when all twelve of us are caroling away, nobody stands out enough to be embarrassed, so it's fun."

Liz followed as Marilyn moved across the long room, pinching a dead leaf from a plant and bending to restore a dropped book to its place on a shelf. She threw open a door in the far wall to reveal a large bedroom, obviously for boys, filled with sports equipment, stacks of books and games, a cabinet of stereo equipment, and two beds. Model airplanes flew at varying altitudes and angles, strung on wire from the ceiling, and a forest mural covered one wall.

"Rod and Jess," Marilyn explained. "They're different as night and day, but they get along really well. They're good boys, both of them. The best," she added softly, as she closed their door and led the way to a long staircase that angled upward across one wall of the dining area.

"I'll just close the little kids' door," she whispered. "All they have are tumbled beds and wall-to-wall toys—they're not into decorating yet." She gave Liz a quick glimpse into Suzanne's lavender and green boudoir, decorated with well-worn dolls on the bed and numerous pictures of boys around the mirror. The little boys' room had a brown and yellow antique car motif, and Becky and Martha enjoyed a pink gingham haven. "All the rooms are so neat," Liz marveled.

"Well, we have a rule—all toys and clothes picked up before bed at night, and all beds made before breakfast. We *have* to—there's no way I could do it all alone. Then everybody has an assigned chore in the morning and one in the afternoon, ranging from mopping the kitchen floor to feeding the dog to things like putting a napkin by everybody's plate for the little ones. It works out pretty well, most of the time." Marilyn grinned. "We have our moments, however. Now—here's our spot."

She opened the door to reveal a quiet bedroom done in shades of beige and blue. The bed was topped with a beautifully crafted quilt—a design of bluebirds flying against a tan sky. One end of the large room was partitioned off by two capacious bookcases of almost ceiling height. Through the space between them Liz could see a cluttered desk, presided over by a computer monitor and keyboard and backed by a map of the world tacked to the wall. Various Oriental knicknacks were placed among plants and groupings of books on the shelves.

"That's Tom's study," Marilyn explained. "We don't have space right now for a separate one, and I've grown accustomed to falling asleep to the sound of his typing."

"Sounds cozy," Liz said with a smile. "How's his book coming? Tuck and Lolly told me about it."

"Pretty well, I believe. What he'd really like is another chance to go to Japan and tour some old Shinto shrines. He's fascinated by some of the similarities between Judeo-Christian beliefs and early Shinto practices. Did you know, for example, that in some of the shrines they baptize little pieces of wood with their ancestors' names on them? Isn't that amazing?"

"Well, I know they revere their ancestors, but why that practice?"

Marilyn shook her head and reached to pat Liz's shoulder affectionately. "Bless your heart, sometimes I forget you're not LDS," she said with a little laugh. "Come on, let's go finish the peas, and I'll try to explain."

They settled in the kitchen again. "The interesting thing about the Shinto practice of baptizing their ancestors' names is that we have a similar practice," Marilyn began. "Basically, I guess, it's all a matter of God being just and fair, and giving all his children the same opportunities, no matter when or where or under what conditions they live on this earth. I mean, how could he, on the one hand, declare that only those who are baptized and follow the teachings of his beloved Son can inherit eternal glory, when only a comparatively few among the billions who've lived on this planet ever even have the opportunity to hear the name of Jesus, let alone comprehend his teachings and receive baptism? What would become of the so-called heathens in Africa or China—or Japan or Chicago or Utah, for that matter. Are they doomed forever to torment in hell or to be lost in a joyless limbo just because they were born in the wrong time or place?"

Liz gazed at Marilyn, considering the question and being surprised once again at the depths in this friendly, unassuming young woman. "So what do you think *does* happen to all the 'great unwashed'?" she asked.

"Well, you've seen what a missionary church we are," Marilyn replied, leaning to open a bin of potatoes close by. "We send out thousands of young people like Dave Ashcraft— and retired couples, too—to spread the good news of Jesus' teachings and sacrifice, and of what we firmly believe to be the restoration of his original church to the earth. We go into every country that will allow us to come, but there's obviously still no way we can reach everyone. So—Heavenly Father has revealed to us that the same sort of missionary activity and teaching goes on after death, too—beyond the veil, as we say—and that eventually every human soul will have had a good opportunity to hear and understand the truth and to choose for himself whether to accept or reject it. Of course, if that opportunity comes here on earth, the convert can be baptized and receive other gospel ordinances. But how do you baptize someone who's been dead for five hundred years?"

"I give up—um—write their name on something, and baptize that?" Liz hazarded, trying to make the connection with Shinto.

Marilyn chuckled. "Close," she said. "First, of course, you have to identify the individual, so that you're reasonably sure of his name and when and where he lived and whose child he was, if possible. You keep a record of him on paper or on the computer, but you don't baptize the record. You do it by proxy—you baptize a living person in behalf of the deceased person, and then the spirit of that deceased person has the opportunity to accept or reject the baptism. If he accepts, he can, as Peter said, 'be judged according to men in the flesh, but live according to God in the spirit.' He said that was why the gospel was preached to the dead."

"That's in the Bible?"

"First Peter."

Liz stared thoughtfully at the pile of potato peelings growing under Marilyn's capable fingers. Her own fingers continued automatically shelling peas. "It boggles my mind," she admitted. "It's all so new to me, yet it makes sense. It's fair, as you said. Is there anything else about it in the Bible?"

"Well, we know the early Saints practiced baptism for the dead. There's a passing reference to it by Paul, when he was trying to prove another point about resurrection. He said, 'Why are they then baptized for the dead, if the dead rise not at all?' Meaning, of course, that the dead *do* rise, and that's why baptism needs to be performed for them. Then, too, you remember after Jesus died on the cross, his spirit went among those who had been dead for a long time, those who, it says, 'sometime were disobedient in the days of Noah,' and preached to them. We believe that was when the Savior organized a missionary program in the spirit world. So they do the teaching on that side of the veil that separates the living from the dead, and on this side, we work to identify the dead and be baptized for them in our temples, so they can have the same opportunities and blessings that we enjoy."

"Oh—you do baptisms in your temples? I didn't know that. I thought maybe people just got married there."

"Oh, that, too. There are several ordinances that take place in the temples. We think of our temples as a sort of link between heaven and earth. Living people go there for ordinances for themselves first and then to perform those same ordinances for folks who have died. We do marriages for the dead, too—for those who were married in life. We call that 'sealing the marriage.' It gives the marriage the opportunity to continue into eternity—but only if the parties are worthy and accept these ordinances that have been done for them. No one's ever forced into anything. That isn't the Lord's way."

Liz's eyes widened, and the motion of her hands ceased.

"You mean—I'm trying to grasp this, I really am—you're saying that couples who have died, who weren't married in your temple, can still have it done for them later, by someone else?"

"Right. Forgive me if I whip along too fast. I forget how different this sounds to someone who hasn't heard it before—I should remember how amazed I was at first. For example, Tom and I were married in the temple for time and for eternity. Why shouldn't my grandparents, who adored each other, be given the privilege of having their wonderful marriage sealed for eternity, if they accept the fullness of the gospel, instead of having it permanently over and done with, as it seemed to be when Grandpa died? So Tom and I went to the Provo temple, knelt at an altar, and made the very same vows and heard the very same promises and blessings pronounced in behalf of Grandpa and Grandma Bussey as we had made and heard for ourselves on our own wedding day. Believe me, it was a wonderful moment for me to be able to do that for them. I felt like they were just as thrilled as we were and kneeling right there beside us. They were always such *good* people, though they had never joined a church. Then, a few years ago, I was baptized for my own mother, who died when I was sixteen. I know she . . ." Tears formed in Marilyn's eyes, and she gave Liz a tremulous, apologetic smile. "Sorry," she whispered. "I can't say much about that." She cleared her throat. "Well," she said shakily, "I've talked your ear off again—it's hanging by the lobe. You'll be afraid to come back. But won't you please come for supper and help us dispose of these peas and potatoes? Look at the mountain I've peeled! Five-thirty?"

Liz stood slowly and shook her head. "Thanks, Marilyn, but I'd better not tonight." She glanced down the length of the pseudo-rustic table and smiled. "Besides, I don't imagine you have to worry a lot about leftovers! And thank you so much—for explaining to me about your temples. That's very, very interesting. I may think of some questions."

"Anytime. Come whenever you can. I love to have you."

Marilyn stood for a long moment in her doorway, watching as Liz walked down the roadway, hugging her arms against her body even in the warmth of the spring sunlight.

Liz's thoughts kept her occupied throughout the evening. Looking up from her growing afghan as shadows lengthened across the grass, she saw Will Parrish stride up the road and knock on the Tuckers' door. She smiled, knowing that he would have a good supper. She strongly suspected, too, that he wouldn't be spending another night with the mice. She saw no more of Will, but the next morning her umbrella stood neatly furled and upright beside her front door, a note fastened to it with a paper clip.

"Thanks again," she read. "It looks as though we can make the house habitable. We'll look forward to having neighbors like you and the Tuckers. Please enjoy the orchard and all that goes with it. Will Parrish."

14

Gradually the blossoms in the orchard faded, their petals swirling downward like a tardy snow flurry in the fitful spring breeze. The young asparagus ferns absorbed nourishment, returned it to the roots, and then died back. They were replaced by tough orchard grass and wild morning glory.

The puppies grew apace and romped through house and yard with wild abandon. Gypsy alternately scolded and joined them till all ended in an exhausted heap and whimpering dreams.

Liz tended her garden. She planted snap beans, cucumbers, squash, and tomatoes, and fashioned hot caps of waxed paper to protect tender seedlings from the chilly mountain nights. She read armloads of books on every subject that caught her interest, created useful and decorative things for her home, purchased a stereo system and a selection of music that appealed to her—and told herself she was happy.

She was delighted when Missy bounded in one Saturday morning and announced she had permission to adopt a puppy.

"Isn't that *neat?*" Missy demanded, plopping on the floor to allow all three dogs to climb into her lap and greet her.

"Now all you have to do is decide which pup you want," Liz said, smiling as the pups settled down to teething on

Missy's knuckles. "I'll probably be an old softy and keep the other one myself. I'm ridiculously attached to them."

"And you're keeping good old Gypsy, too, aren't you?"

Liz sighed. "Yes. She seems to have decided that I'm her person, and I don't have the heart to send her away."

" 'Sides, you love her, too. I can tell."

"Well, it's hard not to, she's so silly and dear. And if you want the whole truth, I'm tickled pink that you're taking a puppy, because that means I'll get to watch it grow up."

"You are a softy, for sure, and that's nice," Missy declared. "Sister Johansen says all you need is a husband and a pack of kids to take care of."

"Sister—you mean down the road, with the red hair?"

"Yep, Francie. She always thinks she knows what everybody should do."

"Missy, I hope—I truly hope you're not going around discussing my business with everyone."

"Oh, no. But everybody likes you—those that know you, I mean. And Francie—I mean, Sister Johansen—she just wonders how come you don't get a job and try to get married and all."

"Does she? I guess everyone wonders."

"Well, Tuckers think you just need a bit of breathing space, and Sister Woodbine says you're busy—uh—evaluating your life, and . . ."

The quotes were too characteristic to be anything but authentic. "Missy, you *are* going around talking about me!"

"Not really. Honest. It's just people always ask me how you're doing, prob'ly 'cause I come here the most, or something."

"Or something," Liz agreed, her lips tightening. "Missy, if anyone asks you about me, you just say I'm doing fine—*period*."

"Okay. I will. Liz, are you mad?"

"I don't know. Maybe a little. Oh, not so much at you, Missy. It's just . . ."

"I know. It's 'cause you're a private person, and all."

"I try to be," Liz said drily. "It's not always easy."

"Wouldn't be, for me," Missy said, shaking her head. "Hey! Did I tell you Dave's through at the MTC? We got to go up to Salt Lake to the airport yesterday and see him leave for Austria. He's there by now."

"I'll bet that was fun for you."

"It was so neat. Mama went too, and we got to eat at McDonald's, after." She looked down at the puppies. " 'Course, it was sad to tell him good-bye again. But I'm still glad he went. He was real excited to go. He's going to send me a doll from there as soon as he finds one that doesn't cost too much. I collect dolls."

"Do you? I used to do that, too. I had all four of the Little Women dolls—Meg, Jo, Beth, and Amy. In fact, I still have them somewhere in the bottom of a trunk."

"Cool! I have a real Cabbage Patch and a Madame Alexander—and a whole bunch of Barbies. My Madame Alexander has real fur trim on her coat. At least, I think it's real. Aunt Lou gave her to me last Christmas. I don't play with my dolls anymore, of course. I'm too old for that."

"Are you? I don't think I was, at your age. My friend and I used to have doll shows and act out stories with them."

"Well, but you had your friend to do it with. It's not as much fun by yourself. I can't wait till the Parrishes get here!"

"Oh, you know about them, do you? I shouldn't be surprised. And I think they do have a girl close to your age. Maybe you'll be friends."

"Maybe. I hope she's not stuck-up."

"Me, too."

"Lots of kids are. Too stuck-up to come out here to play

with me. They say it's too far, or they're not allowed to, or they have dance lessons or piano every day, or something. I think their folks know about Mama and won't let 'em come. One time, Sister Tucker, she gave me a birthday party at her house, and I invited every single girl in my class at school, and only three of them showed up. My best friend didn't even come, and the next day she said, 'Oh, if my mother would've realized it was at Tuckers' house, she'd've let me come.'"

"Oh, Missy—I'm sorry."

"It's okay. We had lots of extra cake and prizes, so it was more fun that way, anyhow. But maybe the Parrishes'll be too stuck-up to come to my house. Or too scared. I don't know why people are scared of Mama—she doesn't even pay any attention to them. Doesn't even notice *me*, most of the time."

"Do you think she'll notice the puppy?" Liz asked, straining to disguise the lump in her throat.

Missy considered. "I don't know. Sometimes she'll sit and watch whatever moves—and puppies move plenty!"

"That's for sure. And try not to worry about the Parrishes. Their dad didn't seem stuck-up at all, when I met him. He was very nice. So probably the kids are too."

"I hope. They won't be here, though, till later in the summer, but Mr. Parrish is coming next week, soon as school's out, to start working on the house. He's real excited about it, Bishop says."

"Is he? Well, that'll be nice. I hope his wife and kids will like it here, too. It's quite different from Virginia."

Missy's head swung up, and she sat still. "He doesn't have a wife," she said slowly, shaking her head. "She died when the baby was still tiny."

"Missy! Are you sure?"

Missy nodded solemnly. "I heard Bishop telling Sister Tucker, when I was over helping her piece a quilt. He said Mr.

Parrish was hoping this place would give them all a new beginning, and something to—to focus on, I think he said."

"I didn't know that," Liz said, her voice sounding suddenly flat and inadequate. "I had no idea. That's very sad—tragic."

"Yep," Missy agreed. "At least I *have* my mama, even if— anyway, that's why I hope they won't be stuck-up."

"Right. Well, I know you'll do your best to help them feel at home here, just like you have for me. You're especially good at that."

"Am I? Really? I know I bother people a lot. I just hope the Parrishes aren't all private people! Mr. Christensen's kind of private, too, only he's *sourpuss* private, not *nice* private, like you. And Tuckers and Woodbines aren't very private at all." She stood up, carefully dumping sleepy, furry little bodies onto the floor. Liz chuckled, watching Missy, clad in jeans and one of Dave's BYU T-shirts, alternately skipping and running up the road. Her laughter was dangerously close to tears, however, as she stepped outside to sit on her back porch and rest her head on her knees, her face turned westward toward the old farmhouse that was just partially visible through the evenly spaced rows of cherry trees.

"I didn't know," she whispered again. Will Parrish hadn't really mentioned a wife, she reflected. Just the children, and she had assumed the wife. More motherless children—would they have the power to rend her heart as Missy so often did? "I'm not involved! I *will not* be involved! I'm here to get my own life together," Liz told herself, trying to stifle all the conflicting emotions that suddenly raged within her—especially the stubborn little voice that kept exulting, "He's not married, after all!"

On Thursday evening, Marilyn Woodbine came running across the field, calling cheerfully to Liz to drop everything.

"Your evening's being replanned, as of now! I have two

tickets to a play at BYU, and Tom doesn't want to leave his writing to go. Suzanne's reading like mad for a book report, and Rod's not into drama, so I need a friend to go. Can you, possibly? It's supposed to be very well done."

"Well, I have been meaning to check out what the university has to offer. Maybe it would shake me out of my comfortable little rut. Why not? What time?"

"We'd need to leave in about forty-five minutes. Will that be enough time?"

Liz laughed. "If it isn't, I'm *too* deep in my rut!"

"Oh, wonderful. I don't know if I can handle it, though— a night out with a friend and absolutely no kids along. I might go off the deep end and treat us to sundaes or hamburgers after!"

"I'll do my best to prevent that by treating you," Liz promised, feeling absurdly pleased to be called Marilyn's friend. She dressed carefully. It was the first time she'd gone anywhere with anyone for months.

It was a heady experience. She and Marilyn chatted incessantly all the way to Provo and nearly made themselves late for the performance by continuing their conversation in the parking lot. Liz found herself telling Marilyn of her growing-up years, things she had not spoken of for ages, even to Dorrie. Marilyn was a good listener—attentive and sensitive to mood and nuance. There was nothing in her nature of the glib sophistication and cynicism that had seemed to characterize so many of Liz's acquaintances among the officers' wives. Even throughout the play, which was delightful, Liz's thoughts kept straying back to their conversation, and she was as eager to continue it over hamburgers as Marilyn seemed to be. Liz felt as though a floodgate in her personality had been wrenched open, loosing a cascade of private thoughts and memories she had thought never to discuss with anyone. She spoke of Brock and their marriage and even touched on her miscarriage—the first time she had mentioned that to anyone except her doctor. She surprised herself at being able to talk about Brock with some degree of objectivity and without the bitter taste of poisoned dreams in her mouth.

"We never were suited to each other, never at all," she admitted, trailing a french fry through the ketchup on her plate. "We were too different ever to have been compatible."

"I can well believe that, from what you've said," Marilyn replied. "What I can't quite understand is how you got together."

Liz smiled ruefully. "It was one of those things you do when you're young and stupid and naive," she explained. "I was in my first year of college, a sheltered little girl from a small Alabama town, living in a rooming house with three other girls while I went to a junior college in northern Florida. One of the girls always had invitations to dances at the Officers' Club at the Navy base nearby, and she would wangle invitations for us, too. I met Brock at one of the tea dances, and he was so different from the boys I'd dated in high school—much more self-confident and sophisticated. I think now that he was probably looking for a girl he could impress and dominate—a pliable sort he could mold into the kind of wife he wanted—and I'm afraid I was all too pliable." She shrugged. "We ran into trouble when I finally grew up and began to think for myself."

"You weren't quite so malleable."

"Right. I decided putty wasn't my color. I think I began to see both of us as we really were and to realize that we were vastly different people—and that that was okay. That was the hardest part—to allow myself to feel okay about not conforming to his pattern for me."

140

"Sounds like you went through your own private liberation movement."

"It was something like that, I guess. I finally realized that if I had met Brock five years later than I did, there wouldn't have been a second date, let alone a marriage."

"But you were happy at first?"

Liz considered. "I think I believed I was. Looking back, it seems like a frantic teeter-totter ride. My whole life centered on catering to Brock and pleasing him. If I succeeded, I was wildly elated at his praise, and if I failed, I was miserable. I revolved around him like a silly little moon, with no light of my own."

Marilyn smiled. "Can't be much fun being a satellite. There's a fine line, I think, between wanting to please someone you love and getting swallowed up in the other person's ego."

"How can you walk the line and keep a balance? I've thought about it often lately. What's to keep me from doing it again someday?"

"Experience!" Marilyn said, with a twinkle. "You'll probably be able to spot another Brock a mile away. What you want is to find a guy who wants to please you as much as you want to please him. Brock just doesn't sound as if he cared much about pleasing you."

Liz made a little face. "He didn't even have the concept."

"How did you manage to break the pattern?"

"Oh—bit by bit I stopped blaming myself every time things went wrong. I began to see that Brock's conviction of his own rightness was just that—it didn't always convince everybody else, including me. I began to ask myself, seriously, how *I* felt about things—all sorts of things—everything from having a family, to—to the style of placemats on our table. We fought about placemats once, if you can believe it."

"I can. But did you have any help through all this—any-one to talk it out with?"

"There was Dorrie Stanford. Though to tell the truth, I never really discussed my problems with Dorrie. She was just there, and I learned so much from watching her and observing her marriage. She was from Utah," Liz added, fishing in her purse for money to pay their tab. They continued their con-versation in the car.

"Tell me about Dorrie," Marilyn requested. "Was she LDS?"

"I don't honestly know. I'm pretty sure her husband wasn't, and I don't recall that she and I ever discussed religion, but she might have been. I do know that she was totally do-mestic. If I said to you, 'blue jeans, potted plants, PTA, cinna-mon rolls, Brownie troop, and needlepoint,' you'd have a bet-ter picture of Dorrie than if I said, 'brown hair, blue eyes, plump figure, and rosy cheeks,' which are also true. She man-aged to be cheerful, relaxed, and busy at the same time. Her husband, now, was completely different. He was your basic 'Type A' personality—restless, driven with ambition, nervous and high-strung and impatient."

"How did they get along?"

"Beautifully. That was what amazed me. He adored her, and she knew it. I think she relaxed him, somehow. She was able to lift the load off his shoulders for a while and make him laugh and unwind a little."

"I think that's a gift, to be restful and able to put people at ease."

"Well, Dorrie has it. The first time I met her, she'd been asked to pick me up for an officers' wives luncheon, because my car was being repaired. We sat together, and after the speaker and the dessert, some of the women around us were complaining and trying to outdo each other, it seemed, with stories about their husbands' stupidity or misconduct. I didn't join in, partly because I was afraid anything I said would get back to Brock, and partly, I guess, because I didn't want to admit my marriage was such a failure. Dorrie didn't join in, either, and I could tell she found the whole thing kind of distasteful, so I suggested we leave. She jumped right up as though she was relieved. On the way home, she asked if I'd mind stopping by her house long enough for her to check on her cat, who had been starting labor, she thought, just before she left, and she was worried about her. She invited me in, and sure enough, Kitty met us just inside the door and really scolded Dorrie for leaving her at such a time! Then she jumped into her box and began to purr—as long as Dorrie was right there. If she tried to leave, the cat was out of the box and telling her about it again. I had to laugh, but now I know how it is, because Gypsy was the same way when her puppies came."

Marilyn chuckled. "Even after ten, I wouldn't want to give birth alone," she said. "I can relate."

"Dorrie said, 'Oh, dear, I'm sorry. Can you stay just until she's had the first? She'll be busy enough then that I can slip away, but she always wants me with her until the first one's born. I guess it's silly, but she depends on me.' "

"So you stayed, of course."

"I stayed for all four kittens, relaxing in Dorrie's rocking chair and enjoying her hanging plants and her stereo. I was so refreshed after that afternoon that I felt I had come home somehow. And I was finally able to identify myself. No—that isn't exactly it, either. I was able to see in Dorrie something of my own suppressed self. She wasn't much like me, but she was like I wanted to be."

"So you felt a kind of kinship with her?"

"Exactly. I had grown up in a small town, as I said earlier, where simple things were talked about and enjoyed, but I tried so hard to put all that behind me and become the uptown sophisticate that Brock wanted me to be."

"Wonder why he didn't marry that sort of girl to begin with."

"I've often thought about that. Pygmalion complex, do you think? He wanted to create and own me."

"Or maybe," Marilyn suggested softly, "he was afraid that that kind of girl, born and bred, would be too independent for him to handle."

"Could be. I've never really thought of Brock as harboring any self-doubts, but you may be right."

"Too proud and defensive to let them show, possibly. You know, it's interesting—you grew up in the South, you say, and yet there's hardly a trace of a Southern accent in your speech."

"Oh, that was one of the first things that had to go," Liz say wryly. " 'Eliza' again. Even the name is similar." She smiled. "But iffen you want, reckon I c'n still spin out a purty fair drawl fer ya."

Marilyn laughed. "Now, I can't believe you ever talked like that!"

"Maybe not, but my Great Uncle Henry sure did."

"Are your parents living, Liz?"

"No. Mom died three years after I married Brock, and Daddy just a couple of years ago. I don't think they ever knew what a mess I'd made of my life. I tried to keep it from them."

"But you didn't head back home to the South after you left Brock."

"No. I came to Dorrie's Utah."

"Bless Dorrie's heart—what an influence she had on you."

"What can I say? She was cool water when I was dying of thirst."

"I hope you've kept in touch."

"We correspond occasionally. I've had one letter since I moved here. She was really surprised that I came to Utah, but I could tell she was kind of tickled about it, too. Maybe we'll get together next time she visits her relatives in Provo."

"I'll bet she wouldn't miss the chance!"

"Well, maybe—but you see, I wasn't to Dorrie what she was to me. I was just an acquaintance, or a casual friend, who came and sat in her kitchen from time to time and absorbed comfort and sanity from her. I didn't give her much in return. I didn't have much to give."

"Maybe more than you knew," Marilyn murmured, pulling into Liz's driveway. "Anyway, I'm sure glad Dorrie was from Utah rather than Vermont or Kansas! Thank you so much, Liz, for coming tonight—and thanks for sharing with me and being my friend."

Liz felt momentarily ashamed. "I really laid it on, didn't I? I should say thanks for listening. You see? I still don't have much to give or share—just old troubles. But I am a little more like Dorrie—I now have a few plants and puppies in my kitchen!"

"You've created a lovely home for yourself, and you have a warm, sensitive personality. I think you're very Dorrie-ish. You just need to keep trusting yourself and let it come out. Good night, Liz."

"Good night."

Liz walked around her yard in the moonlight, wide awake and stimulated by the play and the conversation. Gypsy and the pups romped enthusiastically around her feet, forgiving her absence. It wasn't until she chased the more adventurous of the pups into the orchard to bring it in for the night that she saw the gleam of moonlight on the chrome of a station wagon parked behind the old farmhouse down the hill.

So he was back, as Missy had predicted, and sooner than she had thought—it was barely June.

Over the next few days it became very evident that Will Parrish was, indeed, in residence, and that welcome changes were taking place. Truckloads of lumber arrived, and the whining complaints of saw and drill were punctuated by the staccato comments of hammer and staple gun. Will worked alongside the men he had hired, and once or twice Liz saw Tuck going along to lend a hand. Even Tom Woodbine appeared one evening, hammer in hand, to help finish the new roof before a predicted storm front blew in.

On a Tuesday morning, Lolly Tucker stopped to see Liz and to invite her to a cleaning party in the old house.

"Men, you know how they generally are—real good at making a mess when they work but kind of helpless when it comes down to serious cleaning. Marilyn and me, we thought we'd go down in the morning to do some mopping up—and I expect Missy'll tag along, too. Wondered if you'd be free? It's kind of an interesting old house, and young Will's got his hands full trying to get it ready for his family."

There was no graceful way Liz could refuse, after all the kindnesses she had been shown. And she had been curious about the sprawling old house. As for its owner—he had given her no more than a wave from the distance since his return, so probably he'd take no particular notice of her if she went with the others. That was fine. She didn't want anyone, especially not Will himself, to become aware of the tight quivering of nerves somewhere inside her that began whenever she thought of their first meeting in the orchard. That reaction was something that must remain a closely guarded secret. She agreed to go.

15

At nine the next morning, the five of them—Marilyn's daughter Suzanne having also been pressed into service—presented themselves at the kitchen door of the old house, dressed in jeans and aprons.

"Mop and bucket crew," Lolly called cheerfully as Will came to greet them, lean and tanned in his jeans and white T-shirt, shielding his eyes against the sun with his left hand and rubbing the right against his jeans before extending it to accept Lolly's greeting.

"Ladies, this is beyond the call of duty," he began, but Lolly waved away his objections.

"You know Missy here, Will—and you've met Liz Ewell, haven't you? This here's Marilyn Woodbine, Tom's wife, and their daughter, Suzanne."

He nodded and spoke to each politely and then shook his head, almost in bewilderment. "I've sure appreciated Tuck's help, and Tom's, and they warned me that you ladies might be over, but I hope you don't feel you need to clean up after us."

" 'Course we don't—that's what makes it fun," Lolly told him. "Besides, it gives us girls a chance to get together and gab and to satisfy our curiosity as to just what you men are up to, down here. Now, you can't deny us that!"

Will grinned. "You're right—I wouldn't have the heart. Let me take you inside and show you what we've done, so far." He held back the screened door, which was sagging and sadly in need of repair. "Obviously, we haven't got around to this, yet," he added, as they preceded him into a small entryway that opened onto a spacious old kitchen. It was made even larger by the recent removal of one wall, creating a square, well-lit room with windows on the north and east overlooking the orchard. From one corner of the room, a stairway led down to a cellar, and against another wall stood a blackened old wood stove.

"Would you look at that!" exclaimed Marilyn reverently. "It's the genuine article."

"I thought we'd polish that up a bit and keep it—possibly use it for extra heat in the winter. We've repaired the floor, both here and upstairs, so at least it's safe to walk around." Will indicated the numerous spots where bright new planks shone next to older, grayed ones. "We're putting in all new kitchen cupboards, new appliances, and plenty of durable counter space. Then over here . . ." He strode across the open floor toward the front of the house. "Over here, I thought I'd take out this solid wall and just have a sort of railing as a divider for the living room. Across from that, I'm going to take out the bottom half of the staircase and create a landing, with steps dividing below that—half leading toward the living room and half toward the dining room."

Liz followed the sweep of his hand, visualizing the plan, seeing the effect it would create of openness and warmth.

"A polished banister, going down both sides," she murmured, imagining the wood glowing from a fire in the fireplace across the room. Evergreens at Christmastime, looped along the railing . . .

"Exactly," Will agreed, coming to stand beside her. "Sort

of a colonial look to it. Come on upstairs, ladies, and see what we're up against there. The only other two rooms down here are the two small ones over there. I think we'll eventually make one into a bath and the other possibly a den or study."

They trooped upstairs, where five high-ceilinged bedrooms vied for space under the eaves. An old-fashioned bath with a claw-footed tub was almost as large as the smallest bedroom.

"Talk about possibilities," Marilyn whispered to Liz as they contemplated the brick fireplace in the largest room. Obviously it shared a chimney with the living room downstairs. "What a perfect setting for a romantic evening. I'll bet his wife will love . . ."

Liz's hand flew out to grasp Marilyn's arm warningly and pull her aside. "Apparently there's no wife, after all," she whispered. "Missy says she's dead."

Marilyn's kind face clouded. "Oh, what a shame. But thanks for helping keep my foot out of my mouth. How long— do you know?"

"Less than two years, as the baby is still younger than that. That's all I know."

"What are you two whispering about in here?" Lolly asked, coming up behind them as Missy and Suzanne argued about which room they would choose for their own if it were their house.

"We were just saying that the possibilities for decorating are endless up here. Look at this beautiful woodwork and that rustic fireplace. Think of wainscoting and wallpaper and . . ."

"I think we can lower the ceilings a bit, so there won't be so much vertical space to heat," Will said, following Lolly into the room and looking around critically.

"I can just see striped wallpaper on those dormer angles," Lolly said enthusiastically.

"Braided rugs and a four-poster," Marilyn added.

"I will need help with decorating, when the time comes," Will admitted. "Especially with the living room and my daughter's room. The boys and I can rough it for a while, but I want Megan's room to be just right. She's not exactly thrilled about this move."

"But she hasn't been here, has she?" Liz asked. "I'll bet she'll love it once she sees it."

"That's to be hoped." His voice sounded weary, but he smiled in her direction.

"Maybe among us all we can help her feel at home here," Marilyn said, and Liz nodded agreement, her eyes not leaving Will's face. Why—and how—could he seem so endearingly familiar to her? It was a puzzle, but one she didn't feel ready to solve.

"Well, ladies, you see the mess we're in. There's probably not much point in cleaning up the bedrooms until we've finished the ceiling work, but if you'd like to sweep up the sawdust downstairs, I'd be grateful."

"We'll find plenty to amuse ourselves, don't you worry," Lolly assured him with a pat on the shoulder. "Run along, now, and let us get busy."

He grinned and obeyed. They did more than sweep up sawdust. Under Lolly's direction, the antique bathroom was scrubbed and disinfected, wallpaper was stripped, woodwork was washed, windows were polished, and fireplaces were cleaned. They scrubbed and swept and wiped, and gradually a fresh, clean scent replaced the musty, sweetish odor of mice and old dust.

At one o'clock, Tuck went home and brought back a picnic hamper that Lolly had packed earlier. They all relaxed beneath a stand of old cottonwood trees to eat chicken sandwiches, deviled eggs, and fresh strawberries, followed by chocolate cake and cold milk. While they were clearing up the remains, Will came out of the house with a bemused expression on his face.

"Mrs. Tucker—ladies—I don't know what to say. I didn't expect—you've done wonders in there! I never meant . . ."

Lolly beamed at him. "Of course you didn't. You never even asked. We just barged in and took over. Couldn't stand to let the menfolk have all the fun!"

"I'm very grateful."

"Well, we'll be back another time, when you boys are a little further along, won't we, girls?"

"Please—I can't expect . . ."

Lolly's look stopped him. He stepped forward then and gravely shook hands with each of them. His palm felt warm and dry and callused, and his grip was so firm that Liz hardly noticed the missing fingers. She met his eyes shyly, wondering if he felt the current that she was sure must be flowing between them. If he did, he gave no sign other than a slight tightening of the lips that was almost a smile. She withdrew her hand, and he extended his to Suzanne, who raised her eyebrows in an almost flirtatious glance. Missy stuck her hand out and then half-snatched it back as she noticed his mutilated fingers.

"Oh! What happened to your fingers?" she asked in concern.

Will spread both his hands before him in mock consternation. "Fingers? I'll be doggoned! Must have misplaced them somewhere in all this confusion, do you think?"

Missy grinned at him, obviously relieved that the missing fingers weren't a source of distress after all. He returned her grin and shook hands with Marilyn and Lolly, including them all in another, "Thanks so much, ladies."

Marilyn and Suzanne struck off across the field toward their house, and Liz followed Lolly and Missy up their road, past the orchard where the cherries were already beginning to take on color.

"I call that a satisfying morning's work," Lolly said with a sigh. "Think I'll get me a bath and a little nap before I tackle anything else, though. No pun intended, but I'm just plain tuckered out!"

Liz laughed. "We all had a workout, but it was worth it, wasn't it, to see the place start to shape up. It really does have a lot of potential."

"More than you'd think, from the outside."

"I can't wait till the kids get here," Missy said happily. "I asked him—he said prob'ly in about a month. He wants the house mostly done so they won't hate it."

"Got his work cut out for him, bless his heart," Lolly said. "Lost his wife to cancer, he says, not long after the baby was born. Kids have been living with his sister since then. Said he feels like he's losing them, too—wants to bring them here to live where they'll all be together again. He had to sell their home to help cover medical expenses, and he's been camping out in a little tiny trailer, trying to save enough to start over."

Liz stood silently listening, aware of a slight constriction in her throat. Will Parrish was a good man, surely—why did such tragedies happen to people like him? What fairness was there?

"Liz, I know!" Missy said suddenly. "What if you and Mr. Parrish fell in love and got married? That would make everything all better, wouldn't it? He's real nice, and . . ."

"Missy Ashcraft, don't—you—dare suggest that, ever, either to me or to Mr. Parrish, do you hear me? You just can't go around engineering things like that! I'm sure Mr. Parrish is still grieving for his wife, and you know I'm not interested in getting married again for a long, long time! You're in way over your head on that subject, my dear, so please don't—"

Tears filled Missy's eyes, and she hung her head.

"I'm sorry, Liz, honest. I didn't mean to be pushy. I just thought maybe you'd like him, 'cause he's not like Brock or anything, is he? But if you don't . . ."

Liz, repenting, hugged Missy against her. "I do like him, honey. He *is* nice, and I'm sorry he lost his wife. But that doesn't mean that marriage to me is the obvious answer! That's for TV shows and romantic stories. This is real life, with real people who have their own ideas and needs and feelings. So just please don't meddle, okay? And I'm sorry, too. I didn't mean to hurt your feelings."

" 'S'okay," Missy said in a small voice.

"Liz is right, sweetheart," Lolly added. "Matters of love and marriage are strictly personal. We'll all need to be good friends and neighbors to the Parrishes, but we can't impose our ideas on them."

"All right," Missy said meekly. "I won't. But I do think he's cool." She turned with a fling of blonde hair and trudged up the hill to her house.

Liz looked at Lolly. "Maybe I was too rough with her," she said, "but she scares me. She's perfectly capable of announcing her plans for me to any and all, including Will himself. I'd really prefer to avoid that kind of embarrassment."

"Don't blame you a bit. And thanks so very much, Liz, for helping out today." Lolly reached to pat Liz's shoulder, much as she had Will's, earlier.

"I was glad to," Liz said, surprised at herself that she meant it. She *had* enjoyed the morning—the teamwork, the others' easy acceptance of her, the cheerful results of their efforts. *And admit it, Liz,* she counseled herself, *you enjoyed being near Will Parrish, doing something, however small, that made a difference in his life. But what are you thinking? You're just beginning to find out who you are and what kind of life you want, and here you are— getting emotional over the first attractive man you meet! Is that sensible? As for how you reacted to poor Missy's innocent idea—methinks, my dear, you did protest too much!*

Probably, she reflected, it was just a natural reaction to a year of being alone—a stage that divorced women go through. But who was she kidding? She had been alone, in reality, far longer than a year.

Later in the afternoon, when she had recuperated from her cleaning exertions, she spent a while gently hoeing between the rows of vegetables in her garden. It was pleasant to be out in the incredibly perfect June day, with all silent except an occasional burst of twittering high in the trees and the muted sound of Marilyn's children playing behind their house. When Gypsy chuffed and came to attention, Liz glanced up with surprise to see a man stumping through the cornfield toward her.

"Hello," she greeted cautiously, standing up straight and resting her hoe before her. He paused and bobbed his head.

"How'd'ya do, ma'am?"

"Fine, thanks."

"Beautiful day."

"Yes, it is."

"Seen you out here working your garden, all spring. Figgered I oughta make your acquaintance. I'm Earl Christensen. Live up the road there, other side of Woodbines."

"Oh, yes. It's nice to meet you."

Earl Christensen puckered up his face and nodded. In fact, Liz decided, *puckered* was the word for him in general. The skin around his eyes looked puckered, his mouth was puckered, his words of greeting, though polite, seemed grudgingly forced through lips that appeared to be tasting a green persimmon. She laughed inside, recalling Missy's reference to him as a sourpuss.

"Do you have a garden?" she asked.

His laugh was dry. "Not me, young lady," he said. "Had

enough of that business years ago growin' up. My dad had us kids out in the fields before daybreak, waitin' for the sun to come up so we wouldn't hoe up the corn instead of the weeds. We had so dang much thistle on our place it'd choke a horse. Used to take the skin offa my hands, pullin' thistle. I swore I'd never grow another thing once I got away from home, and I haven't. Wife used to grow a few tomatoes and such, but that was her business. I let her know I was no farmer right off."

"I'd probably feel the same in your place," Liz said. "But I'm really enjoying this little garden. It's my first attempt."

"Well, that's fine. I hope you can keep up with the weeding and watering 'bout the middle of July when the sun's blazing down like the ball of fire it claims to be. But you'll find me shoppin' for my produce in a nice air-conditioned Albertson's store!"

Liz smiled. "Well, I'm going to try to keep up, but you might find me out here weeding by moonlight when it gets really hot."

"You renting this place from the good bishop?"

"From Tuckers, yes."

"And I s'pose you're a Mormon."

"Well, no, I'm not, actually."

"Do tell. You mean you've been here this long, and they ain't got you dunked yet?"

"Pardon?"

"Baptized—by immersion, you know—the only way. Gotta wash the sins off every inch of a body, you know."

"Oh. No—nobody's approached me about that."

"Well, my heck, they're all fallin' down on the job! I'm gonna have to call 'em to repentance."

"So—are you a Mormon, Mr. Christensen?"

"Depends. Don't know, to tell you the truth, whether they've ever taken my name off the books. But I was baptized, right enough, when I was eight years old. Fact, I was dunked three times, 'cause the first two times my big toe popped up outa the water. Like that big toe was really sinful, you know?"

"Really? They baptized you three times, just to be sure your toe was included?"

"Sure did, but I still don't guess it took, do you? 'Cause here I am, just as mean an old sinner as they was afraid I'd be. All that baptizin' and all them beatin's my dad give me and all the fast Sundays I starved through and the Sunday School teachers I tormented, and it didn't do me a speck of good. I still live on coffee and cigarettes, and on the first Sunday of every month I have me a great big breakfast with sausage and hot cakes and eggs, and I jest sit and laugh at those pore hungry folks goin' down there to the church, and I think *why*? Such dang-fool nonsense. 'Course, I figger a good half of 'em are plain old hypocrites, anyway, and just pretendin' to fast, when actually their belly's full as mine. Now, when the wife was alive, she'd cook me up my good breakfast, but she wouldn't never eat it with me, not a bite. Off she'd go, down there with the rest of 'em, and what good did it do her? She got bleeding ulcers, was all, and died of it. I figger if she'd of let up on the religion and jest enjoyed herself, she might still be here. I am!"

Liz didn't know what to say. Finally she asked, "How long has your wife been gone?"

"Been—oh, eight years, now. She was a good woman, mind you. She didn't never preach to me or nag or nothin'. I let her know right off I wouldn't stand for none of that. And she knew I wouldn't never be takin' her to the temple, either, though I suspected she kept hopin' for me to come around and do it. But I had enough of churchy stuff as a kid, just like I had enough of farmin', and I ain't been about to go back to neither one. Guess you think I'm a stubborn old coot, don't'cha?"

"Um—well, we're all different, aren't we?"

"That's for dang sure. One time, one of them little Woodbine boys says to me, 'Don't you belong to our ward, Mr. Christensen? I ain't never seen you there.' I told him, I says, 'Sonny, most of the time, I attend the Scofield First Ward, but sometimes I visit the Strawberry Ward.' He says, 'I ain't never heard of them,' and I says, 'That's too bad, son. You can really find the spirit there.' " He laughed his dry chuckle again. "Strawberry and Scofield's a couple of good fishin' reservoirs, ma'am, if you take my meanin'. Say, what breed of dog's that?"

Liz glanced down at Gypsy, who was sitting straight and still as a ceramic statue by her feet. "I have no idea. She's just a mixture—a stray I found up in the canyon."

"I used to have me a labrador retriever, but she either run off or was stole. It's hard to keep a good huntin' dog—there's always people on the lookout for 'em. That little critter sure seems attached to you. I always say if a dog likes a person, the person can't be all bad."

Liz reached to smooth Gypsy's fur, and felt the slight tremor in the small body. "Good girl, Gypsy," she said soothingly.

"Well, I'd best be gettin' home. There's a wrestlin' match comin' on TV I wanta watch. Been nice to meet you, ma'am."

"Nice to meet you, Mr. Christensen."

He turned and made his way back across her yard and through the cornfield. Beside her, Gypsy gave a low growl, such an unaccustomed sound from her that Liz looked down in surprise.

"What is it, Gypsy? You don't think it was nice to meet Mr. Christensen? You may have a point."

16

The corn in the field grew taller, the cherries ripened, and Missy took her puppy to live up the hill at the quiet gray house. Liz kept busy. Marilyn brought her a home-study catalog, and she signed up for a beginning class in interior design. If she did well, she thought, she might gain the confidence to attend some classes in person. It hadn't been that long, had it, since she'd sat in a college classroom?

In the cool of one late June evening, she squatted in jeans and battered sneakers in her garden, hand-weeding around the green bean plants and lacy carrot tops. She paused to brush a strand of hair off her forehead, realizing as she did so that the gritty sensation meant she had added a smear of dirt to her damp face.

"Elizabeth!"

She looked up. It was Will, calling from the edge of the orchard. "Have you tasted these cherries?"

"Um, no," she replied uncertainly. "Are they ripe?"

"Come see what you think."

Reluctantly she rose, brushing her hands together, and went slowly toward him, bending to swipe at her forehead with the hem of her shirt. He pulled several clusters of dark red fruit from a tree and handed them to her.

"I remember them from childhood as being fantastically good," he said. "But you know how that goes—anything sweet tastes great to a boy. Wonder if our taste buds get more discriminating as we grow up, or what? But these are just as good as I remembered. Guess we ought to wash them, though. Can we use your garden hose?"

She nodded. "Right over there. When were you here as a boy? How old were you?" she asked, holding the fruit out to be rinsed in the stream of water. It ran warm at first, from the sun, then quickly turned ice-cold. Will bent to drink briefly and then flung the hose from him and turned off the spigot.

"How old? Let's see—I must have been eight or nine the first time, and about twelve the second." He gazed off down the hill, as if seeing his younger self playing under the cottonwoods. "I remember my grandpa moving his ladder among these trees, picking the fruit. He worked so fast—it seemed to me he could pick a tree clean in just a few minutes, but that was probably because I was so slow. Plus, I worked on an eat-as-you-go basis. So, what do you think?"

"M-mm," said Liz, savoring the fruit. "The flavor's as rich as the color, isn't it? I don't think I've ever tasted fresh-picked cherries before. A person could get addicted!"

"Aren't they great? My grandmother used to bottle them for winter. I remember seeing her lift a rack of bottles out of her canner. She'd have another ready to go right in."

Liz shook her head. "I wouldn't have a notion how to begin."

"I guess it's getting to be a lost art, like quilting and such."

"Not around here," Liz told him with a smile. "Lolly Tucker quilts, and Marilyn Woodbine talks of putting up hundreds of quarts of this or that."

"With ten kids, I guess she'd need to. Which brings me to the next thing I wanted to say. Elizabeth, I want you and

Marilyn to use all the cherries you possibly can, both fresh for eating and for Marilyn's preserving—all right? Then Tuck's going to help me harvest and sell the rest. He thinks I've got eight to nine hundred dollars' worth here—and that's a windfall, believe me, because funds are running a little low, with all the repairs I've been doing. One thing seems to lead to another. I told Tuck he ought to keep the profit, since he's been the one caring for the orchard along with his own, but he won't hear of it."

"Tuck's that way. He and Lolly are salt-of-the-earth people."

"I'll say."

"Will, I can't speak for Marilyn, but let me buy the cherries I use."

"Oh, hey, no indeed. No way. I want you to have all you can use—and little Missy, too. She sure worked hard the other day, didn't she? Besides, Elizabeth, I'm getting ready to ask you for another whopping big favor." He smiled apologetically.

Liz had trouble keeping her mind on what he was saying. She liked the way he said her name, with just a shade of southern slurring in the middle—Eliz'beth. He'd said it three times, now. His speech was crisp and accentless for the most part, but there was just that touch of Virginia to soften it a little. It reminded her of home.

"A—favor?" she repeated offhandedly, glancing away down the hill. "What did you have in mind?"

"Well, it's Megan's room. I'm about to the point of fixing it up—furnishing and decorating, you know? And I—well, I remembered how much I liked what you had done with your own place, here, and I wondered if possibly you'd have a little time to advise me. In fact, I sort of hoped you might go with me to look at some furniture and such. I just feel so—stupid

160

about these things. I mean, I know what looks good to me—but a little girl . . ." He shrugged. "I feel lost."

"But I don't know Megan—what she'd like . . ."

"I know." He passed one hand over his face, as if in weariness. "The trouble is, I feel I hardly know her anymore either. She's not—she's just not the same warm, happy little girl she used to be. She was always such a delightful kid—easily pleased, affectionate—but now she acts like a stranger. Shy—well, not exactly shy, either—it's more like standoffish. Aloof, you know? Like she couldn't care less about me anymore. And she's totally opposed to this move. Tim's kind of excited about it, I think, but Megan—Megan won't even talk about it."

"Where is she now?"

"With my sister Barbara, in Richmond. Barbara's older than I, and she and her husband have a three-story colonial condo with all the amenities. Their only daughter's away at college, and Barb's been giving Megan dance lessons, tennis, violin, art—all the so-called advantages. I'm grateful, but I don't know who Meggie is anymore. She's growing up and away from me too fast. She's only twelve."

Liz nodded. "That would be hard."

"Megan's always liked pretty things. She's always been a neat and orderly kid and very feminine. I can't help thinking that having a really nice room to come to might give her a lift—be a sort of haven to run to. Does that make sense?"

Liz swallowed. "Lots," she assured him, touched by his care for his daughter's feelings.

"But I . . ." He gestured helplessly. "As I say, I know what I like when it's all finished, and I like your house—but to go shopping totally cold and start putting things together—I just know I'd really blow it. So I hoped you'd have time . . ."

"I'd love to," Liz found herself saying. "It sounds like fun."

"Really? Whew!" He wiped imaginary sweat from his brow.

"That relieves my mind already. D'you have a minute to walk down now and have a look? You might be surprised."

"Oh, I shouldn't—I'm so grubby . . ."

"Well, heck—so'm I, and so's the house."

"You're not, either," she told him. "You've even shaved." *Plus*, she added silently, *you smell of soap and clean clothes.*

"Well," he admitted, "I didn't want to scare you to death, emerging from the orchard. I was starting to look like Blue-beard."

Liz shook her head. "Lincoln."

He grinned. "Been accused of that before, too. Don't know whether to be flattered or otherwise."

"Be flattered. It's a nice resemblance, and not overwhelming. Just a touch."

"Come on, then, and see my log cabin. You look fine—honest. There's just me and the mice, and they've given notice."

She laughed and walked ahead of him through the orchard. They went in through the back screened door, now taut and well-fitting.

"Will! It's beautiful," she said, gazing around the kitchen. There were acres of gleaming countertops framing a shining vinyl floor, and the cabinets were beautifully finished in light wood tones. She looked at Will.

"How much of this did you do?" she asked.

"Oh, quite a bit of the cabinet work and finishing. The more I do myself, the less I pay others to do. Plus, I know it's done right. You like it, do you? Honestly?"

"I do—it's a complete transformation. Any—anyone would enjoy working in a kitchen like this." *Careful, Liz*, she warned herself. *You almost said "any woman."*

"Hope that includes kids," Will said cheerfully. "We'll all

162

be taking turns. I chose ivory appliances. They'll be here in a couple of days."

"Perfect. And what else have you been doing—as if this weren't enough—but I know you've been at it day and night."

He looked at her quickly. "Gosh, I hope the noise hasn't disturbed you."

"Not at all. It's nice to know someone's here."

"Come on in here, then. The stairs are nearly done, but I haven't started on the banister yet. I have laid some parquet by the front door, but I think it'd be cozier to carpet the rest of the living room, don't you?"

Liz knelt to touch the smooth surface of the beautifully in-laid squares of wood. "This is gorgeous," she said softly. "You really are skilled, aren't you?"

He shrugged. "It's my trade. I love working with wood. Building and finishing, and giving kids a start at it."

She looked up. "Have you found a teaching job here yet?"

He shook his head. "I'm waiting to hear from a couple of districts. It looks hopeful. I wouldn't make as much here as in Virginia—but then, I'll have no rent or house payments here, either. All in all, we'll be better off. And we'll be together. Come on up and see Megan's room—maybe you'll get some ideas of what it needs. Careful of the stairs, now—they're still rough."

His hand under her elbow was steady and warm. The room designated as Megan's was clean and bare. Two dormer win-dows looked through the cottonwoods toward the brick church across the road. Liz stood in the middle of the room, half-formed ideas flowing through her mind. A bed between the dormers—or a desk? Window seats?

"What colors does she like?"

"You've got me there. Pink? I don't know. Not too little-girlish, I guess, because hopefully she'll be doing her growing

up here for the next several years. Tell you what—I'm calling
the kids tonight. I'll ask."

"This room has loads of possibilities. The hardwood floor
is still sound?"

"It is. I could sand and varnish it, if you think best—or
should we carpet?"

"I'm not sure yet." It felt strange—and not strange—to be
standing with Will Parrish in the upper story of his house, discussing a room for his daughter. Strange to watch the worry
lines come and go around his mouth and to notice the little
gold flecks in his hazel eyes. She walked out into the hall, and
he followed.

"Do you have a picture of Megan?" she asked. "Maybe if I
saw what she looks like . . ."

"Sure—it's a couple of years old, but it's a good one."

He flipped open his wallet and handed it to her. She took
it and sank down on the top step, where a beam of sunlight
slanted in through a western window. She looked for a long
time at the smiling, mischievous face with its rosy cheeks, teasing eyes, and frame of dark hair. Finally she closed the wallet
and handed it back to him.

"She's a darling. In fact—I don't suppose she's done any
modeling?"

"Modeling? No, I don't think so, although she is pretty
photogenic. Elizabeth, is something wrong?"

Acutely embarrassed at her inability to control the lump
in her throat, Liz put her head on her knees and wrapped her
arms around to shield her face.

"Elizabeth?" He sat beside her on the stairs, not touching
her but so close that she could feel the warmth from his body.
She shook her head and after a minute impatiently dashed
away the stubborn tears that insisted upon forming.

"I'm sorry," she whispered raggedly. "It's nothing, honestly.

It's just that she reminded me very much of someone else—another little girl. It caught me by surprise, that's all."

"Yours, Elizabeth?" His voice was gentle. "Have you lost a daughter?"

"No, no. I feel so foolish. It's silly, really—you'll think I'm a total idiot."

"I won't."

She gathered up her courage and told him about the magazine cover she'd treasured—the dream-child she'd never had. She touched briefly on Brock's refusal to have children and her miscarriage.

"And your Megan is so like that little girl on the magazine," she explained.

"That's why you asked if she'd ever modeled?"

She nodded. "I'm sorry, Will. Really—I'm not usually so teary over nothing." She attempted a laugh.

He stood and reached a hand to pull her to her feet. Still holding her hand between both of his, he looked at her gravely.

"You know, Elizabeth, sometimes you have to open an old wound and clean it out before it can heal. A friend to listen can help in that process. I'm honored that you chose to trust me with what you were feeling. It wasn't 'nothing.' "

"Well, thanks. You're very tolerant. But I'm sure you have enough problems of your own. I have no right to inflict mine on you."

He dropped her hand and cupped her elbow again to guide her down the stairs. "Well, it's kind of funny about that. Seems like if a person's never known any sadness or trouble, he just isn't quite as able to listen and understand. When I—when Kath died—that was my wife, Katherine—the person I turned to the most was an old friend. He was the only one who really seemed to understand how I felt. Not because he'd lost his wife—he hadn't, he was still married—but he had lost his sight in Vietnam. He'd listen to me and talk to me for hours at a time. In fact, I'm sure his wife often wished I would go somewhere else, but she could see I needed him, and she put up with me. I'll always be grateful to both of them. It's a good thing, you know, to have a friend." He smiled a little. "Come on—I've got one more thing to show you, and then I'll walk you home."

He led her through the kitchen again and down the newly replaced basement stairs. "I started cleaning out the basement yesterday, and speaking of canning fruit—well, come and see."

In the sudden glare of a bare electric lightbulb, Liz saw a set of deep shelves about nine feet wide, reaching from floor to ceiling, filled with bottles of fruit and vegetables. Dust and cobwebs had been wiped from the front of the shelves, so that the first row of bottles shone almost as they must have once before. The colors had grown muted over the years—the cherries were brown—but the red of tomatoes was still clear, and the greens and yellows of beans and pickles and corn relish were still recognizable. Will stepped closer and read the date from the top of a lid.

"Nineteen seventy-five. That was the very year my grandmother died. Seventy-nine years old and still preserving all this food. I found that—I don't know—touching, somehow."

"Can you imagine—all that work."

"She did it for Grandpa, but he didn't get to eat it. My Aunt Ceilie came and took him away to live with her. He was in his eighties. I doubt Ceilie even thought to look down here, and Grandpa couldn't tell her. He never spoke a word from the day Grandma died. Everybody thought the stress must have brought on a stroke, but it was more like part of him—a goodly part—had just gone with her."

"Will, how sad."

He nodded slowly, the lines deep beside his mouth again. "Life can be over so quickly sometimes. Makes you want to not waste a minute. But we all do, of course. Lots of minutes. Well—shall we go? You go on up, and I'll get the light."

Sunset was fading into twilight as they walked back through the orchard.

"Don't forget, now—you and Marilyn and Missy—all the cherries you can possibly use."

"That's really generous of you. I'll tell Marilyn."

"And Elizabeth, if you'd rather not be bothered about Megan's room, I can certainly understand."

She smiled at him. "No, I do want to, really. When do you want to start? I'm flexible."

"Maybe—tomorrow?" he asked hopefully.

"Tomorrow's fine."

He regarded her for a long moment while Gypsy rolled ecstatically in the grass at his feet. "Ten-thirty?"

"I'll be ready."

"I'll come for you. Good night, Elizabeth."

"Good night."

Liz went to put away her gardening tools, turning as she closed the shed door to watch Will's tall, well-muscled form disappear into the orchard. He paused fractionally to lift one hand in a casual salute, not looking to see if she returned the gesture.

"You'd never have had a chance," she said to the scornful Brock who appeared mockingly in her imagination. "If I'd met someone like Will Parrish first, I'd never even have seen you."

17

By ten-thirty the next morning, Liz was ready—prepared both physically and emotionally to be cool, cheerful, and practical, and to do all she could to dispel the impression she was sure she must have given the previous evening of a lonely, frustrated woman. She wore a simple blue dress and white sandals. Her skin had acquired a light tan, and her short blonde hair looked like silk. A touch of color on her lips and a spray of light fragrance gave her the confidence she needed to spend a couple of hours in the company of Will Parrish—Will with the deep-set hazel eyes that had a way of seeing things very clearly.

Will's mood too had undergone a change. He bounded onto her porch with an infectious grin and the air of having dropped ten years from his age.

"Ready to celebrate? Where's a good place to have lunch? And I'm not talking hamburgers. I want a thick, juicy steak with all the trimmings!"

Liz returned his smile. "What are we celebrating?"

"I just had a call from the Provo School District, and they're hiring me to teach shop at a middle school. Even the salary worked out better than they had led me to expect, so this is an occasion—and am I lucky, or what, to have a lovely lady to celebrate with? You look cool and crisp today."

"Will, congratulations! It must be such a relief to have that settled."

"A big relief. I can usually find plenty of work as a builder or finisher, but I prefer to stick with teaching. I will have to take a couple of courses to secure a Utah certificate, but that should be no problem. Shall we go?"

Liz locked a mournful Gypsy and puppy into the house and allowed Will to hand her into his station wagon, wondering if Missy was watching from up the road.

"Sorry about the state of the car," he said. "It's—uh—experienced with children."

She looked around. The interior of the wagon was, as he put it, "experienced," but it was also clean. Will drove competently, relaxed but alert, and she found herself unwinding as he told stories from his classroom experiences and his boyhood. She laughed with him, surprised at how soon it began to feel natural to be sitting beside him in his car.

"Sit tight," he told her, and he walked around to open her door when they stopped at the furniture store she had recommended.

"Did you happen to ask Megan about colors last night?" she asked.

He grimaced. "Tried to. I talked to Barb, and she asked Megan. Barb said something about how almost any color scheme could be made attractive, but I could hear Meggie in the background saying, 'Tell him to do it in black, since he's determined to bury me out in the boonies.' "

"Uh-oh—she is upset, isn't she?"

Will nodded. "Stubbornly resistant to transplant. Thinks she'll wilt if removed from Eastern soil. But I think she's hardier than she realizes. She can bloom wherever she's planted if she makes up her mind to. And since she got her stubborn streak from me, I'm going to see to it that she gives

169

the West a fair try. But I do want to prepare a nice garden for her, which is why we're here." He winked at Liz. "And since you're such an avid gardener . . ."

"Avid, maybe, but no expert—with plants or kids. I just happen to like both."

"The first requirement. Have any decorating schemes occurred to you?"

"A couple. But I don't know what we're dealing with in terms of budget, so don't let me get carried away. Probably we should make a list and allow so much per item."

"Good idea. Let's just look for now to collect ideas, and then we'll make our list over lunch."

By the time a rather late lunchtime arrived, a picture was beginning to form in Liz's mind of a finished room. She poked at her salad bar creation while Will attacked a steak with good appetite.

"She'll want a chance to add a few of her own touches, won't she?" she asked thoughtfully.

"I'm sure she will, once she's accepted it as her own place," Will agreed. "You look like a cat with a cream jar all to itself— you must have a super idea."

Liz smiled. "Maybe. Remember that unbleached muslin bedspread with the matching lace?"

"Frankly, my dear, I don't know unbleached muslin from unbleached wool. What sort of color was it?"

"An off-white, not-quite beige, with lots of matching lace."

"Okay."

"Well, I can envision that on that spool bed we saw—the second one we looked at. I thought you seemed to like that one rather well."

"On the mark—that was my first choice. So the spread goes with that, does it?"

"Very well, I think. And—if you wouldn't mind—I'm sure

170

I can find some similar fabric and lace to make matching curtains."

"Oh, now, Elizabeth—I didn't mean for you to have to do anything like that! That's way too much to ask."

"You didn't ask. I'm asking. I love to sew, and I doubt you'd be able to buy what I have in mind. You know how those dormer windows are set back in their little alcoves? Well, that's charming, but it limits the available light, and I think regular curtains would cut it down even more. But the windows are too stark to be left bare, so I thought of making fancy window shades that could be pulled down for privacy and coziness or put up at least partway to let in light and air and the view of those cottonwoods. I have a book that shows how to do French scallop-shirring, and I think that would be effective with muslin and lace to match the spread, and maybe a cherry red ribbon. Then what about fluffy, red area rugs on that polished hardwood—does she like red?"

Liz paused in mid-gesture, suddenly confused at the warmth and amusement she read in Will's eyes. "I'm sorry, I don't usually babble."

She dropped her hands to the tablecloth, and he reached one of his to cover hers and give them a little jog.

"Maybe you should babble more often. I was enjoying it. As for red, I suspect Meggie does like it. At least, she wears it often, and she looks good in it. And the window treatment sounds very nice. If you're really interested, go for it!"

Liz finished her salad in relative silence while Will compiled a list of needed items and approximate prices. He raised his eyebrows at the estimated total but shrugged and said offhandedly, "It's for a sound investment. And I can apply a good bit of the cherry money—so red's an appropriate color, all right."

Back at Will's house, Liz spent the afternoon measuring

the windows and walls and poring over the pattern book until she knew exactly how to spend the allotment Will had given her for materials. He took measurements, too, having agreed to build box-style window seats beneath the two dormers, with hinged lids for extra storage under the cushions.

By noon the next day, Liz had assembled her materials and was busily measuring and cutting. She was annoyed when a knock sounded at her door.

"Not right now, Missy," she called, hoping it really was Missy. Someone else might not be quite so easy to send away.

"It's not Missy," called a voice that she could almost place but not quite. Reluctantly she put down her scissors and went to the door. Francie Johansen stood there, smiling and elegant in white designer jeans and a deliberately casual peacock-blue silk shirt.

"Hello," Francie called, shading her eyes to peer through the screen. "May I come in, since I'm not Missy?"

"Of course," Liz replied, unlocking the catch.

"How are you? I've been meaning to run over and see you for the longest, but my two little rascals keep me so tied down. Oh! Look at your darling little house—how quaint! It's just adorable."

Quaint? thought Liz. *Maybe it is. Maybe I'm quaint, for that matter.* "Thank you," she said aloud. "Come and sit down."

Francie arranged herself along the sofa with an air of sophisticated relaxation, swinging one slim foot in its Italian sandal and rubbing the corner of Liz's afghan between thumb and forefinger as if debating whether to buy.

"Lovely," she murmured. "Now don't tell me you made it or I'll feel totally stupid and unfeminine."

"No danger of that, surely," Liz said with a smile. "I don't know anywhere it's written that the successfully feminine woman has to enjoy tinkering around with strands of wool."

"It may not be written in any of *your* books," Francie said darkly, "but I'll bet it's somewhere in Mormon doctrine, right along with baking bread and putting up peaches."

"Somehow I get the feeling that you don't feel completely comfortable being at home."

"Oh, Liz—I wish I did! But I just don't think I was born to wash diapers and make freezer jam. When I get dressed up and go out to take care of errands—at the bank, or mall, or wherever—I just want to *stay*. Everything's so calm and cool and orderly and quiet, and everyone's dressed nicely. No aprons—not one—no dishcloths. I honestly dread going home to peanut butter on the fridge door and whining kids and 'Sesame Street.' But!" She sat up brightly. "I didn't come to complain. I came to invite you over for dinner next Saturday. Can you come?"

Liz laughed lightly. "But, Francie—you'd just be letting yourself in for more cooking and housework, fixing dinner for company."

"Oh, no, that's different. I love to entertain. It's fun to plan a menu and get things all pretty, if it's for somebody besides three males who aren't even going to notice if there are flowers and candles on the table. Please say you'll come."

"Well, that'd be nice, but frankly, I don't do much in the way of entertaining and socializing these days, and quite possibly I'd never get around to returning the favor."

"Oh, honey, we don't bother with formal social obligations here in our little burg. This is just something I've been wanting to do for a long time, just for fun. Do dress up a little, though, because *I* want to."

"Well—all right. What time?"

"I'll send Eric over for you about seven-thirty, so you won't have to walk down the rocky old roadside in your good shoes. Okay?"

"Okay," Liz agreed. "Thanks, Francie."

"Oh, it's my pleasure, believe me. Well, I'll run. As usual, I've got a hundred things to get done before Eric gets home. See you Saturday!"

"I'll be looking forward to it," Liz fibbed, chastising herself for accepting the invitation. She thought—and not for the first time—*it might have been much easier to have an anonymous lifestyle somewhere in the middle of a city.* But then she wouldn't have her garden and her dogs and this wonderful chance to be outdoors in any weather, day or night, and she wouldn't know Tuck and Lolly, or Missy or Marilyn—or that disturbing man down the hill. *For better or for worse.*

Liz filed the temptation to ponder on whether knowing Will Parrish was for better or for worse and concentrated on crafting the blinds for Megan's windows. She was pleased with the result—they were elegant and dainty, yet they were durable and would be easy to operate.

She and Will surveyed the room critically. The blinds were in place, and Will had done his part in finishing the floor and building the window seats. Liz would make cushions for them, covered in cherry velvet. She had papered one wall, rushing to finish before he varnished the floor, and now that he had declared it ready to walk on and put the furniture in place, he watched while she shook the lacy spread from its plastic confines and put it on the bed.

"No need to put sheets on until just before she arrives, so they'll be fresh."

"And that'll be in about two weeks," Will said. "I'm leaving a week from Monday to go get them, did I tell you?"

"No. You must be excited—it's getting close."

He nodded. "Excited, apprehensive, the whole gamut. You know, Elizabeth, you were right about the spread and the whole effect. I really do like the way it's coming together." His arm went around her shoulders in a comradely hug. "And I was right to ask you for help. It's a triumph!"

"I hope Megan will think so. Are the poppies okay, do you think?"

"Sure—why not? Poppies on the wallpaper and a matching pot of silk ones—are they silk, you said?—on the dresser. A nice touch."

Liz stood still for a moment, savoring a touch she thought even nicer, and then stepped away from the circle of his arm and said, "The throw rugs should be in tomorrow at the catalog pickup at the mall. I have to go into town, anyway—shall I pick them up for you?"

"That'd be great, if you're sure it's no trouble. How much will they be?"

She shook her head. "I still have enough from the budget you gave me—plus some left over for a desk lamp, if that's okay?" She'd spotted a crookneck lamp with a red shade. The money didn't really extend to cover the full price of the lamp, but she wasn't about to tell Will Parrish that.

"Sure, that's fine. You think of everything. I really do appreciate this, Elizabeth. And I'm getting ready to ask you for just one more favor, and then I promise I'll leave you in peace. The moving company called and said my furniture should be arriving tomorrow afternoon. After seeing what you've done up here, I trust your judgment more than ever. If you're available when the truck gets here, would you run down and help me decide where to place things?"

"Happy to."

"I sold a lot of our stuff rather than stored it, but I saved the best pieces. Maybe you can help me fill in later. Elizabeth, did I say how much I appreciate all this?"

"Yes—you did. And you really are welcome."

"I'll get even with you somehow, I promise."

"There's the matter of the asparagus and the cherries," she reminded him as they walked out into the upper hall. A glimpse through the open door of the larger bedroom revealed a tousled sleeping bag, half-falling off an inflated air mattress. The pungent odor of new carpet stung her nose as they made their way down the completed staircase, now divided and banistered in a most appealing way.

"This is going to be beautiful, Will. You've done wonders with it. What do you have coming—sofa, chairs?"

"A sort of brown sofa, two blue chairs, and a fairly new coffee table. Bookcases—in fact, I've probably got a bookcase for every room in the house. I have this thing about books, and Timmy's almost as bad. We never let go of a book once we get it in our grasp. Tim hates libraries, because you have to give the books back."

Liz laughed. "Your kids sound like real individuals. What's the baby like?"

"Nicky? Chubby and solemn, reddish hair and big brown eyes. It remains to be seen what his quirks will be."

"What will you do with him while you're teaching?"

"Some sort of day care, I guess. I'll have to look around for a really good one. Well—thanks again, Elizabeth. You're a lifesaver."

Liz walked home by way of the road. The orchard grass was tall now and still damp from a morning shower. Ripe cherries hung like clusters of garnets, rich and promising among their green leaves.

It was close to one o'clock the next afternoon when the labored sound of the moving van maneuvering into Will's driveway reached her ears. Diffidently she strolled down the hill and stood uncertainly at the edge of the orchard until Will spotted her and waved a greeting.

"This the missus?" asked a burly fellow in a sweat-stained

blue shirt. "Guess you can tell us where the stuff should go, eh?"

"She's a friend," Will said easily, "but that's what she's here for, all right—to help decide where things look best."

The next little while was easy. Liz quickly sized up the pieces as they came in and assigned them their places, assuring Will that he must feel free to disagree or move things about as he chose.

"Will, what a magnificent desk!" she exclaimed, as the men struggled in with a huge, unwieldy oak rolltop. "It's three times the size of mine."

"Yes, I couldn't let that go—it belonged to Kath's grandfather, from their old family home in South Carolina. I'll put it in the study eventually, but where do you think, till then?"

"Um—what about that corner of the dining room, just to the left of the stairs? It'll be out of the way, there, but still visible."

"Good idea. Now for the living room. Let me give you guys a hand there with that sofa—it's a brute."

Liz watched the living room take shape, unable to prevent herself from thinking what she would add if it were her right to do so—a piano, a grandfather clock, a fern stand. She turned away sharply and watched as a set of twin beds, followed by a white crib with decals of balloons on the ends, were carried past her up the stairs. Will was upstairs directing traffic. She walked outside and climbed up the ramp into the dim interior of the van to see how much was left. There was very little left. Other than one wonderful-looking old trunk with a rounded lid, it was mostly the promised bookcases and crates marked Books, Dishes, and Linens. Will wouldn't need her for those. She went home.

18

Liz was reluctantly ready for Francie's dinner party by seven-thirty that Saturday evening, feeling very much over-dressed in a silky, clinging swath of ice green, featuring a shirred panel that curved under her bosom and around her waist to culminate in a tier of small ruffles. It was an elegant dress, undeniably, but she would have felt much more comfortable if she could have worn her crisp pink sundress and jacket and a pair of sandals and walked down the road under her own power. It felt strange to be collected by Eric Johansen. She was not looking forward to this evening, anyway.

"Then why couldn't you have just said a simple 'No, thank you'?" she chided herself for perhaps the twentieth time. "You're a free agent, with no one to answer to but yourself. Yet here you are—accepting unwanted social invitations just as you used to do when you were married. Still the same timid, afraid-to-displease little girl, aren't you? Maybe you haven't come a long way, baby—but I thought you'd come further than that!"

She worked herself into such a truculent mood that it was difficult to smile and greet Eric civilly when he arrived and gallantly admired her appearance.

"Have to admit I wasn't too thrilled when Francie said I

had to wear a suit," he said, "but if it means all you ladies look so gorgeous, it'll be worth it. House is air-conditioned, anyway."

"That'll feel nice. It's been hot today."

"Yeah, I wanted to just install a swamp cooler, but Francie said no way, that with what I make we ought to be able to afford real central air, so I said, 'Well, it's up to you, hon, if you want to spend it that way rather than some other, we'll do it.' She said, 'Well, it's me that has to stay home all day with the babies and cook and clean, so I can at least be cool in the summer.' I said, 'Fine enough,' but I'll tell you what, it sure does cost more than a good old swamp."

"Uh—what's a 'swamp'?" Liz asked, as he opened the car door for her.

"Well, it's a rooftop unit that cools the air by forcing moisture into it and blowing it into the house by a ceiling fan. Works real well in a dry climate, which we have most of the time in the summer."

"I guess that wouldn't help in a humid climate, which must be why I've never heard of them."

"No, they're best for desert air. Be good enough for me. I'm just a simple fellow, but Francie, she's used to nicer things, so I go along. When I grew up here, all we had was a fan in the kitchen and the canyon breezes to cool us off at night, and we survived. Well, looks like the Martins have got here, and the other folks had already arrived before I left."

"How many people did Francie invite?" Liz asked uneasily.

"Think she said there'd be eight of us. Up to me, we'd just fire up the barbecue, but she likes to do things up fancy once in a while."

The cool, clean air of Francie's home did feel welcome after the heat of the afternoon, and Liz took a deep breath of it in the front hall before she stepped up into the living room and put on a smile to greet the others.

"Liz!" Francie squealed, giving her a brief hug and examining her appearance. "You look positively elegant. I'm just so pleased you could come! Everybody, this is Liz Ewell, our neighbor up the road." Francie, resplendent in a royal blue caftan with copper embroidery that matched her hair, pulled Liz into the group as three men rose to their feet. One of them, Liz was aware, was Will Parrish. She forced herself not to glance at him while Francie escorted her around the circle, introducing her to the other guests.

Shaking hands with the Martins, Liz wondered if Francie had invited them for their store-mannequin beauty. Both were slender, graceful people with flawless features—the husband with wavy brown hair, the wife with spun-sugar blonde. Liz wondered giddily if their hands would stay stiffly positioned after she shook them. Next she met a rather short, broad young man with a big, toothy smile that crinkled his eyes into slits over pudgy cheeks. His hand, when he pressed hers, felt pudgy too. She didn't quite catch his name—Brad something, she thought.

"And this is my friend Lynnette Parks, Liz. Lynnette and I used to work together before I married Eric."

"Hello, Liz," said Lynnette, a small, contained person with a mass of curly brown hair cascading down her back. Not really pretty, Liz decided, but she had a certain cool, well-groomed attractiveness.

Francie was tugging her along to stand before Will. "Have you met our newest neighbor, Mr. Will Parrish?" she asked.

You must surely know I have! Liz wanted to say, but she contented herself with, "Yes, I have. How are you, Will?"

"Elizabeth," he acknowledged with a nod. "You're looking lovely."

"Thank you," she murmured, aware of a certain reserve in his manner. Was he as uncomfortable as she was in this setting?

"Your home is beautiful, Francie," she said, moving slightly apart from Will to avoid giving the impression that she assumed she had been invited to be his partner.

"Do you really think so? That tickles me—you're known to be so adept at decorating that I value your opinion."

Liz was at a loss for words. That small cough from Will—was it meant to cover a chuckle?

"Where are your boys?" she asked. "I've never seen them."

"Over at my sister-in-law's, thank goodness," Francie said lightly. "Can you imagine trying to entertain with those little toads underfoot? But those are their pictures over the fireplace."

"They're adorable."

"Thanks. They're certainly full of it, I can tell you."

The two small faces, one still chubby with baby fat, and both topped with blond curls, did indeed reveal a healthy amount of innocent mischief. Liz smiled.

"What do you do, Liz?" asked Lynnette Parks in a bright, conversational tone.

"Well, I . . . ." What did she do? "I'm sort of in between things, right now. I've just been concentrating on fixing up my house and learning to grow a garden—things like that."

"How interesting. Following the prophet's advice, hmm?"

"Prophet?"

"Remember President Kimball? He was always advising people to fix up their property and plant gardens and such."

"Oh? Well, no. I'm not LDS, you see, so I didn't know about that. It just seemed fun, and useful."

"Well, I'm surprised. I looked at you and thought to

181

myself, 'definitely LDS, and probably a schoolteacher or an executive secretary.' "

Liz laughed uncomfortably. "You and Francie," she said. "But I've never been any of those. What do you do, Lynnette?"

"I'm assistant manager of a chain of convenience stores. It's a very demanding job, but I enjoy the challenge."

"Really," Liz murmured. "That's wonderful."

"Have you ever been married, Liz?"

"Um—yes." Something in her rebelled against Lynnette's barrage of questions. Perhaps they were only attempts at polite conversation, but she had no intention of allowing her past to be dragged out and reviewed for the enlightenment of anyone who happened to be listening.

"You're divorced, then, or widowed?" Lynnette pursued, but at the same moment, Will turned suddenly from a table nearby and called her name. She chose to hear him.

"Elizabeth, come and try some of Francie's appetizers, here. Do you like shrimp?"

"Excuse me a moment," she murmured to the inquisitive Lynnette and turned to accept a small cup of spiced tomato juice mixed with tiny shrimp and chopped celery.

"Thank you," Liz responded, and Will seemed to sense that her gratitude extended to more than the shrimp cocktail. He regarded her over his glass as he sipped.

"You disappeared this afternoon," he said in a low voice. "I came back downstairs, and you were gone. I'm sorry if I took too much of your time."

"Oh, no—I just thought you wouldn't need me anymore, since things were pretty much placed . . ."

He raised his eyebrows. "I was hoping to persuade you to share a cold drink with me as soon as the movers were gone. But I'm sure you had things to do at home."

"How does everything look—are you pleased?"

He nodded. "It really helps to have some furniture there. Makes it seem less like such a barn of a place."

"It's a lovely house, really, now that you've repaired and remodeled so beautifully. I hope your kids will appreciate what you've done there."

He shrugged, a small deprecatory grin tugging at one corner of his mouth. "One thing about kids," he said, "I learned early on that you don't expect great amounts of appreciation or gratitude or understanding from them. Kids by nature are takers rather than givers. Hopefully, later, as they grow up, the giving emerges. But while they're young, they're usually so self-absorbed, it's like they live on their own planets. Mine are, anyway, and I see the same thing with the youngsters I teach. Once in a while, you'll find one mature beyond his years, who genuinely seems to care about others and their needs, but by and large, they're prickly balls of low self-esteem and high self-interest, especially adolescents. And babies—babies are the most demanding, impatient little critters in the world. It's fortunate the good Lord made them so cute, or nobody'd want to bother."

"You don't make parenting—or teaching—sound very appealing."

Will chuckled. "It's a funny thing, though, Elizabeth. In spite of all I just said, it's the most wonderful feeling in the world to watch those stubborn, selfish little brutes begin to open up and learn and become. It's just a matter of what you expect. If you go into it expecting the kind of companionship and understanding you'd get from another adult—forget it. You'd be disappointed from day one. You have to accept kids where they are, at each level, and go from there."

"So—are you looking forward to having your three here?"

He drew a deep breath. "Most of the time," he admitted. "But I'll need to keep in mind that all the prickly, angry, selfish feelings are compounded when the kids themselves are hurting. And—mine are hurting. They miss their mother."

"Of course they do. You must, too. And I'm so sorry, Will."

He nodded, staring into his cup of shrimp. "Life goes on, as they say. But I have felt better—much more positive and hopeful since I've been here working on the house. I'm hoping it'll be the same for the kids."

"I hope so, too," Liz replied fervently. "I truly do."

Later at the dinner table, there was sufficient conversation so that Liz didn't feel obligated to instigate any. She merely tried to give pleasant replies to any remarks that were directed her way. Lynnette Parks interrogated first Brad and then Will with her rather obvious questionnaire of details she wanted to establish about each. Brad answered with almost eager good humor, but Will seemed to withdraw and employ some of the same subtle means of discouragement that Liz felt herself hiding behind.

He's a private person, too, she found herself thinking. *Like me.*

At the earliest opportunity that seemed within the bounds of courtesy, Liz thanked Francie and prepared to slip quietly away before she became enmeshed in any of the table games that had been proposed.

"Oh, but you can't leave," Francie protested in a voice guaranteed to call for support from the others.

Just watch me, Liz thought. "I'm sorry, Francie. It's been lovely, and your dinner was truly delicious, but I'm afraid I'm feeling a little tired and headachy. Sorry to be such poor company."

"Let me just give you some aspirin—wouldn't that help?" Francie pleaded.

"No, thanks. I think I just need a good night's sleep," Liz insisted, smiling. "But it's been delightful."

"Well, I'm so sorry. We were all looking forward to getting to know you better. Eric, honey, will you take Liz home? She's not feeling well."

"Oh, sure . . ." Eric began to push his considerable bulk out of his chair, but Will interrupted.

"There's no need for that, Eric. I'll see her home," he said, rising too. "I need an early night myself. This remodeling I'm doing requires all the energy I can muster."

"Well, I'd be glad . . ."

"Thanks, but it's just up the road. Francie, it's been great—dinner was wonderful, and it's been a pleasure, all. Good night."

Liz found her voice. "Yes—it was nice to meet each of you. Good night."

"Thanks so much for coming, both of you," Francie said, as Will offered a crooked elbow to Liz and a hidden wink.

"So that's how it is!" came Francie's playful voice as the door closed behind them. Liz's face flamed.

They were silent as they crossed the neatly manicured lawn to the road. Will shrugged out of his sport coat and slung it over one shoulder, managing in the process to keep possession of Liz's arm.

"In that kind of air-conditioning, you tend to forget it's summer out here," he commented.

"Feels good to me—I was getting a little chilly. Will, you really needn't walk me home. If you don't, maybe Francie will notice and stop her wild matchmaking."

Will grinned comfortably. "If I don't, she'll mark me down as the worst kind of cad. I'm sure she's watching from behind her sheers, aren't you? Shall we turn and wave?"

"It's tempting. But don't pay any attention to her, all right? Tuck and Lolly have already advised me to take her with a grain of salt, and I'll pass on the advice to you."

His arm pressed her hand against his side in a brief gesture of understanding. "Not to worry," he told her. "I've met a number of Francies in my time, and I recognized her right away. She means well, but she's determined to deprive every unmarried guy in sight of his precious freedom."

"Or any single woman of hers."

"Right." They proceeded up the hill in silence, and Will released her hand at her front porch. His gaze strayed down the hill to his home, nestled among its cherry and cottonwood trees, growing into a thing of beauty under his scarred but skilled hands. "I don't know, though, about freedom. Sometimes it's not as great as it's cracked up to be."

"I guess not—not when you've had a happy relationship. A family."

He nodded. "It kind of spoils a guy for the bachelor scene. On the other hand, when you've endured a miserable marriage, it must feel great to breathe free."

"It does."

"Well, don't let the Francies of the world get to you. Good night, Elizabeth."

"Good night, Will. Thanks." She watched him saunter down the hill, whistling. *Are you still watching, Francie? He didn't stay.* She unlocked the door and let Gypsy and the pup out to run happily sniffing the fragrant summer grass. *At least we understand each other,* she reflected. *I know that he still loves and grieves for his wife, and he understands that I'm not in the marriage market. Francie—and Missy—will just have to be content with that. And so will I.*

19

On Tuesday Liz drove to Orem to collect the red-shaded desk lamp and the rugs for Megan's room and then spent the balance of the afternoon at the university library research-ing antique French furniture for one of her home-study assign-ments. Later in the evening, when the sun was slanting in golden shafts through the trees, she took her purchases down the hill and knocked on Will's back door. Will turned from the range, where the mouth-watering aroma of bacon rose from a heavy skillet.

"Elizabeth! You're just in time for supper, if you like bacon and tomato sandwiches. Now, don't tell me you've already eaten."

"I love bacon and tomato—and no, it's been too hot to think about food. I've been living on lemonade and ice water. But you weren't planning for two—do you have enough?"

"See for yourself—there's plenty. And I'd enjoy the com-pany."

"Then let me help. Shall I slice tomatoes?"

"Sure, if you want. Here's a cutting board."

Liz washed and sliced tomatoes at the gleaming new sink in silence, aware of Will moving around behind her, toasting bread and turning bacon. *If Francie could see us now!* she thought with a stifled giggle. She turned with the plate of tomatoes and nearly collided with Will, who steadied her and quickly stepped aside. It reminded her of their first meeting that spring night in the orchard, when she had thought he looked so familiar. She glanced shyly at him. Did he remember, too? He was looking at her, his expression grave, but he said nothing. She began to spread salad dressing on the toast while he stood next to her and assembled the sandwiches. She noted how adept he was at compensating for his lost fingers. How in the world had that happened, she wondered—in one awful accident, or several?

"My plans have changed a bit, by the way," he said in his low, steady voice.

She looked up.

"Things have progressed a little faster around here than I thought they would, so I'm flying back East tomorrow to bring the kids out. We'll all be back here Friday evening. So—" He grinned. "No more peace in the valley."

"Will, that's wonderful! But I had thought you'd be driving."

"I did plan to—I'd like Megan and Tim to see more of the countryside—but it'd be a challenge driving all that way with Nicky, and I'm not sure the wagon is up to making such a long haul again without major problems. I was able to get a pretty good price on tickets, so I figured it might turn out to be cheaper and easier than having a major breakdown halfway through Kansas."

Liz looked up. "You or the car?"

Will laughed. "It's a toss-up which of us would snap first. Plus, the kids have never flown, so it'll be a new experience for them. Tim's ecstatic about that."

"I'll bet. And Megan?"

"I don't know. Silence."

"Mm. Good luck."

"At least the house is fairly ready—Meggie's room, especially—thanks to you."

He poured tall glasses of cold milk. "By the way, Marilyn and company are coming to pick their cherries early in the morning. Why don't you plan to get all you want, too? Tuck's about through harvesting his, and he's bringing his crew over to help with mine. I want just the lower ones on one tree left, so the kids can pick some."

"All I want is a big bowlful to nibble on. Thanks, Will—you're generous."

"Hardly, after everything everyone's done for me. Maybe I should contact Missy's dad. I hate for them to be left out. He's got a heck of a row to hoe, hasn't he? Tuck told me about his wife's situation."

Liz nodded. "I know—it's mind-boggling. But he copes, somehow. He must have—I don't know—a lot of faith, or something."

Will frowned. "Something. Something I'm afraid I probably lack. Help yourself here, Elizabeth—don't hold back."

Liz put a sandwich on her plate.

"Have you seen Missy's mother?" Will asked.

"Yes. She's an attractive woman and seems gentle and pleasant. But she just isn't there. It's as if—I don't know, exactly—as if she lives in a different world. Nothing she says quite makes sense, although it almost sounds as if it should. It's strange—and very sad for the family."

"What does she do all day?"

Liz shook her head. "Virtually nothing, I guess. She'll walk if they take her, eat if they prompt her, and watch whatever moves—any activity, or the television, or the puppy—but she doesn't initiate anything or respond appropriately to questions."

"Makes you wonder if she shouldn't be hospitalized."

"I know. I think she was, for some time. But the family seems glad to have her with them, in spite of it all."

"I guess I can understand that. Although . . ." He shook his head. "When Kath was going—slipping away so that I couldn't communicate with her, I nearly came unglued. It panicked me."

His eyes were bleak with the memory. Liz put down her sandwich and touched his arm. He covered her hand with his and gripped it tightly. "But, do you know, Elizabeth, the worst thing for me was after she died. I was so angry, so very angry—*with her*, you understand—*with Kath* for drifting away like that and leaving me. I knew it wasn't rational or reasonable, it wasn't as if she'd tried to commit suicide or anything—she didn't want to die at all—but I still felt that overpowering fury at her for dying and leaving us. Is that crazy enough?"

Liz returned the grip of his hand but didn't know what to say. A sympathetic lump was crowding her throat, anyway.

"Funny, I'd never been that angry with her in life—ever. We'd had a few little tiffs when we were young and first married but never anything major. I loved that woman, Elizabeth. I loved her so much—it was like having half my soul torn away when I lost her. I thought I was prepared, because we knew it was coming, even while she was still carrying Nicky, and we tried to talk through our feelings and prepare ourselves and the kids. But I . . . I found out you're never completely prepared for something like that. And what I was least prepared for was that anger. I could understand anger toward God, or fate, or cancer, or whatever. But no, I was angry at Kath, herself—and she was the least responsible of all. She was the victim!" He covered his eyes. "I hated myself for that feeling. I thought I must be the most worthless jerk in the world."

Tears ran down Liz's cheeks, and she made no effort to

stem their flow. She felt Will's pain—felt it acutely—and wanted to take it away but had no power to do so. All she could do was share it with him.

"Did she—did Kath—sense your anger before she died?" she whispered.

"No, I don't think so. It didn't really start to hit me until the very end, when I couldn't reach her anymore. And then after the funeral, it seemed to get worse and worse for a while."

"But you've dealt with it now? Has it passed?"

He sighed a brief, shuddering sigh. "Yes, it finally left me. But then I felt horribly guilty and remorseful. I wondered if there was any way she could know—any way she could tell what I was feeling. I didn't want to send her into eternity with anger, Elizabeth! I wanted her passing to be peaceful for her— an easy transition, cushioned with all the love and hope we could muster. I tried—I really did. Then afterwards, I blew it."

"Oh, Will—I'm sure you didn't. I'm just positive you gave her all the love and support you could, and then some. And even if she was aware, afterward, of your feelings—she'd understand, wouldn't she? She'd know it was just a part of your grief."

"Lord knows, I hope so. I've tried so hard to know, to feel something—some assurance that she's okay and happy. I'd like to think she knows where I am, where the kids are, what we're trying to do. You know, Elizabeth . . ." He glanced at her and then quickly looked away again. "You know that first night we met, out in the orchard? Well, I'd just been standing out there in that beautiful place, trying to get through to her, to make her feel and see some of the beauty I saw, and to know something of what I was thinking—that I missed her but that I was trying to put our lives back together. I just felt if I could concentrate hard enough, send enough love—she'd somehow know. Maybe that's silly and impossible, but that's what I was doing."

"Of course. And then I came blundering along and spoiled it all. I'm so sorry, Will. Do you think—you got through to her?"

He shrugged. "I don't know. I don't pretend to know much of anything about life after death, except I have to believe there is one. I do suspect that love doesn't die—but just expands, somehow. I almost convinced myself I felt something out there—a certain warmth or comfort. But maybe it was wishful thinking. I'm good at that."

He noticed her tears then and reached clumsily to wipe the wet streak from one cheek. Her eyes closed at his touch.

"Elizabeth, what can I say? I never meant to unload all this on you! It was the last thing on my mind."

"I don't mind, Will—honestly. It's what friends are for, isn't it? I seem to remember a certain afternoon over there on those stairs, when you were very understanding of my vulnerability."

"Oh, well, hey—anytime. And thanks for listening to the howls of this lonesome polecat. Now, let me warm up your sandwich—and have another, all right?"

"No, thanks. I'm fine." Liz managed to swallow the remainder of her sandwich and milk, and while Will cleared up the kitchen, she carried her purchases upstairs to Megan's glowing little jewel of a room.

With the rugs in place and the lamp turned on, the room looked cheerful and welcoming enough to melt the heart of any young girl, even one who was sure she was about to be "buried alive in the boonies."

Will appeared in the doorway and looked around with a satisfied nod. "You've done wonders, Elizabeth. I think she'll love it. She'd better," he added drily.

"We can only hope," Liz agreed.

"Want to see the boys' room? Not that there's much to see."

He opened a door across the hall, and Liz saw twin beds at right angles in the corner. A durable blue-green tweed carpet covered the floor, and Will had built high shelves above an alcove in one wall.

"For Tim's special things," he explained. "A place to put them out of Nicky's reach for a while. I'm planning some lower shelves under the window for Nicky's stuff. Of course, Nicky won't be moving in here for a while. He'll be bunking with me, so his crib's in my room, but I've learned how quickly they start to grow up. Thought I'd be ready."

"It's nice, Will. It looks like a boys' room."

"I thought I'd let Tim choose some wallpaper—trucks or jungle or football or whatever."

"Aren't you excited to show them the house? I can't believe they'll be here in three days!"

They started down the stairs.

"Neither can I. Excited, yes—but apprehensive, too. I feel like I'm bringing strangers to a strange place. Meggie's changed so much, and poor little Nicky's hardly had a chance to know me. I'm counting on Tim, I think, to pull us all together."

Liz paused beside the back door. "I'll bet the feelings of strangeness will soon melt away for all of you."

"If they do, it'll be at least partly due to folks like you and the Tuckers and the Woodbines. You've all made me feel so welcome here."

Liz bade him good night and walked slowly up the hill, unaccountably pleased at having been classed with such company. Apparently it wasn't possible to live in such a close-knit little community and be completely private and isolated from the lives of those around you. Grudgingly, Liz began to admit that maybe, just maybe, the entirely private life wasn't the most desirable after all.

Early the next morning, cheerful teasing and laughter from the orchard brought her awake, and she knelt beside the window, watching Tom and Marilyn and their children attacking the cherry trees with buckets and ladders. She dressed and went to join them, arriving in the tall, dewy grass in time to see Will's station wagon back out of the drive. He rolled down his window and leaned out.

"Remember, now—take all you can use, everybody," he called, and Tom Woodbine waved in response.

"You're too generous, Will!"

"Can't be," Will replied. "See you all later."

"Have a good trip," Liz called.

"Bound to be interesting." He shrugged, grinning.

Liz watched as the station wagon rolled toward the highway, slowed, and then gathered speed and was gone. Funny she should feel a sense of loss, she reflected, just to know he'd be gone for three days. More than three days often passed with no sight of him, but just to know he was there, down the hill . . . She shook herself and glanced up to see Marilyn watching her from her perch atop a ladder. Liz felt her cheeks redden, but Marilyn said nothing. Only a small, sympathetic smile gave Liz to understand that her secret was suspected.

"I talked it over with Lolly," Marilyn said later, when they were rinsing cherries in the Woodbines' yard and preparing to consign them to bottles. "We decided it might be nice to put up a couple of dozen quarts for the Parrishes, as a surprise. Lolly always does some for Ashcrafts, so I said I'd do Parrishes'. We take turns doing some for Mr. Christensen, too—this is Lolly's year for him. Of course we have to leave his anonymously on his steps, or he won't accept them."

"He's a real grouch," added Suzanne, passing through the

kitchen. "I don't know why you bother doing anything for him. He doesn't appreciate it."

"Well, we just have to assume that he's not a very happy person," Marilyn said.

"It's his own fault if he's not happy! All he does is complain or make fun of us."

"That's how he chooses to behave, but we don't have to let it influence how we choose to behave. Lolly says his wife was a real sweetheart, and she does things for Mr. Earl out of respect for her memory."

"She'd have to have been an angel to live with him. The poor thing probably got sick and died in self-defense! Imagine being cooped up with him in that little mobile home. Anybody'd go crazy."

"Possibly he was different when she met and married him. We don't know enough to judge. Anyway, about these cherries . . ."

"I'd like to help," Liz said quickly. "I want to learn how it's done, so I might as well."

"Great—work with us, then. It'll be a treat to have you. And I don't know what you think of the idea, but Lolly and I talked about maybe having a dinner ready at Will's place for Friday evening when they get back. Of course, they'll probably have eaten on the way, but we thought we'd fix something they could have anytime—a ham and some salads and a cake. Missy and Suzanne want to make a banner that says 'Welcome Home' to put across the back of the house where they'll see it first thing. In fact, my kids thought it'd be great to give them a surprise party, but I said that under the circumstances, Will might just appreciate a chance to slip in quietly with the kids and show them around himself with as little fuss and bother as possible. But the food and the banner—that'd let them know there are friends here, don't you think?"

"I think that will be just right," Liz agreed. "He's nervous about how his kids will like it here—and if everyone descended on them at once, it might just be confusing. They're bound to be tired after that long flight."

"I thought so. Want to help with the dinner?"

"Let me do the cake. You have enough kitchen work to keep you busy for days."

"Oh, that'd be great. Will's nice, isn't he? Tom thinks a lot of him."

"Does he?"

"Mm-hmm. Says he's a steady, decent sort of fellow with deep feeling for people."

"He—yes, he does seem that way, all right."

"Liz, he showed us the room you decorated for his daughter. It's gorgeous. It made me embarrassed that I showed you around our simple place! I should have known, after I saw what you'd done to your house, that you have a real flair for decorating—and that room proves it."

"It was fun," Liz said with a shrug. "I just hope she likes it."

"Well, Will's sure grateful to you. He thinks you're wonderful."

"Now, *wonderful* is a strong word," Liz said carefully. "Maybe *nice* or *helpful* but surely not *wonderful*."

Marilyn smiled at her—a knowing, almost teasing smile. "*Wonderful* was Will's word, not mine," she said quietly.

They worked relentlessly all afternoon, washing, scalding, and filling bottles with the firm, dark cherries that Marilyn said were of the Bing variety. Countless dipperfuls of boiling sugar-water were poured over the fruit, and the jars systematically came from the processing bath in the big blue enamel canner to stand in rows on the towel-covered table, from which a series of satisfying clinks and pops gave evidence of properly sealing lids. The air was redolent with an aroma as rich and fruity as the deep red color of the cherries themselves.

"Ah, Liz, bless you," Marilyn finally said with a tired sigh. "It's been so good to have your help—doubly good, because it's freed Suzanne to keep the little ones out from underfoot. Thank you, thank you. Are you starving? I am."

"Well, I think I've had my fill of cherries," Liz admitted. "What do you do about dinner when you're tied up with fruit like this?"

"I made a huge bowl of potato salad last night, and we're doing hot dogs and marshmallows outside on the grill. And you *must* stay and eat with us this time—it's required."

Liz laughed. "Okay. I accept. What may I do to help?"

"You've done enough, my dear, and so have I. Dinner on canning days is strictly the province of Tom and the kids. You and I are going to scrub our purple cuticles and flake out in lawn chairs."

Accordingly, Liz leaned back in her chair, weary and content to watch the swarm of activity that surrounded the grill where Tom Woodbine presided. It was remarkable, she thought, that all of this life and vitality had come about because of the love and union of two quiet, unassuming people like Tom and Marilyn. Amazing that they both, so interested in things of the mind and spirit, could relate so well to the rowdy give-and-take of their teenagers, the lively exuberance of their middle ones, and the tired and hungry whining of the youngest. She pondered the scene, and a word rose to the surface of her mind: *respect.* Even in the act of physically separating ten-year-old Nathan and Jonathan, who were tussling in a temperamental struggle over the best hot-dog skewers, Tom spoke calmly and listened carefully to each side of the conflict, not judging between them but asking questions that helped to defuse the situation.

Marilyn held Kenny and Kimberly, and five-year-old Becky leaned against her mother's chair. Shyly, she glanced at Liz, who smiled encouragingly at her and finally entreated her to sit on her lap, which Becky did self-consciously, one finger in her mouth.

"Beck, what a baby! You're too big to be held," rebuked Martha, one year older, as she importantly marched by with an armload of paper plates.

"Am I?" Becky asked, twisting to look up at Liz.

"I don't think so," Liz replied softly, tightening her hold just a little. "I think you fit just right." Becky settled back against her with a contented sigh.

After supper, Marilyn insisted that her son Rod carry a case of the day's product home for Liz, who left the bottles standing on the counter of her small kitchen, enjoying the rich color and the satisfaction of knowing that she had helped preserve the fruit. She thought of the faded cherries in the bottles Will had shown her in his basement and felt a kinship with his grandmother. Surely she had felt a similar sense of satisfaction in her work when those same bottles had come dripping from their boiling water so many years ago.

20

On Friday afternoon, Liz walked down the hill with Lolly and Missy, carefully carrying a chocolate cake with white boiled icing. Missy, important with news of a recent visit to see Uncle Max and Aunt Louise, had helped her decorate the cake with pecan halves and pink and green gumdrop flowers.

"We went to the zoo, and it was so neat," she reported. "They had the cutest little baby leopards. I just wanted to pick them up and love them, but of course we couldn't touch them. And we had dinner out at a real Japanese restaurant, where you take off your shoes and sit on the floor." She giggled. "I had a hole in the toe of my sock, and I was so embarrassed. I don't know what half the stuff we ate even was, but it was fun."

"Sounds like you had a good visit," Liz commented, smiling at her.

"I did, but I missed my puppy, so I was glad to get home. Aunt Louise made me a denim skirt and gave me some money for school clothes, too. Did you know we got a letter from Dave, and he's had his first baptism? Isn't that cool? Except he says it isn't really his, because the missionaries have been teaching the man for about three years, and Dave just happened to be there when he finally decided to get baptized. But I think it's neat, anyway."

"Well, it is," agreed Lolly. "And you can never tell—it might just have been something Dave said that helped tip the scales for that man."

"I'll bet it was. Sister Tucker, how long do you think it'll be before the Parrishes get here?"

"Don't know, honey. Some time this evening. But remember, we all decided we wouldn't flock in on them, first thing. Give them time to begin to know their new home."

Missy sighed. "I know. I just wanted to find out if Megan's going to be in sixth grade or seventh, that's all. I wouldn't stay, or anything . . ."

"Missy . . ." said Liz warningly.

"Oh, all right. I'll wait till tomorrow."

"And that's not before tomorrow afternoon at one," added Lolly.

"I don't know if I can stand it," Missy said. She ran ahead to meet Marilyn and Suzanne.

Lolly looked at Liz and shook her head. "I just hope the Parrish girl will be a good friend for Missy. That child needs a companion about as badly as anyone I've ever seen."

"I feel guilty," Liz said, "to have done so little with her this summer."

"You've done more than your share, don't you worry about that. You've been real good for her. But she needs a friend her own age."

"I imagine Megan will, too, from what Will has said."

"Tragic thing, losing a young wife and mother."

"It is. Will's apprehensive, I think, about caring for the kids on his own, but he's determined to keep the family together."

"As it should be," Lolly said, fishing for a key to Will's door.

"Too bad they ever had to be separated at all. Kids probably felt like they'd lost their dad as well as their mom."

Liz nodded silently. She placed her cake in a conspicuous place on the kitchen counter and then went back outside to watch as a colorful banner was tacked across the back of the house. "Welcome Home, Parrishes" had been printed in huge letters.

"Hey, I know!" Missy cried. "We could toilet-paper some of the trees!"

"Best forget that idea," Lolly advised briskly. "I'm just not real sure Will would take that as a sign of welcome."

Missy wrinkled her nose. "Maybe not," she agreed. "Maybe they don't do that in Virginia."

Liz knew when Will and the children arrived. It was after dark, and she was sitting on her back steps while Gypsy and the pup—Tracker, as she had taken to calling him, for his tendency to follow interesting scents all over the yard—took care of their evening needs. All she could see was the broken sweep of headlights through the orchard as the station wagon swung into its accustomed parking place behind the house. She held her breath, listening for their voices. The sound, but not the sense, drifted up to her. She heard Will's deep tones, the lighter, excited ones of a child, and finally a fretful whimper that must be Nicky, unhappy at being awakened, Liz imagined, assuming that he had fallen asleep during the long ride from the airport. Gypsy paused, alert, but refrained from barking, and thankfully Tracker was unconcerned. There were a few more noises—bumping and slamming and calling—and then the night grew quiet as the house down the hill welcomed its new family. Liz whistled to the dogs, and they went inside. At least, she thought, Will wasn't alone anymore.

She didn't sleep well that night, blaming her restlessness on the distant grumble of thunder that kept promising relief from the heat but didn't follow through. When she did sleep, it was a dream-filled slumber that left her headachy and vaguely dissatisfied with life.

"I need a change," she told Gypsy over breakfast. "Will you be good if I spend the day in Salt Lake? You guys won't howl, will you?"

Gypsy paused in her crunching of dog kibble as if considering the request.

"I mean, you know by now that I'm not going to desert you, don't you? And you have Tracker for company."

Liz finished her cantaloupe and toast and aspirin and got ready. An hour later, fortified with the determination to enjoy herself, she drove down the hill with just a glance toward Will's house. All was still quiet, but she smiled to notice a boy-sized pair of jeaned legs astraddle a tree limb in the side yard, feet swinging.

By the time she reached Salt Lake City, the coolness of morning had all but dissipated, and the sky overhead was a rich blue that presaged another day of dry desert heat. The air-conditioning in a downtown mall was welcome, and she browsed contentedly among bookstores, clothing, craft, and home-furnishing shops. She bought an arrangement of blue and peach silk flowers nestled on a piece of driftwood as a sort of housewarming gift for Will and his family and, on impulse, a big sack of freshly made saltwater taffy for the children. She treated herself to an elegant fruit salad for lunch and attended a movie matinee—something she couldn't recall ever doing alone—telling herself that she might as well become accustomed to it or miss every good movie and play that came along. Just the same, she wished Marilyn or Lolly could have been beside her, sharing the laughter. She liked the comic actor who played the lead but had to admit that things were funnier when they were shared. "I should probably get a VCR," she decided. "Then I won't have to miss everything."

The sun beat mercilessly on the city from the western sky when she emerged, blinking, from the darkened theater, and she felt her headache returning. Not wanting to drive home during the hottest time of the day, she went back to the mall and bought an outfit that had tempted her earlier. Storing her purchases in her car, she decided on another look at Temple Square, drawn by the memory of her first night in this city.

She passed through the open gates, surprised somehow at the throngs of people—tourists, she guessed—who crowded the sidewalks and buildings. There hadn't been so many on that rainy February evening. The sturdy but delicate granite temple had lost a little of the fairy-tale charm the lighting had given it on her first visit, but it was still a place that spoke to her of beauty and strength. She let herself be swept along with the crowd, glancing at the beds of brilliant flowers that flanked the wide sidewalks. She followed a group of camera-laden tourists to the same Visitors Center where she had seen the statue of Jesus and the film about life and death and love, both of which had touched her so deeply. It was no longer quite so foreign to her thinking, she realized, to accept the idea that family life could be that close, that warm and meaningful. She could picture Tuck and Lolly in that film, or Tom and Marilyn, or even Wynn Ashcraft and his pretty, lost wife, reunited spiritually in the next life, their years of anguish erased and healed as they clasped each other in a renewal of love and recognition.

On this visit, Liz concentrated on a display about temple marriage—photographs and a recorded voice that, at the press of a button, explained the Mormon belief that a marriage solemnized in the proper place and by the proper authority had the potential of becoming an everlasting relationship if both partners were faithful and true to God and their covenants. This blessing was also available, the voice assured her, to those who had died without the opportunity to have their marriages sealed. It could be done vicariously for them in the temple. Liz frowned. Marilyn Woodbine had told her essentially the same thing, she recalled—had, in fact, mentioned having participated in such ordinances for her own deceased grandparents. It was, Liz admitted, a beautiful concept—if one were fortunate enough to find someone desirable enough to spend eternity with. She thought wistfully of Will, longing for communication with his Katherine, and wondered if he knew of this strange Mormon doctrine. She looked around, spotted a guide who seemed available to answer questions, and approached him.

"I was wondering," she began, "if one marriage partner dies, and their marriage wasn't performed in a temple, can the spouse who's left—um—what's the term? be sealed—is that it?—to the one who died? Or do they both have to be dead and have it done for them then? And do they both have to be members of your church?"

"Let's sit down over here a moment, shall we?" suggested the guide, a dapper, middle-aged man who looked as if he should be hurrying down the city streets with a leather briefcase. He led her to a comfortable grouping of chairs. "Now—are you, by chance, asking regarding a husband you've lost?"

"Oh, no—no. I was thinking of a friend, who lost his wife to cancer about a year ago. He's not Mormon, and neither was she—but they loved each other dearly—and I was just wondering."

"I see. And the answer is yes, the surviving husband would need to be a member of the Church in good standing. He would kneel at an altar in the temple, just as if he were being married, and a woman representing his wife would kneel opposite him and participate in the ceremony as the proxy in her behalf. Their marriage would then have the potential of lasting forever in the eternities. If both partners are deceased, however, neither of them having been members of the Church, then someone would have to be vicariously baptized and endowed for each of them before the marriage sealing would be valid."

"Endowed? What does that mean?"

"The endowment is a temple ceremony in which, basically, an individual covenants with God to keep his commandments and be valiant in serving him and receives the promise of certain blessings in return for doing so."

"But what good would that do if the person were dead? Wouldn't it already be too late for that?"

"No, indeed. You see, we feel confident that the Lord's work goes on even more actively on the other side of the veil that we call death than it does on this earth. But certain ordinances can only be done here—and so living persons perform those ordinances not only for themselves but for persons who have died, so that all may have the same opportunities and be judged by the same standards."

"I see—I think. But, what if someone performed a ceremony that sealed two people together who didn't want to be together?"

The guide spread his hands. "Then the sealing wouldn't be valid. The folks in the spirit world are free, as we are here, to accept or reject anything done in their behalf."

"So—you never know, I guess, whether it's been accepted or not."

The guide's eyes held a serene, faraway look as he considered his answer. "Occasionally," he said, "we're privileged to know. Most often, however, you're right—we don't. We just hope." He went to a rack of pamphlets and selected two, which he presented to Liz. "Maybe these will help to answer your questions."

Liz thanked him and lingered over exhibits and tours until the sun had finally dropped below the horizon. As she drove home, a blessed coolness descended with the soft twilight.

There was a light behind the carefully crafted shades in Megan's room.

"I hope you like it," Liz whispered to the young girl who was Will and Katherine's daughter but who looked so much like the child Liz had fallen in love with on that long-ago Christmas magazine. "That was so silly of me," she told herself. "Even if I'd had a daughter, she'd probably have been blonde and nothing at all like that picture. I can't imagine why I let it affect me so much." She sighed. Reason might try to prevail, but old longings, old yearnings—somehow they survived.

Liz stayed inside all the next morning, her blinds drawn and the house quiet, devoid of the light and fresh air and music she usually preferred. It wasn't until she heard the uninhibited laughter of boys crossing the field behind her house that she recognized her problem: she was afraid to meet Will's children.

"And why is that, Elizabeth?" she queried herself as she peered out the window of her kitchen door and identified the boy that must be Tim—a little taller and with hair a shade darker than the nut-brown thatch of the Woodbine twins. He marched between the rows of young corn with an optimistic bounce and a squaring of his thin shoulders that made Liz feel ashamed.

"They're the ones with new worlds to conquer," she reminded herself. "They're the strangers here." But kids were adaptable. It was adults who struggled harder with change, adults who should be strong, but who were more aware of their own vulnerability. Liz squared her own shoulders and went out to look at her garden.

Down the hill, church was letting out. The Ashcraft family passed. Wynn and Missy waved at her; Helen walked on, gazing straight ahead, smiling slightly. Liz wondered if Missy had made contact with Megan Parrish yet. *Silly,* she chided herself, *they've been here a day and a half. Of course she has!*

She looked across the field as the rest of the Woodbine children swarmed out of their family van and crowded around to greet Tim. She smiled. Nobody could feel strange for long in the face of all that frank interest and obvious welcome.

About four in the afternoon, Liz took the silk flower arrangement and the bag of taffies and walked down the hill, scolding herself for allowing the presence of three innocent children to make her nervous. It was Tim who answered her knock at the kitchen door. His hazel eyes were bright and his grin friendly. There was a generous sprinkle of freckles across his nose and cheeks.

"Hi!" he greeted cheerfully, opening the door to admit her.

"Hi," she returned. "I'm Liz Ewell, your neighbor up the hill. And you must be Tim."

"Yep, that's me. Hey—are you the one that made that cake with the gumdrops and stuff?"

Liz nodded. "I hope it was good."

"It was great!" He went to the foot of the stairs. "Dad! The neighbor lady's here." He turned back. "Dad's just up changing Nicky. He'll be right down."

"That's fine. How do you like it here, so far?"

"I think it's cool."

Liz set her gifts on the counter and smiled at Tim. "Have you picked any cherries yet?"

He indicated a generous bowlful on the counter. "Yeah. Want some? They're real good."

"No, thanks. I have a big sack of them at home. They are yummy, aren't they?"

"Yeah. I never picked any before. Back home we used to have a crabapple tree, but they weren't too good to eat. Us boys—me and my friends—used to have wars with 'em." He grinned. "My mom made us stop, though. She said she was gonna turn our ammunition into jelly. And she did, too."

Liz nodded. "Crabapples make good jelly."

"I reckon. That was a long time ago, though. I don't remember what it tasted like."

"Have you already met the Woodbine kids?"

"Yeah, they're cool. I'm going to their T-ball game, tomorrow."

"Sounds fun." Liz looked up as Will came down the stairs, grinning, a chunky baby boy in his arms.

"Elizabeth! Thanks a million for the great welcome you ladies gave us. That good food made it extra nice to get home, didn't it, guys? You've met Tim, here—and this is our Nicky."

Will turned the little boy around and set him on the edge of the counter, holding him firmly anchored as he twisted and tried to grab a cherry from the bowl. Liz looked at the rosy skin and auburn hair, the shining eyes and healthy, perfect little body.

"He's beautiful, Will. Hi, Nicky," she added, as he examined her solemnly. When his curiosity was apparently satisfied, he remembered the cherries and made another lunge to capture one, but they were just out of reach.

"Good?" he asked, pointing to the bowl.

"Very good," Will answered. "But not too many for Nicky."

"Not now?" Nicky questioned, shaking his head.

"Not right now," his father replied and then raised his voice. "Meggie! Come on down. I want you to meet someone."

"I know—just a *minute*, okay?" came a girl's voice.

"Her hair isn't exactly right, yet," Will explained to Liz, who smiled.

"Let her take her time. How was your trip?"

"Not bad, actually. We had kind of a long layover in Chicago, but other than that, it was pretty smooth, wouldn't you say, Tim?"

"It was super! It was fun to fly—I never did, before. They gave me a certificate."

"It can be fun, all right," Liz agreed. "Oh, by the way, I brought you a little housewarming gift. I thought the colors might go with your living room. And the taffies are to welcome the kids to Utah."

"Hey, neat, Dad. It's saltwater taffy, isn't it, like we used to get in Virginia Beach? I dibs all the cinnamon ones!"

"No way, friend. You'll have to fight me for a couple, at least. Elizabeth, thanks so much! You've already gone way beyond the call of duty, and now this. We'll be spoiled. Let's go choose a spot for the flowers."

Liz chose the coffee table, which was where she had pictured the arrangement when she first spotted it, and Will seemed pleased with the effect. He set Nicky down and stooped to remove a scatter of Sunday comics from the carpet.

"It's starting to look like home—and even feel that way—now that the kids are here," he said, but Liz was looking beyond him. She caught her breath, wondering why the slender preteen slowly descending the stairs, one hand on the railing, had the power to make her heart pound and her palms perspire. Megan wore denim shorts and a yellow T-shirt. She was so obviously Will's child—was that why? She had his dark hair, now pulled back in a banana clip with an artful fluff of bangs above a long-lashed, feminine version of her father's hazel eyes. She gave Liz a charming smile and held out her hand.

"Are you Elizabeth—the lady who decorated my room?" she asked.

"I helped with it," Liz conceded. "I hope you like it."

"I love it," Megan said. "It's darling—especially the window shades and the spread. I didn't expect anything so—you know—classy." She flicked her gaze upward over Liz's shoulder at her dad.

"Well, it sure wouldn't have been that classy without Elizabeth," Will said cheerfully. "You're right on that point. She seemed to just have a feel for what you might like. And look here, Meggie, she's brought us this nice flower arrangement, too."

"Mm, pretty," Megan approved.

"And a bag of saltwater taffy, like from Virginia Beach, only this was made in Salt Lake City," added Tim, holding up the bag.

"Looks like she knows what boys like, too," Megan said.

Liz smiled. "All I know is that when I moved here, all the neighbors were so kind and tried to help me feel welcome. I just wanted to do the same for you folks. I suspect you'll find lots of friends here."

Megan shrugged. "I've only met Missy Ashcraft, so far. She came over, yesterday. But she was real friendly."

"Missy's a one-person welcome wagon, isn't she? And she's been so thrilled to know that a girl her age was moving in."

"She's needed a girlfriend, all right, so it's lucky both ways," Will added.

Megan frowned. "I don't know why everybody thinks that just because two people are close to the same age, they're bound to get along and be good friends."

Will looked surprised. "I thought you liked Missy."

"Well, I did, but I *might* not have! She's a lot different from me and from all my friends back home."

"That's okay," Will said. "People don't need to be clones of each other to get along and have fun. Variety adds spice."

Megan gave her father a look that plainly said "Shows what *you* know" and turned away to glance into a small wall mirror at her bangs.

"I understand the principle of youth conformity," Will remarked to Liz in a low voice. "But I don't feel obliged to encourage it."

She smiled up at him. Nicky clung to his leg, and Will picked him up.

"Can we open these now, Dad?" Tim asked, still clutching the bag of taffies.

"Sure, might as well—but just one apiece for now."

"Hot dog!" He tore into the bag, scrabbling for a green and yellow piece of candy. "I'll bet this is banana, and they're even better than cinnamon."

"Lunch mouth," scorned his sister.

"I'm just a growing boy," Tim replied, unconcerned, and passed the bag to his father, who offered it to Liz. She declined.

"Good?" queried Nicky, pointing at the sack.

"I'll get him one," Megan said and unwrapped a pink taffy for the little boy. Will set him on the floor again, where he was immediately happily absorbed in his treat. Megan took her time examining the candies and selecting the one she wanted, her pretty brow furrowed. Liz looked at Will, surrounded by his attractive, bright children—Katherine's children—and suddenly felt out of place.

"I'll run along, now," she said. "I have some things to see to." She included them all in her smile. "I hope you'll each be very happy here."

Will followed her to the kitchen. "Do you have to go right now? I was hoping we could at least serve you a piece of that wonderful cake you made."

"Oh, no thanks," she told him. "You deserve some time alone with your kids. Enjoy them. They're great, Will, each of them."

"Elizabeth—" His hand, warm on her elbow, detained her. "Thanks so much again—truly." His voice dropped. "Meggie's room has helped a great deal. She's very impressed, not only that you did such a good job but that you bothered to do it at all. And so am I."

Liz looked down in confusion. "My pleasure," she said softly. "And I'm so glad you're all safely home."

He nodded. "So am I. But I can see that we need to keep remodeling and rebuilding—not just our house but our family. It'll take time."

"Well, I think you've made a wonderful start."

Liz walked back up the road rather than through the orchard, as if by so doing she could distance herself from Will Parrish and his family. They were neighbors, that was all—a family trying to reestablish its roots in new soil. She had done all she could—her part was finished. The only thing left was for her to deal with her own feelings. Will had his hands full. The last thing he needed was a divorced neighbor with designs on his affection.

21

Liz threw herself into her gardening, inordinately pleased with herself as her two rows of corn grew tall and her squash plants began to bloom. She was proud of the petunias and marigolds banking her front steps and the impatiens and pansies circling the trunks of the shade trees in her yard.

She took Gypsy and Tracker with her on jaunts up the canyons and to parks where they pulled her along behind them on their enthusiastic, nose-to-the-ground explorations. She made herself read and work on her correspondence courses, but the long, golden summer evenings beckoned her outside, and on any pretext at all she would abandon all inside projects and stay outdoors as long as possible.

There were fewer visits from Missy, now that she had Megan for a friend, but occasionally the two of them would stroll into the yard when they saw Liz outside and chat for a few minutes. Megan seemed to be opening up under the influence of Missy's candor and optimism, and Missy was beginning to be conscious of hairstyles and fashion.

"Doesn't Missy have gorgeous hair?" Megan commented once, as the three of them relaxed on the cool grass, each with a dog close by or in her lap. "It's so silky and light. She's lucky."

"I think you both have lovely hair and coloring," Liz said

diplomatically. "In fact, I often think how nice you look to-gether. You set each other off to good advantage."

"Megan's going to teach me how to do French braids in my own hair," Missy said. "That way, I can do it for school myself. I think French braids look real sophisticated, don't you?"

"I like them," Liz agreed. "And that's kind of Megan. What have you girls been doing to keep busy?"

"Playing," Missy said with a giggle that warmed Liz's heart. "Working some, too, of course. But we've been picnicking and to movies, and yesterday Mr. Parrish took us swimming. Pretty soon he's going to take us hiking, too."

"He said we had to wait for a while to hike much," Megan explained, "until we get used to the altitude."

"Yeah, he said they were still 'flatland furriners.' Isn't that funny?"

Liz smiled. "It is, but he's right. If you try to hike too soon, you'll be all out of breath and miserable. But it only takes a little while. You'll be ready soon to keep up with your dad."

"Yeah, like he's some kind of mountain man or some-thing." Megan rolled her eyes.

"And what do you think of the mountains?" Liz asked.

"Oh, they're pretty—they're so big. I like it when we go for rides in the canyon on a hot evening—it feels so much cooler there. But it's so dry here! I have to keep putting lotion on, and I've had three nosebleeds."

"It takes a while to get used to a new climate, that's true," Liz said. "I had a few nosebleeds, too, but I like the drier air. I always lived in humid places before, where your shoes mildew and your crackers go mushy."

"Yuck!" said Missy. "I'd hate that."

"Where-all did you live?" Megan asked curiously.

"I moved here from Hawaii in February, but I grew up in

Alabama, and I've lived in California and Guam—and even for a short time in Virginia."

"Her husband was in the Navy," Missy explained.

"Oh, did he—die?"

"No," Liz said gently. "We divorced."

"Oh. Did you ever go to Virginia Beach?"

"Sure did."

"We used to always go there for a week in the summer," Megan said. "We'd rent a little apartment and play on the beach while my dad golfed. Then at night we'd go to a carnival and ride the rides and try to win things. Sometimes we'd take the ferry or the tunnel across Chesapeake Bay to the eastern shore and hunt for antiques. My mom liked that."

"Sounds like fun," Liz said.

"Yeah. It was." Megan's voice was small, and she stared at the grass as she ruffled it with her palm. "And we had this thing we did, where we had to eat a different kind of food every night, and we all had to try something new. Like one night we'd have Chinese and the next night Italian or French. One night, up on the eastern shore, we had fried oyster sandwiches with hot pepper sauce."

"Oysters—gross!" Missy protested.

"They were kind of good, if you didn't look at the insides of the oysters after you bit into them. That looks awful. And one night at a French place, my dad had snails."

"*Escargots*," Liz said, smiling at Missy's expression. "They're yummy with garlic butter."

"Dad said they were good, but none of us dared try 'em. That was three years ago—our last vacation."

Liz wanted to gather Megan, who suddenly looked lost and desolate, into her arms, but she didn't dare. "It sounds as if you have some really great memories," she said instead, trying to keep her voice warm and cheerful. "Now here you are out West, having new experiences and making new memories."

"I reckon," Megan said, her tone indicating that her present situation could never yield memories to match the ones already stored in her heart.

And that's probably true, Liz admitted. Things were and would continue to be irrevocably different for Megan, growing up without her lively, beloved mother, transplanted here to this arid climate, the only girl in her household. *I hope Will can be all she needs him to be, the next few years,* she thought. *It won't be easy.*

Three days later, Will himself strolled into Liz's yard at sunset and eased his long frame onto the grass beside the lounge chair where she was reading a long letter from Dorrie.

"Hello!" she said in surprise. "How've you been keeping?"

His grin was slow and rueful. "We're hanging in there," he said. "It's interesting, trying to get much done on the house with three other people around, each with an agenda of his or her own. Nicky's settling down, now. I think he really missed Barbara at first, which is natural—she's the only mother-figure he's known. It's lucky the other kids are here, because at least he knows them, whereas he must have wondered who the heck I was—some strange guy who kidnapped him from his home. Good thing he's a rather placid little guy or we'd be in trouble. He had a few restless nights, but he's sleeping better now, and smiling and laughing more than he did at first."

"He's so adorable. Where'd the auburn hair come from?"

"Kath's side. He is cute, isn't he? Even if I shouldn't say so. But this is really the first chance I've had to try to bond with him and get acquainted. I just want to sit around and play with him all the time."

Liz shrugged. "Do it. It's probably the best thing you could do, don't you think?"

"It feels right. I hope so. But the two older kids have been agitating for some action. So, I've come to ask a favor—again—which I know I promised I wouldn't do, after all you've done already."

Liz smiled and put down her book. "Ask away."

"Well, I've done a rash thing. I've told Megan and Tim they could each invite a friend to go with us to this place called Lagoon, and then I realized that that's going to leave me a lone adult with five active kids, and I decided maybe I'd invite a friend, too. Does that sound horrendous to someone who enjoys peace and quiet and privacy? I'm probably doing you no favor, so don't hesitate to say no if you . . ."

"What's Lagoon?" Liz asked, amused that he seemed to be rattling on like an insecure teenager asking for a first date.

"Oh, well, it's an amusement park north of Salt Lake. Meggie's been remembering one we used to go to in Virginia, and I asked Lolly if there was such a thing around here. I guess there are rides and swimming and a pioneer-style village with a Wild West shoot-out—that sort of thing. I thought we'd go next Wednesday. Megan's taking Missy, and Tim's invited one of the Woodbine twins. I was worried about the other feeling hurt, so I told Tim he could ask them both, but it turns out one of them has a doctor's appointment that day anyway. We'll invite him to do something another time. I know it probably sounds like a lot of hassle and noise, but . . ."

"I'd love to go."

"You would? Are you sure, Elizabeth? Do you know what you're saying?"

"I'm positive. It's been eons since I've done anything like that. It sounds fun. Shall I help pack a picnic?"

"I thought we'd just pick up some fried chicken and take plenty of fruit and drinks—maybe buy whatever else we want there. We'll need to bring swimsuits and towels and plenty of sunscreen for Nicky—and for you and Missy, too, don't you think? I thought we'd leave about ten in the morning and make a day of it. It's about as close to a vacation as we'll be taking this summer."

"Are the kids excited?"

"Out of their skulls. I think they thought that sort of activity was behind them forever—that there wouldn't be any fun in Utah."

"I suspect they're pleasantly surprised. Megan seems to be in a pretty positive mood whenever she and Missy stop by. Do you think she's reconciled to the move by now?"

Will shrugged. "Most of the time, I think. And when school starts, I think she'll settle in even better."

"And Tim? I don't see so much of him."

"He lives at Woodbines', or they at our house. Kindred spirits from the first. And that's what Tim requires, along with a good supply of books—friends to hang out with every spare minute."

"I'm so glad Missy and Megan hit it off."

"Yes, well—they did, but again, I wonder when school starts if Megan won't drop Missy when she makes other friends. I hope not, but Meggie's a grade ahead and that means a different school for this year."

"But maybe the fact that they live close here, kind of apart from other friends, will help to keep them together. That and the fact that they have time this summer to get well acquainted before they meet other people."

"I hope so. And you're kind to care, Elizabeth. Meggie thinks you're rather wonderful."

"She does?" Liz's surprise was genuine.

"She does. She's always talking about how nice you are and how smart and creative and pretty."

"She said that?"

"That and more. Of course, Missy adores you, and that has probably influenced Megan's thinking, too. Or it could be that my daughter has inherited her father's instinct about people and recognizes quality when she meets it, as he does." Will's smile was teasing, and Liz felt hot color rise in her cheeks.

"They're sweet," she whispered. "I enjoy it when they come over."

Will sobered. "Well, they are missing a mom's influence in their lives, and I, for one, am grateful for you—and Lolly and Marilyn, too, of course. I think I'm very glad we're here."

"I'm—glad you are, too."

Will's hand rested briefly on her arm as he rose to his feet. "I'll look forward to Wednesday," he told her, and he left.

Liz gazed off over Tuck's orchard and fields, her letter lying forgotten in her lap.

"So will I," she whispered.

On Tuesday it rained—gusty thundershowers that rattled the windows in her little house and made Gypsy and Tracker cower close to her in fear.

"You guys think this is a storm? You ought to see what it can do in Hawaii or Florida!" Liz chided them. For her, the rain was a welcome break from the dry heat that had all but baked her lawn and garden for three straight weeks. She stood in her doorway and breathed in sweet gulps of the cool air.

"Liz, what if it rains tomorrow!" Missy mourned on one of her now-rare solo visits.

"Then I imagine we'll just pick another day to go," Liz soothed. "Will—Mr. Parrish—won't disappoint you kids, I'm sure."

"I think it's so cool that you're going! It'll be so fun—I haven't been for a long time. And you know what? It'll be just like we're one big family—I mean, there'll be a dad and a mom and all us kids. Let's pretend that's how it is, Liz, okay? Just for fun?"

"Now, Missy . . ."

"I know, I know. But I'm going to pretend it anyway, just to myself."

"Please keep it that way."

"Okay. I promise. But you are looking forward to it, aren't you, Liz—just a little?"

Liz smiled. "Of course I am, honey. And I hope it stops raining, too."

"Will you ride Colossus with me?"

"I don't even know what Colossus is, but it sounds fearsome."

"It's awesome, that's what it is! It's like a roller coaster, but it goes all the way around twice. Promise me you will, Liz, if no one else will . . ."

"No promises until I see it in action, and that goes for all the rides. I'm fairly adventurous, but I'm not suicidal."

"You'll love it. It's great. Oh, I almost forgot. I brought you the newest letter from Dave to read." She fished in the pocket of her jeans and brought forth a thin, rumpled aerogram covered with cramped writing.

"But Missy, isn't this private, just for your family?"

"Not really. We're keeping all his letters in a notebook to make a kind of journal for him when he gets back. Here, read this part—it's so cool."

Liz tilted the letter toward the silvery light from the doorway.

> We went to visit Herr Schwann on Monday—a man we had just started to teach. He had been really interested on our first visit, and more humble than most of the folks we meet here. He invited us back before we even got through the first discussion, and asked a lot of good ques-

tions, so we knew he was sincerely interested. Well, on Monday when we got to his house—actually it's an apartment—he wasn't there. We were really surprised, because he didn't seem like the type to skip out on us, though a lot of people do that rather than be rude and just say they're not interested. We were just leaving the building when Herr Schwann's wife came rushing up to us, all out of breath, and begged us to come with her to the hospital. It turns out Herr Schwann had suffered a heart attack the night before, and was in pretty bad shape, but he still somehow remembered that we were coming, and sent his wife to get us.

We went with her, of course, and when we got there, we had to say we were Herr Schwann's religious leaders to get in to see him, and show our ordination cards as ministers of the Gospel. Poor Herr Schwann was hooked up to all these machines and monitors, and could hardly speak, but he managed to tell his wife that he wanted us to pray for him. I explained to her about administering to the sick, and she said yes, that was what they wanted, so Elder Hauptmann anointed and I gave the blessing. It was so neat— Dad, you'll understand this—how I could feel the priesthood power flowing through me into Herr Schwann, and I heard myself promising him all kinds of wonderful things, including swift and complete healing, and responsible callings in the Church of Jesus Christ through which many lives would be blessed! If it had just been me talking, I'd have been scared to death, because he looked so gray and weak, and I'd probably just've asked for him to be comforted, and healed if possible. But it wasn't just me talking—it was the Lord, and I knew it, so I just relaxed and let him speak through me, and tell Herr Schwann what he wanted him to know. By the time I got through, Herr Schwann didn't look *so gray—he looked pinker, and he seemed to be breathing easier, and sleeping.*

Well, the next day we went back to check on him, and his wife couldn't get through thanking us for our blessing. She said he was a lot better—so much that the doctors were confused, and couldn't understand what had happened. I guess it had been touch and go there for a while, but now he was way ahead of their best hopes for getting well. We explained to her about the priesthood and the gift of healing, and that we felt it was largely due to Herr Schwann's own faith that it was able to happen that way. Now she can't do enough for us—she's always feeding us and wanting to wash our clothes and do anything she can to help us with our work. It's so great to know that the Lord can use us as his instruments here in Austria—or wherever. I'm sure glad I came!

Liz handed the thin paper back to Missy and cleared her throat. "That's really something, Missy, something to keep and treasure. Thank you for letting me read it."

"Isn't that neat? Well, I want to show it to Bishop and Sister Tucker, too, so I'll go now. I think it'll stop raining by tomorrow, don't you?"

"I hope so, Missy, but I haven't heard the forecast."

"I think it will," Missy called back over her shoulder as she cleared the steps and ran through the lavender twilight, avoiding puddles like hopscotch squares.

"Ah, the optimism of youth," Liz remarked to herself, shaking her head. Nevertheless, she laid out her clothes, bathed, and made an early night of it, just in case Missy was right.

22

By Wednesday morning only a few wispy shreds of clouds remained of Tuesday's storm, and the air was scrubbed fresh
and spiced with foresty scents from the canyons. Liz dressed in
light blue jeans and a pastel plaid shirt, agonized over the
choice of which swimsuit to take, and packed and repacked
her canvas tote. She doubted if the combined level of anticipation of all the kids equaled hers, and she confessed to herself the source of her excitement: a whole day spent in Will's
company. Hours and hours of opportunity to observe him in-
teracting with his children, having fun, relaxing—hopefully,
she'd have a chance now and again to chat with him herself—
it was heady stuff! She had missed him during the busy days
since the children had come but hadn't wanted to intrude on
their fragile family life during its rebuilding. But now—how to
fathom Will's reasons for inviting her to join them on this outing? Was it to help with the kids, or just to have another adult
along for company—or had he, perhaps, missed her a little,
too? She hoped he had, and no amount of self-scolding on her
part could shake that hope.

The sparkling day and the holiday atmosphere combined
to keep everyone's spirits high on the nearly two-hour freeway
drive. The children told silly jokes and sang silly songs, and

Will whistled cheerfully to fill the few silences. Liz felt free to relax and enjoy the breeze ruffling her hair. For the moment, nothing was expected of her, not even conversation, and she could watch the way Will gripped the steering wheel and observe how the tan of his arms contrasted with the white of his casual shirt. Nicky, between them in his car seat, dozed peacefully.

Liz glanced at the girls, who shared the middle seat with a picnic cooler. Missy grinned happily at her, and leaned forward to whisper, "I'm pretending You-Know-What!"

Liz smiled. "Keep it to yourself," she whispered back.

Oh, Missy—I can pretend, too, she thought. *And I'll also keep it to myself.*

Once in the park, the first order of business was to establish a "home base" for everyone to return to for meals, drinks, and catching up to the others. Then they toured the park as a group, discussing which rides to go on, and Will and Liz watched as the four older ones braved a ride called the Tidal Wave. They came away flushed and laughing. Then Megan took Nicky for his very first ride on a merry-go-round. The little boy was wide-eyed and serious, nearly ready for tears when he caught sight of the others waving as he circled away from them, even with his big sister holding him firmly in the saddle.

"Is he having fun yet?" Will asked wryly at Liz's shoulder. She smiled up at him.

"I guess he's learning something about the thrill of danger that goes with the pleasure of the ride," she said.

"Funny how we humans like to be a little scared, isn't it? So anxious to jump on a wild and dangerous machine, and so ready to get off when it releases us."

"Slightly crazy," Liz agreed. "Maybe it's youth. I find I'm

not *quite* so anxious to get on some contraptions as I would once have been."

"Let me know which still appeal to you, and we'll be sure to work them in, okay? Meggie can tend Nick while we have some fun, too."

"Oh, I'm having fun. This is delightful," she told him. "But I'll probably work up the courage to ride anything you want to tackle."

"Brave words, lady! How do you know I'm not a roller-coaster maniac who stands up and gives a rebel yell on the first plunge?"

Liz laughed. "I trust you to have more sense than that."

He quirked his eyebrows at her. "One can only hope," he said cryptically.

They walked through the picturesque pioneer village with a nervous Nicky clinging to Megan and refusing to be put back into his stroller, and planned to return when the Wild West shoot-out would be staged. They decided to concentrate on rides for a while, have lunch, attend the shoot-out, go swimming, have a snack, enjoy one of the evening entertainments offered, go for a final round of rides, and then head home.

After making sure that everyone knew the way back to "camp" and had a watch to keep track of time, Will allowed the two boys to head for the fun house while the girls raced for the log flume ride. He and Liz strolled with Nicky through the arcade, where Will threw a baseball accurately enough to win Nicky a small toy duck in a sailor suit.

"Looky, Nick," Will said, kneeling to present the toy. "Here's Mr. Duck, who wants to ride with Nicky." He walked the duck up the edge of the stroller, making quacking noises and then, "Whoops!" as he allowed the duck to fall and start climbing again. For the first time, Liz saw a smile tug at the corners of Nicky's mouth. Will saw it, too, and repeated the performance. This time the little boy laughed out loud and bounced in his stroller. Liz laughed, and Will glanced up at her.

"His first laugh for me," he said. "He often giggles at Tim or Meggie, but I've been such a stranger he just gazes at me like he's trying to place me and can't quite succeed."

"He's just been reserving judgment until he got to know you better. And now—a moment of triumph!"

"No kidding. Amazing how intimidating toddlers can be when they just look and look and won't smile. He's never resisted having me pick him up, but he doesn't reach out to me, either, like he does to the kids."

"It'll come," Liz soothed. "Probably sooner than you think. Maybe even today."

They resumed their stroll, with Nicky absorbedly bouncing the duck up and down.

"It's a magical sort of day, isn't it? You almost feel anything good might happen. I'm glad you could come, Elizabeth."

"So am I," she replied, thinking she had never meant any statement more sincerely. "It's a spectacular day," she added, thinking of more than the weather.

They relaxed on a worn quilt spread on the grass near their cooler, sipping lemonade and allowing Nicky to explore under his dad's watchful eye. He wandered around picking up twigs and bits of plant material to hold up for their inspection. Once he started to put a leaf in his mouth but then shook his head vigorously.

"No, no!" he told himself decisively, as Liz and Will shared a stifled laugh.

"Self-control at such an early age!" Liz said. "What a remarkable child."

Will nodded. "It's really something, getting to know him, watching him unfold, you might say, and realizing that I'm his dad. He's different from the other two. In fact, they were very different from each other, right from the start, so I shouldn't be surprised, I guess. But there's something unique about Nicky. He seems to accept what life gives him and to think everything over before he reacts. Meggie always reacted first and thought later—maybe, if she got around to it. Tim always wanted something going—he had to be doing, at every juncture. He likes to be a participator. Even when he reads, he shows a lot of facial expressions and talks back to the books— he's a participator then, too. But Nicky seems to be an observer. He zeroes in on things and really sees them."

"Maybe he'll grow up to be a scientist or a philosopher— or an artist."

"I wonder what they'll become, each of them." He paused. "I hope Kath knows what a wonderful little guy she produced with her last shred of strength."

Liz swallowed. "I'll bet she does. That reminds me, Will— are you familiar with the Mormon view of eternal marriage?"

"Not really. My grandfather was a Mormon, but somehow the family didn't choose to follow his faith. What do they believe?"

"Well, I'm not LDS either, so I'm sure I don't completely understand the concept. But I was talking to one of the guides at Temple Square about it, and he explained that they feel that a marriage can be 'sealed,' they call it, even after one or both of the partners has died, so that the husband-wife relationship can continue on into eternity and not just be a death-do-you-part sort of thing, as we're accustomed to. It's one of the things they do in their temples."

Will looked at her with interest. "That's unique, isn't it? But I guess it's just for members of their church."

Liz nodded. "Apparently, if the partners weren't baptized into the LDS church, that's also done for them by proxy in the temples. Then the man said the people are free to accept or reject the baptism and the marriage part in heaven—the spirit world, I think they call it. And living Mormons who get married in the temple are married for time and eternity."

Will cocked his head, regarding her seriously. "That's a nice concept, isn't it? I'd like to feel Kath and I will still be together in the next life, but I've never known of a religion that openly taught such an idea."

"I hadn't either. But when I heard it, I thought of you—and Katherine."

"Did you? That's sweet of you, Elizabeth."

"Well, I think it's pretty special when a marriage is good enough that the partners want it to last forever. I couldn't even stick with mine for more than eleven years."

He smiled. "There are mitigating circumstances."

"I suppose. Hmm—do you know what I just realized?" Liz looked up in surprise. "I just realized I haven't even thought about Brock for weeks now, it seems like. It's almost as though he's receded so far into the past that he doesn't matter much anymore. At first, I could hear his comments echoing through my brain on everything I did, but I think he's finally beginning to be silenced!"

"That must be a welcome relief. Who needs a running commentary of disapproval, anyway? To be honest, though, I have a hard time seeing what's to disapprove in you. Brock must have been a hard guy to please."

Liz shrugged. "We were just far too different to be compatible. We never should have married, but I guess we were both too young and infatuated at the time to realize it—or to care. Then, as we grew up, we grew apart—miles apart. And yes, it *is* a relief that he's retreating. To be fair, I suspect that the commentary my own mind created for him was even more scathing than the real thing would have been."

Will's gaze followed Nicky's progress along the edge of a picnic table, where he pointed wide-eyed to the array of baskets and coolers on top. "It's interesting—you're glad that Brock's fading, while I'm afraid of losing memories of Kath. The sound of her voice eludes me more often now, except for certain phrases, and more and more often I find myself remembering how she looked only in certain poses or in photographs. I can remember how young and trusting she looked at our wedding ceremony, and then I remember her a year later, all flushed and perspiring when Meggie was born. And of course, the last time—she looked so pale and thin in her casket I hardly recognized her. But I can't seem to bring back at will all the other expressions or her laugh. I wish I had taken videos of all of us through the good times, but I didn't. And I don't know—maybe it would be morbid to go back and look at them all the time, anyway. Unhealthy, backward-looking—you know?"

Liz nodded. "I know. I'm like that with my mom and dad, too. I seem to remember certain things they said or ways they looked, and I wish I could remember more. Once in a while I do—something will trigger a flashback to an event I'm surprised is still there in my brain. I guess our memories are selective. And I suspect that even when we say, 'I'll always remember this day,' we can't be sure we will."

"I read somewhere that our earliest childhood memories are those that have the strongest emotional content—anger, or fear, or delight—whatever. And I think that's probably true. My earliest memory is of being really mad at my sister because she wouldn't share with me something she was eating."

Liz smiled. "And I remember being lost from my mother in a supermarket when I was two, and I was terrified. So—maybe the trend continues, do you think? You mention remembering Katherine's expression during key events—wedding, childbirth, funeral—strong emotional times, each of them. So probably that's why I tend to remember the clashes with Brock—a lot of our strong emotions were anger and frustration."

"Let them fade, then, as quickly as you can."

"Right."

They were silent for a while. Nicky picked up a stray pink napkin and toddled over to stand before Liz, holding it up for her inspection. Impulsively she held out her arms to him. He regarded her solemnly for a moment and then ceremoniously turned around and backed up to plunk his padded bottom into her lap. Liz's heart turned over. She folded her arms gently around his little body and rested her cheek lightly atop his head. It had been so long since she'd held a child—other than a few brief minutes with Marilyn's little girl, it had been years—and the experience was sweet beyond belief. She closed her eyes to savor the moment, and when, as she expected, the little boy soon pushed himself up to go exploring again, she looked up mistily to see Will watching her.

"He's just so precious," she explained, clearing her throat.

"You should have a family, Elizabeth," Will said. "You deserve to be a mom. Do you think you'll ever see your way clear to try marriage again?"

Oh, Will, why are you, of all people, asking me this?

"I hope so. I—think so. I just need to learn to trust my own judgment again, I suppose."

"Well, I have faith in you. You won't choose another Brock, I'm sure of it."

"No. No, I don't believe I would. I think I've come that far at least." She drew a deep breath. "What about you, Will? Do you think you'll ever love another woman, after Kath?"

He looked down at his hands, loosely clasped, and rubbed the stumps of the missing fingers as if he still felt the pain of their loss as well as that of the greater loss he had suffered. "I know one thing," he said slowly, "I don't expect to find another Kath, and I guess that's as it should be. It would probably be better to marry someone who *didn't* remind me of her at every turn—someone who would just make her own place in my life." He looked up and smiled. "I think I'm maybe an inch closer every day to being able to consider that."

"Good," Liz said, not trusting herself to say more.

"Whoa, Nickers, I detect it's time for a diaper change." He spread a baby quilt on the grass and shucked the little boy out of the offending diaper while Liz watched, amused and touched.

"You're pretty efficient at that," she told him.

"Oh, I'm a whiz with disposables," he replied with a grin. "But can you imagine how I'd be with safety pins and thick cloth? Completely buffaloed."

"There don't seem to be many things that buffalo you."

"Stuck zippers, small buttons, playing the violin." He shrugged.

"I didn't know you played the violin!"

He winked at her. "I never did. But if I tried, I'd really be in trouble."

"You *are* in trouble!" Liz looked around for something handy to throw. Tim and Nathan Woodbine arrived on the scene just in time to see Will duck a flying paper cup. Tim flashed a toothy grin. He plopped down on the grass and started playing with Nicky.

"We rode the Flying Carpet and the Tilt-a-Whirl. Have we got time to go on Colossus once before lunch?"

Will consulted his watch. "If the line's not too long, you can probably make it, but come straight back here. We're getting hungry, aren't we, guys?"

Nicky looked up hopefully. Liz felt remarkably uninterested in food. She was too full of memories being made.

23

Among the memories that Liz took home with her from that summer outing was that of swimming with Will and the children. Shy at first to be seen in her swimsuit, she was glad for the light tan she had acquired in the relative privacy of her yard. Will, surprisingly, had worn a white T-shirt in the pool, and she could only assume he didn't want to sunburn. He took Nicky into the water in a little inflatable toy. Nicky was solemn at first, but he watched the antics of his brother and sister and gradually began to pat at the water and make it splash, which pleased him enormously.

"Bat?" he asked of Megan, who laughed delightedly. "No, Nicky, it's not a bath—it's a swimming pool. Can you say pool?"

"Poo?" asked Nicky, which sent all four youngsters into a fit of giggles. Pleased with himself, Nicky bounced in his inflatable toy and said it again.

When they tired of water play, Liz and Will stretched on towels to dry and warm themselves. Nicky reclined in his stroller, happy and sleepy with a bottle of milk.

"I think the kids are having a good time, don't you?" Will asked lazily, his eyes closed against the sun.

"I'm sure they are," Liz told him.

"How are you holding up?"

"Holding up! You make me sound like a granny."

Will grinned, his eyes still closed. "You don't look like any granny I ever knew," he said. Liz couldn't decide how to reply to that and felt her cheeks burning from more than the sun. Will opened one eye to check her reaction, chuckled, and reached over to squeeze her hand briefly. "That was a compliment," he added softly.

"A girl can never have too many of those," she replied.

When it was time to leave the swimming area, Will stripped off his damp shirt and reached for a towel to take to the shower. He turned slightly away from Liz but not before she glimpsed a jagged, angry welt of scars in the upper middle of his chest.

"What in the world . . ." she breathed to herself, realizing that there were many things about this attractive, thoughtful man that she didn't know—and perhaps never would. That realization brought the only breath of sadness to the otherwise perfect day.

They were all tired on the ride home. The children each slept soundly, and Liz savored again the chance to be with Will in the relaxed atmosphere of companionable silence or easy conversation.

He glanced across at her. "Still glad you came?" he asked.

"Very, very glad," she assured him. "It was, as the kids said, a blast."

"For me, too. The most pleasurable day I've had in a long time. I'm as tired as if I'd worked for twelve hours, but I feel more alive than if I'd slept all afternoon. And you have a lot to do with that, Elizabeth. You're comfortable to be with but not the least bit dull. It's a nice combination."

"Well, you've been a super host. You made it fun for all of us."

"Wouldn't be much point to the outing if it weren't fun. I always hate to see families at a place like that—or anywhere—angry and squabbling and glaring at each other. I just cringe and think, 'No, no, stop it. Life's too short!' "

Liz stored away the memories of their conversations against a rainy day of loneliness when she could take them out and re-play them over and over at her leisure, reminding herself that at least they had had that time together.

After the day at Lagoon, Megan and Missy stopped by to visit Liz more often than ever, and sometimes it was Megan and Tim, occasionally with Nicky in his stroller. Liz talked with Tim about the books he was reading and with Megan about clothes and the violin lessons she had begun taking from a teacher Marilyn Woodbine found for her. Megan seemed more content and reconciled to her life in the country, for which Liz was grateful, and she knew Will was, too. Will con-tinued working on his house, cleaning out the basement, re-pairing and refurbishing the room that would be his study, and preparing to add a second bath off the kitchen.

The Woodbines hosted a neighborhood barbecue on the eve of Pioneer Day, which Liz learned was the anniversary of the day the Mormon pioneers first entered the Salt Lake Valley. When Tim and Megan learned that there was to be a large parade in Salt Lake City the next morning, they teased and coaxed their father to take them, until finally he relented, in part, saying, "Only if Elizabeth will come, too," whereupon they both descended on Liz, begging her to agree.

"Well," she said with a mock frown, "I *was* going to bathe the dogs and clean my refrigerator . . ."

"You can't—it's a holiday!" Tim told her. "And we missed the Fourth of July parade in Provo. We can't miss this one! You can wash the dogs any old time. Besides, if you come and keep

Dad company, he won't watch us so close, and we can have more fun!"

Liz laughed. "It's nice to feel useful. I guess the dogs will agree to wait a day, and I've never known the fridge to complain."

"Yes!" Tim and Megan exulted together, and Will smiled at her in the background. Megan, of course, invited Missy, and Tim asked Jonathan, the Woodbine twin who had missed out on Lagoon.

There was no rain-washed coolness to temper the heat on the 24th of July, and the day dawned sunny and clear with the temperature rapidly rising. The city was crowded with tourists and parade-goers when they arrived, many of them having staked their claim to their vantage points by camping all night along the parade route. Will, Liz, and the children left their car and walked for several blocks, looking for a spot that would afford at least partial shade and a good view of the street. Once settled, Tim and Jonathan solved both problems for themselves by climbing a nearby tree and straddling sturdy limbs. Nicky was not content to stay in his stroller, and it took the combined efforts of Will, Liz, and both girls to keep him amused. His idea of fun was to climb out of the stroller and toddle off among the sea of strangers in any direction, chortling in glee at efforts to retrieve him. Finally Will bought him a bright, helium-filled balloon that, tied to his wrist, amused and delighted him and kept him more willing to stay put. When a contingent of motorcycle policemen, sirens wailing, performed their intricate maneuvers before them, he clung to Will and stared in solemn amazement. The firing of a Civil War-era cannon nearly brought tears, but Liz smiled at him, and Megan leaned over to whisper, "Boom!" in his ear, and he apparently decided there was nothing to fear.

The floats were varied in their size and professionalism,

ranging from the exquisite and elaborate to the small and homemade, many of them depicting scenes from Mormon history—the miracle of the seagulls devouring the crickets that were destroying the pioneers' crops, the crossing of the plains with covered wagons or handcarts. There were, naturally, several bearded Brigham Youngs. One entry that touched Liz was an actual handcart, piled high with simple belongings, pulled by a ragged, barefoot young man who feigned exhaustion. When his strength would flag, another young man, dressed in the shining white robes of an angel, would step up to the rear of the cart and push it along. A banner on the side of the cart read, "Count your many blessings; angels will attend, help and comfort give you to your journey's end."

Liz noticed that Will's eyes followed that entry, too, and he turned to say to her, "Remind me, later, to tell you what I found yesterday."

There were numerous marching bands, all of which Liz enjoyed, but far and away her favorite was the Utah Pipe Band, the pipers' kilts swaying to their measured tread, and the lilting melody of the bagpipes skirling above the solemn drone, seeming to speak at once of both the joys and the sorrows of life. She glanced at Will just as he turned to grin at her.

"Music of my ancestors, lassie," he said. "Do you like it?"

"I love it," she told him.

"If you truly do," he replied, "I have a couple of albums you might enjoy hearing."

"Of pipe music? Wonderful! I've never thought to look for such a thing, but I always thrill when I hear bagpipes being played. Brock hated the sound. Said it set his teeth on edge. But I love the pipes."

Will nodded. "They're like cats."

"Beg your pardon?"

"Like cats. No middle ground—most people love 'em or hate 'em."

Liz laughed. "I'd never thought of it that way."

After the parade, Will treated the group to hamburgers and shakes, and they spent an hour looking around Temple Square, where Missy assumed the role of guide. Will stood thoughtfully before the display about eternal marriage that had so intrigued Liz but made no comment. They climbed the carpeted ramp to view the Christus statue, but the place was so crowded with visitors that it didn't have the same effect on Liz that it had had on that rainy February evening when she had first seen it. Will stood with a hand on the shoulder of each of his older children.

"Very impressive," he murmured, before they turned to descend the ramp.

"Isn't it neat?" Missy asked, in hushed tones. "But you know what? One time, this guy came in with a hammer and knocked off some of the fingers before he got scared off. Isn't that awful?"

"That's sick," Tim responded. "Who'd want to do that to Jesus?"

"Think what they did to him in real life," Megan reminded him.

"Oh, yeah. But I don't get that, either. If he was so kind and good, how come people hated him?"

"I know why," Missy said. "It was because they thought he was lying about being the son of God—making it up, you know? And that was against their law. They had all kinds of prophecies that should have told them who he was, but they weren't paying attention. They were looking for—like, a king with an army, or something, to come in and fight for them. At least . . ." She looked suddenly embarrassed at having everyone's attention. "That's what my Primary teacher said."

"Sounds about right to me," Will commented, smiling at her. "Way to go, Missy."

Missy blushed but looked pleased at the praise.

They drove out for a quick look at the Great Salt Lake, where the children shopped for souvenirs in a railroad car that had been converted into a gift shop, while Will and Liz enjoyed the stiff breeze that had sprung up and endured the pungent odor of the briny water. Nicky napped peacefully in his shaded stroller.

"You said you found something yesterday," Liz reminded Will. "What was it?"

"Oh, right. I've been cleaning out the basement during the last few days, and I came across some boxes of old books stored down there. One of them, if you can imagine, was my grandfather's journal, kept partly while he was serving a mission for the Mormon church, mostly in North Carolina, and then off and on for pretty much the rest of his life, I think. I knew he was a member of the Church, but I had no idea he'd been a missionary. It's fascinating."

"Really! What year would that have been?"

"The journal starts in 1915. I can't imagine how it got stuck in with a stack of old books and packed away like that. It's a family treasure."

Liz shook her head. "Must have been overlooked. Have you read it all?"

Will shook his head. "No, I've just started. He talks about tramping through muddy roads in the rain, and being pelted with pine cones and rotten vegetables by little kids, and then being so grateful to be given a dinner of cornbread and 'pot likker' on some farm family's back porch. The pot likker, he says, was the broth left from a pot of turnip greens the family had had for dinner."

"Full of vitamins, at least," Liz said with a smile.

"True. Then he remarks that whatever hardships he has to endure, they'll never match what *his* grandfather went through, walking across the plains with a handcart. That's why the handcart in the parade reminded me. I'm going to have to see what I can find out about that. I didn't realize I had an ancestor who was a pioneer. Somehow, all that got lost by the time my generation came along."

"It'll be interesting for your kids to know about."

"It will. Maybe it'll give them a sense of belonging and identification with Utah so they won't feel so uprooted."

"They seem to be doing okay, though, aren't they?"

"Tim's happy, and Meggie's doing a lot better, though she still has sullen moments and times when she misses her friends and her Aunt Barbara."

"And Nicky seems to be thriving."

Will grinned. "Bless his adaptable little heart. He actually seems glad to see me these days. And I've fallen completely in love with him."

So have I, Liz admitted only to herself. *And maybe with his father, too—for all the good it does me.*

"I'm so glad, Will," she said aloud.

24

A few mornings later, Wynn Ashcraft's car pulled into Liz's drive while she was watering the flowers by her front steps.

"Hello," she called, and threw down the hose to go over and speak to him. He didn't get out of his car but leaned out the window.

"Mrs. Ewell, I'm real sorry to disturb you, and I hesitate even to ask you this, but Missy's prevailed upon me to promise her I would."

"What can I do for you—and Missy?" Liz asked curiously.

"Will Parrish has shown me through his house, and seeing the fine job you did on his daughter's room—well, with my wife's condition, you understand, I'm afraid fixing up the place has been the last thing on my mind for years now. Is there any way—could you advise us on some inexpensive ways to spruce up Missy's room—make it look more suitable for her? It wouldn't need to be as fancy as Megan's, but I'd like it to be nice. Of course, I don't know your schedule, and I don't mean to impose . . ."

Liz smiled. "My schedule's pretty flexible, and I'd enjoy helping with Missy's room. She's a sweetheart."

"Well, I'd sure be grateful. Please feel free to go on up anytime Missy's home, and she'll show you what's there. My wife won't—you know—interfere, or anything."

"I understand. Why don't you give us a budget to work with, and Missy and I can plan the room together?"

"That'd be just great. You're very kind, Mrs. Ewell. I'll let you know about the budget as soon as I work it out."

"Fine. And please—just call me Liz. Everyone does."

He smiled gravely. "Thank you then, Liz."

She waved as he backed his truck out of her drive and headed off to work.

"Maybe I should start asking for extra credit on my correspondence course," she remarked to Gypsy, who had monitored the conversation, "for all this practical experience I'm getting."

About ten, she walked up the hill and knocked on the door, to be greeted by an exuberant hug from Missy.

"My dad talked to you, didn't he, and you're going to fix up my room!"

"Well, it sounds like fun to me. He's going to give us a budget to work with, and you and I will do the fixing up together. How's that?"

"That's so cool! Come on in, I'll show it to you. Maybe we ought to do before and after pictures, do you think? You know my mom," she added with a wave toward the sofa where Helen Ashcraft sat, neatly dressed in slacks and a flowered shirt, watching television.

"Yes. How are you, Mrs. Ashcraft?"

Helen smiled, but her gaze followed Missy. She didn't speak.

"Come on back here," Missy directed, and Liz followed her down a bare hallway to a rather small corner room. There was threadbare beige carpet on the floor, a painted chest of drawers missing two handles, and a Hollywood-style twin bed, neatly made with an old quilt and piled with stuffed animals and dolls. Some magazine pictures had been pinned to the scarred and flaking off-white walls, and the only light came from an overhead fixture. The windows were covered with worn beige drapes that hung unevenly, their hems pulled loose and fastened in places with safety pins.

"I don't have anyplace to put my junk," Missy said, opening a closet door to reveal a jumble of books, shoes, and other paraphernalia. "So when my dad says to clean my room, I just shove everything in there and shut the door."

"Hmmm," said Liz, looking around critically. "There's plenty of room for some storage areas—bookcases and such. I think we can do some interesting things, Missy! What's your favorite color?"

Missy shrugged. "I like green a lot. And blue, and yellow. Look, this is my Madame Alexander doll that Uncle Max and Aunt Lou gave me." She took a plastic-covered doll from the top shelf of her closet and uncovered it for Liz. The doll wore a yellow taffeta dress and cape, trimmed in brown fur.

"My, she is elegant, isn't she? Maybe we can make a place for you to display her—and what if we were to build your color scheme around her dress—use a lot of yellow? Would you like that?"

Missy nodded, her eyes bright. "That'd be neat! Then it'd always look like the sun's shining, wouldn't it?"

Liz took out her tape measure and notepad and made notes while Missy went to the kitchen and mixed a pitcher of lemonade. They sat in the living room with Helen, who sipped her drink politely, gazing at Missy with a puzzled expression.

"She's been looking at me like that all day," Missy whispered, as she refilled Liz's glass. "I don't know why. She usually doesn't pay that much attention to me."

Liz jumped when Helen spoke to Missy. "You know, dear,

you resemble my little daughter so much, you could almost be her older sister."

Missy stared at her mother in blank incomprehension, but Liz stifled a gasp.

"How—how old is your daughter, Mrs. Ashcraft?" she asked, her voice suddenly husky.

"She's only three, but this child's resemblance to her is amazing."

"That's—very interesting. What's your little girl's name?"

"Melissa Jane—but we call her Missy. I—I'm not sure where she is right now. She must be with my husband. Do you know where my husband is? Wynn Ashcraft?"

"Um—he's at work," Missy said, her voice small and constricted. "I could—I could call him."

Liz nodded at her, and Missy disappeared into the kitchen. Helen continued to look about her.

"This sofa's already getting shabby," she remarked, caressing a worn spot on the arm. "It should have lasted longer than this. I can't understand it."

"Things don't seem to be made the way they used to be," Liz murmured, her heart pounding. What sort of miracle was she witnessing? Liz sent up a silent prayer for help.

Missy appeared in the kitchen doorway, motioning frantically to Liz.

"Excuse me a moment," Liz said and went to Missy, whose eyes were round and terrified.

"Liz, what's going on? I called my dad, and he's going to come home as soon as he can. Something's weird about Mom—she never talks like that—about me. What's happening?"

Liz hugged Missy to her. "I'm not sure, honey, but I think maybe her thinking is clearing up—maybe just for a little while, I don't know—but it sounds like she thinks you're still little. Were you about three when she got sick?"

"Yes."

"And you didn't live here then, did you?"

"No, we lived in Pleasant Grove."

"So she sees a resemblance in you to the little girl she thinks is still three—and she recognizes the furniture but not the house. I think—maybe we shouldn't tell her who you are, right away. It might be quite a shock for her to realize that she's lost the last eight years."

"You go talk to her, Liz, okay? I think I'll stay in here until my dad gets home."

"Okay. Don't worry, honey, everything'll be all right." Liz hugged Missy.

Missy's voice came, muffled and tearful, from Liz's shoulder. "I'm scared!"

"I know. I am too, but it's just because we don't know what to do or what to expect. Why don't you—um—put away the clean dishes, and I'll go in and visit with her."

"O-okay."

Liz took a deep breath to still her own trembling before she walked back into the living room and sat down. Helen sat turning her lemonade glass round and round in her hands, a slight frown between her eyes.

"I'm afraid I'm feeling a little strange—I don't know what's wrong," she said apologetically. "I wonder—do you happen to know where my husband is?"

"He's on his way here to be with you," Liz said. "We called him, and he's coming."

"Oh, thank you. I appreciate that very much. I'm sure he'll be able to straighten everything out for me. Somehow, I feel rather confused. I must be ill—maybe it's the flu, or something.

I'm so sorry to put you to this bother, but as soon as Wynn gets here, we'll go home and not disturb you further."

"You're not disturbing me at all. Please don't worry about a thing."

"It's just that I can't seem to remember where my little boy and girl are. I don't normally leave them, and . . ."

"I'm sure your husband will know where they are."

"Yes, of course he will. He's such a good man, Wynn is. So kind and patient with me and the children."

"That's wonderful."

"Yes." She fingered the worn sofa arm again. "You must think I'm silly. I realize now that this sofa just looks like mine, but of course it's yours. It's uncanny, though, how you've decorated your home so much like mine. I actually have that same picture on my wall, and a chair very much like that one, too. It's amazing. Please forgive me for saying the sofa was old and worn—I didn't mean to be rude. I was just confused because I don't feel quite myself today."

"It's all right—don't give it a second thought," Liz said, feeling that she had been sucked into a surreal world.

"I don't even know—how did I get here?"

"Um—you were here when I came," Liz temporized.

"I see. And your little daughter was so kind to give me a cold drink. Are you sure my husband knows how to find your house?"

"Yes, I'm sure he does. Would you care for more lemonade?"

"Oh—no. No, thank you."

Drive fast, Mr. Ashcraft! Liz thought. *Fast and carefully, and bring the wisdom of the gods with you. Or maybe just God.*

"Excuse me a second," Liz murmured and headed for the kitchen again to check with Missy.

"She thinks this is my house, and that you're my daughter,"

245

she whispered to the little girl, whose normally rosy cheeks had gone ashen. "I really do think she's come out of an amnesiac state—loss of memory, you know—and she's confused because things are different from the way she remembers them. The furniture looks familiar to her but older, of course, and she thinks it's mine."

"Oh, Liz—I'm so glad you're here. What should I do?"

Liz shook her head. "Anything you can think of that won't jar or upset your mom and that will make you feel better."

Missy shrugged. "I don't know what to do. I don't know how to *be*."

"I know. I don't either. We'll just play it by ear. When your dad comes, I'll try to go out and explain what we think is happening. Has anything like this ever happened before?"

Missy slowly shook her head. "I always thought it'd be so wonderful if she came back to us. But it's scary!"

"I know it is. But if it lasts, and she's able to adjust and understand what's happened, it may come to be wonderful."

Missy's eyes held Liz's. "Will you—stay with me, Liz?"

"As long as you need me, honey."

Missy drew a long, shaky breath. "Okay."

On her way back to the living room, Liz paused before a framed picture of the Ashcraft family on the dining-room wall. It had been taken only a few months before, when David was still at home. She hesitated and then took the picture down and set it on the floor, facing the wall.

"Would you like to lie down, Mrs. Ashcraft?" she asked as she reentered the living room.

"That might be wise," Helen replied. "Just until Wynn gets here, and then we'll be on our way."

"All right." Liz found sofa pillows and settled Helen in a comfortable position on the couch. Helen closed her eyes, but the slight frown remained, and occasionally she would shake

246

her head slightly, as if trying to clear it and make sense of her world. Liz sat quietly across the room, silently praying for Helen, and then Missy, and then the whole family.

Finally Missy, who had been watching out the kitchen door for her father's car, alerted Liz to his arrival. Liz slipped out the door as Wynn Ashcraft bolted out of his car and ran toward the house, Missy's puppy bouncing at his heels.

"Is Helen all right? What's going on?"

Liz told him, as concisely and as calmly as possible, what had taken place. "She thinks this is my house," she concluded, "and that you will take her home."

He stared at her, his eyes deep with concern, and then nodded. "I think what I'll do is take her with me, but we'll go straight to her doctor for an evaluation. I called and alerted him, and hopefully he'll know how to proceed. Dear heaven! I can't believe, after all these years . . ."

His voice broke, and he hurried into the house. Liz followed him, and Missy hung back behind her, watching in awe as her father knelt tenderly beside the sofa and took his wife in his arms.

"Wynn, I'm so glad to see you! I'm not feeling very well—will you take me home now? I don't know what's wrong with me, but I feel all confused, and I don't know where the children are! Do you know?"

"Yes, honey, I know. They're just fine. You've been sick for quite a while—it's no wonder you're confused. But everything'll be fine, sweetheart, in a little while. Are you ready to go, now?"

"Yes, please. I feel better already, now that you're here." She smiled lovingly at him, and Liz could see how hungrily he absorbed her affection. His lips trembled as he tried to return her smile.

"Wynn? Have you been sick, too? You don't look well at all. Have you seen a doctor?"

He shook his head. "Maybe—maybe it would do us both good to stop off at the doctor's office on the way home," he said gently.

"I think so. Now, I've intruded on this kind lady's hospitality far too long. Thank you so much," she added, turning to Liz. "You've been very kind, you and your daughter. You won't believe, Wynn, how much her little girl looks like our Missy! It's uncanny. I hope we'll see you again." She held out her hand to Liz, who pressed it warmly.

"I—hope so, too," she replied. "Best of luck to you both."

Wynn Ashcraft nodded to Liz over his wife's head. "Thank you," he whispered.

"I'll look after things here," Liz told him softly, and he nodded again, managing a wink at Missy. He escorted Helen outside to his car, and Liz stood with her arm around a sobbing Missy, watching them drive away. Then something inside her crumbled, and she cried too, holding Missy while all the mixed emotions of the moment were given vent.

"She—she didn't even know me!" Missy cried, as her sobs subsided into trembling little gasps.

"Oh, Missy—I think she knew you better today than she has for years."

"But—but she thinks I'm three—and she doesn't even know that Dave's grown up and gone on his mission, does she?"

"Not yet—but soon she'll learn that, if her mind continues to be clear. Think how confusing it must be to wake up after all these years and find that things—and people—have grown older while she was in a sort of dream state. For a while, you wouldn't know what was real and what wasn't."

"Kind of like that Rip van Winkle story?"

"Kind of like that, I think, yes."

"She—she loves my dad, huh?"

"Very much, it seems to me. And she was very concerned about you and Dave, wondering where you are, and all."

"Yeah." Missy considered things silently for a moment. "Why'd you take the picture down?"

"Because I was afraid that if she saw the picture of all of you together, eight years older than she thought you were, it would be too hard on her—and I wouldn't know what to do or say to help her with that. I think it's good your dad's taking her to the doctor. He'll know how to explain things to her, a bit at a time, and help her through it."

"Wow. That'll be scary for her, too, won't it?"

Liz nodded. "I would think so. At least, it would be for me."

"Wow," Missy said again, solemnly. "I'm sure glad you were here today, Liz. I wouldn't've thought of that, about the picture and all. I'd've prob'ly just blurted out who I was, and everything, and mixed her up worse."

"Nobody would've blamed you, if you had," Liz comforted. "But I'm glad I was here, too. What do you want to do now?"

Missy thought for a minute. "The first thing I have to do is go tell Bishop and Sister Tucker. Will you come with me? You explain it better'n me."

"I'm yours as long as you need me," Liz repeated. By mutual consent, they walked down the road with their arms around each other's waist. Missy seemed to need the solace of physical contact, and Liz drew comfort from it, too.

25

Lolly answered the door, her smile changing to concern as she saw that Missy and Liz had been crying.

"Come in here, you two. What's wrong?" she asked, drawing them into her polished little living room. She listened carefully to the first part of Liz's explanation and then held up one hand. "Tuck needs to hear this," she said. "Let's go find him—he's down to the peach orchard."

She led the way through the rows of cherries, finished for the season with their budding and bearing, to the younger and smaller peach trees, which Tuck was nurturing as they developed their still-green fruit.

Tuck removed his hat and wiped his perspiring head with a handkerchief as he listened gravely to their report.

"Seems to me the first order of things is a prayer," he said. "Would you ladies object to kneeling with me here in the grass? We're private right here as anywhere."

Liz dropped to her knees rather self-consciously but was soon lost in Tuck's prayer, touched by the simple and natural way he spoke to his Father in Heaven in behalf of the Ashcraft family, and by the great concern and affection he evidenced as he mentioned the needs of each one. She opened her eyes momentarily, startled to hear herself mentioned, too, with Tuck

giving thanks for her, and her presence among them, and her
help to the Ashcraft family as well as others in the neighborhood. Tears, somehow so quick and ready these days, warmed
and flooded her eyes again, and she pressed her hands against
her face in an effort to stem the tide. Had she ever heard herself prayed for? Had anyone ever done so? There had been
Missy's sweet childish prayer when the puppies were born—
she remembered being included then—and probably her
mother, at some time or other, had prayed for her when she
was a child. But it was a remarkable experience to hear her
landlord and neighbor express thanks for her presence and her
help as if she really mattered to him—really made a difference
in his life and in the neighborhood. Did she? What had she to
offer these people?

She missed Tuck's "amen" and found herself scrambling to
her feet moments after the others had risen, with Tuck assist-
ing Lolly.

"Now, I know who Helen's doctor is, and I'm going to
leave a message at his office for Wynn in case I'm needed, and
I think we'd better stick close to the phone until we hear from
him, don't you, Missy? He'll be in touch as soon as he can, I'm
sure. And don't you worry, honey—everything's going to be
just fine."

Missy nodded and gave him a hug. "You're the best,
Tuck—I mean, Bishop."

He grinned. "Answer to either one," he assured her. "You
know, Missy, I'm remembering what your brother Dave was
told by the Lord when he was worrying whether to serve a mission or not. Do you remember what the Lord said to him,
when he went up in the mountains to pray?"

Missy frowned. "Um—something like, 'Don't be afraid to
go and serve me, and everything will be all right with you and
your family'?"

Tuck nodded. " 'All shall be well with thee and thine.' I wrote it down in my journal the night Dave came and told me about it. I want you to keep that in mind, Missy, as things unfold with your dear mother. The Lord knows each of you, and he honors his covenants with his servants. Dave's one of his servants, and he's out there doing his best to serve his fellow-man and his Heavenly Father. Don't ever doubt that you'll all be blessed because of that service—that sacrifice. I've seen it happen time and again."

Missy nodded. "Thanks, Bishop. I feel lots better now. I was real scared at first."

"Of course you were, sweetheart—that's perfectly natural."

"Liz said she'd stay with me today, and that makes me feel better, too."

"Thank you, Liz. That's mighty good of you."

"My pleasure," Liz said, surprised at how sincerely she meant it.

She and Missy stopped to feed Gypsy and Tracker and then went back to Missy's house to wait for Wynn's call. They passed the time by making brownies and a casserole and playing Yahtzee.

"Oh, that was fun," Missy said with a sigh, when they both grew tired of the game. "Dave always used to play that with me, but Dad hardly ever feels like it."

"It's been years since I've played," Liz said. "Where's Megan today?"

"She's gone with Sister Woodbine and Suzanne to some music workshop at BYU. She's real good on the violin. I wish I could play something." She sighed again. "What d'you think's happening with my mom, Liz?"

"I just don't know, honey, but I'm sure she's in good hands."

"Yeah. I wish Dad would call."

"He will as soon as he can. It's hard waiting for something like this, isn't it?"

"Uh-huh." She grinned. "It's like waiting to hear if Sister Woodbine's had her baby yet. Seems like it always takes forever."

Liz smiled. "Probably feels that way to her, too. It's hard to believe she's had ten."

"I know—she's so skinny and young-looking. She's nice, too, but she's always so busy with stuff."

"Missy, I'm glad you and Megan are friends. That's made your summer more fun, hasn't it?"

"A whole lot more fun! Only, I'm worried that people will take her away from me when school starts."

"I know what you mean. And of course, she will make friends at school, just like you have friends at your school."

"I know. And I don't really mean I don't want her to. I just mean I hope she doesn't dump me for them."

"I hope not too. But I think you two are getting close enough this summer that you'll always be one of her friends. She's a nice girl, and I think she likes you very much."

Missy nodded. "She is nice—except if she gets real mad at somebody she can be kind of snotty. She likes you a lot, too."

"And Tim's a sweet boy."

"Tim's cool. And Nicky's a doll."

"He is, isn't he? Adorable." Liz steeled herself against the wave of longing that swept her when she remembered holding Nicky, warm and solid, in her arms.

"And Mr. Parrish likes you, too."

"Well, yes, we're friends, I think."

Missy looked sly. "A little more than friends, I'd say."

"Why do you say that?"

"Well—'cause I saw how he put his arm around you on the rides at Lagoon—and how he looked at you sometimes."

Liz felt herself blushing. "Now, Missy—"

"I know, I know. I'm just saying what I think. And I think he likes you—a lot!"

The ringing of the phone saved Liz from having to reply to that, and Missy answered on the second ring, her face suddenly serious again.

"Dad? What's going on? How's Mom? She is! Why? Oh . . . okay. But what does the doctor think? Does she know who I am yet? Uh-huh . . . Okay. Okay. I will. Love you, too. Thanks for calling."

Missy turned back to Liz. "He said the doctor put Mom in the hospital for uh—observation, or whatever—so they can check her out, and all, but he's kind of excited about her, and she's still trying to figure out what's going on. She knows she's been sick, and she asked Dad not to leave her, so he's staying there all night long. He said he'll call again in the morning. Oh—and they haven't told her about how old everybody is, so she still doesn't know who I am, or anything. He said she's sleeping right now."

"I'm glad she's getting good care," Liz said. "What are you supposed to do tonight?"

"Dad said maybe I could stay with Megan, or—or somebody."

"What if you and Megan both stayed at my house? We could have a good old-fashioned slumber party, just the three of us."

"Liz! Could we? That'd be so cool!"

"We'll do it. Did your dad say whether he'd talked to Tuck?"

"Yeah—he said Tuck's going to go down this evening, and they're going to give my mom a blessing."

"Oh? What does that mean?"

"Well, it's a special prayer that's given for someone who's

sick or really needs extra help from Heavenly Father. Remember how Dave wrote about Herr Schwann and the blessing they gave him when he was so sick? Two men who, like, hold the priesthood put their hands on the sick person's head and put a little drop of this special oil on, and say a prayer for the person to get well. And usually they do."

"Has your mother had that done before?"

"Yes, lots. But see, it works according to everybody's faith, and it has to be the Lord's will, too."

"I see. But why wouldn't it always be the Lord's will for people to get well? He healed many, many people in the Bible."

"Yep, and in the Book of Mormon too. My dad always says that maybe Mama stayed sick to teach the rest of us something—like patience and loving her anyway—stuff like that."

Liz bit her lip. "I'd say you've all learned those things remarkably well."

"Do you think so? Then maybe that's why she can get better now."

Liz didn't venture an answer to that. She and Missy collected Missy's sleeping bag and pillow, wrapped a plate of brownies for snacking, and walked through the afternoon heat to Liz's house, where Missy's pup greeted his mother and brother with yips of delight and absurd antics. When they saw Marilyn Woodbine's van parked at home, Missy called Megan's house to invite her to the impromptu slumber party.

Megan accepted readily, and at six-thirty she and her father walked up to Liz's house, their arms full of bedding, pillows, and boxed games.

"I was invited, too, wasn't I?" Will teased, depositing Megan's gear in a corner of the living room. "What's the occasion, anyway. Is it a birthday, or just time for a girls' night out—or in, as the case may be?"

"There may well be an occasion for celebrating—we're not entirely sure, yet—but I'll let Missy tell you about that," Liz said.

"Well," Missy began, blue eyes wide, "this morning my mom—you know how she always is sort of in her own little dream world? Well, this morning she just kept looking at me so funny, like she was trying to figure something out, and when Liz came over, Mama started talking to her about how much I looked like her little girl who was only three, and how the sofa looked like hers, but was older and shabbier, and she was worried because she didn't know how she got there, or where Dave and I were. I called my dad at work and he came right home, and she recognized him and everything—but she thought we were at Liz's house, and she wanted him to take her home. He took her to the doctor, though, and the doctor put her in the hospital. They haven't told her yet that she's been—you know, like asleep—for eight years."

Will's expression grew serious, and he turned his gaze to Liz, who nodded confirmation. "Missy's dad is staying with her mom tonight—she asked him not to leave her—and since Missy's staying with me, we thought it'd be fun to have Megan, too, and make a party of it."

"That's incredible," Will said softly. "After all this time."

"Wow!" said Megan. "And she didn't even know who you were?" she asked Missy wonderingly.

Missy shook her head. "See, she can't figure out why things—and people—look the same but different. She told my dad he ought to see a doctor, too. I guess she thought he looked sick, but really, he's just eight years older and thinner than she remembers. And of course, I'm eleven, instead of three. And she doesn't even know that Dave's all grown up and gone on his mission."

Will looked at Liz. "That's going to be a lot for her to assimilate—losing eight years of her life. That'd be tough."

Liz nodded. "She knows she's been sick, but she thought maybe it was the flu or something that was making her all confused."

"And boy, I'm sure glad Liz was there with me when it happened, 'cause I was scared to death. I didn't know what to do or say or anything—but Liz figured out right away what was going on."

"That'll be so great to have your mom back," Megan said, a touch of wistfulness in her voice.

"I know," Missy replied, "but it'll be weird, too, because it's like we don't really know each other. I don't remember much at all about how she used to be, and she sure doesn't know anything about me anymore! What if she doesn't even like me?"

"She'll like you," the three of them chorused together, and Missy gave a little laugh.

"It'll be a matter of getting acquainted again, for both of you," Liz told her. "Your dad will do all he can to catch her up on things, and you'll have to be patient while things are getting back to normal. She'll be wondering what you think of her, too."

"Well, I'll—love her," Missy said, but there was a note of uncertainty in her voice.

"You'll just need to give it time," Will added. "I expect the doctor will talk with you and your dad, too, and give you some ideas on how to make things go smoother and easier for all of you. Well, what a great thing to celebrate! Better than a birthday."

Missy nodded. "It's kind of like a—a rebirthday, isn't it? Like she's getting a new life today?"

"I'd say so," Will replied, giving her shoulders a hug. "I'm happy for you, Missy—and I hope everything goes wonderfully for all of you. Boy, what do I smell—can that be pizza? You girls do know how to have a good time, don't you? We poor guys are going to be toughing it out with plain old ham sandwiches tonight."

"Liz and I made it ourselves, and it's got real pepperoni and gobs of gooey cheese," Missy said, grinning at Megan.

"Mmm," said Megan. "You mean the stretchy kind that's all soft and melted, with spicy sauce and a crisp, chewy crust?"

Liz laughed. "I think we'd better relent, Megan, and feed your dad a piece so he'll go away happy."

"Well, just so he goes away," Megan agreed. "It's girls only, tonight, so we can talk."

"Yeah—about boys!" Missy added.

"Missy! Are you interested in boys already?" Will pretended shock. "Megan isn't, I know that."

"I am, too!" Megan protested, cuffing his arm. "Just because I don't talk to *you* about them . . ."

"Well, Elizabeth doesn't care about that sort of stuff, so at least she'll keep you both firmly in line," he said, with a wink for Liz, who smiled serenely.

"Come into the kitchen, and I'll send some pizza and brownies home for you and Tim," she invited. He followed her, watching while she prepared two paper plates for him to carry.

"It's good you were there with Missy today," he commented. "She'd have been treading deep water without you."

Liz nodded. "It felt pretty deep to me too. I sure hope the improvement lasts, for all their sakes."

"So do I. And thanks, Elizabeth, for what you're doing for the girls." He gave her a brief hug, and she felt his cheek rest momentarily against the top of her head.

"It'll be fun," she replied. "I think Missy needs a little distraction tonight so she won't brood and worry too much."

"Be good for Meggie, too. She gets weary of being around only us males all the time."

Liz smiled. "So she's glad to come over here, where she and Missy can *talk* about males."

"Well—the twelve- and thirteen-year-old variety. That's a whole different story from dads and brothers."

"I see. But you don't think I'm interested in such talk?"

His grin was slow, lighting the hazel eyes that were so much like his daughter's. "I'm kind of hoping your interest is geared more *toward* the dads and brothers, I guess—who, by the way, will surely be enjoying these goodies tonight. Thank you—and you ladies have fun, now."

Liz watched him go, feeling again the soft pressure of his face against her hair, wishing wishes and hoping hopes to which she didn't dare give words. "Certain dads and brothers are very much in my thoughts," she whispered, and she turned to take up pizza and salad for the girls.

The evening was fun and lively, and Liz almost felt twelve again herself as they snacked and talked and tried different hairstyles on each other, and played Clue and Pictionary and Monopoly late into the night. When they finally settled down, Gypsy, nonplussed at finding her mistress stretched out on the living-room floor between Missy and Megan, fussed around for a bit and then curled up nearby to keep an eye on things. Missy's pup snuggled by her in such a matter-of-fact way that Liz suspected she knew his sleeping arrangements at home, and Megan coaxed the other pup to cuddle close to her, saying, "Come on, Tracker, I need a doggie, too!"

Liz lay awake for some time, exhausted, but with her mind replaying the events of the day that had begun so quietly with the early-morning watering of her flowers. She had just re-viewed Tuck's prayer in the orchard when a discreet snuffling sound on her right alerted her to the realization that Megan

259

was crying. She listened to be sure, hearing Missy's deep, even breathing on her left, and Gypsy's gentle snores. The sound came again, only this time it was accompanied by an unhappy whimper, muffled as if Megan had pulled her pillow over her face. Liz rose to her knees and reached over to touch Megan's shoulder.

"Megan?" she whispered, as she felt the girl's shoulder shake with suppressed sobs. Liz patted her and then gently massaged her back.

"I'm—I'm sorry," Megan gasped squeakily, between sobs.

"It's okay to cry when you need to," Liz told her softly.

"I don't want to—to wake Missy."

"Shall we go to the kitchen?"

Megan gathered herself to her feet, trailing a sheet, and followed Liz to the kitchen, where Liz shut the door and turned on a small light over the range. Megan buried her face in her arms on the tabletop and allowed her sobs to erupt unchecked. Liz busied herself getting out milk, sugar, and spices.

Finally Megan's tears subsided, and she blotted her face with a paper napkin. "I'm so sorry—sorry I—woke you up," she said shakily.

"You didn't—I hadn't been asleep. I was just thinking over everything that happened today."

"Oh. Good."

"Have you ever had hot spiced milk?"

"Is that what you're making? No, I never heard of it."

"My mom used to make it for me when I couldn't sleep. It just has a little cinnamon, nutmeg, and sugar. Vanilla if you like it. It's yummy and relaxing, and nothing stimulating like chocolate or coffee to keep you from sleeping. Want some?"

"I reckon. I mean, I guess so. Nobody says *reckon* around here, do they?"

Liz smiled. "I reckon not."

Megan smiled tremulously and accepted the mug of milk Liz handed her.

"I don't want to sound too Southern when I start school, or everybody'll make fun of me. I'm trying to get rid of my accent."

"I did that, too. But I wish you wouldn't—it's charming."

They sipped in silence.

"This really does taste good," Megan remarked in surprise. "Um—aren't you going to ask what I was crying about?"

"Usually when people cry at night, it's over some private hurt," Liz said. "I'd be glad to listen if it's something you want to talk about, but you don't have to tell me."

"It's just—sometimes I'm not very nice, I guess."

"Oh?"

"I ought to just be happy for Missy, that she's probably getting her mom back, and all. Only, I kept thinking, it's not fair. We've been kind of alike, Missy and me, because we neither of us had our moms, and we could—you know—sympathize and understand each other. Now, it'll be all different. Her mom will be there, and she'll want Missy with her, of course—and that's wonderful, I don't mean it isn't—but my mom will still be gone. Always. And I—I miss her. I really do. Not—you know, not every minute, but lots, still. So, I was just thinking how crummy it is of me to be jealous of Missy, but I was anyway. That's all."

Liz nodded and took a long sip of her milk. "You're afraid of losing the one good friend you've made in this new place, and you feel kind of guilty because you're envious of Missy's good fortune in having her mom restored to her?"

Megan sighed raggedly. "That's about it. It's mean of me, isn't it?"

"Seems like natural feelings to me. It's been my own experience that grieving for somebody comes in waves after the first misery has passed. You feel better for a while, and then it hits you again, and again—but each time it's a little less painful. Sometimes, though, something comes up that brings on an especially painful wave, and I suspect that's what happened to you tonight. And no—I don't think you're mean. You don't wish Missy's mom any harm, or Missy either. You're just wishing you could have your mom, too."

"Yeah, that's it, exactly. My mom was so nice. She was fun and pretty. I don't see why she had to die."

Liz shook her head. "I don't know why either. By the way, don't think that Missy has all smooth sailing ahead of her. She'll need you to be her friend to talk to during all the adjustments her family will be making, if her mom continues to improve. And she worries, too, about losing your friendship. She's afraid that when school starts, you'll make lots of new friends in your grade and forget about her."

"Really? Did she say that? I wouldn't. I mean, I hope I make friends at school, but I won't forget about Missy. She's been so nice to me this summer."

Liz smiled. "She couldn't wait for you to get here. She needed a friend close by. Suzanne's just a little too old for her."

"I know. Oh—that reminds me. Something good happened to me today, too—I think. At the music workshop I went to with Suzanne and her mom, they talked me into trying out for this youth symphony they're forming, and I *think* maybe I'll get in!"

"That'd be great!"

"I know—it'd be fun. But it'd take a lot of time, too, and maybe Missy'll be jealous of that. Do you think?"

"Friends, even best friends, can't be together *all* the time. But you can talk and encourage each other in any good thing you do."

"Do you have a best friend, Liz?"

Liz considered the question. "I did when I was your age. Her name was Marcy Strickland, and we did everything together. But when she was sixteen, she was killed in a car accident."

"How awful!"

"Yes, it was. That was when I first learned about grief— how it comes back in waves. At least, that's how it was for me. Now I just remember Marcy with affection. I think of our happy times, and I'm glad I knew her. But for a long time it was painful to think of her at all."

"What about now? Do you have a best friend now?"

"I guess my best friend around here is Marilyn Woodbine," Liz said slowly. "Although I like most everyone I've met. Marilyn's honest and friendly and caring. She reminds me just a little of a lady I knew and liked a lot in Hawaii. Her name was Dorrie—and she's the reason I'm here now."

"Why? Did—did your husband fall in love with her or something?"

Liz laughed. "No. Not at all. Dorrie grew up here in Utah, you see, and she always told me such good things about it that I decided to give it a try when I was looking for someplace to go—someplace I'd never been, where I could live quietly and privately and think things over after my divorce. Utah sounded just right."

"So do you like it here?"

"Very much. Even more than I expected to when I first came."

"Yeah, me too. I thought it'd be really dumb—all dry and deserty and no people around or anything to do. I reckon I gave my dad kind of a hard time about it. But I was scared."

"I know."

"But then when I got here and saw my room—well, that

made a lot of difference. It made me feel like somebody cared how I felt."

Liz smiled. "Somebody did—your dad."

"Right. But somebody else—somebody I didn't even know—went to a lot of trouble to make it extra nice."

"Well, that somebody had a good time doing it, although she fretted and worried that you might not like it, after all."

"She doesn't need to worry anymore." Megan stood up and gave Liz a hug. "I really appreciate it, and so does my dad. He thinks you're great."

"Well, I think he's great, too. You all are, in fact."

Megan yawned, covering her mouth daintily. "I think I can sleep now. Your spiced milk worked. Thanks for that, too."

"Missy missed out, didn't she? Too bad she dropped right off to sleep."

Megan shrugged. "She gets you all to herself lots more often than I do. It was my turn." She made a little face. "See? I *am* the jealous kind!"

"You don't need to be," Liz told her. "There's plenty of room for you in my life—and I'm glad you're in it."

Megan smiled, contented at last.

26

True to proper slumber party protocol, it was nearly time for lunch when Liz and the two girls awakened the next day, so Liz let them help her prepare a brunch of waffles with fresh blueberries.

Missy leaned back with a satisfied sigh. "I think we're prob'ly the best cooks in the whole world."

"Well, go ahead and brag on yourself!" teased Megan, prodding Missy with her foot.

"Might as well—nobody else here to do it," Missy said complacently. "That's what I do at home when I do a good job on the kitchen, or something. My dad says you ought to take pleasure when you do a good job and compliment yourself."

Megan frowned. "Isn't that being kind of conceited?"

"Not really," Liz said, smiling at both of them. "Most of us need to feel as good about ourselves and our accomplishments as we can. Then we feel ready to do more or to try new things."

"Well, what if you do really bad at the new thing?"

"That's okay, too. We don't have to be wonderful at everything. I'm a terrible typist, for example. And pianist. I hit wrong keys even while I know I'm doing it. I can't seem to stop myself. But I feel pretty good about my sewing skills, and I'm happy about learning to grow my first-ever garden this year, so it balances out. What are you best at, Megan?"

"Umm—playing the violin, I guess. And I like to draw. And I'm not too bad at ice-skating. But I hate playing team sports, like baseball or basketball, where everybody yells at you if you miss something, and it makes you feel dumb and guilty. What about you, Missy?"

"Well, I like to cook, and I've learned a lot about that from Liz. And I like—I guess it's not a talent, but I like to be with people and talk and visit. Oh, and I got the highest score in my grade on the math part of our achievement tests this year. But that's because I like math—it's like figuring out puzzles. My dad has some of his old books from high school, and sometimes when I don't have anything else to do, I try to work some problems in them, so I guess I've learned some stuff from that. But I wanted to take gymnastics one year, and I was so klutzy and so scared that I finally quit. And Aunt Lou tried to teach me to embroider, but—" She made a face. "It looked awful. Plus I didn't like it. It was too—too little, and it had to be just right, you know?"

"Too tedious," Liz supplied.

"Yeah, that's the word."

"Isn't it a good thing we all have different talents?" Liz commented. "If we all could do everything perfectly, nobody would be special, and we wouldn't appreciate each other as much."

Missy nodded. "Heavenly Father knew what he was doing, all right, when he gave us all different talents before we were born."

"Before?" Megan questioned. "You mean, *when* we were born?"

Missy shook her head. "No, before. When we were his spirit children and lived with him before we came to earth. My dad says that prob'ly some people like—like Beethoven, you know, or some great artists prob'ly brought a lot of knowledge and experience with them about music or art, 'cause they did a lot of it up there, and Heavenly Father let them kind of remember how to do it so they could bless the whole world with their talent. But, maybe that's just my dad's idea."

"That's an interesting thought, Missy," Liz said, impressed as she had been on other occasions with Missy's interest in religious principle and theory.

Megan frowned. "I don't know anything about living with God before we were born. I never heard of such a thing!"

Missy shrugged. "Oh, prob'ly it's something other churches don't know about. Heavenly Father's told our prophets a lot of stuff that other people don't know."

"Why?"

"Umm—I don't know. I guess so that we can share it with other people. At least, that's why my brother Dave is on a mission—telling the people in Austria what we know about Jesus and Joseph Smith and everything."

Liz smiled at her. "You're a pretty good missionary yourself, Missy," she said. "Now, what are you girls planning for today?"

Missy thought a minute. "I think I'm going to go clean the house real good. You don't need to come, Liz. I feel okay today, and I want to be there in case my dad calls or comes home. But I'll let you know what he says, okay?"

"That's fine, honey. How about you, Megan?"

"Reckon I'd better get home, too. Dad'll have some chores saved up for me, I know, since I was gone all day yesterday and half of today."

The girls gathered up their belongings, and when they were gone, Liz looked around at her suddenly quiet house and yawned.

"It was fun to be twelve again for a while," she told Gypsy, as she stretched across her wonderfully comfortable and yielding bed. "But it catches up to you."

It was three-thirty when she woke and showered and let the dogs out to run. The sky had grown overcast, and a gentle wind was moving the treetops; it made a refreshing break from the baking summer sun, and Liz stayed outside, weeding her garden and flower beds while the coolness lasted.

"Hi, Liz, you're more ambitious than I am," called a tired voice, and Liz looked up to see Francie Johansen sauntering up the driveway.

"Just taking advantage of the cooler air," Liz said, dusting off her hands.

"Me, too. Thought I'd better go for a walk while the boys are asleep. My doctor told me to walk more."

"Oh?"

"Yes. Can you believe I'm pregnant again?"

"Are you? Congratulations!"

"Fine for you to say," Francie said, easing onto the top step. "I'm only four months along, and I already feel fat and ugly."

"Well, you look gorgeous, as always. Really, don't you want another baby?"

"Oh, I love the little toads, once they get here, of course. I just hate the process."

"I always thought it'd be kind of wonderful to feel a baby kicking inside and realize that it's a real person in there getting ready to experience life. But maybe I'm naive."

"Maybe," Francie agreed wryly. "Well, I don't mind the kicking so much, most of the time, and I thought it was kind of cute when Gabe used to get hiccups inside me. Guess he didn't like what I ate! But what I hate is feeling heavy and tired and looking like a blimp and throwing up and running to the bathroom every ten minutes—not to mention labor and delivery.

Believe me, there are times when surrogate motherhood seems like a pretty marvy idea. Or adoption."

"How does Eric feel about another baby?"

Francie rolled her eyes. "Tickled pink, of course, but what does that have to do with the price of beans? Men don't have to *do* it—they just sit back and watch!"

Liz smiled. "Do you want a girl or another boy?"

"If it's a girl, that'll be the only good thing to come of it all. I don't want to know, though, because if I find out it's another boy, I'll be depressed the whole blessed time."

"But your little boys are so cute! I see them playing outside when I go walking sometimes. You must enjoy them."

Francie sighed. "I guess I do, when I'm not mad at them for some mischief or other. I just don't have all the patience I could use. That's my problem. I like being with adults and doing important things like secretarial work or banking. I like dressing up and earning my own money and not having to stay home all day changing messy diapers and wiping up spills. And just when I can see my way clear to going to work again in a couple of years—bam! I'm starting all over again."

"Well, lots of mothers work these days, even when their children are small."

Francie's mouth drooped. "Eric won't hear of it—not until the youngest is in kindergarten, at least. So here I go, for another six years of slavery."

"Wouldn't he even agree to a part-time job?"

"He says we don't need the money, and it would just wear me out. Then the Church upholds him, of course—he's a man." Her voice changed to a mocking sing-song. "Mothers should stay home with their children if at all possible. A woman's place is in the home," she chanted. "Fine for men to say!"

"Francie," Liz said, after a moment, "if you feel this way, why did you get pregnant again?"

"I didn't mean to. I just got—careless. And one mistake is all it takes for me, seems like. Oh, well. You don't want to hear me complain, I'm sure. I know it's not very attractive of me."

"I'm sorry if you're unhappy, but I have to admit I envy you. I'd love to have a baby."

"Want to trade places?"

Liz smiled. "Oh, come on—you wouldn't trade your nice new home and good-looking husband and cute kids for my situation, would you?"

"Eric is kind of a hunk, isn't he? That's what got me into this to begin with. No, I guess I wouldn't really trade. I just want the kids to hurry and grow up so I can do something else."

Liz stood up. "Come on in, and I'll wash my hands and get us something cold to drink."

"That sounds good. I can't stay long, though. I have to finish my walk and get back. Eric doesn't like me to leave the boys, even when they're asleep."

"Would he watch them for a while in the evenings? You could walk with me then—that's when I go." *What am I saying?* she asked herself wildly.

"Oh, Liz—that's sweet! Maybe he will."

Francie followed Liz inside. "Speaking of handsome hunks, how are you getting along with our neighbor down the hill?"

"Oh, fine. We're friends. He's nice."

"That's pretty vague."

"Well—there's really nothing more to tell."

Liz poured two tall glasses of grape juice and added ice and a squeeze of lemon.

"Have you dated him at all?" Francie asked.

"Mmm—probably not. I did go with his family to Lagoon one time and to the Pioneer Day celebration in Salt Lake. I had fun, but it wasn't exactly a date, in either case. Other than

270

that, I went shopping with him once, to help choose things for his daughter's room, and he bought me lunch. But I don't think that qualifies, either, so—I guess the answer is no."

"Aren't you attracted to him? I just think you make the cutest couple. I thought for sure when you two left my dinner party together, you wanted some time alone."

Liz smiled. "He walked me here and then went straight home," she replied, neatly dodging Francie's question about attraction.

"You know," Francie said thoughtfully, twirling the ice in her glass, "maybe he just doesn't know whether you like him that way. Maybe you need to flirt a little."

"You think so?"

"Well, some guys are kind of dense. You have to use the sledgehammer approach to get their attention."

"Will's not dense. I think he's just still grieving for his wife. He was really in love with her."

"Well, sure—and he will grieve, until he finds somebody to take her place, you know? Hey, if you're interested, you'd better let him know, because when school starts, you can be sure there'll be plenty of young, available teachers who won't be shy about flirting with a nice guy like him!"

Oh, Francie—how do you manage to unnerve and irritate me every time we meet? And why in this world did I offer to go walking with you? I'll regret that seven days a week, I know I will!

"I'll keep that in mind," she said meekly. "Thanks for the advice."

"Oh, I'm good at giving advice," Francie said airily. "I just don't take it very well. Hey, thanks for the drink—I feel better now. See you soon!"

Liz cleaned up the breakfast dishes and sat down to read, trying to drive the unsettling conversation with Francie from her thoughts, but it was useless. She could concentrate for only a paragraph or two before her mind insisted on suggesting to her all the things she had really wanted to say to Francie, and finally she said them out loud: "Francie Johansen, I think you're short-sighted, selfish, ungrateful, and a busybody. You need to grow up and appreciate what you have! And yes, if you want to know, I'm mightily attracted to Will Parrish, but any relationship that may or may not develop between us is absolutely none of your well-meaning business!"

Gypsy and Tracker looked at their mistress with alarm, wondering if they were being scolded for some doggy misdemeanor, but Liz was apparently addressing the west wall of her living room, so they wrote it off as another incomprehensible bit of human behavior. Liz, somewhat relieved after her outburst, went to stand on her front porch, where she saw Missy running down the road toward her.

"Liz, guess what!" Missy arrived, panting, on the steps, eyes shining. "My mama's even better today, and the doctor told her how long she'd been—you know—away, and my dad said she took it pretty well, and almost right away she realized who I was—that I was her daughter, I mean, instead of yours. He said she cried for a while, and the doctor was real thrilled with that, because he said it was the most natural way she could act and that she'll prob'ly grieve for a while over all the lost time and then start feeling happier."

"Oh, Missy, that's wonderful!" Liz hugged Missy exuberantly. "Does the doctor have any idea why she came back all of a sudden?"

Missy shook her head. "He told Dad he can't understand it, but he doesn't think she'll go back into her dream world again, though he can't be positive."

"So, are they going to let her come home?"

"In a few days, probably, when she feels ready. But I get to go see her tomorrow!"

"Oh, good! But how do you feel about that?"

"Not even scared like I was before. It's funny—now that she knows who I am, it's okay. But I want to look real nice! If I wash my hair, will you curl it the way you did last night, and fix my bangs? And I'll wear the dress Sister Tucker made for Dave's farewell."

"You'll look beautiful—she'll be so proud of you! Have they explained to her where Dave is, yet?"

Missy nodded. "They had to—she kept asking about him. She just couldn't believe it, Dad said. She said, 'But to me, he was just about to be ordained a deacon!' "

"That means he was how old?"

"Almost twelve. A little older than I am now. She cried because she missed all his teenage years, but she's glad he went on a mission."

"Can he come home to visit her?"

"I don't know. They don't usually let missionaries do that. But this is kind of special, so maybe."

"This is all so exciting! Have you told Tuckers or Megan, yet?"

"Dad was going to call Tuckers after he called me, and I'm going to run see Megan right now. Dad's coming home tonight, so I'll give him that casserole stuff we made yesterday. Well—gotta go! I'll be over about ten tomorrow, if that's okay."

Liz watched her go. The roller coaster at Lagoon, she reflected, had fewer highs and lows than she had experienced in the last couple of days. "And I thought a little country neighborhood like this would be the ultimate in quiet living and solitary contemplation," she remarked to Gypsy. "Shows what I know!"

273

27

In the cool of the evening, when Liz was relaxing with her home-study workbook under a tree, Marilyn came hurrying into the yard, her eyes alight.

"Liz! I don't know where I've been, but I just heard the news about Helen, when Megan came over to borrow some music. Is Helen really herself again?"

"It's looking good for her so far, according to Missy's latest report," Liz said, putting down her book.

Marilyn sat down on the grass. "Tell me about it. Megan said you were there when it all started?"

"I was." Liz told what she knew of Helen's story, including her own feelings, and by the time she was finished, Marilyn's fingers were pressed against her lips and tears stood in her eyes.

"Isn't that something!" she breathed. "I thought Helen's condition was irreversible, for sure. It has to be a miracle!"

Liz nodded. "Seems like one to me—and I didn't know they still happened."

"Oh, they do still happen. More than we have any idea, I suspect, because they're usually not publicized. It makes sense, when you think about it. The Lord hasn't lost his power to bless his children, and he loves us as much as he did the people in his day—so when there's a need, and faith to be rewarded, it can still happen."

"You don't think there's a natural explanation?"

"Well, there may be. But again, who's in charge of the laws of nature more than the one who set them in motion? Did the doctor have an explanation?"

"Not yet, at least," Liz conceded.

Marilyn nodded. "Often the medical people are confounded. But I've found that lots of doctors are believers, too, and they know when their skills have been superseded."

"Well," Liz said thoughtfully, "I don't know of anyone who would deserve a miracle more than the Ashcrafts."

"I know. They're a great family, aren't they? Just honest and humble and patient, all these years, in the face of such trying circumstances. Wynn's been incredible—he's just kept on loving Helen."

"Well, she loves him, too. I could tell that from the way she greeted him—wow—was it only yesterday? It seems like weeks ago."

Marilyn smiled. "That's how it is when a lot happens in a short time, isn't it? I'm so glad you were with Missy when her mom woke up. I somehow think that was planned, too, don't you?"

Liz shrugged. "I really don't know. I mean—who am I that God would choose me to be there?"

"A kind and sensitive person who cares about Missy," Marilyn replied promptly. "And someone bright and perceptive enough to realize what was happening to Helen and ease the way."

Liz was silent, remembering the many times she had called out, "Not today, Missy!" when she hadn't been in the mood for a visit.

"You've been really good for that little girl," Marilyn

275

added. "Lolly has, too, of course, and I've done what I could, but Missy seems to regard you as—oh, a favorite aunt, or something—someone she can run to with questions about almost anything."

"And I've learned a great deal from her," Liz responded, "although I'm afraid I've been selfish a lot of the time and too busy guarding my precious privacy to always see her need. But she's been sweet about that, too."

"She's a good-natured kid. She takes no for an answer considerably better than most of mine. I have a few champion wheedlers who regard a no as a challenge to their ingenuity and endurance!"

Liz smiled. "Sounds normal to me. But Missy's a remarkable girl, with all she's been through, and I am really fond of her. There are times, though, when she exasperates me. She gets a little carried away with her interest in—um—my personal business."

Marilyn laughed. "You mean she wants you to marry Will Parrish."

"Oh, dear. Has she talked about that to you?"

"Only to say how cool she thinks Will is, and how perfect it would be if you two were to fall in love. It's natural for young girls to think up romantic schemes, that's all."

"I know it is. But Missy scares me—she's almost capable of planning the wedding and sending out announcements before there's ever been a proposal!"

Marilyn chuckled. "Oh, Missy can handle a simple thing like a proposal, too—have no fear."

"Deliver me!"

Marilyn gave Liz a sideways look. "Liz, I realize I'm risking being as nosy as Missy by asking this—and if you decide to answer, you can know it'll go no further—I'm not into gossip about your private life—but *are* you interested in Will? I've almost thought I detected something once or twice that made me think so."

Liz didn't answer immediately, not from an unwillingness to have Marilyn's hunch confirmed but from a desire to word her answer truthfully.

"Let me put it this way," she said at last. "If I had met Will Parrish before I met Brock Ewell, I'd never even have seen Brock. At least, I *think* that's how it would have been. Who can say for sure what I'd have done or thought at a younger and sillier age? But Will's so solid and so genuine. He reminds me of the kind of wood he likes to work with—seasoned and straight and valuable, not warped or green or wormy."

Marilyn clapped her hands in delight at the comparison. "I love it!" she said, her eyes warm with humor and affection. "That's perfect. And for the record, let me say that I agree with Missy's evaluation—I think it'd be cool, too, if you both got together. How about his family—do you like the kids?"

Liz nodded, gazing at her hands. "I'm trying not to let myself get too attached to them—and I could, easily. But what we all have to realize is that Will is still in love with Katherine. He's still trying to deal with her death."

"It may take some time," Marilyn agreed. "But maybe even sooner than he thinks, he's going to want to marry again. It's not good for a man to be alone too long. And those kids could use a mom—not that Will's not doing a great job with them, he is—but I notice how little Tim hangs around me in the kitchen when he comes over, and Megan chided Suzanne one day when Sue said something rather cheeky to me. She told her to be glad she has a mom who cares how she does things and that it's awfully lonesome without one. And she's right—it is."

"It's sad she had to learn that so early in life. And I don't kid myself that I could ever really take her mom's place, even if things were to develop between Will and me."

"She likes you, though, and that's a start. She told me so."

"That's what Missy said, too—and I'm glad. Let me tell you a story, Marilyn."

Marilyn hugged her knees and looked up expectantly. Liz told her of Megan's resemblance to her dream daughter pictured on the magazine cover of that remote December issue.

"And I felt so foolish," she concluded, "when Will showed me Megan's picture, and I actually started to cry. He was totally understanding and kind about it, but he must have thought I was a hopeless neurotic!"

Marilyn gazed off into the orchard. "Maybe I tend to attach too much significance to things like that," she said slowly, "but has it occurred to you that maybe Meggie's resemblance to the picture that had such an emotional impact on you might not be simple coincidence? That maybe—just maybe— you reacted to the little girl in the photograph *because* she resembled the girl you're meant to care for and mother?"

"Do you truly think that's possible?"

"I do—and I'll tell you why." Marilyn smiled. "Of course you know by now that I'm so happily steeped in Mormon doctrine that it colors all my thinking."

"That's natural."

"Well, you're familiar with our belief that we existed as spirit children of God before we were born into mortality, aren't you?"

"I've heard it spoken of—by Missy, for one."

"So I just wonder if perhaps you were given a touch—a glimpse of memory, you might say—through the veil of forgetfulness that comes upon us at birth, to allow you to recognize Megan, whom you knew and loved in that existence and maybe even agreed to care for here. Please understand, this is just the gospel according to Marilyn that I'm quoting here, not proven truth. But it makes me wonder. Have you ever met anyone for the first time and felt sure that you've known the person before, though you can't for the life of you remember where or when?"

Liz considered. "There've been times when I thought so. When I first saw Will he seemed incredibly familiar to me, but then I decided it must be his slight resemblance to Abe Lincoln."

Marilyn smiled. "He is a little bit Lincolnesque, isn't he? Only handsomer."

"But do you seriously think I might have known him—and Megan—in some former life?"

"I truly believe it's possible. I think we made covenants in that existence, promising we'd fulfill certain callings or responsibilities here—whether they be in some kind of religious service, or motherhood, or marriage, or sharing our talents with the world, or whatever. I know it's a unique doctrine, but I believe it."

"It's interesting, and it makes a certain sense."

Marilyn looked at Liz with a speculative expression. "I don't usually speak of this, but I feel close to you, Liz, and I think you'll understand, whether you're able to fully believe in what I'm saying or not."

Liz sat up straight. "With that introduction, you'd better tell me! I told you my little story."

"It's just this. As you can imagine, people often criticize Tom and me for having so many children. Actually, we had about decided, after the twins were born, that we should stop. We had five, and that seemed a large family at the time— especially to me, since I had grown up in a small family. Then one night I had a dream. I saw six children—four girls and two boys—beautiful kids. They were standing together in a group.

279

One of them spoke and said, 'You promised.' That was all, just 'you promised,' and then I woke up with that dream firmly implanted in my memory. At first I thought it meant we would have one more child, because we already had five, and there were six of them—but then I realized we had four boys and a girl, and they were four girls and two boys! Gradually I came to accept the idea that we were going to more than double the family we had then. Tom understood, and we prayed a lot about it and felt really warm, positive feelings every time we did, although there were other occasions when I would cry and doubt and ask, 'Why me?' and 'How can we afford it?' and 'When am I going to have time to be me?' But, as you know, we've had the two boys, and three of the girls . . ."

"You mean you think you'll still have another?"

Marilyn nodded. "One more girl, I feel sure of it. I had quite a hard time when Kenny was born, and I thought surely I wouldn't be able to go through it all again, but one night when he was about six months old, I dreamed again—this time of just the one little girl. She didn't say anything, just smiled at me, and I felt that everything would be just fine and that she still would come. I hope it won't be too long. We aren't doing anything to stop her, but so far, no Marilea. That's the name we've chosen for her."

"Forgive me, but I have to ask—what if you give birth to a boy?"

Marilyn laughed. "I'd probably figure that somebody else sneaked in and wanted to come to our family—and I'd still look for Marilea."

Liz looked at Marilyn in awe. "That's truly amazing," she said at last.

"It has been to me. But those dreams were so real, and so different from the ordinary, crazy dreams that you sometimes remember for a while. They were impressive enough that they prodded me into action—I learned to sew and to bake bread and to can fruits and vegetables—and Tom learned to garden, which wasn't an interest of his at all. We did some serious financial planning, set educational goals for ourselves and the kids, and looked for a house that would accommodate all of us, with plenty of play area and a good neighborhood. I can tell you, it's been quite a challenge—and continues to be—but I wouldn't trade it for anything, not even my good old career in social work."

Liz shook her head. "Going for eleven! And Francie Johansen's in the dumps because she's pregnant with her third."

"I know. Poor Francie. She sees herself as a career woman and feels that life—or Eric, or the Church, or somebody—is determined to keep her from her destiny. And I guess if I were pining for my career, I'd be miserable, too. But I've learned that it's best to stay flexible, because plan as we might, life has its little surprises. I've learned, too, that my Heavenly Father knows me better than I know myself, and I can trust him to guide me through whatever comes."

"I admire—and envy—your faith. I'm trying to gain a little of that for myself. Well, as usual, Marilyn, you've given me a lot to think about! And I'll let you know if I hear any more about Helen."

"Please do—that's so thrilling. And as for Mr. Lincoln down the hill, I personally think the man's smitten with you and simply doesn't realize it yet!"

Liz felt the warm color rise in her cheeks. "If he ever does realize such a thing and say so, you—not Missy—will be the first to know!"

Marilyn chuckled. "What a coup that would be!" She unfolded herself with remarkable agility and stood up. "I'm so glad you moved here, Liz. I needed someone like you."

Liz was left to ponder that while Marilyn skirted the corn-field on her way back to her house. The corn, she had learned, belonged to the Woodbines, who were furnished the use of the ground by the Tuckers. A large garden behind the Woodbine home flourished with squash, tomatoes, beans, and cucumbers, tended dutifully by Tom, the reluctant gardener, and several small employees.

"Ten children," Liz murmured to herself. "Ten, and prob-ably another to come, if Marilyn's right. She could open her own school! And in a way, I guess she has. But is she *right*? Did we really exist before we were born and make promises that we've forgotten? That sounds like a pretty chancy sort of promise, if we're bound to forget all about it once we're here! What promises might I have made if I existed then? And Will—did he agree to be Katherine's husband, knowing he would lose her? Did Francie promise to be a mother, or is she really out of her element, as she claims? Did Wynn and Helen know what they would have to endure?"

Gypsy and Tracker, certain that Liz must be talking to them, scrutinized her face, listening for familiar words or phrases.

"Silly dogs!" Liz chided, laughing at their identical expres-sions. "Am I meant to have only you guys as my children?"

They swarmed into her lap, finally identifying what they considered to be an invitation, and offered what solace they could. Liz rubbed their ears absently, thinking of Francie's sug-gestion that Will might need some encouragement to think of her in romantic terms. She let her mind replay their times to-gether, trying to decide whether his gallantries had been those of a man who liked and respected her—in itself a rare and wonderful thing—or whether they indicated a deeper interest on his part. It was a conundrum. Everything he had ever said and done, she reflected, could be taken either way. She put her head back and dozed, both course work and puzzling thoughts momentarily forgotten in a peaceful interlude of dappled sun and evening shade across her face.

She opened her eyes some time later to see Mr. Earl Christensen standing at the edge of her lawn. Her hand, resting on Gypsy's back, felt the sudden tensing of the little body.

"Oh, hello," she said, sitting up. "How are you, today?"

"Could be worse, I guess. On the other hand, I could be better, too. I'll tell you what—these dang 'golden years' they talk about must be fool's gold! You start to fall apart and have all kinds of aches and pains, and you can't even enjoy sleepin' at night—wake up way before sunup with nothin' to do but lie there and think and wonder how long you got left, and what kind of thing's gonna do you in. Call that golden? Not me. So how you doin'?"

"I'm fine," Liz said, almost feeling she should apologize for her health and well-being. "Just fine, thanks."

"They gotcha, yet?"

"Pardon?"

"The dang Mormons—have they gotcha yet?"

"I'm not a member of their church, no. But I think it's fascinating, and I really like all the folks around here. They've been so good to me that I have to respect their beliefs."

"Well, see, that's how they do it—treat you so good it shames you into listening to 'em. But I don't let it get to me, I'll tell you. I just let it run like water off a duck's back. Ain't no bunch of pious do-gooders gonna take away my smokes and my six-pack and my freedom to do what I want with my time and money! Tell you the truth, I feel sorry for 'em, all cooped up and hedged around by what they call the commandments of God!" He shook his head and spat into the grass. "They talk a good line about freedom, but the pore things don't know what freedom is."

"I don't know. They seem to me to be an unusually happy group of people, on the whole. I keep thinking their faith must have something to do with that."

"Aw, they don't know no better. They just think they're happy."

Liz smiled. "Seems to me if a person thinks he's happy, then he must be."

Mr. Earl Christensen pursed his lips and peered at her. He obviously found her wanting—perhaps in good sense. "Hmph," he snorted, batting the air with a dismissive wave of rejection, as though he threw her words back at her. "They've gotcha, all right. You just don't know it yet."

Liz watched him stump off up the lane, then looked at Gypsy and shrugged.

28

As it turned out, Liz didn't need to initiate the next meeting with Will, and it was enough of a date to satisfy Francie, Missy, and Marilyn, all rolled into one. Marilyn allowed her children to host a neighborhood summer sleep-out in their yard, which took care of all the children except Nicky. Quick-thinking Marilyn suggested to Megan that Nicky would be welcome to share the room of Kenny and Kimberly, who were too young to sleep out with the others—just in case her dad would appreciate an evening to himself.

That Will did appreciate such an opportunity became obvious when he promptly sought out Liz and invited her to dinner.

"I thought," he explained, standing with one foot on the bottom step of her porch, "that this is a pretty rare chance, these days, to enjoy a little grown-up conversation and company without benefit of coaching from the peanut gallery. We can find a place that doesn't even serve cheeseburgers or pizza, and if you feel really daring, we could come back and listen to my bagpipe albums while I read to you from my grandfather's journal."

Liz laughed in delight. "I can't think of anything more wonderful."

Will's eyebrows rose. "Seriously? I was half-kidding. I'd be delighted to take you to a movie—play—concert—ballgame—whatever's on that appeals to you."

"They all sound fun, but bagpipes and grandfather interest me most."

Will grinned. "How gratifying! Seven?"

"Seven's fine."

He turned to go and then paused. "Um—I thought I might not mention my plans to the kids. I'll just tell Marilyn, on the side, where we'll be, in case I'm needed."

" 'A word to the wise is sufficient,' " Liz quoted. "I know Marilyn's wise, and I'll be, too—even though Missy will be highly insulted later if she finds out we did something without her knowledge!"

"My point exactly," Will said wryly. "Meggie, too. See you at seven."

All day, Liz hugged the anticipation of the coming evening to her as she might a warm shawl in a cold wind. There was no fear of a cold wind, however. The August day was golden and still, with green accents below and blazing blue above.

She was ready when Will came, and he looked approvingly at her brightly flowered silk shirt and white slacks. She felt festive and daring enough to scent herself with a white ginger cream perfume she had bought in Hawaii but rarely used.

Will had polished the station wagon, she noticed with a flicker of amusement, and he himself looked rather polished, too, his hair carefully but casually combed, his tan contrasting with the pale yellow of a crisp, new-looking shirt and the whiteness of his teeth. He took her to a Mexican restaurant in Provo, not far from the university campus, where the food was excellent, the atmosphere relaxed, and where no one seemed to mind if customers lingered over their meal and talked well into the evening.

"Tell me about your family," he asked her. "Tell me about your growing up. I want to know how you came to be you."

"Well, I was an only child," she said. "A year or so after I was born, my mother developed problems that prevented her from having any more children. We lived just a couple of miles outside of Brewton, which is a small town in Alabama, not far from the Florida line. My dad had a farm implement business there and did a little farming on the side at our place—nothing too ambitious—just our home garden and some extra vegetables to sell. We lived quietly, and it seems like we always had some relative or other staying with us—maybe because we had extra room and not too many noisy kids around, just myself and an occasional friend or cousin. My dad's mother stayed with us the last five years of her life, and then my mother's older sister came, and mom nursed her through a long recuperation from surgery. My dad's uncle stayed with us for a while, too, when I was just small. I liked him. He always told me stories, and taught me things, and let me play with his walking stick, which was one of those old carved kinds, you know, with a hound's head?"

"I've seen those," Will said, nodding. "So you had a fairly quiet childhood with a lot of adult company."

"Yes, and I thought that was fine until I became a teenager and started to resent and mistrust adults, even while I was doing my best to become one."

Will laughed. "Exactly. I wouldn't care to go through those frustrating years again, would you? Although looking back, mine seem to have been much happier than I thought they were at the time."

"Were you a rebellious teenager?"

"No—my folks didn't give me much reason to rebel. They were careful to be so fair and understanding with both Barb and me, that we had to search really hard to find something to

287

complain about. I guess we found a few things, but, by and large, it was a struggle to work up a good, full-blown rebellion. How about you?"

Liz smiled. "I was into open submission and quiet stubbornness. I would agree with my mom that I was too young to wear makeup, but as soon as I was on the school bus, out came the mascara and lipstick. I can even remember my favorite shade—'Cherries in the Snow.' It was about like the red we used in Megan's room. It must have looked positively garish on a pale, skinny little kid!"

"Yeah, but I'll bet it made you feel grown-up and attractive like nothing else."

"Oh, absolutely. The only challenge was getting rid of all traces of it before I got home from school."

"That pale, skinny little kid surely turned out okay," Will said, his eyes warm. "Somewhere along the way, she learned to do her makeup and her hair just right, so that now she's one very attractive lady."

Liz fought the desire to deny his assessment and said simply, "Thank you."

When they emerged from the restaurant into the summer evening, the red had faded from the western sky and been replaced by the first stars. A gentle, fragrant breeze filtered down from the mountains, tempering the day's heat into a pleasant warmth.

Will reached for Liz's hand. "These Utah summers are something, aren't they?" he remarked. "I like the way they cool off at night. Makes for comfortable sleeping, unlike the muggy air and clammy sheets you can get back East this time of year."

Liz murmured something in agreement, but her mind was busy registering surprise and a whole range of other emotions. It was the first time Will had really held her hand. She tried to convince herself that it was just a friendly, companionable impulse that had prompted the gesture, but her heart willed it to be otherwise. By mutual consent, they walked for a while around the relatively quiet campus, enjoying the grounds and the atmosphere and the new dimension of their relationship.

The drive home was leisurely, too. Liz felt absurdly young and vulnerable—almost shy in her replies to Will's easy banter and casual questions. Only when he asked for the latest news regarding Helen Ashcraft did she forget herself enough to open up and speak easily.

"Missy stopped by this morning, and I curled her hair for her first visit to her mom in the hospital. She was so excited— and even more so when she came back. I gather the visit went really well. She said Helen just held her and cried, and then told Missy how beautiful she was, and how proud she was of her, and how sorry for what the family had had to go through all these years because of her illness. Then she had Missy talk to her and tell her everything she could remember about each year of that time. Missy's going back again tomorrow and taking their photo album to share with her and try to catch her up on their lives."

Will shook his head. "As if she really could," he said. "But isn't that incredible? How must it feel, to wake up and find you'd missed—how many years? Eight?"

"Eight years," Liz agreed, her voice subdued. "It awes me, too. And it makes me want to appreciate and enjoy every minute of life and health and normal thinking I have."

Will glanced at her. "A good point," he said quietly and again covered her hand with his on the seat between them.

They sneaked from the station wagon into the house like a couple of conspirators, Will barely closing the car door and cocking an ear toward the Woodbine yard across the fields, where young, excited voices could be heard calling, "All-ee, all-ee in free!" and "You're it!"

They crossed the nearly dark kitchen and went into the living room, where Will turned on a couple of table lamps and invited Liz to sit down. She chose one end of the sofa, beside a lamp, and Will pulled a comfortable chair for himself into the pool of light. Then, he excused himself to put a tape on and to bring a tray with two mugs of iced ginger ale to set on the low table before them.

"Mexican food always makes me thirsty," he explained with a grin. "Also—you might find Grandfather's journal pretty dry stuff." He picked up a black book with worn binding, the front labeled simply "Record" in faded gilt.

"I don't exactly know where to begin," Will murmured, carefully turning yellowed pages. Liz waited patiently, her attention caught by the haunting strains of music emanating from the tape player.

"What is that melody?" she wondered aloud, not really asking Will. "I know I've heard it somewhere . . ."

He looked up quickly. "That's called 'The Skye Boat Song,' or 'Over the Sea to Skye,' and it tells of Bonnie Prince Charlie being rescued and carried swiftly from the shores of Scotland to the Isle of Skye."

"It's beautiful."

He nodded. "It is. Stays in your memory for days. Would you rather just listen? We don't have to read this now."

"No, I want to hear this, too. Go ahead whenever you're ready."

"Here's something I found interesting—maybe you will, too. He's still on his mission back East:

> We tramped through the woods this rainy day for a good eight miles or more, coming to only three or four homes along the track, none of which would receive us, until at last there was a cabin in a clearing, with a good ample porch along the front and blessed smoke rising from the chimney,

290

and the smell of food cooking. It was enough to cheer our spirits and raise our hopes that we at least might be fed before we turned around and retraced our soggy footsteps back the way we had come. We opined that given the welcome (or lack thereof) we'd received from the neighbors along the way, there would be little hope of sharing our message with the inhabitants, but if only they would feed us, we would leave a blessing on the house, indeed.

We must have presented a sorry sight, to be sure, in our dripping coats and hats, but I hadn't thought we looked horrible enough to occasion the fright I saw in the face of the young woman who stepped out onto the porch, holding a huge hound by his collar close against her skirts. Though clearly a Lamanite by birth, her face was as nearly white with shock as any I have seen, and her eyes huge and dark. Elder Brown and I stopped still in the yard and removed our hats, trying to smile and win her confidence sufficient to prevent her loosing her dog, which by the curl of its upper lip didn't appear overjoyed to see us.

"Good day, ma'am," Elder Brown said. "We've walked many miles to bring you a message from God. Could we possibly sit and dry ourselves while we deliver it? We'd be most grateful."

The young woman looked at us, unsmiling, for what seemed an eternity. Then she murmured, "Just a minute," and disappeared into the house. Elder Brown and I looked at each other, hardly daring to hope we might be received. After a minute, she came back out, without the dog, and in a trembling voice told us that her father said we could come in. We thanked her, and leaving our hats and coats to drip on the porch, we stepped inside the little home. Beside the fireplace sat a gray-haired man with keen eyes and a beaked nose. He rose and came forward to peer at us, ignoring our outstretched hands.

"How do you do, sir?" I said, smiling as cordially as I could. He didn't smile in return, but turned to his daughter and said something I didn't understand. She looked at us nervously. "My father wants to know why you are laughing at him," she whispered.

Elder Brown and I immediately disposed of our smiles. "Please tell your father we are not laughing at him, but merely greeting him in the manner of the white man," Elder Brown said. "We are honored to be asked into his home, and we have a message for him regarding his ancestors."

Showing only the barest flicker of surprise, she turned and translated this for the old man, who broke into a torrent of speech and pointed at a box on a shelf beside the fireplace. She obediently went to the box and extracted a folded paper tied with ribbon. "My father wishes me to tell you that we own our land," she said to us. "This is our deed to it, and it is recorded in the courthouse in the white man's way. Our ancestors were forced to flee and leave their lands, but my father says that can no longer be—that this paper protects us."

"You are Cherokee?" I asked, remembering what I had heard about their people being driven from the South to reservations in Oklahoma.

She lifted her head proudly. "Eastern Cherokee," she replied. "My father's father paid for this land with white man's money that he earned, himself."

"Please explain to your father that we are not here about his land. The ancestors we have come to tell him about lived many generations before those who walked the Trail of Tears—many years before the white man ever came to this country."

She repeated these words in Cherokee, and the old man peered at us again before he spoke.

"He wishes to know how white men of this day can know anything of his ancestors who lived so long ago," the young woman stated.

"We have a book," Elder Brown explained. "It was written many hundreds of years ago by good men who lived on this land—this continent. Then it was hidden away in the earth until about a hundred years ago, when it was found and translated into English by a man chosen by God to do so. It tells the story of your ancestors, and other people who came to this land—where they came from and what happened to them."

"I have not heard of this book," she said, and I noticed that her fright was beginning to be replaced by curiosity. "What is it called?"

"The Book of Mormon," I told her. "It's like the Bible. Do you know the Bible?"

"The Bible is true," she said promptly. "I have studied it since I was a child."

"The Book of Mormon is true, too," I said. "It's scripture, just like the Bible, except it tells of God's dealings with the people on this land of the Americas. It also tells of a visit of Jesus Christ to this continent."

Her father was making impatient questioning sounds, not liking to be left out of the conversation, and she turned and gave him a rather lengthy explanation. I looked at Elder Brown, wondering if he, like I, was beginning to feel the swelling and trembling and warmth inside the chest that I have come to associate with the testifying of the Holy Ghost in this work.

Finally she turned back to us. "I have told my father what you said," she told us. "Also, I have told him that I

*believe you have a true message for us. If you have a copy
of the book you mention, I will know for sure."*

*I think we both were surprised at this, but I recovered
first, reached into the knapsack I had dropped at my feet,
and handed her a Book of Mormon. She took it reverently
in her hands, and her eyes filled with tears, though she kept
her chin up. She said something to her father, and he
replied, nodding his head.*

*"This is the book I was given in my dream, last night,"
she told us. "I saw two men coming to the house and handing me this book, and I was told to read it. It frightened me
when I saw you coming, just like in my dream, but I knew
I shouldn't send you away. My father says he wishes to hear
about the book, but first you must eat."*

*I was so excited I had almost forgotten about being so
hungry and tired, but she gave us a meal of stew and cornbread and fried apple pies that I will never forget. Afterward
we sat for three hours or more, teaching and explaining the
Book of Mormon and the gospel to that man and his daughter, and they were most attentive and intelligent, asking
many searching questions. It is worth my whole mission and
all its difficulties and disappointments, to have had this one
afternoon, though I hope there will be many more. We are
invited back. Praise God! I have heard of dreams or angelic
visitations preparing the way for missionaries, but this is the
first time it has happened to me! I am overwhelmed with
joy. Elder Brown and I hardly touched ground the whole
eight miles back to town, and though the rain continued to
come down, we were warmed and filled and happy as I
have never before been happy.*

Will looked up from the pages and smiled at Liz. "So what
do you think?" he asked gently. "Is this a treasure, or what?"

"Well, don't stop!" Liz said in mock indignation. "Did he convert his Indian maiden and her dad?"

Will gazed across the room. "Remember the grandmother I told you about, who bottled all the fruit and vegetables for her husband, and who left such an empty space in his life when she died? Well, she had big brown eyes and very dark hair before it turned gray—and she was from North Carolina."

"Will! Are you serious? Yes, you are. I remember now that you told me you were part Cherokee, that morning when I gave you breakfast! He not only converted her, he married her, didn't he? What a marvelous, marvelous story. And he tells it so well! I'm right there with him—I see the rain, and the cabin, and that proud old man by the fire. Wow! Thank you for sharing that with me."

"Can't think of anyone I'd rather share it with, except the kids, and they'll appreciate it more when they're a little older, though I plan to read it to them soon."

"And you said it was dry stuff!" Liz chided, as Will took a long drink of ginger ale.

"It is," he said, indicating his empty mug. "There—I'm rehydrated. Care to hear more, or is that enough for one evening?"

"I'd love to hear more—and I'm loving the bagpipes, too. What's that sprightly tune?"

"I think that's called 'Mairi's Wedding.' It almost makes *me* want to get up and dance, and a worse dancer you've never seen! Speaking of weddings, let me skip over the rest of Granddad's mission—he had mixed success—and get to the part about his own wedding. That's kind of interesting."

Liz curled up in the corner of the sofa and sipped her drink, enjoying the story, the music, and more than anything else, the man who provided them. It was a joy to listen to him read and to watch the play of emotions over his face as he did so.

He read of the occasional exchange of letters that had taken place between the young missionary returned to his Utah home and the Cherokee girl in that faraway cabin in the wooded hills of western North Carolina. The young man had thought seriously of marrying a certain young lady of his acquaintance, but compared to the direct, forthright honesty of Lucy, as the Indian girl's English name turned out to be, the flirting and giggling of his Utah girlfriend seemed flapperish and insincere, and he soon knew which he'd rather spend his life with. He wrote to Lucy and proposed marriage. She accepted, but conditionally—they would have to wait until her father died, as he was old and ill, and she felt duty bound to care for him in his own home for as long as he lived. Grant Parrish, as Will said his grandfather had been named, had had to be content with that. He waited for nearly two years until a letter came saying that the old gentleman had passed away, the farm was now in possession of Lucy's older brother, and she was free to come to Utah. Grant expressed his excitement and his misgivings at bringing Lucy out West and showing her Salt Lake City and the farm he had purchased in southern Utah County. Lucy had never seen a real city, only the town where she had boarded with a white family and gone to school, her father having realized that she needed to speak and read English to help him survive in what was increasingly a white man's world. But Lucy accepted it all with equanimity. She had made her decision to marry the young man she had seen in her dream, who had brought her the knowledge of her ancestors and a confirmation of the faith she'd already developed in Jesus Christ, and she set about loving and serving him and bearing his children with the same unflinching sense of duty with which she had cared for her father. Grant took to referring to her in his journal as 'my Lucy,' and his love for her was apparent. There were disappointments, however. His Lucy was

296

able to bear him only two children—a daughter and a son—and this supposed inadequacy she sorrowed over. She felt inadequate in other ways, too, around the women in her new neighborhood. Grant recorded that he more and more often found her in secret tears over some real or perceived slight from the women at church, who should have been her dearest friends. Gradually she stayed away from meetings more and more—sometimes attending long enough to partake of the sacrament and then slipping away to go home and study her scriptures in private. Grant grieved over that and reasoned with her, and counseled with the Church leaders, but Lucy's spirit had been wounded, and like a forest creature, she withdrew into her own place. In time it became a rare thing when Grant or the children could lure her outside their own house and yard on any pretext at all. She seemed content enough there with her little family, but would receive no visitors. Her home became her prison, and her prison her world.

"How sad, Will. Do you remember her as being withdrawn?"

"As a child, I didn't notice anything like that. She welcomed Barb and me, as her grandchildren, and I think my mother got along with her all right—but we were family, you see. I do know she never went anywhere with us when we visited. She would just say, 'I'll stay home and have your supper ready when you get back.'"

"Do you think she was agoraphobic?"

"Could have been, I guess."

"Bless her heart! She suffered far more from transplant shock than Meggie ever could, didn't she? And this was her home."

"This very house was built for her," Will agreed. "And reading this has made both my grandparents come alive for me in a way nothing else could." He tapped the cover of the black book. "I, of course, remember them as elderly people—but now I think of them as *whole* people with complete lifetimes."

"And so do I," Liz agreed. "Will, thank you for this wonderful evening. I can't remember when I've enjoyed anything more."

"It's been great for me, too. Come on, I'll walk you home."

They strolled slowly up the road, a nearly full moon lighting the way. The air had grown sweater-cool, and Liz shivered in her summery shirt. Will noticed and put his arm around her, rubbing her bare arm with his hand to warm her. She closed her eyes against the tide of feeling for him that rose within her and forced herself to think of something to say.

"I hope the kids are warm enough, sleeping outside."

"They'll be fine—they have sleeping bags. Elizabeth?"

"Yes?"

"Could we do this again, some time soon? Just us, I mean— not that we need to do the same thing. It's been so great to spend some time with you. Forgive an overworked word, but you're very special—very nice to be with."

"Well, so are you—and I'd love to repeat the evening whenever you like."

He gave her a long smile, his eyes shining darkly in the moonlight, and then bent to kiss her cheek. "One for Missy," he said softly. He kissed the other cheek. "One for Meggie. And one for me." The one for him was on her lips—brief and gentle and such a surprise that Liz barely found her voice to whisper, "Good night," as Will turned and left her.

29

For the next few days, Liz savored every moment of the magical evening she and Will had spent together. Even her walks with Francie in the cool twilight couldn't destroy her equanimity, although Francie's complaints about the symptoms of her pregnancy were frequent and vociferous. Liz gritted her teeth and tried to sympathize.

Helen Ashcraft came home, and Missy skipped joyously down the hill to tell Liz and everyone else how wonderful it was to have her mom now for company and how Helen wanted to get acquainted with everyone, but not just yet. She still felt fragile and shy in her newly resumed identity.

"But we called Dave," Missy confided to Liz. "It was really neat. He sounded like he was just in Springville or Spanish Fork, not clear over in Austria. He was so excited to talk to Mom, and she just cried a lot, like she keeps doing, because his voice had changed and she couldn't recognize it. But Dave, he started reminding her of things he did when he was younger—things she would remember—and he made her laugh, and he told her he was really still just the same kid, only bigger, and that he still loved her. And she kept saying, 'Oh, honey, I never meant to go away and leave you—I couldn't help it. Please forgive me.' "

Liz wiped her own eyes. "Missy, it's such a miracle! You realize that, don't you?"

"Sure. My dad and me, we're fasting this coming Sunday—not to ask for anything at all, but just to give thanks. My dad says this is the fifth greatest gift God ever gave him."

Liz looked up in surprise. "The fifth? What in the world are the first four?"

Missy ticked them off on her fingers. "The gospel, Mom marrying him in the first place, then Dave, and me."

"Oh—of course. Um, Missy—when you speak of 'the gospel,' what exactly do you mean?"

"Well, like—everything, you know—like how Jesus died for us, and paid for our sins, and all the commandments, and the scriptures—you know what I mean? And how Joseph Smith was a prophet, and the Church is true and all. That stuff."

"And when you say the Church is true, do you mean that just the Mormon church is true, or all the churches that believe in Jesus, all put together, are true?"

Missy frowned. "Well, Dave says all churches have some of the truth and do some good in the world, but our church is the same one Jesus started when he was on earth, except it was lost for a while, you know, after his apostles died, and people started to forget what was right and to argue and change things, and get all separated into different churches. That's why Heavenly Father picked Joseph Smith to bring back his true church, because by that time, people had things all mixed up and nobody knew for sure what was right and what wasn't. So God made Joseph Smith his prophet and told him what was true and gave him the Book of Mormon to go with the Bible to help straighten things out and to show that Jesus really was God's son, like the Bible says."

Liz looked at Missy fondly. "You seem to have things pretty

straight in your mind, kiddo! How is it you know all these answers to questions that millions of grown-ups struggle with all
their lives?"

Missy blushed. "Did I sound smart-alecky? I didn't mean
to."

"No, honey. You just sounded sure of yourself and what you
believe, and I wondered how you came to be that way at your
tender age."

"Well, before Dave left on his mission, he and Dad would
talk a lot, at night, you know? About stuff he'd learned at
BYU. And sometimes I'd listen. I guess I learned a lot that
way. Plus Primary, too. I've had a real good teacher this year.
It all seems pretty simple to me, the way she explains it."

"You're lucky," Liz said softly.

Missy shrugged and grinned. "You can learn all about it,
too," she said. "All you have to do is study and pray."

Liz nodded. "Okay, I'll keep at it."

"That's super! Megan's dad's been reading the Book of
Mormon."

"He has?"

"Yep. Megan said he found out his grampa was a Mormon
missionary, and it made him curious."

"Oh, yes—the journal he found. I wonder if he's finished
reading that."

"He has," Missy told her. "And he started reading it to the
kids. Megan thought it'd be boring, but she says it's not."

"No. No, it definitely isn't that."

"Did he read it to you, too? When was that?" The alert
interest in Missy's eyes warned Liz of danger.

"Oh, he read me a passage, a while back. I thought it was
interesting."

"Are you guys still just friends?"

"Yes, we're good friends."

"You're not planning to get married, yet?"

"Missy! You're treading on dangerous ground again. But since you ask, no—the subject hasn't come up, between us."

"Oh. Well, it's just that Megan wishes you would."

"Megan does! Did she tell you that?"

Missy nodded solemnly. "She talks about it all the time."

"Truly? She'd like her dad to marry me?"

"Sure! She loves you bunches."

"Well, that's really sweet of her. I'm fond of her, too."

"But you don't want to marry her dad?"

"Missy, I'm not even going to answer that."

"Okay, it's cool. Well, I'm going to run home now. Mom and I are cooking dinner together. She's going to teach me to make a kind of meat loaf that Dad really likes."

Liz nodded, her heart suddenly too full to allow her to speak. "Thank you," she whispered in a brief prayer as she watched the happy girl whistle for her dog and hurry away.

Two nights before school started, Will invited Liz to attend a get-acquainted barbecue hosted by the principal of his school for the faculty and staff. It was a pleasant affair, and Will, one of six new teachers, introduced Liz as "my neighbor and good friend, Elizabeth Ewell." Liz smiled, remembering Francie's prediction about all the young, single female teachers who wouldn't hesitate to flirt with a man like Will. There were several of those on the faculty, all right, and some were quite attractive. But Will stayed close beside her all evening, attentively bringing her anything she showed the least interest in eating or drinking.

"Now, Will, we don't want you to sacrifice any more fingers while you're with us—that's going beyond the call of duty. All right?" the principal remarked with a chuckle, as they stood in line for dessert.

Will's grin was wry. "I'm planning on keeping the ones I

have left," he agreed. "And I'm hoping to inspire safety-consciousness in all the students. Sometimes a negative example works best, don't you think? I'm well equipped to provide that!"

The principal clapped him on the shoulder and moved away.

"How exactly did that accident happen?" Liz asked, as they perched on the bench of a picnic table.

Will shook his head. "Just one of those sudden, unexpected things," he said. "Boy, this is good apple pie, but it needs a slice of cheese. Do you like cheese with apple pie? I'm going to see if they have any left from making the burgers. Want some?"

"No, thanks. You go ahead." Liz watched him stride away in search of the cheese, feeling that she had somehow touched a nerve that made him uncomfortable. Was he embarrassed because of his mutilated fingers? He didn't act as if he were, and yet he was obviously discomfited by mention of them.

She didn't bring up the subject again, and the rest of the evening proceeded normally, culminating in a long, leisurely conversation in her living room. It seemed they could talk endlessly on practically any topic, exploring each other's thoughts and attitudes, discussing his children, his work, her interests, their backgrounds and experiences. It was easy to relax with him, Liz realized. He was tolerant, easygoing, and rarely judgmental—so different from Brock. When she saw him to the door, it seemed natural to lift her face for his goodnight kiss, which was just a shade more lingering than the first had been but not nearly as lingering as she wished it to be. Gypsy took a personal interest in this gesture, stretching as tall against Liz as she could, as if to force them to include her in their embrace.

"Don't worry, Gypsy," Will said, ruffling the dog's ears

fondly. "I won't hurt your mistress. I care about her too, you know."

Liz went to bed that night bolstered by this declaration and fortified by the remembrance of Will's kiss.

On the first day of school, Liz felt absurdly lonely, just knowing that Will and his children would be gone most of the day. Missy was absent from the gray house up the hill, leaving Helen alone, and Marilyn Woodbine had to cope with all the needs of her youngest three with no help from the older ones. *How does Lolly stand it,* she wondered, *having had a houseful of lively children and then none, as they grew up and left? The first quiet days after the last one leaves for good must be awful.*

She went outside with the dogs to pick her ripe tomatoes and the two zucchini that had suddenly lengthened to a usable size. A coolness had crept into the air over the last few days that presaged autumn, yet all was still green and growing and in need of water. Liz dragged the hose and positioned it to soak the thirsty squash plants and then straightened up to see Helen Ashcraft walking slowly around her yard up the hill, gazing at the straggly and neglected areas that might once have been flower beds. She bent to pull an overgrown weed and toss it away. It was the first time Liz had seen Helen outside alone, or indeed, purposefully doing anything, and she felt a great swelling of gratitude inside her. Helen saw her and tentatively raised one hand in a wave, to which Liz responded cheerily. To her surprise, Helen left her yard and came slowly down the hill, Missy's puppy ambling happily in her wake. Liz walked down her drive toward the road to greet them.

"Hello," Liz said, when Helen was within earshot. "It's good to see you home again. How are you?"

"Very well, thank you," Helen responded. "You're Liz, aren't you? I've been wanting to thank you for everything you've done for Missy. She—" Helen's voice choked, and she dropped her face into her hands as the tears came. Liz paused only a second and then went to put her arms around Helen, who allowed herself a moment to cry before she found a tissue in her pocket and mopped at her eyes.

"I'm so sorry," she said. "I guess I'm still a little weak emotionally. I cry over everything."

"Oh, so would I, in your place," Liz told her, her own voice a little wavery. "Please, come and sit down and let's visit. Would you like to go inside?"

"No—no, if we could just sit out here? It feels so good to be outside on a morning like this."

They sat in the sunshine on the front steps. Helen smiled shakily at Liz. "As I was trying to say—I deeply appreciate your goodness to Missy. And to me, when I—when I first woke up and was so terribly confused."

"I've been glad to do whatever I could. In fact, I wish I'd done more for Missy. I'm afraid sometimes I get kind of wrapped up in my own interests and don't see what needs doing for other people. But I'm glad I was there to witness the miracle of your waking up. Believe me, that was a thrill like no other I've ever experienced."

Helen nodded. "It's still difficult for me to comprehend all that's gone on in the last eight years. Everyone seems so delighted that I came back from the condition I was in, but to me, all was confusion. Honestly, it's devastating to realize you've lost eight years of your life, to see that your children have virtually grown up without you, that you've been worse than useless to them . . ." Her tears began again, and she blinked them away impatiently. "I'm so sorry. Probably I shouldn't even try to talk to people until I'm more stable. Forgive me."

"It seems to me that crying is the most natural and probably the most healing thing you could do," Liz said gently. "It'd be a terrible shock to go through what you did. I could see how bewildered you were, recognizing your furniture but seeing it older than you remembered, wondering where your children were, why the house was different."

Helen nodded again, smiling. "Not recognizing Missy but wondering at her remarkable resemblance to the little girl I thought was your daughter. And then, when Wynn came, I— he looked older, of course, and worn—I thought he must be terribly ill! And all the time it was I who . . ." She shook her head. "They've told me about the bee stings, and so forth, but even so, I don't really understand what happened to me or how I came back—and neither do the doctors. I'm—I'm grateful I did, even now. It would be worse to—to one day 'wake up dead,' as they say, and realize I'd lost the whole remainder of my life. But still, I hope everyone can be patient with me while I try to adjust."

"I don't think there's any problem with that. You have a wonderful family—they've loved and cared for you through all your illness in a really remarkable way, and they're walking on clouds now because you're back."

Helen bowed her head. "I know," she said. "They're incredible, aren't they? Wynn's so patient and dear, and Missy is—she's all I ever wanted her to be. And my boy—my big, grown-up missionary—how I'd love to see him!"

"Well, you can be proud of him. He's a fine young man— handsome and decent, bright, sensitive."

"Wynn's done a great job with the children. I guess I wasn't very necessary to them, after all. They've done fine without me. I know, of course, that that's partly due to all you good folks who've helped with them when Wynn was at work. Missy has told me how good you've been to her. She told me about your plans for her room, too, and I wondered if you'd like to go ahead with that project?"

"Whatever you want," Liz answered. "I know we'd both like you to be involved, too—or just take over, if you'd prefer."

"I'd like to help, but I'd value your advice and assistance in actually shopping for things. I don't feel at all confident to drive or to shop by myself yet. It's amazing how different things can seem after eight years—away."

"Absolutely. Just let me know when you're ready to begin."

"I think I'd like a few weeks more to get back into a normal daily routine, and then I want to begin trying some creative things. They tell me I'm in good general health, but I still tire so easily—probably because of the emotional strain."

"That can be exhausting," Liz agreed.

Helen was quiet, gazing pensively up the hill at her house. "Liz, may I ask you, as an honest observer—how did I behave?"

"I expect Wynn and Missy have told you . . ."

"Yes, but—I'd like to hear from someone outside the family, how I acted. I can't imagine . . ."

"You were always very gracious, very polite. It was just as if you lived in a different world than the rest of us, and so what you said didn't always make sense to us. One time you remarked to me that you felt the calendar was too full of days, and another time you said something about the mountains falling. It was as though you had some fears that you didn't quite know how to express. But please don't think you ever did anything—you know, bizarre, or anything. You were just in a sort of dream state. Sometimes you would sit for a couple of hours and just watch TV, or watch the puppy playing, or whatever moved—and not say or do anything. But you would eat, with a little prompting, and help to care for yourself when they told you to. I guess you don't remember anything at all of that time?"

"Not a thing. I don't remember the hike and the bees, either. My last memory that I've been able to identify was

307

shopping for a ball and bat for Davey's birthday—and that was almost two weeks before the bee incident. So I didn't—you know—make embarrassing scenes or anything?"

Liz shook her head. "Not at all, that I know about. You've gone to church and for walks with Wynn, and you went to see Dave off at the airport and had lunch at McDonald's afterward, according to Missy—and I've never heard of any embarrassing incidents."

"Oh, thank heaven. I was afraid they were just sparing me the awful details." Helen smiled shakily. "Thank you again, Liz, for everything. I hope we'll be friends."

Impulsively, Liz leaned over to hug her. "We *are* friends," she told her. "And you have other friends waiting in the wings—Lolly Tucker, Marilyn Woodbine—and all the good women in your church. You're surrounded with friends."

"If they're all half as understanding as you, I'll be truly blessed," Helen said. "Bishop Tucker's been so kind, I'm sure his wife must be, too. I'm trying to get up the courage to go to church, but maybe I'd better meet a few people individually, first."

"What does your doctor say?"

"He says to proceed at my own speed and do whatever I feel ready to do."

"I'm glad you felt ready to talk to me."

"So am I. Missy assured me you were approachable—although she did say you liked to be quite private, and I hope I haven't invaded that privacy."

"Not at all." *I'm labeled forever,* Liz thought wryly.

They stood up, and Helen smiled as the three dogs came roughhousing across the lawn, running circles around each other, but still interested in what their people were planning to do.

"I can tell they're related," Helen remarked.

"Yes, I gave Missy her pup," Liz said.

"Thank you for that, too. He's given her a lot of pleasure and company, and I find I enjoy having him around, too, especially now that school's started."

"They are good company," Liz agreed, watching as Missy's pup reluctantly separated himself from the antics of his mother and brother to trail after Helen as she waved good-bye and walked back up the road.

Liz went to change the position of the hose so that it would soak her ever-thirsty stand of corn. Her attention was caught by the slamming of a car door, and she looked up to see Mr. Earl Christensen coming through the field from his and Woodbines' road. His eyes squinted against the sun, and his mouth was puckered as he leaned forward to ask in a hoarse half-whisper, "Was that that crazy woman here talkin' to you? I never seen her talk to nobody or go anywheres by herself before. What'd she want, if it made any sense, which I doubt?"

Liz smiled sweetly. "She was just thanking me for being nice to her little girl while she wasn't able to care for her. She's better, now, of course—certainly not crazy—and she made perfectly good sense."

Mr. Christensen tilted his head as if he thought the change of position would aid his hearing. "You telling me she ain't crazy no more?"

"It's like a miracle, Mr. Christensen. She suddenly woke up out of some kind of half-dream state, and she's just as rational and normal as you and I. The doctors don't really understand how it happened, but it's the most thrilling thing I've ever seen."

He stared at her, disbelief and avid interest fighting for control of his features. "Nah—you're pullin' my leg, right? I expect you think it's none of my business, and I expect you're right on that—but I've seen that woman before, tried to talk

309

to her when she was outside with her poor bedeviled husband, and she was crazy as a loon. They don't just suddenly 'get better' from something like that."

"That's why I said it was like a miracle. And I'm sure you'll have a chance, sooner or later, to talk to her yourself."

"Well—won't last, I'll betcha, even if she is some better for a spell. No such thing as miracles, anyway."

Liz shrugged. "Helen Ashcraft believes in them—and so do her husband and kids." *And I'm beginning to, as well.*

Mr. Christensen frowned and shook his head in disapproval. "Not likely," he muttered, as he turned back toward his car.

"Whatever else life may be," Liz told Gypsy and Tracker as they went inside the house, "it's never boring. At least, not with you guys and these neighbors."

30

L iz didn't see Will or the children for several days, nor did she wish to intrude on them, but she began to feel lonely. It was with delight that she spotted Megan pushing Nicky in his stroller up the road to Missy's house on Saturday afternoon.

"Megan!" she called. "Stop in for a minute, and I'll give you a plate of cookies to take with you."

"Oh, that's all right," Megan responded. "You don't have to always feed us."

"No, come on—these are good, and I was planning to share them with you guys and the Ashcrafts, anyway. I made a double batch just for that purpose."

Megan turned the stroller up into the driveway but made no move to take Nicky out or to go inside. She stood and waited while Liz hurried inside to wrap a paper plateful for each family.

I feel like the wicked witch in "Hansel and Gretel," she muttered to herself, *using goodies to lure children to my house. Is this what I'm going to grow into—a lonely old woman baking cookies to curry the favor of the neighborhood kids?*

"So how's school?" she asked, withholding the cookies while she waited for Megan to answer.

"It's okay."

"Just okay? Is it very different from your school in Virginia?"

"It's fine."

It was unlike Megan to be so uncommunicative, and Liz wondered what was wrong. "Are you sure it's fine?" she asked kindly. "You don't seem especially bouncy today. Is anything wrong?"

"I'm sorry. No, nothing's wrong. School's fine."

"And how has it been for Tim and your dad?"

"Okay, I reckon. Tim seems to like it, and I guess Dad has a couple of kinda wild classes that he's having to tame before he can even let them think about using any tools. But other than that, it's fine."

Liz stooped down to greet Nicky, who grinned and batted at her with one plump hand. "I think it'd be scary to try to teach a bunch of unruly kids to use power tools, especially after his own experience."

Megan frowned. "What do you mean?"

"Well, I'm thinking of the accident that cost him his fingers. That's bad enough, but trying to keep a class full of rowdy boys from doing the same thing—that's a lot of responsibility."

Megan looked at her strangely. "Is that what Dad told you, about how he lost his fingers?"

Liz straightened. "Well, yes—I think so—isn't that what happened?"

Megan shrugged, her eyebrows arched elegantly. "I guess that must be what he wants you to think," she said, reaching for the cookies. "I'd better go, now. Missy's waiting for me. Thanks for the cookies."

"You're—welcome," Liz said, staring after her in perplexity, watching the girl's determined march up the hill, cookies riding precariously atop the fringed awning of the stroller. "Now what was that all about? And if Will didn't lose his fingers in a shop accident, what was it, and why the secrecy?" She went inside and sat at her place at the small drop-leaf dining table where she and Will had breakfasted that rainy morning nearly six months earlier, trying to recall his exact words. What were they? He'd made light of it—something about had she ever known a shop teacher with all his fingers—was that it? But had he actually said that was how he'd lost them? She wasn't sure. And then at the faculty barbecue, he'd avoided telling her about the incident, although surely the principal had the same impression she did, judging from his remarks. It was strange—strange that Will, usually so honest and forthcoming, should deliberately mislead people on such a subject. Why did it matter how he'd lost his poor fingers?

Suddenly she was at Lagoon, again—the sun warm on her back as they prepared to leave the swimming area, and Will turned partly away from her as he stripped off his wet T-shirt, but not before she'd caught a glimpse of the angry welted scar on his chest. Was whatever had caused that scar the same incident that had taken his fingers? Then why not say so? What was the big mystery? And why had Megan been so curt with her? Liz folded her arms on the table and rested her head on them.

It's not fair! something inside her protested. *Just when I was starting to feel the tiniest bit of confidence that Will was beginning to care for me, and that things might work out with his children if he did—this happens. Have I said or done something to offend or alienate them? Is it just Megan's moodiness, or more?*

Liz moped about the house for a while, debating the possible consequences of ignoring the situation versus confronting Will about it, and chose to postpone making a decision. Instead, she took herself to a shopping mall in Orem and indulged in a new fall wardrobe—several sweaters and pants, a longish corduroy skirt, some long-sleeved shirts, and one rather elegant teal woolen dress that would serve for dressy occasions, if dressy occasions should happen to be part of her fall and winter schedule. She added a comfortable pair of loafers and some waterproof boots for slogging around in the snow and then treated herself to a solitary dinner at a Chinese restaurant, during which she browsed among the four paperbacks she had picked up. One was a newly published mystery she would share with Lolly, but even it failed to hold her interest for long. She kept wondering what Will was doing this Saturday evening, and whether Megan had reported to him their rather stiff conversation of earlier that day. She grimaced as she broke open her fortune cookie and read, "Sorrow and joy are two sides of the same coin." *Don't I know it!* she thought wryly.

She took her purchases home and dropped them on the floor by her bed. Normally it would be a source of pleasure to reexamine and tuck away a collection of new clothes, but somehow she didn't have the heart for it. She put some soothing music on her stereo and went to bed early, dropping into a restless and troubled sleep.

On Monday afternoon, she avoided Francie's company and took a long walk by herself, enjoying the fresh air and the breeze that whipped at her hair. She circled around by Woodbines', debating whether to stop in, but Marilyn spotted her and decided the matter for her, calling to her from the kitchen door on the side of the house.

"Come and talk to me while I languish," Marilyn said. "I've bottled a million pears today, so Tom and the kids are doing their dinner thing, bless them."

They sat on the porch steps.

"Knowing the kind of volume you do things in, I'm afraid to ask how serious you are about the million pears," Liz said with a smile.

314

Marilyn stretched. "I guess it only feels like a million," she said. "I hate doing pears—they take forever. They have to be peeled, and the cores scooped out—and the juice drips off my elbows and makes me itch. But we love them best of all the bottled fruits, so I figure it must be worth it. I did get some lovely big ones this year, and they worked up faster than the cheaper tiny ones would, so I guess I shouldn't complain. And I'm not, really. I'm just tired."

"Why didn't you call me to help? I would've come."

"Hmm," said Marilyn, giving her a sideways look. "Does the offer still hold? I have some more that should be ready in a couple of days. Pears don't all ripen at once, so they usually take a while to finish. I want to make some old-fashioned pear preserves, too—the kind you cook forever until they're dark and syrupy. There's nothing better with warm bread and cheese."

"Yum. I'd love to help, honestly. Just let me know."

"You've got yourself a deal. So—how's your life?"

Liz shrugged. "I feel like everything's on hold, right now."

"How so?"

"Has Megan been over lately?"

"She was here last night for a while."

"Did she say—is anything bothering her?"

"Well, she seemed a little quiet, now that you mention it, but I didn't think anything of it. Why do you ask?"

"It's just that she had become so sweet and affectionate, and I thought we had a good friendship going, but Saturday she was downright chilly to me—almost rude—and I wondered what in the world I've done to upset her. I honestly can't think of anything."

"Have you asked Will if she's said anything to him?"

"I haven't talked to Will for over a week."

"Oh."

"I feel funny going and asking. I mean, Will and I parted on very good terms the last time I saw him—and as far as I can recall, so did Meggie and I—and suddenly there's this blanket of silence and this very definite coolness on Meggie's part. I know Will's been busy with school beginning and all—so I don't know if not hearing from him means anything or not. I'm just confused." Liz was tempted to mention the mystery about Will's fingers, too, but felt constrained by respect for his feelings.

"Would you want me to talk to Megan and see what I can find out?"

"I don't know," Liz said miserably. "That might make it worse if she knew I was concerned. I don't want to blow this up into anything bigger than it is. Maybe it'll just pass."

"Could be. I'll keep my eyes and ears open, though, just in case."

"I'd appreciate that."

They chatted of other things until Marilyn's children proudly called her to dinner, at which point Liz declined their invitation to join them and crossed the field to her own place. She allowed herself only one quick glance down the hill at Will's house before she went inside. All seemed quiet. Were they having dinner? Working on lessons? Perhaps reading from Grandfather's journal?

None of your business, Elizabeth. They'll invite you to be part of their lives when and if they want you to be. It was not a comforting thought.

September first was a gray day with a steady but light rainfall that cooled the air considerably. Liz was grateful for the coolness that eased the heat from the canning kettles in Marilyn's kitchen. She was also grateful to be there, doing something useful that occupied her hands. Marilyn chatted companionably while they worked, and, seeming to sense that

Liz didn't feel especially talkative, carried most of the conversation herself, avoiding painful subjects. They spoke of gardening, books, music, world events—and when the pears were done, they made sandwiches and fed the children. Then, while the little ones napped, they concocted huge salads for themselves that Marilyn served with homemade French bread and old-fashioned ice cream sodas.

"Oh, Marilyn—thanks," Liz said, as they leaned back in their chairs, tired and replete. "I needed this, today—all of it."

"So did I," Marilyn replied. "It's such fun to have a friend close by. I mean, I love Lolly, but she's busy with Tuck, and a generation older than I. Helen, of course, hasn't been available—and frankly I have a hard time communicating with Francie, except on a very superficial level."

"I hear you. Have you talked with Helen, yet?"

"I haven't."

"She's really sweet and almost apologetic for having been ill—as though it were her fault."

"What an adjustment to have to make—for the whole family—although it's a happy one. Bishop Tucker was saying that they'll probably be going to counseling as a family for quite some time. Can you imagine? It's almost like having someone resurrected from the dead!"

"It is, isn't it? Missy seems happy, but now she'll have another parent to answer to and possibly not quite as much freedom as she's had to run here and there."

"But also not as much need to do that. And not as much responsibility around the house for meals and such. I wonder if she'll feel displaced at all as Helen takes over more and more of the housework and cooking?"

Liz nodded. "Probably that's one of the things they'll address in counseling. Helen is already teaching Missy some cooking skills and recipes."

"Isn't that amazing? How must she feel? How would I feel, if I woke up eight years down the road, and the little girl in there napping was suddenly eleven years old, and Rod was twenty-five, and Suzanne twenty-two?" Marilyn's eyebrows quirked. "Hmm—doesn't sound too bad, actually!"

Liz laughed. "I'm sure there are times when you feel like jumping ahead a few years."

"The notion comes, but it soon passes. To tell the truth, I don't want to miss a moment, even the tough ones. And I look at Rod and Suzanne and realize how quickly time really does pass. It doesn't seem so long ago that they were the ones napping after lunch."

"Sunrise, sunset . . ."

"Exactly. That song dissolves me to a puddle of tears because I'm living the truth of it. So is Helen, of course, but in a greatly exaggerated sense."

"No wonder she cries easily. She says she can't seem to stop."

"I hope people will treat her well and not like some kind of nine-day wonder. She's bound to be sensitive about that."

"She is," Liz agreed. "She asked me to tell her how she acted during her illness. She was afraid she had been an embarrassment to her family, but I tried to set her mind at ease on that point. Well, just talking about Helen's situation puts my few problems into perspective! I have nothing to complain about."

She rose to go, and Marilyn gave her an impulsive hug. "Any problems of the heart can be painful to go through," she said. "I hope yours resolve themselves in the very happiest way—and soon."

"Thanks. I just hope I haven't offended or hurt anyone. I never meant to."

"It may be that Will's just doing some thinking, as well as

being busy with school. As for Meggie—she's an adolescent girl. Maybe there doesn't need to be any more explanation than that."

"Maybe you're right."

Liz walked home smiling to herself, warmed and cheered by Marilyn's friendship, hoping her theories were correct.

As the days went silently by, however, she felt increasingly certain that all was not well in her relationship with Will and his family and increasingly bewildered as she tried to identify a cause for the breach.

She walked by their house one evening after sunset, and through the open doorway, saw Will framed in the lamplight of his living room, apparently engrossed in a book, sitting on the sofa where she had sat while he read to her from his grandfather's journal. The sight of him caused an almost physical pain that stopped her in her tracks, and she felt so strongly drawn to him that she nearly stepped up to the door and called his name. Just then she heard Megan's voice, calling, "Dad! I need help with my math," and she forced herself to continue her walk as he arose from the sofa and went to his daughter's aid.

31

As September progressed, the colors changed on the higher reaches of the mountainside—first a sprinkling of red here and there among the green and then a preponderance of red, then yellow patches appeared, and finally all faded to russet as October approached. The valleys were still predominantly green, however, and Liz's marigolds were at the height of their glory. Production on her squash and tomato plants had slowed in response to the dry days and cooler nights. Tuck's apples were harvested and either sold or placed in cold storage, and Liz had a large box of them taking up the lower shelf in her refrigerator. She had gone to trade books with Lolly, as had become their custom, and received in addition all the fruit she could possibly use.

"It's one thing we have to share," Lolly explained when Liz protested. "Good neighbors like you don't need to go buying apples at store prices when we have such an abundance. Now, sit down and tell me how things are going for you."

Reluctant to hurt Lolly's feelings by hurrying away, Liz sat down and told her about the correspondence course she had just completed and of the new ones she had enrolled in—Comparative Religion and Introduction to Psychology.

"Well, my goodness, you're ambitious!"

"Not really," Liz said with a small smile. "If I were really ambitious, I'd be out developing a career instead of just puttering around at home. And—maybe I will, one day. I'm really interested in home decorating—interior design—that sort of thing. But there are so many things I want to learn in addition to that. This first course just whetted my appetite."

"Funny thing about us humans—we like to keep on learning, don't we? I think that's one reason I love to read so much. I'd like to get out and travel all over the world, if I could, and find out how everybody lives and thinks. But Tuck, he's pretty much a homebody—has to be, with the farm and all—so when I get cabin fever or want to get out and go, I just start another book. I love to read about England and Scotland, Greece, Russia and China, and—well—lots of places. But you've done some traveling, haven't you?"

Liz nodded. "A little, mostly because of the Navy. I've lived in five states besides Utah and traveled to Europe and Brazil for vacations. But there are lots of other places I'd like to see, too—the New England states, Canada, the Pacific Northwest, Ireland, Spain, Japan, Egypt. It would be fun to go almost anywhere, I think, if you were with somebody compatible. Someone you enjoyed being with—sharing things with."

Lolly nodded. "That goes for all of life's experiences, don't you think? Tuck and me, we can have fun going for a ride, or watching an old movie on TV, or sorting apples. And much as I'd like to see all those places I mentioned, they wouldn't mean half as much if he wasn't with me. You get kind of dependent on each other when you've been married as long as we have."

"I'm sure that's true," Liz said wistfully. "When the marriage is solid and good, anyway. And when it isn't, the most exotic or beautiful place in the world seems kind of—blah."

"Is that how it was for you in Brazil and Europe?"

"Brazil was still pretty good—at least I thought so. Europe was miserable."

"Bless your heart. I'd sure like to see you find somebody wonderful."

"Yes, well . . ." Liz shrugged. "Maybe someday, if I really get lucky."

"I don't mean to come across like Missy, but secretly I kind of hoped you'd take a shine to Will Parrish. He seems such a fine fellow to me."

"He is," Liz said. "But I don't think I fit the bill for him."

"Now, how can that be? He said . . ." Lolly bit off her words with a guilty little smile. "I am meddling, aren't I? Oh, dear— Missy must have learned it from me! I'm sorry."

"It's okay—go ahead and meddle just a little more. What was it Will said?"

"Oh, it was a while back. He was kind of asking questions about you, you know—in a way that made Tuck and me think he was more than a little interested."

"What kind of questions?"

"Well, let's see—something about how did you feel about children—and I knew he meant his children—and whether your ex-husband pays you regular alimony. I said I thought he did—that's right, isn't it?"

"Yes. The Navy sees to that."

"And then he said something that wasn't exactly about you, but it made me think of you—how'd he put it? He said 'I feel so grateful that my granddad's house was right here instead of anywhere else. I can't imagine any place or any people better for me and the kids than this place and all you people. Especially for me—I feel like a new man since I've come here.' That's pretty much what he said."

"Oh—well, but—he surely was speaking of all the neighbors, collectively—not me. You and Tuck have been good to him, and so has everyone else."

"It wasn't me and Tuck, nor the Woodbines or Ashcrafts, and certainly not Francie and Eric or Mr. Earl Christensen that brought back the shine to that boy's eyes, my dear—it was you. Ever since he got acquainted with you, he started to heal from his sorrows. We could see it, both of us. Tuck remarked on it, himself—and he's a pretty fair judge of folks' feelings and character, having the spirit of discernment like he does—being a bishop, you know."

Liz wasn't sure how to answer that. "The thing is, I haven't talked to Will or the children much since school started," she finally admitted. "In fact, I think they're angry or upset with me about something. I have no idea what."

Lolly frowned. "Is that so? He sure hasn't mentioned anything like that to me."

"Lolly, Will hasn't spoken to me for over a month," Liz said miserably, afraid that tears would well up and overflow if she stayed much longer in Lolly's motherly presence. "The last time we were together, he was very warm and friendly and talked about asking me out again soon. Then—nothing. And Megan started acting really chilly. I don't understand it."

Lolly pursed her lips and closed her eyes. "Trying to think exactly when it was he mentioned you," she said. "Believe it was only about two weeks ago, best I can recall. Hmm. Tell you what—why don't you take the initiative this time? Go straight to Will and ask him if you've offended him or his family in any way?"

"After all this time, I know I must have."

"Well, just let him know you didn't mean to, and that you don't know what it's all about. He's a decent man—he won't bite your head off."

Liz sighed. "I'll—think about it. And thanks, Lolly—for everything. For caring."

"Of course I care! And look at it this way, honey—isn't it better to find out what's troubling him than to give up and never know? Likely it's just some simple misunderstanding you could clear up in a minute."

"I hope so," Liz said fervently. "If it isn't, I might—well, I've thought of moving away."

"Now, don't do that! My word, child, you can't do that. We all love you too much!"

Liz read the sincerity in Lolly's eyes. "Why?" she asked softly.

Lolly hugged her tightly, patting her back as she might pat Missy's in a comforting moment. "Because you're a beautiful and unique daughter of God," she whispered. "Because you're you."

Liz closed her eyes and allowed herself a moment to absorb the warmth, physical and emotional, that came from Lolly's gesture. Then she gently detached herself and turned away.

"Thank you," she whispered.

For five days, she battled with herself about taking Lolly's advice. Then one golden Sunday afternoon after lunch, when she assumed Nicky would probably be napping, she made herself walk through the orchard toward Will's back door, Gypsy and Tracker sniffing on expeditions of their own. She had seen Missy and Megan heading toward Missy's house not long before, and it was one of those strange, quiet Sundays that the Mormons seemed to have from time to time, when no meetings were held in their chapel. She paused just inside the orchard and took a deep breath. Then she sent up a silent prayer for help as she plunged through the orchard grass and across the yard.

Tim answered her knock, his eyebrows rising in uncon-cealed boyish surprise when he saw her.

"Uh—hi," he said uncertainly and called over his shoul-der, "Dad! Miz Ewell's here."

"How're you doing, Tim?" Liz asked, mustering up a smile for the little boy. "How's school?"

"It's good," he answered. "Dad!" He glanced quickly at her. "I'll go get him," he told her.

"If he's not busy," Liz replied as he turned away. She waited, her pulse hammering in her throat, until she heard Will's footsteps approaching.

"Elizabeth—how are you?" he said, his face unsmiling but concerned. "What can I do for you?"

Love me. Forgive me, for whatever . . . "Could we talk for a few minutes?" she asked. "Or am I interrupting something?"

"Not at all. Come on in—or shall we sit outside?" He ges-tured toward a pair of lawn chairs at the edge of the orchard.

"Outside's fine." She turned and led the way to the chairs. Will leaned forward in his, his hands clasped loosely before him, a small frown creasing his forehead. Gypsy came and rolled over at his feet, and he rubbed her belly absently.

"So how've you been, Elizabeth?" His voice was gentle.

"I'm all right. Just—confused."

"How's that?"

"Well, we haven't talked for a long time, have we? In fact, it's been over a month—nearly a month and a half. It—it may surprise you that I've kept count, but I have. I know you must be busy with school, but—but then, the children haven't been over, either, and Megan's been noticeably cool—and so I guess I'm slow, but I've finally realized I must have done something to offend all of you."

"Have the kids been rude? I won't allow that."

"Not—rude. Just not happy and talkative like they used to

be. Truly, Will, I don't know what I did, but I'm so sorry for whatever it was . . ."

"To my knowledge, you haven't done a thing to offend any of us. I'll speak to them."

"No, please don't. There must be something. Maybe I should ask Megan, herself. I'll do that sometime soon. Don't worry about it." She forced her voice to be bright. "And how is everything going for you? Is school a success?"

"We're all adjusting. I'm enrolled in a couple of night classes to go toward my Utah certification, so I've been pretty occupied. And I've—had a lot on my mind."

What, Will? Please share with me . . . "Anything that I can help with?"

His smile was small and wistful. "Nothing that I could ask of you," he said. "Just some things I need to work out for myself."

Liz tossed aside her pride. "I've missed you," she said. "Really missed you—a lot."

Will ducked his head and examined the denim fabric stretched over his knees. "I've missed you, too," he said in a low voice.

"What did I do, Will, to upset our friendship? What did I say?"

He shook his head, but didn't look at her. "Not a thing. Not one thing, Elizabeth. I'm sorry."

Then it must be that you've regretted how far you let our relationship progress—that you've realized you don't really feel for me what you thought you might be feeling on one romantic summer evening—and you're trying to back off gracefully. Or maybe you've met someone else, as Francie predicted.

Liz stood up. "I'm sorry too, Will. I'll go now. Please don't say anything to the children. It's all right."

He rose and looked at her, misery evident in his eyes.

"Elizabeth, I value our friendship. I'm glad just to know that you're there, up the hill. I'm not angry with you for any reason."

"All right. Thanks. Good-bye, Will."

"I'll be seeing you."

Yes, and I'll see you—and I'll still wonder what's wrong, and why you don't want to be frank with me about it—and I'll think about what we might have had together—and it'll drive me wild, and I won't be able to stay here. I'll have to find somewhere else and start all over, only this time I won't be so romantic to think that just because I find someone attractive and—yes, lovable—that he'll feel the same about me. I can get over you, Will Parrish, but I can't do it here.

Liz bought a paper and quietly set about searching for a rental house that had room for Gypsy and Tracker to run and a policy that allowed them to. It wasn't easy to find anything in that category that she could afford or that she would feel comfortable inhabiting. Most places that allowed two dogs were either so run down that the owners knew the dogs could do no noticeable damage or so expensive that any potential doggy damage was well compensated in advance. She spent hours driving from one community to another, following leads and looking at houses, but none of them spoke to her the way the little brick bungalow had. It was, she admitted, a depressing sort of search—looking for a house she didn't want, so that she could move away from people she didn't want to leave. The searching occupied her days, however, got her out into the fall sunshine, and gave her a sense of purpose, albeit a sad one. Evenings were spent before her fireplace, reading, studying, and listening to music behind closed door and shades. She admitted to herself that she had gone against the blueprint she had adopted for restructuring her life by allowing herself to be drawn into the lives of her neighbors. Now they were a part of her and she of them, and it was painful to separate herself from the little community she had grown to love. Several times over those days she called out, "Not today, Missy," when she saw the sun glinting on the girl's fair head as she approached the door. It wasn't, after all, quite so important to be kind to Missy, now that she had her mother back. Tuck and Lolly seemed absorbed in their preparations for winter, and Marilyn was occupied with PTA, church, and the needs of her numerous children. Liz avoided walking with Francie by simply being unavailable whenever Francie could go. And as for Will and the children, she tried to pretend they didn't exist—that they weren't just down the hill doing homework and munching apples and reading Grandfather's journal and making plans and being a family.

It didn't do to picture Nicky, cuddly in warm pajamas, climbing out of his crib—or Tim, frowning and chewing absorbedly on his lower lip as he read an engrossing book— or Megan, trying valiantly to be too sophisticated to show how desperately she missed her mom. It certainly didn't do to imagine Will, the lines deepening beside his mouth as he dealt with whatever was troubling him, the light in his hazel eyes dimmed and almost extinguished as he struggled alone with his problems. Yet that was exactly what Liz did, night after night when the fire in the grate had died down and the ever chillier canyon breezes whined at the corners of her house. Gypsy and Tracker would roll over and sigh or whimper in their dreams. Liz, watching them, wondered if she whimpered in hers.

There was a car in her driveway one late afternoon when she came back from one of her fruitless searches—a white Pontiac with a bumper sticker that proclaimed it to be a rental car. It was empty.

"Who in the world?" she wondered, as she pulled to one side and parked. She could hear Gypsy and Tracker's discordant duet coming from the house, sounding as though they had barked themselves hoarse. Liz allowed herself a moment of hope that the visitor might be Dorrie Stanford, looking her up as she had promised she would on her next visit to her relatives in Provo.

It wasn't Dorrie. Liz stopped dead in her tracks as an all-too-familiar male figure sauntered around the corner of the house. Brock hadn't changed in any apparent way—he still ambled with his hands in his pockets, his eyes narrowed as he examined, evaluated, and judged what he saw. He stopped when he saw her, and then slowly came forward, a small, sardonic grin twisting his features. With just that expression, Liz felt once again weighed in the balance and found wanting.

"So, Lizzie, it's true what I've always heard."

"What are you doing here?"

"Yep, it's true. I've always heard it said that you can take the girl out of the country, but you can't take the country out of the girl. So here you are, running true to form, hiding in this incredible backwater, and following the bent of your noble ancestors—growing a tomato patch. Still have a liking for yappy dogs, too, I hear." He gestured toward the house, where Gypsy and Tracker's cries had grown more agitated.

"What do you want, Brock?"

"Oh, I just decided I'd like to see how you're spending the very generous alimony check you receive every month." He cast another disparaging look around and shook his head. "Either the rents are horrendous here in 'Ew-tar,' or there's some sort of value here that doesn't meet the eye."

A small, cold lump formed in the pit of Liz's stomach. "I think you may assume the second."

"Or maybe you're saving up for something big—another European vacation or a mountaintop mansion?"

"I don't know why you'd be interested, unless you're hoping to persuade the judge to order a reduction in alimony."

"Nah—I didn't come to fight about money."

"Why *did* you come, Brock?"

"I came to see you, Lizzie—to see how you're getting along on your own. Aren't you going to invite me in?"

"Why? So you can make fun of how I've decorated my home? I don't think so. As you can see, I'm doing just fine. Actually, I am planning to move, soon, so you needn't think this is my permanent residence. But I've enjoyed living here—it's been wonderful in many, many ways. I . . ." Liz was embarrassed and angry that her voice, breaking, betrayed the image of iron control and aloof coolness she wanted to present.

His grin reappeared. "So—you haven't changed all that much. Still the emotional little woman. But I'll say this—you're looking good, Lizzie. The mountain air must agree with you."

Liz was silent. She didn't need his compliments, couched as they were in thinly disguised criticisms. She had received compliments—validations—from someone else whose opinion she had learned to value far more than Brock's.

"Hey! I just thought it might be nice to—you know—go out to dinner, for old times' sake. I have a few days' leave before I report in at the naval air station in Pensacola. I've been transferred, so I decided to stop over and look you up. That's really why I'm here."

"I don't think it's necessary to go to dinner, thank you anyway. But you'll find plenty of restaurants and motels in Provo to make you comfortable."

"For pete's sake, Liz, can't you even be civilized? What's wrong with a little dinner together? Do you have a date or something?"

Liz raised her eyebrows. "A date—an uncivilized woman like me?"

"All right, I'm sorry. That was uncalled for. But you're being stubborn and unreasonable. I had no idea you were so bitter."

"I don't feel bitter, Brock. I wish you well. I am simply not interested in spending time with you. I'm sorry."

Liz became aware of Missy, crossing the yard behind him, her blue eyes alert and curious. When Missy heard the name Brock, she stopped, teetering forward on her toes, and then changed her direction and headed speedily down through the orchard.

Brock stepped closer and half-sat against the fender of his rented car. "You know—the truth is, I've missed you, Liz."

Liz didn't reply. She gazed off at the purple mountains, knowing that Missy would tell at least Megan, and possibly Will, that Brock was here. But why would they care? She was nothing to them.

"I really have missed you, babe. Maybe we didn't—uh, you know—appreciate each other enough, before. But just looking at you now, I see why I've been missing you. You look different, somehow. I can't say exactly what it is—have you lost weight? And your hair looks good that way."

"Excuse me, I need to let the dogs out."

Brock's smirk returned. "Should I get in my car? Are they vicious?"

"You never know. It depends on whether they take a liking to you or not." Liz opened her front door and the dogs tumbled out, whining in pleasure at her presence and then aggressively lunging to check out the new arrival. Liz smiled to herself to see that Brock was backed up against the white car, his hand on the door handle. The dogs sniffed and barked, circling around him, glancing back at Liz for their orders. She deliberately waited a few minutes before calming them. They rushed to relieve themselves, then came back to stretch out on

331

their tummies between Liz and Brock, watchful, trying to sense the reason for the hostility they felt emanating from Liz. She waited, her eyes daring him to denigrate her dogs' breed or appearance.

"So, I—guess you felt the need for some watchdogs way out here by yourself, huh? A lot different from the places we've lived, isn't it?"

"It certainly is," Liz agreed readily.

"Why Utah, Lizzie? Why here?"

Liz shrugged, unwilling to share with him the need she had felt for this sane haven. "Why not?"

"Well, it's the back of beyond! I had a devil of a time even finding you."

"I'm still not sure why you bothered."

He looked at his shoes, spit-polished fringed loafers. "Truth or consequences? Okay—I came to see if there's any hope of us getting back together again. I thought maybe you'd be over your little temper tantrum by now and tired of the single life."

Liz couldn't stop what came out next. "Why? Didn't things work out with Lieutenant Godfrey?"

The quick color that rose in Brock's neck told her she had hit home. He hadn't known, then, that she'd been aware of his affair with Lieutenant Nancy Godfrey.

"That was over a long time ago, Lizzie. It didn't mean any-thing to me, anyway."

"Then why did it happen?"

"Oh, just—because our relationship was hurting, and she was available and willing—when you weren't."

"Have you ever really given any serious thought as to why I was no longer—as you put it—available and willing?"

"Oh, these things happen when people have been married for a while. You get bored with each other, tired—it's natural. You feel a need for something—or someone—new. It passes."

"Well, I gave you your opportunity for something new. You still have it. Why would you want to go back into a tired, old relationship that wasn't even working anymore? And why should I want to?"

"Aw, Lizzie, look around you. Then think of what we had in Hawaii—our place in Jacksonville—even the house in Guam, way back—and tell me your current lifestyle is better than that!"

"My current lifestyle *is* better than that—for me. I don't live in tropical splendor, but I enjoy the mountains here—the change of seasons. I like the life I've created for myself. I like the people I've met. I like the freedom to express my own personality in everything I do, without worrying whether I'll clash with your opinions or displease you. I like myself better now than I ever did when I was married to you. So I'm sorry, Brock, but I don't see why I should leave all this and go back to a relationship that gave us both pain."

"It wasn't all pain, babe—we had a pretty good thing going there, for awhile. You know we did."

"Until I began to grow up and know myself—and know what I wanted from life. We shouldn't ever have gotten married, Brock. We're far too different. It's nobody's fault—just a fact of life."

The sun was going down, and a chill crept into the air. Liz shivered. What was she doing, out here talking to Brock? Why didn't he go away? The whole thing felt surrealistic. It couldn't really be happening, could it? The thing that happened next made it even more unreal. She heard a cheerful whistled song from the direction of the road and glanced that way to see Will Parrish swinging easily along, turning up her drive.

"Evening, Elizabeth," he called. "Sorry to interrupt—didn't realize you had company. Wondered if you might have a minute to advise Meggie on a sewing problem for her home ec class. She's pitching fits, and I'm no use to her. No hurry, though—just whenever you're available."

"Oh, sure, I'd be happy to. Um—Will, this is Brock Ewell, my former husband. Brock, Will Parrish, my neighbor down the hill."

"How d'you do?" Will greeted, extending his hand for a brisk handshake.

Brock nodded, his speculative gaze bouncing back and forth between Liz and Will. Liz thought that surely the pounding of her heart must be evident through her light jacket. *Please, both of you, go away,* she cried inwardly. Gypsy and Tracker were rolling on the grass at Will's feet, and Liz wondered whether Brock saw any significance in that beyond the fact that they recognized and liked a familiar neighbor.

"So, Lizzie, if you're too busy to run out for a bite of dinner, I guess I'll be on my way," Brock said, and Liz was surprised at the unaccustomed sound of uncertainty in his voice.

"I really do have some things I need to do," she said quickly.

"I'll be off, too," Will said, giving a little salute that included them both. "Just whenever you have a minute, Elizabeth. No hurry. Nice to meet you, Mr. Ewell."

"Right," Brock said, watching Will's clean stride carry him back down the hill. "Interesting fellow," he commented, his eyes moving curiously back to Liz. She made no reply; she had no intention of discussing Will Parrish with Brock Ewell.

"So—no hope. Is that what you're telling me, Lizzie?"

"I'm sorry."

"What do you suppose we could've done differently, to have made our marriage work—is there anything?"

She was surprised at the question. It deserved an answer. She shook her head. "Maybe if we'd had a family. But even then, I suspect we wouldn't have agreed on how to bring them up. I think it's just a matter of irreconcilable differences."

"That's a big word. So you're still set on kids, are you?"

"More than ever."

Brock kicked the tire of his rented car. "Okay! Well, I guess I have my answer. But don't think, Lizzie, that I'm going to keep coming around and begging. This is it."

"Oh, I sincerely hope so. Go and find someone who thinks more like you do, Brock. She'll make you much happier than I ever could." Liz snapped her fingers at the dogs and turned to go into her house. She looked back as Brock swung open his car door. "By the way," she called. "Did I ever tell you how much I detest being called Lizzie? I think I must have—fifty or sixty thousand times, for all the good it did!"

The white car blasted backwards out of her drive, sending dirt and gravel flying as it tried to gain sufficient traction to move forward. There was a screech of burning rubber as the tires grabbed at the surface of the highway, and Brock was gone. Liz breathed a sigh that coincided with the diminishing roar of the engine and only then gave in to the trembling that had been threatening to overtake her for the past half hour.

32

When the trembling stopped, Liz made herself phone Will's house. He answered.

"I just wanted to say thanks, Will, for checking on me. At least I assume that's what you were doing. I don't suppose Megan really does need help with home ec, does she?"

Will chuckled. "Heck, she doesn't even take the subject this year. But when Missy told me your—er—Brock was here and you didn't seem exactly thrilled to see him, I thought I'd at least try to supply you with a reason to excuse yourself, if one was needed. I'm—um—sorry, though, if I intruded."

"No," Liz said with a weary sigh. "The intrusion was more welcome than you know. Brock doesn't take hints easily."

"Well, can't exactly blame the guy for wanting to reclaim a good thing." Will's voice was pensive. "Or—am I assuming wrongly? Is that not why he was here?"

"Oh, so he said—among other things. With Brock, it's hard to tell what really motivates him."

Liz heard Missy's voice in the background: "I thought he'd be ugly! But from what I could see, he wasn't."

Liz thought of Brock's tanned skin with the tiny lines at the corners of his eyes, his firm-muscled body and white teeth and close-cropped hair. *No, Missy, he's not ugly. Not where you can see, anyway.*

She almost missed what Will was saying. "—ought to at least consider giving the guy another chance, if he still cares for you?"

She closed her eyes and shook her head slightly, as though Will could see her. "I truly don't think there's any danger of that," she said softly.

"Well, you'd be the best judge on that matter," Will said. "Missy and I hope we helped, and didn't fumble too badly."

"You and Missy both have my gratitude."

"Happy to be of service. Good night, then."

"Good night." Liz put down the phone and gave a small laugh. "Interesting scenario," she remarked to Gypsy. "One man who doesn't love me rescues me from the unwanted attentions of another who doesn't either. I'm really batting zero. I do believe it's time, as the folk singers say, to be a-movin' on."

She found a house, eventually, and reluctantly paid a deposit on the rent. It was on the outskirts of Payson and not as private as she would have liked, but it did allow the dogs and had a fenced backyard for them to run in. It would not be available, however, until the first of December, so she gave Tuck and Lolly notice, asking that they not tell anyone else of her plans or her reason for moving. She steeled herself against the tears she saw threatening Lolly's composure and walked back across the road, only to dissolve in tears herself as she entered her living room and thought about the Christmas tree she had planned to place before the big front window—a green, old-fashioned one, sparkling with varicolored lights and tinsel, smelling of forest and spice—nothing at all like the orange and silver concoction Brock had favored, claiming it complemented their furniture.

"Oh, Gypsy," she mourned. "We won't even have one

337

Christmas here." And how bleak that holiday would be in her new house in Payson, where she knew no one! She had even thought of hosting a simple party for the neighbors, with trays of homemade goodies and hot spiced apple juice, small gifts for all the children to take home, and Christmas music from her stereo in the background. Foolish dreamer that she was, she had pictured everyone there, including Helen Ashcraft, shyly learning to know her new friends, basking in her husband's adoration—and Will, looking relaxed and content, perhaps realizing that Liz was someone he wanted to have as a permanent part of his life . . .

"Oh, well—dreams come and dreams go," she said with a sigh and set about packing her summer clothes into boxes, finally having to shut Tracker out of the room, as he "helped" by dragging things out of the boxes and shaking them, puppy fashion, as soon as she put them in.

About the first of November, a rainy spell settled in, and Liz was reminded of the February day when she had first come to Utah, unsure of herself, smarting from the pain of her divorce and all that had led to it but eager for a new beginning, a chance to learn who she really was and what she wanted from life. So what had she learned? Not what she had expected, that was certain! She had learned that her heart could stretch to feel compassion for a lonely, motherless child and a mother who didn't recognize her own daughter. She had learned to admire and—yes—envy a young woman who was both burdened and blessed with the care of ten active children and still confidently hoped that yet one more would appear. She had learned to love her landlords almost as surrogate parents and to lean on their faith and wisdom to bolster hers. She had remembered how to study, how to strive for excellence, and how to develop and use her talents for her own enjoyment and that of others. Perhaps most important, she had learned that she was still capable of

falling in love—that she was willing to tackle the considerable
challenge of taking on a complex man like Will Parrish, with
his secrets and sorrows, and willing to be a mother to his children. She had been more than willing, in fact—had been eager,
and that eagerness, that dream, was taking a long time dying,
even though she tried at every turn to put it out of its misery.

She had come to know, too, something of the peculiar
brand of Christianity that most of her neighbors espoused, and
she was sufficiently impressed that she wanted to learn more,
but quietly, privately, not with the pressure and encouragement she felt sure would accompany formal missionary lessons.
It was something she would look into when she was relocated
and settled.

Gently, carefully, she worked at detaching herself from
those around her, reasoning that she could have the process
completed by the first of December, when she would quietly
slip away and hardly miss or be missed by the small collection
of people she had grown to love.

"Honest, Liz, you're privater than ever," Missy complained
one rainy afternoon when she stopped by on her way home
from the school bus. "Are you mad at everybody?"

"I'm not mad at anybody," Liz responded, wincing inwardly
to think that her careful detachment techniques were being
misinterpreted.

"Well, everybody's worried about you."

"Why should they be? Who's everybody?"

"Me, Sister Woodbine, Lolly—everybody. Mama even asks
why you don't come up and visit. She thinks maybe you feel
funny around her."

"Oh, I *don't*, Missy. I think she's a lovely person, and I'm
so happy for all of you that she's better! You were right to begin
with, honey. I'm just feeling 'privater' than usual."

"And last summer you used to do stuff with us kids, and

Will and all. That was fun, but you haven't done anything with us for ages."

"Well—I know, but everybody's busy these days. There isn't much time for frolicking around like there was before school started."

"And one time, when I went with Parrishes on a hike up to Timp cave, I thought you'd have liked that, and I asked why you didn't come, and Mr. Parrish just said something like you probably wouldn't want to. Didn't he even ask?"

"No," Liz said quietly. "But that's all right, Missy. He needs time to be with just his family."

Missy shrugged. "I'm not part of his family, and neither are the Woodbine twins, but we all went."

Liz forced a smile. "Well, there—you see? Both of the Woodbine twins got to go because there was room for them! When I went places with the Parrishes last summer, the twins had to take turns going with Tim."

Missy made a face. "One at a time's enough for me, any-way. But did you and Mr. Parrish have a fight or something? I figure you must have, but Megan won't talk about it."

"No. No, we didn't have a fight. Everything's fine."

Missy regarded her for a long minute. "I don't think every-thing's so fine," she said. "But I know—it's none of my busi-ness. Hey! Did you know that Megan and Tim have been going to church with me? Megan wants to get baptized."

"Really? Do you think she will?"

"I hope so. Her dad's thinking about it and deciding."

"Oh—well, that's nice."

"Yep. And Dave has had four baptisms—and that's real good for where he is."

"Wonderful."

"We're all real excited. Mama can't wait for Christmas! He gets to call home again then—and on next Mother's Day, too."

Liz smiled, relieved to be on safe ground again. "That's a terrific present," she agreed. "Tell your mother I'm happy for her, and I'll see her soon."

"Promise?"

"All right. Promise."

She fulfilled that promise a couple of days later when the rain let up and the afternoon sun warmed the air enough to make it tempting to get outside. She took Helen an apple pie she had made, and they chatted amiably for nearly an hour. Helen showed her Missy's room, which had begun to take shape under Liz's ideas and the family's labor. Helen had added a whimsical touch of her own with a bit of white-painted trellis attached to the wall behind Missy's bed, and silk ivy climbing the lattice-work. The drab, uneven drapes had vanished from the windows, replaced by white folding shutters that let in the sunlight.

"It's looking wonderful!" Liz complimented. "It's sunshiny and cheerful, just like Missy."

"Isn't she precious?" Helen murmured. "And she's been so good—so willing to accept me as a new person, almost, in her life. Our therapist is impressed, too. He says she's a remarkably mature little girl emotionally. I can only thank Wynn—and God—for that blessing."

"It could make things harder than they are if she weren't that way," Liz agreed, thinking of Megan's stubborn streak.

After their visit, Liz strolled back down the hill, enjoying the crisp, sunny late afternoon. She saw Will's station wagon turning into his drive, but no one waved. She didn't know if she had been noticed or not. It didn't matter—couldn't be allowed to matter. She lingered outside for a while, letting the dogs run while she gazed pensively at her faded flower beds, wondering who would be there next spring to see the first crocus emerge and whether any of her marigolds would reseed themselves. It was a bittersweet thought and nearly brought her to tears, but her reverie was interrupted by Lolly, who burst out of her house calling for Liz as she ran down her drive, moving more quickly than Liz had ever seen her move.

"Liz, hurry! Come with me! Francie's little boy has drowned himself in the bathtub! Hurry!"

Liz started jogging even while she spoke. "But I—I'm not any good with things like that—I don't know CPR or anything. I—oh, that's terrible!" She looked toward Francie's house, where the front door stood open. Francie ran out, cupped her hands and yelled something Liz couldn't quite make out, and then rushed back inside.

"Get Will," Lolly instructed breathlessly. "And hurry, both of you!" She kept running, while Liz stopped still in the road and looked toward Will's house. He was lifting a sack of groceries out of the back of the station wagon.

"Will!" she cried. "Can you come help us? Francie's little boy has drowned in the bathtub!"

He looked at her intently. "Dear heaven!" he said, and set the sack down with a thump. "Megan! Watch Nicky. Tim, bring in the rest of the food. Stay here."

"What's going on?" Megan questioned, frowning out the back door.

"Watch Nicky," Will repeated, and broke into a run, barely bothering to check for cars before he crossed the highway.

Liz followed, arriving in Francie's living room in time to see Lolly force Francie into a chair and go to the kitchen telephone, which was dangling by its cord. Francie's face was white, her eyes wide with shock, and her breath ragged. Will had found the drowned child—the younger one—and placed him on a towel on the sofa. Liz's chest constricted. The little boy was marble-pale, almost gray, his eyes partially closed and his body limp and unmoving.

"Get me a blanket," Will barked, and she ran to find the child's crib, jerked a soft blanket from the foot panel, and rushed back to the living room.

"Tuck it around him," Will instructed, as he probed the child's mouth to see if he had choked on anything. Finding nothing obvious, he tilted the little head back and covered the mouth and nose with his own mouth and puffed gently, watching the chest for expansion and deflation. Liz watched raptly, vaguely aware that Lolly was repeating the location of Francie's house into the phone and that Francie was beginning to cry in great, gulping sobs. There was a movement just at the edge of the hallway, and Liz turned to see the older child, his eyes saucer-wide, his body trembling inside the bath towel he had clutched around his shoulders. She went to him.

"Tell you what—let's get you all dry and dressed," Liz said, turning the child away from the living room. "You must be Gabe—is that right?" She guided the boy to the room he shared with his little brother and briskly toweled him dry, fluffing the blond curls that lay plastered to his head.

"Tyler was being so silly," the little boy said, as Liz held his underpants for him to step into. His high voice trembled, and she wanted to gather him against her and comfort him, but she realized he didn't really know her and was trying to be brave.

"What was he doing that was silly?" she asked, rummaging in the chest of drawers for a clean pair of jeans.

"He—he kept playing in the bathtub, when I told him to get out. He kept playing scuba-diving and wouldn't come up, even when I said Mom would get mad."

"I—I see. So you got out of the tub, and he didn't?"

"Yep. And I didn't want to get in trouble, 'cause Mom had yelled and told us to get out, but he wouldn't."

Wouldn't—or couldn't? "Where was your mom?" Liz asked.

"She was just in the kitchen, talking to somebody. I got

out, boy! But Tyler kept on being silly and playing scuba, like the guys on TV."

"And then your mom came in and found him doing that?"

"Yeah, and boy, was she upset! Now Tyler's playing like he's asleep or something so he won't get in trouble."

"Well—you know, Gabe, I don't think Tyler's playing right now. I think he—uh—swallowed some water and it's made him sick. He might have to go to the doctor. That's why your mom's so worried. Can you be a really good boy for a while, so we can help Tyler and your mom?"

"Sure. I can read my books or watch TV."

"Oh, that's wonderful—that'll be a big help. Where are your books?"

"There's some here and some down in the family room."

"Where do you want to read?"

The little boy thought a minute. "Here. On my bed."

"Okay. I'll come back in a little bit and talk to you, all right?"

" 'Kay."

Liz finished buttoning his shirt and settled him on his bed with a pile of books. Then she went back to the living room. Francie was shaking all over, and Lolly was still on the phone, relaying instructions to Will, who continued working over the tiny boy. Liz looked in what she correctly assumed to be the hall linen cupboard and found a quilt to cover Francie.

"Where—where's Gabe?" Francie gasped, clutching at Liz's hand.

Liz rubbed the icy hands gently. "He's all dressed and looking at books in his room."

"Where's Eric?"

Lolly called from the kitchen, "We'll call Eric as soon as the paramedics get here, honey. We have to stay on the line with them until they're here."

"Are they coming?"

"They're on the way. Try to relax a little, Francie. Take slow, deep breaths if you can. You don't want to go into premature labor."

"N-no. Is—Tyler breathing?"

Liz glanced toward Will, who paused a moment, watching the still chest, and then resumed CPR. "Will's helping him breathe," she said softly.

"Why? Why'd this happen, Liz?" Francie asked. Liz shook her head silently. "It's because of all I said, isn't it? All—all I said—about not wanting kids—about wanting a career. That's why, isn't it?"

"I don't think so, Francie. Just lean back and try to relax. Do you want to lie down?"

"That must—must be it. But I don't mean it. Liz, you know I don't! I love my kids. I really do. My mother—my mother always says how—how wicked I am, to talk—like I do. She must be right. God must be angry. Lolly? God's punishing me, right? That's why this happened, isn't it?"

"It was an accident, honey—just an accident," Lolly said soothingly from the kitchen. "And help's on the way."

"Tyler's such a sweet baby. He—he didn't deserve—he's so sweet . . ."

"He's adorable. So is Gabe," Liz said.

"They always take their bath together—it's easier to do them both that way. But the phone rang, and I—I thought they'd be okay for a sec. It was my friend I used to work with, and I hadn't talked to her for ages, and I just—I just kept talking, because I could hear the boys splashing and laughing and I thought they were all right. Then I yelled at them to get out, and Gabe said, 'Okay, Mommy,' and the splashing stopped, and I thought they were both out, only they weren't. Oh, Liz, they weren't—Tyler was still in there, with his face in the w-w-water! What'll I do? I thought he was out!" Francie's voice, like her breathing, was ragged and shallow, and her eyes were wide and staring as she contemplated the unthinkable.

"It'll be okay, Francie. You did the right thing—you got help right away. Can you hear the sirens? The paramedics are coming now." Liz went to open the door for the two uniformed young men who sprang from the ambulance and efficiently took over. Lolly, freed from her post at the phone, went to Francie.

"Now, honey, you're going to want to go with them when they take Tyler. Where's your purse?"

"Purse? On—on my—um—dresser. Where's—where's Eric?"

"I'll call him and tell him to meet you at the hospital. And we'll take care of Gabe," she added, as the little boy appeared, hovering in the background to see what the uniformed men were going to do with his brother.

Liz knelt beside him, and he sidled against her, letting her hold him for a minute.

"Are they policemen?" Gabe asked. "Are they going to put Tyler in jail for being bad?"

"No, honey. They're more like doctors. They're going to help Tyler feel better and take him to the doctor. Mommy's going, too. Can you be a big boy and stay with uh—Sister Tucker or me, till Mommy or Daddy gets home?"

Gabe considered. "Do you got any toys?" he asked, wrinkling his nose as if he didn't think it likely she had.

Liz smiled faintly. "I'm afraid not."

"Then I'll stay with Sister Tucker. She gots lots of toys at her house."

Liz nodded. "That's right. She's a grandma, so she would have toys. Let's find your jacket, and you'll be all ready to go whenever she is."

That done, she went back to the living room. Lolly had gotten Francie's coat and purse and was standing by her chair while Francie cried softly into her hands. Liz looked at Will, who returned her glance almost as though he felt it, and slowly shook his head, his face grave.

Liz bowed her head. *Oh, please let Tyler live!* she cried inwardly. *And help Francie to cope. And—all of us.* She went to stand by Lolly, and Gabe followed.

"Don't cry, Mommy," he said shyly, and Francie put her arms around him and cried harder.

"What we need here is a good priesthood blessing," Lolly whispered to Liz. "But with the time element being so crucial, I guess that'll have to wait until the hospital. Tuck's not home, and I don't think Brother Woodbine or Brother Ashcraft are, either. Anybody else'd take too long getting here. But Eric'll see to it. I called him."

When the paramedics were ready to transport Tyler, Liz and Lolly helped Francie to her feet, but one look at her little son attached to the portable ventilator and she sagged between them, her head lolling back, and they eased her back into her chair.

"Francie here's fainted," Lolly told the paramedics. "She tends to be a little on the hysterical side, and she's about seven months pregnant."

"Tough shock for a young mother," murmured one of the men, coming to examine Francie. "We'll transport her, too, and keep an eye on her. You've done well, keeping her warm and trying to comfort her. It's a good thing she had you folks nearby. This gentleman may very well have saved the baby's life."

"How is the baby?" Liz asked softly.

"We've got a fairly steady heartbeat now, but he's still unconscious and not breathing on his own. It's too early to tell how much damage was done, but we'll do our best. Lots of times these young ones pull through this kind of experience far better than an older person would."

He quickly checked Francie's vital signs and listened for a fetal heartbeat. Finally he stood up, nodding in satisfaction. "I think she'll be okay. We'll go ahead and transport."

When the ambulance had pulled away, Lolly looked at Liz and Will wearily. "Thank you, you two. I don't know what we'd have done without your help. God bless you both! Well, Gabe, shall we go see if Sister Tucker has any cookies and milk for a big, brave boy like you?"

Gabe nodded solemnly and took Lolly's hand.

"I'll just straighten up here a little and then go home," Liz said. "Lolly, will you let me know as soon as you hear anything?"

"I surely will, hon. Will, you were a godsend. I'm so thankful you were available."

"So am I," Will said, closing his eyes tiredly. "I hope I did enough, soon enough. It was—touch and go."

"You couldn't have done any more, or any sooner," Lolly told him. "It's in the good Lord's hands now—and the doctors' and nurses'."

Liz didn't wait to see them leave but turned and went into the bathroom off the hall and began picking up towels and mopping up the water that had been splashed onto the floor. There was only about four inches of water in the tub. She sank onto her knees on the soft rug and gazed at it, amazed that a sturdy little boy like Tyler could drown in so little water and in the presence of his older brother. She let the water out, dried the bright rubber and plastic bath toys, and placed them on a corner shelf, barely able to contain her own tears as she rinsed the tub and tidied things away. She stood up to place the boys' soiled clothing in a hamper and turned to see Will standing in the doorway, watching her.

33

Oh, Will, I thought you'd gone," Liz said, her voice hoarse with unshed tears.

"Elizabeth," Will said in the softly slurred way he had—*Eliz'beth*—that had always caught at her heart. She turned her face away from him, unable to keep the tears at bay. "Elizabeth, I have no right to ask this, but—I need to talk to you."

"All right. What about?" she whispered, pretending to be busily wiping around the sink with a wad of tissue.

"You're planning to move."

Her head jerked up. "Lolly told you? She promised she wouldn't!"

"Don't be angry with her. She knew I needed to know."

"I can't imagine why."

"Can't you?"

She was silent, struggling to gain control of her voice so that she could speak without wavering. Finally she said, "A couple of months ago I might have thought I had an idea, but after all that *hasn't* happened since then, I don't know why it would make any difference at all to you."

Will nodded, and gazed morosely at the floor. "I deserved that. But Elizabeth, won't you come and sit down? We can be private here for a little while, I think. I have some explaining to do."

Liz dried her hands and straightened the towels on their rack. "I didn't think Francie and Eric ought to have to come back and see the bathroom like it was. It'd be too hard."

"That's kind of you. This was a tragic thing, wasn't it? I sure hope the little guy makes it—and in good shape. You worry about brain damage when they stop breathing."

"Will, you were wonderful."

He shook his head. "Just doing what I've been trained to do. I hope it helped. Come and sit down, Elizabeth. This has been hard on everybody. You look worn out, and I know I am."

Liz allowed herself to be drawn into Francie's living room, where they sat in two wing chairs on either side of the fireplace.

"I—I have so much I want to say," Will began. "I hardly know where to start."

Liz took a deep breath. "Maybe you could begin with why you dropped what I thought was a good and promising relationship. It really meant something to me, Will, and I would have sworn it did to you, too."

"Probably more than I let you know," Will said. "You've done more than anyone—anything else—to help me start to heal from the pain of losing Kath. With you, I began to feel that life might be good again, not just bearable, but—happy."

"Then what happened? I knew I must have said or done something to turn you away, but I never could think what."

Will looked straight at her, and she couldn't bring herself to look away. "You never said or did anything amiss, Elizabeth. I told you that when you tried to talk to me before, and I truly meant it. The entire problem was with me. I didn't stop caring for you—and I still haven't—and I'm so sorry to have caused you any pain. I think I didn't realize—couldn't believe—that I actually felt as strongly as I did. It seemed too soon—I didn't expect it to happen like that. What Kath and I had was so real and good that I wondered at myself. I felt maybe I was betraying her or just fooling myself. Plus, I had a hard time believing that you were really as—as involved in the relationship as I was beginning to be."

Liz bit her lip. "Couldn't you tell? I tried to let you know."

He nodded, a brief smile tugging at the corners of his mouth. "I picked up on your messages, yes—but I made myself set them aside."

"But why?"

He looked down. "It all started, I think, with something I read in my grandfather's journal."

Thanks a lot, Grandfather, Liz thought wryly.

"He wrote an entry toward the last of the book—as an older man, after my grandmother had become a recluse—that shook me up a bit. He quoted somebody who said, 'Never take something away from someone unless you have something better to replace it with.' He went on to say that for all the love he had for his Lucy, and for all the truth of the gospel of Christ that he felt he had brought her as a missionary, he had to acknowledge that he might have actually done her a disservice by marrying her and bringing her to such a different environment and lifestyle than she had experienced growing up. She was away from all her family, all her people, all her familiar customs, and though she tried valiantly, she never really felt accepted here. He never even saw his way clear to take her back for a visit—and after a while, she just withdrew. She never scolded him, or asked for anything, or complained, but he saw her, day by day, becoming more and more reclusive, and he felt—he felt it was because of his own selfishness in bringing her here and asking her to give up her whole life for him. He knew she loved him, and he loved her—but he felt he had injured and stifled the very person he loved best."

"That's sad, Will—but what does it have to do with us?"

"I asked myself what would I be taking away from you if we were to marry—and whether I had something better to offer you in place of it."

"And?"

"Well, you were just coming to grips with an unhappy marriage and a divorce, just beginning to blossom and find your way—and I was afraid I would stifle your growth and development. Maybe you were meant to go a different direction entirely. You've made it plain how dearly you hold your privacy, and I'd be pretty well ignoring that if I brought you into my busy household. Plus, I'm quite sure my teacher's salary, stretched five ways, could never compare with the alimony you receive from a naval officer—all of which you're free to use any way you want."

"So that's why you asked Lolly about my financial situation."

"Yes. And then there's the very real possibility that you could meet a guy with a lot less baggage to bring into a marriage than I have—possibly someone with no children, so that you could just have your own family together—someone without a burden of sorrows and memories to intrude on your life together. I began to realize that I'm not such a bargain—that I very likely would be taking quite a bit away from you that I couldn't replace with something better."

Liz shook her head. "I'm not believing this," she said softly.

"Elizabeth, it's true! You're so beautiful and bright and giving. You have so much to offer. There are hundreds and thousands of men out there who would jump at the chance to find a woman like you! Guys with all their fingers, even—and an unscarred body and mind. Men who . . ."

"All right, Will, since you brought it up—that's another thing I haven't understood. You let people think your fingers were injured on the job, in a shop accident, but when I mentioned that to Megan, she just gave me a funny look and said that must be what you wanted me to believe. What am I supposed to think? And why is it so important how they were injured?"

He shook his head. "It's not important. And I would have told you, sooner or later. It's just a rather painful incident in my life that I'm not very comfortable talking about. So I hide behind the shop accident theory, which is what almost everyone assumes when they find out what I teach, anyway. I never actually tell people that that's what happened."

"I'm sorry. You don't need to tell me, if it's painful."

"I do need to, because I don't want there to be any mistrust or dishonesty between us."

Liz's heart took a forward leap. Was he saying he wanted their relationship to continue? "I'm listening, then," she said gently.

"Do you remember my speaking of my good friend Kirk, who spent so much time listening to me after Kath died?"

"I do, yes—you said he was blind?"

"He's the one. Well, Kirk lost his sight in the same incident that cost me my fingers, and put some pretty ugly scars on my body. It was in Vietnam."

"I had no idea you were there."

"I know. It was—well, no war is easy or pleasant, but this was—unspeakable. It was close to the end, and I was just a kid—had barely finished being trained as a medic. It was my job—and Kirk's—to go in and bring out the wounded. I saw such sights, Elizabeth, you can't imagine—and I wouldn't want you to. But to make a long story short, there was this area where some fighting had just taken place. You couldn't even

call it a village—just a couple of huts where our guys had suspected some of the enemy were hiding, and a detachment had
gone in to clean them out. There was shooting, and we waited
for somebody to come out, but there was just silence for a long
time, and we figured everybody was dead or injured. Then we
heard somebody call, 'Help! Medic!' and we started toward the
huts. Just then a little kid came running out—not even as old
as Tim—carrying a baby in his arms."

"A baby," Liz breathed. "Children in the middle of all that
disaster."

"Oh, yeah, they were everywhere. It seems like half the
war was fought in people's backyards, so to speak. Lots of families had evacuated, but not everybody. Some tried to hold on
to the pitifully little they had. So this kid came toward us,
holding out this baby, wrapped in a shawl soaked with blood.
'Help sister, Joe,' he said. 'Help baby sister!' "

"Oh—how awful. How sad!"

"Right. The little guy looked so pitiful and so terrified—of
us, I thought—and we could see the baby was gasping for
breath. I took the baby and laid her on the ground and started
to turn back the shawl, and Kirk leaned over to examine her,
and—well, he lost his eyes and part of his face and saved my
life in the process, I guess. I lost parts of my fingers and had a
couple of big holes blown in my chest and side."

"Will, are you saying they had—booby-trapped that baby?"

"I guess they knew she was dying. They apparently planted
a small explosive device inside her clothing and forced the
little boy to bring her out to us. No wonder he was looking so
panicked and in such a hurry to run away. We found out later
that a couple of Vietcong had the kids' mother tied up inside
the hut, threatening to kill her if the boy didn't cooperate."

Liz shuddered. "Oh, I can't bear it! To use little children—
what kind of monsters . . ."

Will nodded. "The kind produced by war, and by unrelenting pressure to win at any cost. It's never a pretty picture, whatever the nationality and the politics. Kirk and I were lucky to survive. The surgeons were able to reconstruct Kirk's face pretty well, but his blindness has cost him his hopes of a medical career. As for me—I'm okay now, but I don't relish telling that story very often. Megan doesn't even know all of it. I've just told her and Tim that it was a war injury. I've told other people that, too, but I find many of them press for details or tell me their horror stories, so it's become easier to be the wounded shop teacher and laugh it off. Now you know."

Liz swallowed. "Thank you for telling me. But Will—one question. Why did you decide to tell me all this, now?"

He gestured toward the empty fireplace. "Because my heart's been feeling about as cold and cheerless as that empty grate. So many times, I've nearly come and begged your forgiveness, but I felt it was in your best interest to—to let you go, to let you find something better than I can offer. You don't know how hard it was not to give in and take you in my arms that day you came to see me."

"It was pretty hard on me, too."

"Elizabeth—forgive me, if you can. I never wanted to hurt you in any way. This thing, today—the feelings that came over me as I was trying to keep that little boy alive—somehow it all brought everything into focus, and I knew I had to talk to you. Then when Lolly confided in me that you were planning to leave—because of me—I decided it had to be now."

Liz studied his face. "Didn't it ever occur to you through all this that my feelings ought to have some bearing on your decisions?"

Will hung his head. "I thought you'd soon get over any fondness you'd developed for me or the kids. And then when I scolded Megan for being rude to you, she burst into tears and confessed how hurt she'd been when Missy told her you weren't interested in marrying me—that you just wanted to be friends. I honestly hadn't realized how attached Megan was becoming, although I shouldn't have been surprised . . ."

"Wait a minute! Missy told Megan that I wasn't interested in you?"

"That's what Meggie said."

Liz took a deep breath. "I might have known that would backfire," she said with a shaky laugh. "I tried so hard, Will—" She stopped to fight back tears. "I tried so hard to keep Missy from being such a promoter of romance between us. I was afraid she'd embarrass us both and interfere with the natural progress of our relationship. She kept trying to get me to say that I was interested in you—and I tried to keep her firmly in her place, telling her we were just friends, and it wasn't her business, anyway . . ."

"Which it isn't," Will agreed. "I know what you mean. Missy and Megan have both pestered the life out of me, trying to get me to say I'd propose to you."

"Oh, I'm sorry, Will . . ."

He grinned. "I'm not, because that's exactly what I kept being tempted to do, but I was afraid that Missy knew whereof she spoke and that you really weren't ready to tackle another serious entanglement."

She looked up, her eyes luminous with tears. "Do you want the truth? I think I've been in love with you since our second meeting—remember our breakfast together that rainy morning? But I tried to fight it—first, of course, because I thought you were married, and later, because I thought you were still in love with Katherine."

He nodded. "About that, Elizabeth—I do love Kath. I always will. She was a major part of my life and the mother of my kids. I've been struggling with that ever since I started getting to know you, and I've finally discovered something I didn't know before: my love for her doesn't weaken or make impossible my love for you. In fact, I think she taught me to love, and I know she'd want me and the kids to be as happy as possible. I've discovered that we can't be as happy as possible without you, Elizabeth. We all need you—and want you—in our lives, in our home. Is this something you could even begin to consider, after all I've put you through these last few months? Can you make do with a teacher's salary, and can you take on three rampant individualist kids and their foolish, stubborn dad? Is it even possible?"

Liz thought the tightness in her chest would cut off her breath. "I think it might be," she whispered.

Will took a deep breath and reached to grasp her hands. "And you're sure you don't want Brock back? He's a fine-looking fellow, and he cared enough to come after you and try again."

"I sent Brock away—and I'd have done the same even if you and I had never met. It was such a shock to see him that I almost felt physically ill, standing there talking to him—and I was so relieved when he left that I was weak and trembly. Please believe that I would move to Outer Mongolia before I'd go back to him!"

"Well, if you really want to move, may I suggest a slightly larger house in your own neighborhood? The master bedroom needs some serious redecorating, but I also can recommend a wonderful decorator—the same one who did my daughter's room. I know she'd take a personal interest in the project."

"Would—would the owner allow pets? I have two dogs. And what about the possibility of additional children, if that should occur?"

Will chuckled. "The owner would welcome your silly

dogs—and . . ." His eyes grew serious. "He would most defi-nitely be delighted at the prospect of additional children."

"He sounds like a most unusual landlord."

"He is kind of an odd duck—but he loves you, Elizabeth, and he'd do his level best to make you happy."

"Oh, Will! He just did."

Will stood up and drew Liz into his arms. She stayed there for a long time, not even noticing the November afternoon turn to evening, hearing only Will's murmured endearments against her hair.

But they both heard the timid knock on the front door, and Tim's voice calling, "Dad? Are you still here? Dad?"

"Right here, Tim. In the living room. Everything's okay."

The foyer light came on.

"Dad? How come you're here in the dark? What's going . . . Oh! Whoops, never mind." Liz caught a glimpse of Tim's de-lighted, embarrassed grin as he saw them together and backed out of the doorway. She also heard his exultant "Yes!" as he closed the door and bounded toward home.

Will shrugged. "As I said, I can't promise you a high degree of privacy."

Liz reached her arms around his neck and looked into his eyes—eyes where once again a light had been kindled. "I think I can adjust," she told him. "Privacy, like freedom, isn't always all it's cracked up to be."

Epilogue

A warm May breeze carried with it a note of birdsong as it stirred the quiet air in the chapel. Liz stifled a yawn. It was difficult to get enough sleep these days. She returned the knowing smile of her friend Marilyn two rows ahead and to her right. Marilyn looked tired, too. Who wouldn't be, at eight-and a-half-months pregnant and with a houseful of ten children already clamoring for her time and energy! Liz looked down her own pew at Will, drawing a picture on the back of the folded bulletin to amuse auburn-haired Nicky, who was going on four and interested in having hands-on experience with everything. He grabbed the pen from his dad to add his own touches to the sketch. Will turned his head suddenly, as if he had felt Liz's attention, and gave her a warm and private smile. Between them, Megan smoothed the skirt of the dress Liz had helped her finish sewing the day before. Tim was on the front row with the deacons, looking earnest and important in his first suit.

Liz's gaze touched others in the congregation—the Ashcrafts, all four of them, looking as happy as anyone she had ever seen—or maybe it'll soon be all five of them, she amended, noting the possessive way David captured the hand of the young woman seated next to him; the Johansen family, with Gabe and Tyler wisely situated on either side of Francie, and baby Laura, named for Lolly, investigating the contents of Eric's suit pockets. How Francie had matured, Liz marveled, thinking of the eighteen months since Tyler's accident. From somewhere deep inside, and surely from her Heavenly Father, Francie had garnered the strength to cope with the long days of Tyler's coma and eventual rehabilitation, as well as the advent of her little daughter. A slight jerkiness in some of Tyler's movements seemed to be the only residual effect of his brush with death, and he rode his tricycle with all the verve and abandon of any child his age.

Liz let her mind wander during part of the opening hymn, watching Suzanne Woodbine at the organ, as poised and decorative as she was competent, looking older than her sixteen years. A corsage on her dress identified her as one who had attended her school's prom the night before. Her father, Tom, first counselor in the bishopric, also watched her with satisfaction from his seat next to Bishop Tucker on the stand. Rod Woodbine, recently ordained to the office of elder, was at the sacrament table, helping there because of a shortage of young priests in the ward. He was looking forward to his mission call.

There were many in the congregation Liz had learned to know and appreciate, and she now felt comfortable in this place, among these people. They had become her brothers and sisters as well as her friends. She listened to the opening prayer and then watched as Tuck—*Bishop Tucker, Liz*, she reminded herself—came to the podium.

"Brothers and Sisters," he began, "we have today the infant daughter of Brother Will and Sister Elizabeth Parrish to be blessed. Her daddy will pronounce the blessing, and she will be given the name of Lucy Elizabeth. We invite all those who have been asked to participate in this ordinance to come forward."

Will stood, and Liz smoothed her sleeping daughter's silky dark hair with one finger before handing her to him—the first of his children to be born in the covenant. The others were sealed to him now, and to Katherine. Liz had acted as proxy for her that day in the temple, the same day her own marriage had been made potentially eternal. And there had been no jealousy, no envy—just an incredible flood of love and warmth that had touched everyone present.

"We are in the presence of angels, brothers and sisters," the dear old man performing the sealing had told them, and no one doubted. Their presence had been almost tangible, almost visible.

Liz had known before that day that Will loved her, but it seemed that he cherished her even more tenderly since she had done all she could to give him the eternal companionship of his beloved Katherine as well as her own.

She watched him walk to the front of the chapel, where he was surrounded by other priesthood holders—Bishop Tucker, Tom Woodbine, Eric Johansen, and Wynn Ashcraft. Just before he bowed his head and began the blessing, Will sought her out and sent her a look of love and gratitude that melted into tears the smile of encouragement she had intended for him. She bowed her own head, aware that her old friend Dorrie Stanford, on her left, had slipped an arm around her shoulders and that Megan, on her right, had reached to squeeze her hand.

How far we've come! she thought gratefully. *How very far— and yet we're just beginning. Bless you, Dorrie, and thank you for flying to be with us today. More than that, thank you especially for creating a desire in me to begin with, to come to this place—this place of healing and love.*